To Bob &
hopes you m— —— —
you.

THE WAKE OF THE WOONSOCKET

The continuing adventures of Rory Dunbrody, CSN,
and Tobias St. John, USN

third in a series

with much aloha,

a novel by Les Eldridge

Les Eldridge

LEEWARD ★ COAST ★ PRESS

-- Printed in the United States of America.
ISBN# 978-0-9794847-1-1.

To the memory of my father, Charles Dillon "Bob" Eldridge, and of my mother, Natalie Josephine Oakley Eldridge

Author's Note to the Reader:

The **Wake of the Woonsocket** is fiction, but most of its characters actually existed. I have tried to be true to their characteristics as we know them from history. They were involved in most of the events that take place in the novel, but occasionally I have collapsed time (and merged the accomplishments of characters) in the interest of the story.

For the reader who is not a sailor, nor Irish, nor yet Hawaiian, it may help to scan the glossary. As the story tracks two often separate story lines, the chapter list identifies the primary character (Rory, Tobias) in each.

About the Author:

Les Eldridge has retired from careers as a college administrator, county commissioner, corporate executive, mediator, and administrative law hearings officer.

Also by Les Eldridge:

In the Dunbrody-St. John Series -
> **The Chesapeake Command (2005)**
> **Gray Raiders, Green Seas (2007)**

The Wilkes Expedition, Puget Sound and the Oregon Country (1987), a history, co-authored by Frances Barkan (also editor), and Drew Crooks.

ACKNOWLEDGEMENTS

My special thanks to those critical readers who read and edited the manuscript, Dick Van Wagenen, Sherie Story, Don Law, Jack Howard, and my wife, Mary Eldridge. Mahalo to my kumu, Laulipolipo'okanahele (Nova-Jean Mackenzie) for her continued guidance, and to my friend, Herb Kawainui Ka'ne for his support and assistance.

Thanks for the help and advice of Don Lennartson, Chuck Fowler, Jane Laclergue, David C. Johnson, Fred and Sandra Romero, and Peggy Bruton and David Bruton. Research and production were enhanced by navigator Lt. Nino Fedele of Princess Cruise Lines, Herbert and Anne Kupers, Tom Kenny of Galway City and John Ryan, Barry Ryan, and Mark O'Hara of Clifden, Connemara, County Galway, and Randy Stilson of The Evergreen State College Library.

My thanks to Hari Jones, curator of the African-American Civil War Museum, John Hightower and Tracy King of the Mariner's Museum, Newport News, VA, Ron Ruhl, Bob and Betti Fogel, Jim Sherman, Mark Terry, Judy Gibson, Pat Brady, Roger Ottenbach, Leroy Hurt, Bill Baker, Martha and Paul Capra and Susan Rohrer for their invaluable assistance.

My friend and photographer, Lloyd Wright was indispensable. Leeward Coast Press, in the persons of Layout and Graphics Editor Patrick Eldridge and Publisher Robert Payne, made it all come together.

CONTENTS

Map #1) England, Ireland

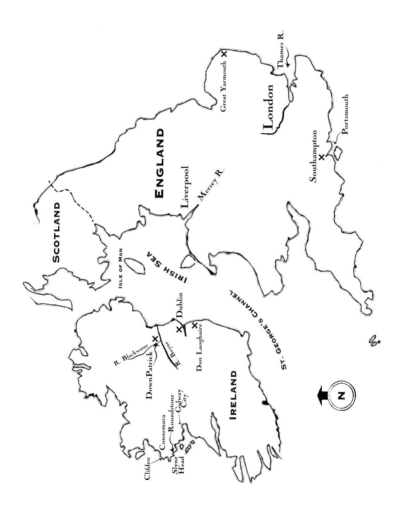

Map #2) Madeira

LONGITUDE: 77° 30' W
LATITUDE: 30° 50' N

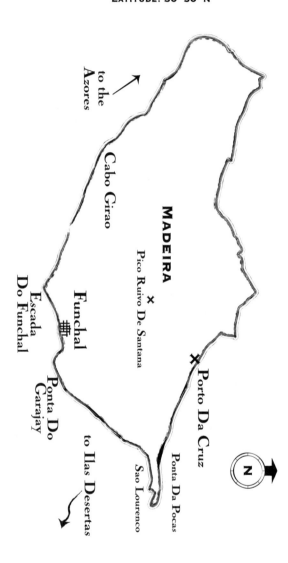

to the Azores

Cabo Girao

MADEIRA

Pico Ruivo De Santana ×

Escada Do Funchal

Funchal

Ponta Do Garajay

to Ilas Desertas

Sao Lourenco

Ponta Da Pocas

Porto Da Cruz ×

N

Map #3) Texas-Mexican Coast

TEXAS

Galveston ⊙

Detail: Mouth of the
Rio Bravo

to Piedras
Negras

PADRE I.

R̲i̲o̲ ̲B̲r̲a̲v̲o̲ (*Rio Grande*)

Matamoros ×× Bagdad

LAGUNA
MADRE

Rio Bravo   Brownsville   Boca Chica

PADRE I.

Matamoros

Bagdad   Woonsocket   Albion

LAGUNA
MADRE

MEXICO

GULF OF MEXICO

YUCATAN

Mexico
City ⊙

× Xalapa
Veracruz

× Puebla

N

Map #4) Virginia

THE SUFFOLK CAMPAIGN

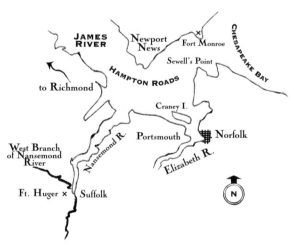

xi

Map #5) Caribbean Sea

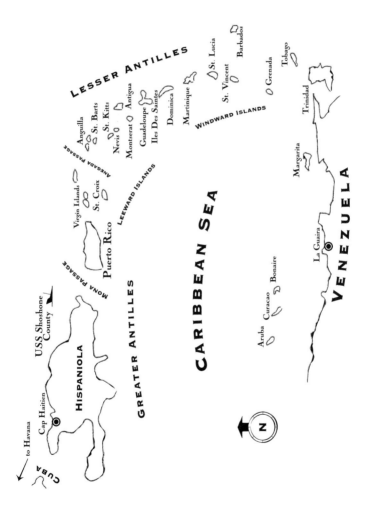

Map #6) Charleston, S.C.

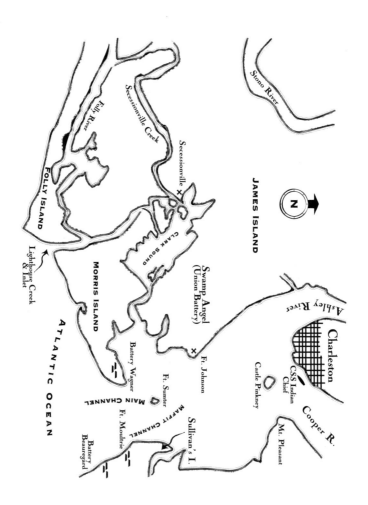

Map #7) New York City

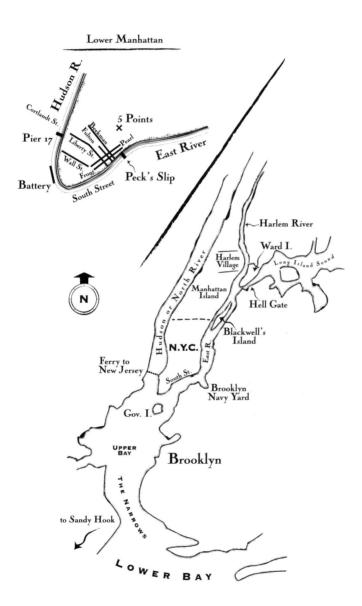

Lower Manhattan

Hudson R.

Cortlandt St.

Pier 17

5 Points
X

Beekman

Fulton

Liberty St.

Pearl

East River

Wall St.

Front

Battery

South Street

Peck's Slip

N

Harlem River

Ward I.

Harlem
Village

Long Island Sound

Hudson or North River

Manhattan
Island

Hell Gate

Blackwell's
Island

N.Y.C.

East R.

Ferry to
New Jersey

South St.

Brooklyn
Navy Yard

Gov. I.

UPPER
BAY

Brooklyn

THE NARROWS

to Sandy Hook

LOWER BAY

Map #8) New Berne

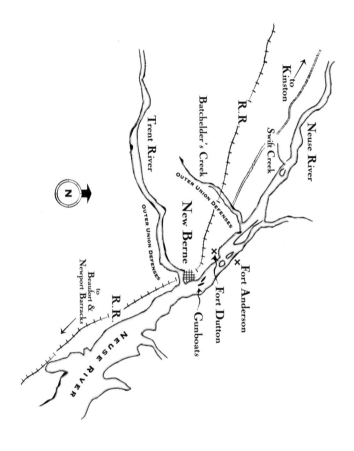

N

Trent River

Batchelder's Creek

R.R.

to Kinston

Swift Creek

Neuse River

OUTER UNION DEFENSES

OUTER UNION DEFENSES

New Berne

to Beaufort & Newport Barracks

R.R.

NEUSE RIVER

Fort Anderson

Fort Dutton

Gunboats

Map #9) Wilmington, N.C. to Cape Fear

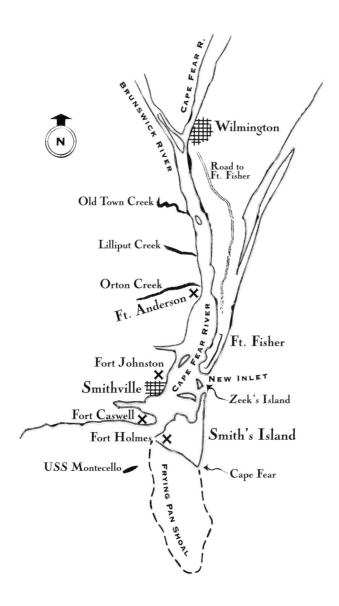

CHAPTER 1
HOME TO CONNEMARA,
JANUARY 1863

Rory hung on to the swaying boarding ladder with one hand and fired his Navy Six Colt revolver with the other at Klaus Dieter von Klopfenstein's grinning duel-scarred face. The Prussian hacked at the boarding ladder with a huge saber as the waves swung the ladder away from the hull and then crashed it back into the iron bulwark. "Click!" The pistol was empty and battle lust shone in the Prussian's eyes as he swung the saber again and again.

"Jasus, Mary and Joseph!" Rory sat up in bed, drenched in sweat. "What a nightmare that was," he exclaimed as he shook his head violently from side to side, trying to erase the image of his nemesis von Klopfenstein, aide to Major General George Edward Pickett, Confederate States Army. *I must keep that daltheen out of my dreams 'til we can cross swords for real*, he thought as he rose, stripped off his soaking nightshirt and ran water into the basin in his Liffeyside hotel room. *Thanks be t' St. Patrick that Klaus is in Virginia and I'm here in Temple Bar!*

Two hours later, bathed and dressed, Lieutenant Rory Dunbrody, Confederate States Navy, boarded the day car at the Dublin train station, and settled back to watch the countryside slip by on his way to the west of Ireland. He had just left his cousin Richard Dillon Fitzhugh of the Bank of Hibernia. *Grand of Dillon to show me a way to use our Confederate cotton certificates to get a raider purchased*, he thought. *And grand to see our Uncle Francis, too.* Francis Dillon had taught his nephews to ride when they were young boys at Dillon's Stables, near Downpatrick and the confluence of the Boyne and the Blackwater, in County Meath. Now the cousins, grown men, were conspiring to let Rebel raiders loose on the high seas.

A long day later, the Great Southern and Western railway deposited Rory at the station in the city of Galway. His Uncle Liam greeted him as he left the train. Liam Dunbrody and his wife, Caitlin, had raised Rory. Liam was brother to Rory's father, Patrick Dunbrody. Patrick's wife, Deirdre Dillon Dunbrody, had died giving birth to Rory in 1837, in North Carolina. Patrick, building a new shipyard in New Berne, and with two older children, Tim and Siobhan, to raise by himself, had sent his newborn to be raised by brother Liam in Clifden, Connemara, County Galway.

"Rory, my boy, you're a sight for sore eyes! You're not in uniform?"

Rory wrapped his arms around his uncle. "There's a reason for that, Uncle Liam, sure, and there is. It's so good to be home."

"Only the second time since you left as a lad of fourteen,"

"That's right, you came to meet me in London in '54, when I was on my way to the Mediterranean as a US Navy midshipman."

"Grab your sea bag and we'll take a hack to the *Claddagh*. The *Caitlin* is waiting to take us to Clifden."

Before Rory was in his teens, Liam had taught him seamanship and sailing in the type of sailing craft Rory now saw secured at the stone wharf in the *Claddagh*, the shallow boat basin in the center of Galway City, the old fishing village. *Caitlin* was a forty-two foot Galway Hooker or *bhad mhor*, with a foredeck and cargo cockpit. The single-masted cutter was wide of beam, with tumble-home sides to give her more cargo capacity and still sail in the shallow *Claddagh*. She was suited to the choppy seas between Galway Bay and the Aran Islands. Many of the hookers of this largest size earned their keep by carrying turf to the Arans or to County Clare. Others were used around the peninsula of Connemara, where roads were poor, to carry hay, sheep, cattle or miscellaneous freight. During the Famine, they kept many coastal villages alive.

"Where is your *gleoiteog*, uncle?" Rory was asking after Liam's second hooker, a smaller one of 25 feet used for fishing.

"She's at Cleggan. The fishing's been good." Liam was considered a very rich man, to own two Galway Hookers. The boats had been the only thing between the Dunbrodys and starvation during the Famine. Rory could remember the Society of Friends setting up soup kitchens in Clifden for the starving tenant farmers. *Maybe that's a reason Tobias and I get on so well, him bein' a Quaker and all,* he thought. Rory smiled at the thought of his close friend, Tobias St. John, now in the US Navy.

They boarded the *Caitlin* and Rory greeted several crew members, some of whom remembered him from his youth. The *Caitlin* was named for Liam's wife, Rory's aunt and surrogate mother. Galway hookers were rigged as cutters, with two headsails or jibs, a long, offset bowsprit, and a large gaff-headed mainsail on a boom extending beyond the stern.

"We'll lie up in Cashla Bay tonight, land our cargo and take on new cargo at Roundstone in Bertraghboy Bay tomorrow, and sail around to Clifden in the morning," said Liam as they cast off from the wharf. "I might as well mix business with the pleasure of seeing you."

Rory laughed as he hauled on the main halyard with two crewmembers, hoisting the rust-red mainsail. "You've not changed a bit, uncle mine."

When the boat was under way, Rory sat aft with his uncle, explaining his need for officers willing to sail with a Confederate commerce raider. Rory had been assigned to the staff of Commander James Dunwoody Bulloch in Liverpool, and had arrived a scant two weeks ago, in late December 1862. Bulloch's duty was to acquire and arm Confederate raiders, and get them to sea.

"I have one or two ideas of lads who might be interested in a billet aboard a Rebel cruiser, Rory," said Liam. "Times have been hard in Galway since the Famine. Families have had to scratch for a living. I'll make some contacts and put them in touch."

The hooker was soon under way with the high coast of Connemara to starboard, and as they reached Cashla Bay, Inishmore to port. The clear light of January reminded Rory how the colors changed with the seasons on this coast, the browns of winter, the greens of summer, and the mystical red hue of fall, like a mirage along the cliffs.

The morning of the third day, Liam decided to take the hooker through the Slyne Head "shortcut," through Cornwell Sound to Joyce Sound Pass, some two miles east of Slyne Head, known as the "Irish Cape Horn" for its steep and dangerous seas. The careful mariner would leave Slyne Head a mile or two to starboard as he rounded it into Clifden. The "shortcut" would save hours of sailing, but it required a wild ride through the pass on a race tide bore. Rory involuntarily clutched the mullard at his side as he thought about it, and then sheepishly released his grip on the big timberhead securing the sheets.

That afternoon, the tide bore behind him, Rory looked out toward the Atlantic from the hills above Clifden Bay, hills he had seen rising over him as he and Uncle Liam had sailed into Clifden Harbor that morning. In his youth, before rejoining his father Patrick in North Carolina, he had seen small famine ships leave from that harbor, carrying starving Irish to Canada and the United States.

Liam and Caitlin still lived in the small stone cottage where Rory had grown up. The big central room looked west toward the harbor, with a kitchen at the east end looking toward the Twelve Bens, the mounded peaks in the interior of the Connemara peninsula. The main room was home to Caitlin's harp, standing in one corner. Rory had thought of it often, whenever he flew his green flag with the gold harp. "Remember, Rory," Caitlin would remind him, "Queen Elizabeth called for harpers to be hanged wherever found, she was so afraid of the harp's power to rouse the spirits of the Irish."

Conversation over lunch with his aunt and uncle had ranged from life at war in the American south to the oppression experienced by Irish tenant farmers laboring under English landlords. "We're lucky to have held on to our language and religion over that last century," said Liam. "And 'though progress is sometimes made, it can be undone in an instant by a change in Crown policy or Parliamentary action. We'll never be safe until we're free."

"Sure, I remember the Young Irelanders rising in 1848, when I was a lad, toward the end of the Famine. It was so weak, and unplanned, it came to naught," Rory recalled.

"Ah, but it led to the founding of the Fenians," said Liam. "Here and in America, we're much stronger."

"Many of you in Galway, are there, Uncle?"

"Indeed, and aren't we the hub of the last Irish speakers in the country? The *Gaeltacht* is very prevalent here." The *Gaeltacht* was the name attached to pockets or areas of Irish speakers, mainly on the west coast. Connemara's was one of the largest.

"Your playmate from your youth, Mary Kate, is a great energy in the movement, Rory," said Aunt Caitlin. "You should say 'hello', before you leave."

"And so I shall, dear auntie," said Rory. "Just after I help with the dishes,"

"Ah, go on with ye," Caitlin said. "Your hours in Clifden are numbered. Make the most of it. When this war ends, you can find time for a more leisurely visit. There will be dishes a plenty then, too."

Rory appeared at the door of the small Clifden bookshop on Market Street where Mary Katherine O'Shaughnessy worked, just before the hour for tea. Mary Kate was stocking bookshelves when Rory entered the shop, standing behind her. "Pardon me, miss, but would you be interested in a bite to eat?" She turned with a shocked look at the sound of his voice, her long auburn hair swirling in a half circle behind her.

"Rory Cormac Dunbrody, shame on you for sneaking up on a girl after twelve years away!" She cocked her head to one side, her arms full of books. "I suppose the best I can expect from you is bread, cheese and an hour's chat. I'll get my coat." Rory waited, gazing around the cluttered bookshop, its shelves extending from floor to ceiling. Ladders running on rails gave access to the highest shelves.

They walked to Anthony Gorham's store on Market Street for tea. Gorham, like Liam, was a successful hooker owner. After tea, they strolled through the nearby square and sat facing each other on a bench beneath the trees. "Your uncle's a marvel, Rory. He's been helpin' me organize the local Fenian group."

"Quite the Irish patriot you've become, Mary Kate."

"You lived here during the Famine, Rory. You saw how little the British did to stop the starvation. Apparently the Act of Union that made Ireland a part of Great Britain didn't include helping to keep us alive.

You'd be a Fenian, too, if you still lived here."

"You'll be careful, now, Kate, will you not? The Fenians are
known to be anti-clerical and the Church is as formidable an enemy as the
Saxons."

"The Church," she sniffed, scornfully. "They were the worst
of the lot, landlords, constabulary, Trevelyan, and all. Not speakin' out
about the pitiful deaths of their own flock, so scared of having the right to
practice Catholicism revoked again. And then sayin' not to go to America
because it's Protestant and we'd lose our faith. Have any of those Irish lads
you fight with lost theirs?"

"Not so I've noticed, Mary Kate." Rory smiled, wanly. "Cousin
Dillon told me the younger priests aren't so anti-Fenian."

"Sure, like before. The parish priests care, and the bishops want
to keep their station and privilege. It hits hardest here, with so many Irish
speakers. The Church discourages the Gaelic, and it's spoken mainly by
the poorest among us. But you're right about being careful. The Irish
Constabulary already has its eye on Liam, and they're a nasty bunch." The
Constabulary, or "IC" was the well-trained paramilitary arm of the British
authorities who were headquartered in Dublin Castle, under the Lord
Lieutenant of Ireland.

Mary Kate looked at Rory with a dazzling smile. "Y' look grand,
Rory. The sea life must agree with ye. Is there someone waitin' for you in
America, now?" Mary Kate asked, wistfully.

"If I ever find my way back, aye, there is." Rory smiled benignly
at his childhood friend. "She's bright and strong-willed, with her own
opinions, much like someone I know in Clifden."

"Ah, go on with ye. Y'd best not be stayin' too long in
Connemara, else Liam will have you gatherin' weapons for the Fenians."

"I'll be back again, t'be sure, Mary Kate. This war won't last
forever, and I'm thinkin' I'll be lookin' for work when it's done."

"Not confident about victory, Rory?"

"Out-numbered and out-spent, sure, that's the way of it for the
Confederacy, sad to tell. But I've still my duty to do. It's been a delight
to see you, dear. You be careful, now." They rose together, and embraced
for a moment, then turned and walked separately away from the bench.

"Heaven save us," Rory thought, "what a striking woman she grew to be! Tall, that gorgeous red hair, and the smile, 'twould melt a man like candle wax."

The warmth of the Dunbrody home in Clifden was a welcome reminder to Rory of the joys of his childhood under this roof.

Liam and Caitlin, much to their dismay and disappointment, were childless, and raising Rory had been a delight for them. "We get letters for you from your friend Tobias, on occasion," Liam said. "Tell us how your system is working." Tobias St. John, born into slavery in Antigua, was now a Union sailing master. He and Rory had vowed to maintain their friendship, despite the war that separated them, by communicating through the Clifden Dunbrodys.

"So far, so good," said Rory. "We're both careful to read and then destroy them, and as they come to us from you, no one suspects that each of us is 'communicating with the enemy,' as the Articles of War warn against."

"Rory, dear," said Caitlin, "that sounds so ominous. What would happen if you were found out, writing to a friend on the other side?"

"Death, or other such punishment as a court martial may impose, auntie mine, is the result prescribed in the Articles of War. We might skate by with less. Each side's Articles are almost identical, as both services have the same parent, the U.S. Navy. We're both grateful for your help in keeping our friendship current."

"Is he safe, do you know, dear?" Caitlin's concern was palpable.

"As safe as any man in harm's way, Aunt Caitlin, as John Paul Jones would say. Tobias has risked blowing up aboard a ship with its magazine at the end of a burning fuse, and he's been a spy whose efforts enabled the capture of three blockade-runners. And those are only the dangers I know about. Maybe 'safe' is not quite the right term."

"What does he know about your war, son?" Liam asked, with raised eyebrows.

"He knows I almost sank with my first command at Hampton Roads. The USS *Monitor* destroyed my tug while we tried to pull *Virginia* off a sandbar," said Rory, wincing at the memory. "I lost a fine friend and bo'sun that day. And I told him about sinking two Union gunboats on the

Piankatank. It's no secret. Our raider unit got the Thanks of Congress, sure and we did. But I didn't tell him about luring the *Cumberland's* boats into a trap in North Carolina, or rescuing a lost company of infantry from Virginia's eastern shore. The both of us are careful only to tell deeds of public knowledge. We'd not be true to our oaths if we did otherwise. Someday you'll meet him, after this war is over, and see what a grand fellow he is."

"We heard from your da and Siobhan, dear. It's so sad they had to flee their home in New Berne." Caitlin was stirring the potato soup on the stove as she took her part in the conversation.

"Ah, sure, The Da and Sis are flourishin' on the Roanoke River in upper North Carolina, still building ships. I saw them just before I left for Liverpool. It's lucky their shipyard foreman was willin' to stay behind when the Yankees took New Berne, livin' in their house and keepin' the yard operatin' at the same time. Maybe they'll have something left when the war ends."

"You don't think the South will win, then, Rory?" Liam asked.

"No, and neither does Da," Rory replied. "And that's a telling statement from a man who's always as optimistic as is Patrick Conor Dunbrody, the lad who sees rainbows everywhere. The North has too many people and too much industrial strength."

"What news of your brother Tim?"

"He's a major now, accordin' to Da, who gets more of Tim's letters than I. He's still in Grant's western command."

"God keep him safe and well," said Caitlin.

"Amen," echoed Liam and Rory together.

Liam sailed Rory back to Galway city in the *Caitlin* along the rain-swept cliffs of Connemara. The bleak and slate gray skies crowded down on the cliffs as the mists curled and swirled over their crests. Uncle and nephew sat in the sternsheets and talked as the hands tended the sails. Liam's eyes were on the wind and his hand on the tiller as they talked. Many an unwary sailor had been knocked unconscious and overboard by an unexpected gybe in the flukey winds off the Connemara cliffs.

"You've grown to be a fine young man, Rory. Your aunt and I are very proud. She does worry for you, you know."

"Uncle Liam, sure, it makes me glow inside to have you say that. Auntie should be worryin' about you, what with your Fenian shenanigans and plannin' for a risin'. The County's rife with informers, as ever was."

"I'm bein' careful, but you're right, it's a risky business, for all that. But it must be, Rory, if we're ever t'be sure of our land and language. Ever since they buried Terence McManus, the brotherhood here has been more focussed, more together. And O'Mahoney's American Fenians are a legal organization there. If only they'd send us more money."

"Sure, they've been a wee distracted, what with 200,000 Irishmen on both sides of the Civil War."

"Bless them, at least they're gettin' good military experience. We'll need it to throw off the yoke of the British!"

"No doubt in me mind, Uncle. Maybe I'll be back someday to help."

"One war at a time, son." Liam smiled affectionately at his tall nephew. They landed at the stone quay of the *Claddagh* and decided to walk to the station. They made their way leisurely up the cobbled street lined with shops and public houses.

As they approached the train station, a tall constable of the Irish Constabulary barred their path. "The two of you need to be comin' with me to the station," he proclaimed, a hand on the butt of his holstered revolver.

"Do we now, Sean Daugherty?" Liam responded. "Is it transport of some livestock you're needin', then?"

"This is serious business, it is, Liam," said Constable Daugherty. "Don't be getting' all flippant with me, now, and makin' it more difficult than it needs to be." He turned to Rory. "And who might you be, and what would be your business in County Galway?" he asked, with a steely gaze designed to intimidate.

Rory couldn't suppress a laugh. "Sure, and will you be apprehendin' me now for all the times you had to chase me away from Mrs. Flynn's apple cart? It's Rory Dunbrody, constable. 'Leftenant' Dunbrody, Confederate States Navy, and a little deference to me rank, if you please."

Daugherty's jaw dropped in amazement. He quickly recovered

his military bearing. "Young Rory, is it then, and grown, and all? Well, you're not in uniform, and this is serious business, so you'll have to come along until we can verify you're what you say you are." And he turned on his heel, obviously expecting them to follow the fifty yards up the street to the Constabulary station house.

Rory and Liam exchanged a glance of resignation, and followed Daugherty through the station house door. Daugherty gestured to two chairs at a table, and, as they sat, Rory handed him his commission. "You would have saved us all time if you'd asked to see my commission from the Congress," he said. "I'm guessin' now, constable, but I doubt Lord Russell is in the mood for further contretemps with the Confederate government after the Trent affair. Detention of a commissioned officer wouldn't sit well, I'm thinkin'."

"Dammit, Rory, Dublin Castle is all in a lather over the organization of the Fenian Brotherhood. The bishop is denouncin' the Fenians from the pulpit, and threatenin' excommunication. And we have sources that tell us your uncle's in the thick of it. This is no joke." Daugherty looked at Liam. "I've the right of it, don't I, Liam?"

"Sure, constable, and are your informers not paid by the claim, now?" Rory leaped back in to the debate before Liam could answer. "Of course they're accusin' Uncle Liam. And anybody else they can imagine, so they can get paid."

Liam leaned forward, quieting Rory by placing a hand on his arm, and turning to Daugherty. "I'm a simple sailor, constable, just transportin' cattle and doin' my fishin', and such, and if you had proof to the contrary, I'd be in Mountjoy Gaol." Liam smiled disarmingly.

Daugherty heaved a deep sigh, and drew a piece of paper from the desk. "You need to be careful, Liam. Dublin Castle's in charge here, not your neighbors like me. Now, let me copy the particulars of this commission, and you can be gone."

Once on the train, Rory dwelt on his detention for a while, and then decided there was no point in belaboring the unpleasant and threatening experience. *Nothing I can do about it, and that's a fact.*

The train back to Dublin bore Rory swiftly away from hearth and home. The metronomic click and clack of the wheels over the rails cast Rory's memory back to other trains he'd ridden, into New Berne, into Richmond, into New Orleans. *I wonder how Commander Semmes is faring?* Rory had helped the exacting and irascible commander of CSS *Alabama* escape from New Orleans in his first command, CSS *Sumter. With luck, I'll be aboard a ship of my own with a chance of encounterin' him on the high seas,* Rory smiled to himself. *Sure, fantasy's an important part of navy life,* he mused.

His aunt and uncle, after quizzing him about his war experience, had questioned him about his new southern love, Carrie Anne, and had seemed to take special pleasure in trying to entice him to compare her to Mary Kate. He'd not mentioned that he'd killed Colonel Thomas Donovan in a duel over Carrie's affections. Rory had sensed that Caitlin would not approve, and might transfer that disapproval to Carrie Anne before she'd met her. *Once she gets to know her, Aunt Caitlin will love Carrie Anne, to be sure,* he thought.

He had told his surrogate parents more about their brother Patrick's successful shipyard at the confluence of the Trent and the Neuse rivers, of his father's part in the cruise of the *Rose of Clifden* and the capture of the *Cumberland's* boat crews, and of the good friends he'd made in the Confederacy, Taylor Wood, John Tucker, and the wild cavalryman, John Singleton Mosby. That they seemed assured that he was making his way well in a dangerous world was a great comfort to him.

CHAPTER 2
ABROAD IN THE SCEPTERED ISLE
JANUARY 1863

The packet bore him from Dublin back to Liverpool. Rory regretted missing a visit to Dillon Stables on his way through the width of Ireland, but his mission was urgent. The morning after his return, Rory again met Bulloch and Prioleau at Messrs. Fraser, Trenholm & Company. It was not a long walk from his lodgings on Water Street, crossing Chapel Street a few blocks from the river. "Your report, Dunbrody?" Bulloch and Prioleau looked at Rory expectantly.

"Sir, here is a letter from the Hibernian Bank to the company, offering to issue bonds on the cotton certificates, and suggesting a ninety-day delay clause in their effective date, to accommodate the needs of the commissioners with respect to the Erlanger loan. If we can find a ship, officers and crew, and arms and stores within that time frame, or beyond, we've the funds to pay for it, if these terms are acceptable."

"All seems in order, James," said Prioleau, looking over the letter. "I see they suggest a ship chandlery here in Liverpool, to make our involvement less obvious."

"My Uncle Liam is already seeking officers and seamen ashore who'd like a chance at prize money, sir," said Rory.

"Very well, lieutenant, this is an excellent start. Are you ready for the next challenge, finding the ship?"

"Yes, sir, I am and I'd like to try making contact with some on my list of acquaintances from the Royal Navy, as well, to help in the hunt for hungry sea officers," Rory replied.

"Splendid. I've prepared a list of potential ship purchase sites, together with a few vessels we know to be available. You'll travel first to Portsmouth and Southampton. After Portsmouth, you'll return through London and Greenwich, with the opportunity for contact with the Royal Navy officers on this list. Geoffrey Phipps Hornby is in London now, and we've prevailed upon your acquaintance, the Baroness St. Regis, to host a gathering that will include Hornby and other RN officers, as well as some of our own. We've also arranged a meeting with Commissioner Mason in London, four days from now. I want you there to reassure him of our navy's connection, through you, to the Hibernian Bank. We'll have to convince him of the wisdom of our 'delayed bond' approach."

"Aye, aye, sir. I'd best be packing, then. I see the list takes me to Glasgow and Tynemouth after London."

"Yes, and we'll have to exercise great care that our meeting with the commissioner is in a private place. I want to keep Adams' spies from seeing you with him, and with us. This Thomas Dudley, Adams' consul in Liverpool, is at the heart of an exceptionally effective network to infiltrate our ship acquisition effort here. We must be always on guard against his agents. Mr. Prioleau has arranged for a visit to his tailor and haberdasher. You'll have need of more formal civilian attire in London than you have now." Bulloch smiled, a tinge of affection in his glance at the lieutenant almost young enough to be his son. "You're wishing you were in uniform at least, and on your own deck at best, my boy?"

"Sure and you're right, commander, but I'll do my best. After all, how often does a young Irish lad get to mingle with the British gentility, and persuade them to do his bidding?"

After two trains, Rory reached Southampton. The following morning he wandered the quays of the great port that had seen the *Mayflower* leave more than three centuries before. His eye fell upon a 160-foot barque-rigged screw steamer, her bow pointed south toward France across the Channel.

Sure, I may have found one right off the bat, as my baseball-playing-friends from Virginia might say, Rory said to himself as he consulted the detail in his materials provided by Fraser, Trenholm and Bulloch.

Royal Navy dispatch vessel Mesopotamia, built eight years ago by

Laird, one of the first equipped with a lift screw, and up for sale to buyers now, probably will be snapped up by blockade runners, read Rory to himself. *I'll be in London day after tomorrow, and we'll be meeting with Mason. That'll leave plenty of time to start the purchase process. Now to get aboard her and confirm what I hope I'll find.*

Rory spoke to the Royal Navy rating standing next to the sentry guarding the gangway of HMS *Mesopotamia.* "I represent O'Rourke's Ship Chandlers of Liverpool. Please take my card and inquire of the officer of the deck if I may board and assess the barky to see if we want to make a purchase bid."

"Aye, aye, guv'ner," the rating replied, and walked up the gangway.

Moments later, Rory was aboard with the run of the ship, inspecting the frames and planking. She was a wooden vessel, with reinforced framing through fore and aft stringers and diagonal planking overlay that gave the hull an unusual strength without much added weight. The foredeck and afterdeck could, with additional shoring, accommodate eight-inch pivot rifles. *She'd be perfect for what we need,* thought Rory, admiring the inverted, back-acting steam engine amidships. Two boilers and 30-inch diameter cylinders would yield 10-knot speed under steam. The propeller-lifting mechanism had been built by John Penn and Sons of Greenwich. She was pierced on her gundeck for four 32-pounders a side.

With a nod to the gangway sentry in his white-duck uniform and musket, Rory returned to his hotel, grabbed his sea bag and boarded a train for nearby Portsmouth, the cradle of the Royal Navy. In his room in Portsmouth, at the Lady Hamilton Lodging and Public House, he unpacked his Confederate gray dress uniform, unable to resist frequent glances out the window at the might of Britain's navy anchored in the harbor. His schedule from Bulloch showed him due aboard HMS *Warrior,* Britain's first ironclad, at nine the next morning. Bulloch had arranged for his visit to allow him to inspect the huge prototype ironclad to sound out her officers on their ideas for British officers who might be willing to take furlough in order to serve aboard Confederate men o' war.

The stone steps leading down to the water at The Hard had been descended by British naval heroes from Jervis to Nelson. "The Hard" was the stone quay at Portmouth Harbor's edge. Rory, resplendent in gray and gold, felt a definite sense of this history as he walked down the steps to the captain's gig of HMS *Warrior*, sent to transport him to the huge ironclad anchored in Portsmouth harbor. The *Warrior* dwarfed all but the largest vessels in the anchorage, the 100-gun "first-rate" ships of the line. Indeed, she had the same sail area as an 84-gun second rate. Rory could see massive ship's boats cradled amidships, as well as boats hung by davits fore and aft. The bulk of 110-pounder pivot guns fore and aft were visible, augmented by eight more broadside breech-loaders on dumbtrucks on the main deck alone. *And then she's got the broadside guns on the gun deck! What a tremendous armament!* Rory had never seen such fire power.

 Warrior was more than twice as long as *Mesopotamia*, and displaced six times the tonnage. *And Mesopotamia's not a small ship,* thought Rory. The gig pulled alongside a small float abeam of the *Warrior's* mainmast, and Rory climbed the gangway, holding his sword's scabbard with his left hand to avoid tripping on it. He was greeted by Commander George Tryon, the executive officer.

 "Welcome aboard, Lieutenant Dunbrody. We've heard much about you here aboard *Warrior!*" He motioned Rory to follow him aft along the 400-foot length of the ironclad's deck. They passed the captain's bridge, a raised steel platform extending across the ship, and then a round deck house with small ports, connected by voice to the combat helm below on the gundeck, with small ports so that the captain was fully protected while under fire. They descended the companionway just forward of the massive, four-wheeled sailing helm, and then aft along the gundeck to the captain's cabin.

 Now who can be tellin' tales of Dunbrody aboard this behemoth? Rory wondered, as he stepped through the door to the day cabin of Captain the Honorable Arthur Auckland Leopold Pedro Cochrane, third son of Admiral Lord Cochrane, British frigate captain and founder of the Chilean navy. Cochrane rose from his seat at the head of a table laden with breakfast treats, flanked by his officers, and came forward to shake Rory's hand. The cabin stretched to the port bulkhead, and included a sitting area as well as the dining table, with a smaller sleeping cabin behind a bulkhead on the starboard side. The cabin was illuminated by light streaming through the skylights.

"Delighted to have you aboard, lieutenant," Cochrane said.

"I'm honored, sir," said Rory. "I had the privilege of being presented to his lordship, your father, in '56 when I was a middie, sir.

"Splendid," replied Cochrane, who was dressed in a short-waisted mess jacket, his orders and campaign medals glittering on his chest. Cochrane had commanded at the victory of Fatshan Creek in the Opium Wars with China in the late fifties. "I'll introduce my officers, and you'll see a guest you'll no doubt recall."

Rory looked past Cochrane to see a familiar face. *This would be the Dunbrody story teller,* he thought. "Mr. Tremaine, good to see you, sir, but, I see it's Commander Tremaine now," said Rory, noticing the three gold rings around the sleeves of Wickstrand Tremaine's mess jacket.

"Right you are, young Dunbrody. We're both guests here. I'm visiting from my command, *Irrepressible,* across the harbor."

"The commander's been regaling us with tales of you on the northwest frontier, taking on those Indian chaps by the dozen, lieutenant," said Cochrane. "You've met my Number One, Commander Tryon. Let me present my other officers." Rory met engineers, deck officers, and the navigator, still called, as in the American navies, "sailing master." "And this," Cochrane concluded, "is our gunnery lieutenant, Jacky Fisher." A short, twenty-two year old officer rose, smiled and shook hands.

What an amazing countenance, thought Rory, looking at a face that conveyed at once amusement, determination, arrogance and camaraderie. "A pleasure to meet you, lieutenant," said Rory, noticing that Fisher wore the same Opium Wars campaign ribbon as did his commanding officer. *So, they go back a way,* he thought.

"All these stories of hunting Haida through the deep woods, Mr. Dunbrody," said Fisher. His mouth turned up into a lopsided smile. "You've fair got our blood a-pumpin'!"

"All true, Mr. Fisher," said Tremaine. "Have you any word of your friend, St. John?" He asked, pronouncing Tobias' name in the British manner, "Sinjin", as did Tobias. "Did you hear I met him in English Harbour?" He asked Rory.

"I hadn't heard that, commander, but I saw him go aboard USS *Vincennes* to cut the fuse to the magazine. Her captain had misread a signal, and Tobias saved the ship from destruction. I was aboard CSS *Manassas,* and had him in my telescope. Later, I talked to a pilot in Wilmington who described how Tobias masqueraded as a slave pilot and led three blockade runners straight to the Yankee fleet. And Lincoln awarded him their new Medal of Honor. Sure, and it's for valor, like the Victoria Cross."

"It seems he's doing well, then, as you and I might have expected," Tremaine offered.

"Indeed he is, sir. Tobias is a sailor's sailor, t' be sure," Rory said, proudly.

"I say, Dunbrody," said Fisher, "you sound delighted at these exploits, and this chap's on the opposite side."

"He's my friend, lieutenant. He saved my life, once, and we've fought the enemy, back to back, in combat. You can't break those bonds, not with politics, not with rhetoric. Sure, it's the pity of this war, between the States, that brother fights brother. My own brother Tim's a Union infantry captain. I'll never love him the less."

"Jove, eloquently put, lieutenant," said Fisher. "I understand, I truly do."

"And St. John's record is all the more admirable," said Tremaine, "when you know that he's a black, and has had to deal with that burden in the promotion wars."

"I say, Damon and Pythias, and that's a fact," exclaimed Fisher. "Captain, may I give Mr. Dunbrody the tour of the ship?"

"Captain Cochrane," said Tremaine, "I beg that I be allowed to accompany my comrade in arms while Fisher acts as guide."

"Most assuredly, commander," Cochrane replied. "But first, let's take advantage of my excellent chef. Help yourselves to bacon, kippers, eggs, and a bit of champagne in honor of our Confederate guest."

The tour of the great ironclad was a wonder to Rory. *Warrior* was the first warship built entirely of iron, as opposed to iron plating laid over a wooden hull. The four-inch armor extended from her gunwale down her black side to five feet below the waterline. The armor extended amidships for 200 feet, ending in armored bulkheads fore and aft. Her huge engine cylinder diameters were almost four times those of *Mesopotamia*. The two red funnels amidships contrasted dramatically with the gleaming black hull. Fisher's enthusiasm for his classic war vessel was contagious.

After the tour, Rory had a word with Tremaine, Tryon and Cochrane in the great cabin, regarding possible officer recruits for the Confederacy. "Sir, what about Cadwallader?" Tremaine asked Cochrane.

"Excellent suggestion, commander," said Cochrane. "Poor Armistead has three sisters to support, and no income to speak of, beyond his pay. He's on the beach, now, and openly talking of furlough. I'll draft a quick note of introduction, lieutenant, and send you along to his lodgings."

"Sure, I'd be most grateful, sir," said Rory. "Would y' have any thoughts on engineer officers?"

Tryon leaned forward in response. "I have just the man, lieutenant, my cousin, a crackerjack third assistant engineer in the merchant service and just returned from India with his wife, who is about to give birth. Conroy Allison is looking for a chief engineer's berth to maintain his family. We have Commander Bulloch's address. I'll ask Conroy to contact him."

"Thank you, sir. The commander will be grateful."

"You'll be seeing Captain Hornby in London, will you, Dunbrody?" Tremaine asked.

"Day after tomorrow, commander," Rory responded.

"He'll have a name or two, without a doubt," Tryon commented.

With Cochrane's note in his travel case, Rory made his way to the Southsea lodgings of Lieutenant Armistead Cadwallader, RN. Cadwallader was tall and spare, with his sandy hair receding markedly. When he had read Cochrane's note, he beamed and welcomed Rory into his sparsely-furnished quarters. "The Honorable Artie, God bless'm," Cadwallader exclaimed. "I knew I could count on his good offices. He notes he's explained to you my circumstances, lieutenant, so I shan't equivocate. I've three sisters in Great Yarmouth for whose welfare I'm responsible, and it's peacetime. A berth aboard a ship with prospect of prize money would be a godsend!"

They talked of Cadwallader's experience, which was considerable, and included service in the Crimea. Rory explained that he had been part of a U.S. Navy observer group during the Crimean war when he was a midshipman. Rory outlined the hoped-for sequence of acquiring ship and crew, and promised to wire Cadwallader with instructions as the scenario unfolded. Rory and Cadwallader parted with a firm handshake and elevated spirits. *Sure, I can report with prospects of a sound ship and a veteran combat officer and engineer recruited,* Rory exulted as he boarded the train for London.

The beautiful Baroness St. Regis greeted Rory as he arrived at her London home for the evening reception honoring the Confederate States Navy. She wore a striking formal gown of red silk. Her butler took his winter overcoat and uniform cap, and Rory took her arm as they walked to the drawing room of her London town house. The baron and baroness had long been known as sympathetic to the Southern cause, and had been glad to oblige Bulloch when he had explained his need to gather Royal Navy officers in one place in order to facilitate recruiting to man the raiders about to go to sea.

"I'm so sorry the Baron has been called away, and must miss the opportunity to meet you, lieutenant," said the baroness, her eyes a-twinkle. "With the recent French détente, we've invested in an extensive vineyard in France. Some crisis necessitated his presence." She and Rory had been passengers on the packet that had borne him to England, and he'd been taken with her looks, even then. She'd made him promise to see her during his stay in Great Britain.

"I'm sad to have missed him, m' lady," said Rory as he admired her face and figure. *What a great female she is,* he thought, *fifteen years my senior or no.*

"Let me introduce you to some other guests, so you may get right to your clandestine pursuits," she said in a conspiratorial tone.

"Aye, ma'am, clandestine's the very thing on my mind!" She gave his arm a squeeze and led him to a group of Royal Navy officers. He smiled at Bulloch and Prioleau, across the room. A servant brought him a glass of champagne. An RN captain turned and smiled in recognition.

"It's young Mr. Dunbrody, and not an Indian in sight," he exclaimed.

"Captain Hornby," Rory responded. "Good to see you, sir. I've only just left Commander Tremaine."

"Ah, yes, Wickstrand has been telling me of all the excitement that took place in Puget's Sound after I brought *Tribune* back to England. It seems you had quite a brouhaha with the Haida. It doesn't surprise me, having seen you in action as I have." Geoffrey Phipps Hornby, Captain, RN, had been on the British Columbia station when Rory and Tobias had been in those waters aboard USS *Active* in 1859. They had worked together to avert a British-American conflict over the status of San Juan Island.

"You were very helpful, sir, in the Gulf of Georgia. I'm here to ask for your help, once again. My new country's navy needs officers. Sure, I was hopin' you might point me in the right direction."

"I'm happy to oblige, lieutenant. Congratulations on your promotion, by the way. I'm told you've seen considerable action during the War between the States. Let's sit down over there. You can catch me up, and I can suggest some contacts among our furloughed officers."

"Aye, aye, sir. It would be my pleasure." Rory and Hornby found themselves a secluded corner of the large room and spent the next half hour in enjoyable conversation.

As they concluded, Hornby said, "I knew you were an officer destined to rise! There's quite a bit of support for the South in England, you know. I'm afraid your cause will not be greatly aided by our government, nonetheless. President Lincoln's emancipation proclamation last month has muted any outcry from our textile workers over the unemployment brought on by the cotton shortage. Emancipation's a very popular policy among most of our population."

"As it should be, in my opinion, sir," said Rory. "I'm a southern officer because of my family's location, not out of any sympathy for slavery."

"I never would have thought otherwise, knowing your deep friendship with Mr. St. John," Hornby replied. "Do you hear anything of your friend?"

"Yes, sir, we've a careful communication system in place. He's received the Medal of Honor, a bit like your Victoria Cross, for action off the mouth of the Mississippi. I was in the opposing fleet and watched him through the glass as he went aboard a ship with her magazine about to blow and cut the fuse. And I know he's been behind the lines to capture our shipping."

"Well, you're quite a pair, Dunbrody. I hope this war ends with the both of you all shipshape. How has your officer search gone so far?"

"I've recruited an engineer though Commander Tryon and a sea officer at the suggestion of Captain Cochrane of the *Warrior*, sir. Lieutenant Armistead Cadwallader."

"Excellent. A good man. I know of him. I've a name for you, as well. Lieutenant Ian Sutherland, a fine Scottish officer, is looking for a berth. I'll just note his address, and you can pursue him as you like."

"We're very grateful, sir. I'll pass it on to my commanding officer, Commander Bulloch. He's right over there," said Rory, pointing in Bulloch's direction.

"Ah, yes, Bulloch! I've heard much good about him. Oh, I say! There's an old mustache you must meet! Sir Richard Francis Burton, explorer and secret agent extraordinaire. There, by the bar, which is quite where one would expect to find him. He's rather well known for his drinking forays. But, if you've studied swordsmanship, as I know you have, he's a practitioner you'll no doubt enjoy."

"Sure, you were there, sir, when I had my little bout with the Proosian sabreur."

"I was, and I'll describe it to Burton after I introduce you. Come!"

Burton was a striking figure in his early forties, with a drooping mustache and a hideous scar on his left cheek. A native lance had pierced his face during his search for the origin of the Nile. Hornby made the introductions and described the fencing match between Rory and Klaus Dieter von Klopfenstein, George Pickett's aide on San Juan Island in 1859. When he described Rory's last lunge, launching himself to the side and striking the Prussian with the flat of his saber, Burton laughed. "Well done, young man. A horizontal fleche! I've included that strike in the book I'm working on. I call it the 'Book of the Sword.' First of three volumes, I hope." He and Rory were soon deep in discussion of swordsmanship and secret thrusts, "*botte segrete*" while not straying far from the bar. They also were of a mind on the topic of slavery, Burton being an outspoken and frequently published opponent of the "Peculiar Institution."

I'd best report to Bulloch while I can still speak, thought Rory, as he watched Burton down another scotch whiskey. *This bravo can drink, and that's a fact!*

He excused himself and sought out Prioleau and Bulloch, in a far corner of the room. "I know we meet tomorrow, sir, but I wanted you to know I've found a perfect ship in Southampton, the *Mesopotamia*, a former RN dispatch vessel, and I've three British officer prospects."

"Good work, Dunbrody. I'll pass the word to Commissioner Mason, and we'll discuss it all tomorrow at our hotel. Come with me and meet Mason. He's the one speaking to the baroness."

Their dark-haired hostess was wearing her hair up in a coif that exposed her neck in a way Rory found most evocative, particularly as he was feeling the results of going drink-for-drink with Sir Richard. She was speaking to a dour-looking man with a nose spread broadly across his face. James M. Mason wore his hair, which receded considerably, at shoulder length.

"Commissioner," said Bulloch, "may I present Lieutenant Dunbrody, who'll meet with us tomorrow. He has good news for us."

"I'm delighted to hear that, lieutenant," replied Mason. "We could use some good news right now. I understand you've been able to travel without the agents of those damned Yankees Adams and Dudley following your every move. Pardon my language, baroness."

"Quite all right, commissioner," said St. Regis. "How have you managed to move so freely, lieutenant?"

"Sure, I've not been in uniform much until tonight, m' lady, and with my brogue, and meeting secretly with my superiors, and all, the Yankees and their agents haven't tumbled to me as yet."

"I think that will come to an end tonight," said Mason. "They're watching this house, and will follow all who emerge, particularly those in uniform."

"Well, gentlemen," smiled St. Regis as she arched her eyebrows, "I think we can protect Mr. Dunbrody's anonymity, if it would be useful to you all."

"It would, indeed, baroness," said Bulloch. "Dunbrody's ability to move without hindrance is a great benefit to our operations. What do you propose?"

"As the party draws to a close, all the carriages waiting in the drive will leave, I'll wave my goodbyes from the entry, and the lights will be turned down. It will appear as a household ready for repose. No agent will lurk freezing in February weather for no apparent purpose. Meanwhile, my coachman and carriage will be at the back. Lieutenant Dunbrody will quietly depart through the servants' entrance and be whisked back to his hotel, to appear in the morning unrecognizable in civilian attire."

"A splendid plan, baroness," said Prioleau. "The South is in your debt!"

"We all must do our part, gentlemen. I'm just glad we can help."

Rory was feeling the whiskey superimposed on the champagne. *Sure, I may have had too much of the drink taken, but not so much that I can't recognize an opportunity being presented*, he said to himself. A group in gray uniform across the room caught his eye. "Baroness, gentlemen, please excuse me. I must say hello to some former shipmates."

As he walked toward a group of naval officers in gray, Rory's smile was met by a wide grin from Midshipman James M. "Jimmie" Morgan, whom Rory had last seen at the battle of Drewry's Bluff in Virginia. They had been shipmates aboard CSS *McRae* in New Orleans at the beginning of the war. "Jimmie, me lad, you're afloat and well!"

"Hello, sir, it's a pleasure to see you again," said Jimmie. "I wouldn't describe my condition as 'afloat,' however. 'On the rocks,' maybe. I'm aide to Commander Matthew Fontaine Maury, and we're looking for a ship or two." Morgan turned to the Confederate lieutenant next to him. "Have you met Lieutenant Fauntleroy, sir?"

"I certainly have. I haven't seen you since you commanded USS *Massachusetts* in Puget's Sound, lieutenant," said Rory. "Are you looking for a ship?"

"Midshipman Dunbrody, now a lieutenant! Yes, I'm looking, but until Commander Maury assigns me, I'm ashore like Morgan here."

"It seems we're all in competition for the same thing, ships and billets," said Rory.

"I think it's the financing that's causing us the biggest problem," said Jimmie.

"Maybe I can make a suggestion, for the good of the service," said Rory. "We're trying to convince Commissioner Mason to sign cotton certificates with a delay clause, so we can have a chance of finding a financial institution to issue bonds against them. I'm assuming you're held up by the Erlanger negotiations as we are?"

"I think that's right, sir," said Jimmie. "I'll mention this to the commander. He might be interested."

"We'd all like to be at sea, and that's a fact," said Rory. "Good luck to you both."

As the evening drew to a close, Baroness St. Regis motioned to Rory. "Wait in my husband's study, like a dear, while I say my goodbyes. Then we'll get you ready for departure."

"Yes, m' lady. Clandestinely," said Rory.

"My dear, if we're to be co-conspirators, you must call me Evelyn. Wait here, now, and make yourself at home." She smiled warmly at him as she returned to the drawing room.

Rory took off his uniform jacket and threw it over a desk chair. He sank into a comfortable overstuffed chair and closed his eyes. Sleep overcame him easily. He awoke to the scent of Evelyn, Baroness St. Regis, in his nostrils, and her lips upon his. "Don't get up, dear boy, I'm just going to make myself comfortable for a time, 'til we can send you safely home." She turned down the light, and Rory's next sensations were the rustle of her gown, and the feel of her smooth skin as she filled his arms. His pang of conscience was dulled by a pang of yet another type.

An hour later, out of sight of her waiting coachman at the servant's entrance, she kissed him on the lips. "Stay safe, dear boy. You're a national treasure."

Rory drifted off to sleep in his hotel room. He was sure he'd not been followed from the St. Regis town house. *Jasus, what a shameful interlude, and me bethrothed, and all,* he reflected groggily. *Sure, I'm a better Catholic than I thought, the way the guilt's upon me.*

Out of uniform the next morning, Rory walked the short distance to Bulloch's hotel for the meeting with Mason. He'd checked out, and was prepared to entrain for Tynemouth after the meeting concluded. His uniform and his dress saber were in his sea bag. He walked to the elevator, rode to Bulloch's floor, and knocked on the door of Bulloch's suite. Bulloch answered his knock. He joined Mason, Prioleau and Bulloch at a table in the sitting room. "Our friends from the U.S. Minister have a room down the hall. Your departure will be noted, and you'll be followed," said Bulloch.

"Not to worry, sir. I've a plan to lose him on the way to Victoria Station."

"I'll be eager to learn if it works. Let's hear your report, lieutenant," said Bulloch.

"Aye, aye, sir. I found a dispatch bark, HMS *Mesopotamia*, in Southampton. She's perfect. Up for sale, does ten knots, pierced for four 32-pounders in broadside, and able to take an eight-inch pivot fore and aft. Here is the contact information," he said, handing Bulloch a portfolio. "If Hibernia Bank can issue bonds, and O'Rourke's can arrange for the modifications, we could have her at sea in weeks. We could shore up below decks for the pivots at quay-side without attracting attention. If we could bring the pivot rails and the artisans aboard, we could move to Spithead, anchor, and have the installation done in days."

"Good work, Dunbrody," said Bulloch. "Commissioner, I believe we could provision a tender with arms and supplies, and rendezvous in Madeira. I've assigned a captain, Ashton Canby, just sent out by Secretary Mallory. He could go with the tender. Now all we need are British officers and crew for *Mesopotamia*."

"Sir, I've recruited Lieutenant Archibald Cadwallader, RN, who's furloughed and eager. Commander Tryon suggested his cousin, Conroy Allison, as chief engineer, and he'll contact you. Last night, Captain Hornby gave me the information on Lieutenant Ian Sutherland. It's in the portfolio. The sea officers are both veterans with fighting experience, sir. Captain Hornby said Cadwallader would be ideal to command *Mesopotamia* until Captain Canby can join us in Madeira."

"Excellent," said Bulloch. "Your Uncle Liam has given us two fine prospects, Diarmund McGuiness, a merchant lieutenant, and a bo'sun, Brendan O'Toole. With you, we have a bo'sun, an engineer, a captain and four lieutenants. I also can assign three midshipmen."

"Lieutenant Cadwallader said he could find most of the crew off the Portsmouth docks, if we could provide a few from Liverpool."

"I'll see to it, lieutenant," said Bulloch.

"Commissioner," said Prioleau, "can we persuade you to sign the certificates with a ninety-day delay clause? If you agree, everything will fall into place."

"I'm comfortable doing so, gentlemen. The Erlanger loan will surely be in place by then. Hibernia Bank involvement seems ironclad, and will avoid the U.S. Minister's suspicions."

"We have Dunbrody to thank for that," said Prioleau.

"Once the ship purchase is complete, I'll have the repair attributed to preparation for the wine trade, and the first port of call listed as Oporto." Bulloch smiled at Rory. "You can go out with her, Dunbrody. I seem to remember you're experienced at installing pivot rails."

"Yes, sir. I'd suggest pivot ports fore and aft, sir. It's the kind of alteration that can be explained away. The more we can do at dockside, the better we'll be."

"We'll ask the bank and O'Rourke's to begin arrangements immediately, commissioner," said Bulloch. "Lieutenant, we'll ask you to carry on your search for other vessels. When you are through in Tynemouth and Glasgow, report, and then we'll assign you to Southampton. What's your plan for avoiding being followed from this meeting?"

"Sure, sir, I'll be takin' a water taxi from here to Chelsea Embankment. I'll hire two of the best watermen I can find. A guinea will persuade them to give a finishing sprint, and give me a good lead. If I'm followed, I'll be able to wait in an alley, and either lose him or bruise him, sir!"

"I'll leave it up to you, Dunbrody. Next week, I meet with Lucien Armand, a Bordeaux shipbuilder. I'm convinced that Great Britain will continue to make it more difficult for us to acquire British ships. We need to explore the French possibility. Some day, I may ask for your services again to help with the French."

"Commander, I enjoy serving under you, sir. But I hope my duty keeps me at sea. Will the French not follow the British lead in tightening their application of neutrality laws?"

"Eventually, they may. But Louis Napoleon has much more control of his country's course of action, independent of law, than is the case here. Britain is primarily a nation of law, while Napoleon III has more latitude in directing his country's course, less hampered by the law. He is very interested in surrounding what he hopes shall become 'French Mexico', that is, Maximilian's Mexico, with 'weaker' states, so his putative puppet, Maximilian, can eventually exert more influence in the hemisphere. So he supports the notion of a divided America, a Union and a Confederacy. We may turn that to our advantage."

"Thank you, sir. I never understood that complexity, at all, at all."

"Polish up your French, lieutenant, against the day we need you."

"Aye, aye, sir. *Mais oui*," said Rory with a smile.

CHAPTER 3
AN AGENT COMES TO MURPHY'S
FEBRUARY-MARCH 1863

Rory emerged from Bulloch's hotel room and quickly brought
the collar of his winter cloak in front of his face to conceal his features
from the spying eyes of the Union agents keeping watch. Hurrying
down the stairs and through the lobby, he ran toward the nearby dock at
Millbank and placed a guinea in the hand of a waterman standing beside
his double wherry. The waterman's mate was already seated on the bow
thwart. "I'm in a bit of a hurry, lads. There's another guinea in your
future if we can get upriver to Chelsea Embankment without anyone
gaining on us!"

The stroke oar pocketed the guinea coin, nodded knowingly at
Rory, and growled, "shove off, Alfie," to his bow oar. The four sculls of the
wherry caught the water precisely together as they rapidly left Millbank
astern.

Rory looked aft to see a man on the dock with two other
watermen. *Look at him, pointing straight at our wherry,* he thought. "Are
you faster than that double at the dock, lads?" He asked.

"Never a worry, guv'ner," the stroke oar replied. "We'll gain half
a length every twenty strokes on that sorry pair!" And, indeed, it appeared
they'd gained some distance on the pursuing boat as they eased alongside
the dock at Chelsea. Rory made the promised payment and ran to the
nearest horse-drawn hack. He estimated he had a two-minute lead on his
shadow. *Not enough he won't see where I go, but too far to pick me out of a
crowd,* Rory thought and smiled in spite of himself in anticipation of the

next segment he had planned.

"Murphy's Pub in Kilburn," he said to the driver, "and a handsome tip if no one overtakes us on the way."

"Right you are, sport, but I won't linger dropping you off. It's a place for those with your accent, not mine."

"Fair enough," said Rory to the driver.

As the trap pulled up to the pub, Rory paid the driver and clutching his sea bag, ran in the door. As he did so, he glimpsed a hack three blocks behind him down the road. "God bless all here," he said loudly as he entered, and received a chorus of "God save you kindly's" in response. He shoved his cloak in his sea bag and approached a crowded table toward the rear of the pub. "Sure and I'd be grateful if I could join you now. There's a Saxon behind me who'd like to put me in Old Bailey."

"Sit you down, then, boyo, and look inconspicuous," said a big man with a Dublin accent. "We've got to take care of you country boys from Galway."

A mirror on the back wall enabled Rory to watch as his pursuer entered the pub, looking most uncomfortable, as an Englishman in the midst of fifty Irish ought. The Dubliner at Rory's table got up and moved forward to the bar. "I smell a Sassanach!" He roared, and pointed toward the Union agent.

"Out with him, then, and the curse of Cromwell on his head!" Patrons shouted and rose menacingly. The agent, his mouth agape, turned on his heel and fled the bar, to a roar of laughter.

"Now what would such an evil man want with the innocent likes of you?" The Dubliner was smiling broadly as he rejoined the table.

"Sure and isn't he the worst kind of gombeen man you'd ever encounter?" Rory replied. "And now that I'm shut of him," he said with a grin, "I've more than enough to buy a round for the table!"

A week later, Rory's report on prospective vessels at Tynemouth and Glasgow was in Bulloch's hands. He had identified two more possibilities for cruisers. In the interim, Bulloch had purchased the *Mesopotamia,* and Cadwallader, who would command on the trip to Madeira, was at work hiring a crew and preparing for sea in Southampton.

Rory's parting from Bulloch was bittersweet for both men.

"You've done outstanding work, Mr. Dunbrody," Bulloch said as he sat behind his desk in the offices of Fraser, Trenholm and Company. "I now have a new pipeline to desperately-needed British officers who can 'front' for us, plus two ships Mr. Adams doesn't know I'm looking at. Plus, the *Star of the South* will soon be at sea. And behind it all, your cousin maintains a financial curtain the Yankees haven't seen through, as yet! Well done, lieutenant! I'm going to miss you."

"And I you, sir. I know how much you'd like to be at sea, and I admire you for continuing in a duty that's not your first choice. I can't thank you enough for making me second lieutenant of *Star of the South*," Rory concluded.

"You'll just have to capture enough Yankees for the two of us, my boy." Bulloch's affection for his young subordinate was obvious, despite his reserved demeanor.

"Aye, aye, sir, I'll make a point of it."

"One more thing, lieutenant. I've instructed Mr. Cadwallader to sign aboard at least one Portuguese hand. I don't recall your skills extending to that language."

"No, sir. Spanish I learned aboard *Wabash* in Nicaragua in '57, but not Portuguese. Perhaps I'll learn a word or two on the voyage to Funchal."

That afternoon, Rory left his lodgings in Liverpool for Southampton, making sure his seabag contained his treasured flag of Brian Boru, a gold harp on a green field. He had flown that flag, the storied "harp without a crown," on his first command, the *Old Dominion,* and, if he received a second command, would fly it again as a tribute to his Irish forebears. Rory was soon hard at work supervising the shoring up of the fore and after decks to support the weight of rifled pivot guns aboard the former HMS *Mesopotamia*, soon to be the CSS *Star of the South*.

Captain Ashton Canby, marked by the Union spy network as a Confederate officer, would stay far away from his new command, but would join the ship in Madeira. The ship would sail under the command of its eventual first lieutenant, Armistead Cadwallader, a properly accented Royal Navy officer on furlough ostensibly to bring *Mesopotamia* into the wine trade. Lieutenants Dunbrody, Sutherland, and McGuiness, with

Boatswain O'Toole, would lead a mainly British and Irish crew, a common situation for Confederate raiders acquired in English ports. No known Confederate would go near her. If they could avoid suspicion for the two weeks needed to cut gun ports for the pivots and install the pivot rails, the Confederate Navy would have another menacing cruiser at sea.

The four sections of the bulwark, fore and aft, were cut and designed to be cleared away to open the eight-inch pivots' fields of fire. They could have been fashioned, one might argue, to enable easier access to the hatches of a wine transport, but a keen and suspicious eye would question that purpose. To guard against sudden discovery, Boatswain O'Toole organized a watch crew to observe any passersby on the harbor side who seemed too interested in the *Mesopotamia's* gunwale alterations.

Rory breathed a sigh of relief as the *Mesopotamia* left the quay side on the Test River at Southampton and moved several miles seaward down Southampton Water to the somewhat sheltered and broad waters of the Solent and Spithead, where she anchored in order to install the pivot rails that would enable the eight-inch guns to rotate, finding targets over a 270-degree arc. Once again, Boatswain O'Toole's watch crew kept a lookout for overly-interested small vessels passing by, or observers on the distant shore with telescopes or binoculars.

Rory was somewhat uneasy about the risks of the week it took to install the pivot rails. The CSS *Alabama* had been got to sea just ahead of a detention order from British officials responding to Union complaints about the warlike nature of the ship. The detention order would have put the question of whether the ship could leave Great Britain into the courts, and have delayed departure for a year, even if the case had been decided against the Union. The *Mesopotamia*, like the *Alabama*, had no military stores or arms aboard, and was commanded by a British subject not commissioned in the Confederate Navy. Even so, each ship would have endured a lengthy court case if she were detained before getting to sea. So when Rory was summoned to Cadwallader's cabin late one afternoon, and saw the telegram on his desk, he feared for the worst.

"We've just received word from Commander Bulloch that a detention order will be served on us by day's end tomorrow. Someone in the Union's pay has seen enough to generate a government charge."

"Sir, if they serve that order, we'll be delayed for months, at best."

"Are the traverse rails secure enough to go to sea?"

"Yes, sir. Just a matter of a few more bolts. We could finish tonight by lantern-light."

"Then we'll weigh anchor as soon as you finish. The earlier, the better. I'll send Mr. Sutherland ashore to telegraph Commander Bulloch. The stores are all loaded. I know he has the tender with all our ammunition and cannon aboard ready to sail from London." The store ship *Martha,* with Captain Canby aboard, would rendezvous with *Mesopotamia* in Madeira. The *Alabama* had carried out its transfer of weaponry in the Azores, and Bulloch had decided to change locations to avoid Union cruisers on the chance they had remarked on previous practice.

"Sir, the crew all have women aboard, expecting to get the mens' advance pay before we sail." The "ladies" of the seamen were careful not to leave their men for a moment, after the sailors' extended time ashore. Financial obligations had been incurred, and under the traditions of sailors and "Portsmouth Judies," were expected to be met before the ship's departure.

"Damn all," Cadwallader swore. "Mr. Sutherland, I'd be obliged if you'd go ashore and charter a tug to accompany us as we leave Spithead. When we're out of sight of the harbor side, we'll transfer the women to the tug. Mr. McGuiness, Mr. Dunbrody, set up the pay table amidships. I'll get the pay notes from the safe."

As Sutherland took the jolly boat ashore, the word spread among the crew and they gathered in a clump of humanity, with their women, on the main deck where Rory and McGuiness had set up a table. The crew list and articles of the cruise were laid out on the table with the currency stacked on a smaller table flanked by two boatswain's mates, pistols at their hip. The ship's purser sat at the table with McGuiness beside him. Rory could hear the women badgering the men over the amount of advance being offered. Muttering grew to shouts. "That's no fair pay for croosin' the Bay of Biscay! You'll work off the dead horse before you clear Ushant!" The day the men had worked enough to work off their advance was known as "working the dead horse". On that day, a straw filled horse effigy was often hoisted to the yardarm and dropped into the sea.

Rory whispered to Cadwallader. "Sir, they're workin' themselves into a frenzy. You might announce a midnight dinner and a double grog ration, and then have them sign for their advances. Alter the mood, so to speak."

"Damn cogent idea, Dunbrody! Mr. McGuiness," he bellowed, "belay the pay and signing, just now, if you please!" Cadwallader's voice could have been heard in the maintop during a gale. Everyone paused to listen. "We've all had a long day, and need some reconstitution. Pipe 'up spirits' and set up the mess for a midnight dinner. We'll sign and sail after we've regained our strength!" Murmurs of approval from the sailors and the women accompanied the preparations for the grog ration and the best meal the cook and his mates could provide on short notice.

An hour later, the officers and petty officers began the pay and signing again, and the women, their men's wage advances secured close to their hearts, calmly prepared to board the tug. At a safe distance from Portsmouth, the tug came alongside, and took aboard its cargo of harborside beauties. The port official serving the detention notice the next morning would search the anchorage in vain for the *Mesopotamia*. She had weighed anchor under that name for the last time.

CHAPTER 4
RENDEVOUS IN MADEIRA
MARCH-APRIL 1863

Dawn found the *Mesopotamia* under all plain sail, courses, top-sails, topgallant sails and royals, driving west down the English Channel and toward the treacherous Bay of Biscay. The ship's purported destination, Oporto in Portugal, was a ruse, as was the ship's purported use, as a wine trader. Cadwallader intended to gain sea room away from the Bay of Biscay as soon as he cleared Land's End, the southernmost and westernmost point of England. The island of Madeira was 200 miles more westerly than the entrance to the English Channel, and 500 miles south of Oporto's latitude.

Cadwallader and his crew were glad to be giving the stormy waters and lee shores of Biscay a wide berth. Any time of year in the Bay could be difficult, but early spring was particularly so. As they passed the Lizard and Land's End, they continued bearing southwest, rather than come south toward Oporto. It was one of the ironies of war that their course away from the storms of Biscay enabled the USS *Tuscarora* to sight them later that afternoon.

Tuscarora had been on patrol off Liverpool, alert to any attempt by Bulloch to get raiders to sea from the port most famous for Confederate construction, when she'd received word from United States Minister Francis Adams that a possible Rebel raider was poised for flight from Portsmouth and Spithead. The *Tuscarora* had headed south through the Irish Sea at full speed, in the midst of a storm front, and sighted *Mesopotamia* barely a mile ahead at three in the afternoon.

Aboard *Mesopotamia, Tuscarora* was sighted at the same moment. "Sail, ho!" The lookout at the mizzen top shouted down to the quarterdeck. Rory had the watch.

"Where away?" He called in response.

"Two points off the starboard quarter, just coming out of that squall, sir. Not more'n a mile, I'd say, sir. A man o' war, by the cut of her jib." The Union ship was behind the Rebel, and slightly to her right.

"Call the captain," Rory said to the master's mate of the watch. "I'm going to the main top."

Rory ran to the mainmast shrouds and climbed quickly up the ratlines (the nautical equivalent of ladder-rungs) to the small platform or "top" just below the bottom of the highest of the four sails on the main mast, the royal sail. With one arm around a shroud bracing himself, he focused his telescope on the vessel little more than a mile astern.

Rory shouted down to the quarterdeck. "Sir, she's a *Wyoming* Class screw sloop of war. I'm guessing *Tuscarora*. She's been on station in the Irish Sea." Rory realized he had much more information to impart, and tucked the telescope into his waistband. Grabbing a backstay, he wrapped his legs around it and slid 100 feet to the deck, controlling his descent with his hands. He ran to the quarterdeck. "Sir, she's rated at 11 knots, but I'll wager it's 9 and 1/2, her bottom being fouled by a year at sea. Her forward pivot's an eleven inch muzzle-loader, and the pivot's range is about a statute mile."

Cadwallader laughed in spite of himself. "Jove, Dunbrody, you're a treasure trove of information! Were you first in your class at your naval academy?"

"Sure, and I was, my captain." Rory smiled in return. The two officers realized that they'd be lieutenants together soon enough, when Captain Canby joined the ship, and were establishing a bond closer than the usual more-formal captain-subordinate relationship. "I believe we can outrun her, sir, sure and I do. She's at extreme range for her bow chaser. It's only three hours 'til sunset, and the glass has been dropping this last hour. It's goin' to blow harder, sir, judgin' from the squall lines to weather. We'll lose her after sundown."

"If she doesn't land a lucky shot first. Well, lieutenant, I don't want her coming within range with us mounting pivot rails and with a commissioned Confederate officer on board. We'll carry this press of sail as long as possible. The game's afoot! Hoist the Red Ensign!" The British merchant flag, red with a union jack in the canton, rose to the spanker gaff. "Mizzen top, there. Let us know the range and bearing!"

"Aye, aye, sir", came the response from aloft.

"They'll be havin' a back-and-forth about whether to fire on the British flag, I'm guessin'", said Rory.

"If they know we were about to be detained in Portsmouth, they won't argue long," Cadwallader responded.

A dull "boom" punctuated the captain's last remark. A spout of water erupted from a wave top a moment later, only 250 yards astern.

"Short, and to starboard, sir," said Sutherland, watching intently.

The *Tuscarora* fired every forty seconds throughout the afternoon. Her forward eleven-inch smoothbore Dahlgren was shooting from a platform tossing in fifteen foot seas. Shots fired on the up-roll gradually crept closer to the *Mesopotamia,* but *Tuscarora's* progress was slowed by the difference between her quarry's hull, free of marine growth, and her own, trailing seaweed after months at sea.

After an hour of the chase, with tension mounting, Rory heard shouts and swearing from the foredeck. One of the deckhands was haranguing his shipmates. "See to that brou ha ha, if you please, Mr. Dunbrody," said Cadwallader.

"Aye, aye, sir," said Rory as he ran to the foredeck. He could see Boatswain O'Toole's massive form moving in the same direction.

"Avast, there!" cried O'Toole as he climbed the companionway to the pitching foredeck. A dozen men paused at the sound of his command voice. One continued to shout. "Belay that caterwaullin', and shut yer gob, Bancroft!" O'Toole advanced menacingly on a spare and toothless Cockney.

"Well, Mr. Bo'sun," Bancroft responded, fire in his eye, "we signed on for the wine trade, not the Battle of Trafalgar. The captain should heave to and let the Yankee escort us back to Spithead. We've got our month's pay, and we've more than earned it!"

Rory laughed as he stepped beside O'Toole. "Sure, Mr. O'Toole,

I've heard some sea-lawyerin' in my day, but this whimperin' whelp isn't my idea of a British tar! Men, listen. It's no secret we're made for cruisin' in search of prizes for the Confederacy. Every true sailor aboard knew that when we shored up the gundecks. We're bound for Madeira, not Oporto, and when we get there, every Jack who wants prize money and bonus pay will have his chance, and them that don't, we'll pay their voyage back to Portsmouth. But if that Yankee stops us, no one will have a chance for riches. So those who want out, help your shipmates that want the chance until we reach Funchal!"

"You knew all that, Bancroft," said the captain of the foretop, "but yer knees turned to jelly when you heard the Yankee's first shot. Stow it! Be a man and get back to duty!" The rest of the crewmen growled their agreement, but Bancroft kept shouting.

"This Mick is goin' to drown us all!" he wailed.

"That's the limit, Mr. O'Toole. 'Mick,' indeed." Rory winked at his fellow-Irishman. "Can't have truck with insubordination. Confine him below, if you please." He pointed to the main deck hatchway, and O'Toole motioned to his two burly boatswain's mates. Bancroft was borne below, his feet barely touching the deck as he was hustled below by the boatswain and his mates. *Sure and he shouldn't be tossin' the term "mick" about, with half the crew Irish,* Rory thought.

The *Tuscarora* could barely be seen in the gloom when a shot from its bow chaser cut the mizzen topgallant yard in two. "Mr. Dunbrody, fish that yard, if you please." The captain's words were still ringing when Rory and several topmen began lowering the two fragments of the yard to the deck. O'Toole, meanwhile, had a detail of men remove the tattered remnants of the mizzen topgallant sail from the ends of the spar as they lay on the quarterdeck. The two ends of the broken yard were butted up against each other. The carpenter and his mates lashed shaped timbers, called "fish", to the yard around the break where the shot had torn it in two. Topmen bent a new mizzen topgallant sail to the repaired yard. The men tailed on to a halyard and hoisted the "fished" spar to its former place, and the new mizzen topgallant sail was soon filled and drawing. *Sure, it's grand to have an experienced crew. I hope we can persuade most of them to join our raider's voyage,* Rory thought.

38

Darkness had fallen, and Cadwallader shortened sail in the increasing wind. *Mesopotamia* darkened ship and changed course to the west, running in heavy seas on a beam reach. Daybreak showed an empty horizon. They'd outrun and outguessed their pursuer.

A number of days later, the lookout called, "Land, ho!" from the foretop. The mountains of Madeira were soon in sight from the deck, the 6100-foot peaks of Pico do Arieiro and Ruivo de Santana the most prominent above the clouds that wreathed their slopes. Rory could see a 1300-foot monolith rising from the shore. "Sail, ho, ship at anchor, sir, three points off the starboard bow." The lookout had spotted the *Martha*, at anchor in the small bay off the northern town of Porto da Cruz. Funchal, the main port, was on the south side of the island, across the mountains.

The *Martha* had two anchors out, in order to hold both ships. Cadwallader brought *Mesopotamia* neatly alongside the store ship, and quickly ran bow, stern, and spring lines to *Martha,* whose crew was starting the laborious and back-breaking process of swaying up kegs and barrels, full of stores, from her hold to her yardarms. Slings were attached to the containers by *Martha's* crew, and led to the *Mesopotamia's* deck, where the raider crew hauled them down, through her hatchways, to the hold.

Rory found a pleasant surprise among the junior officers that Bulloch had put aboard *Martha* to accompany Canby. "Midshipman Ormsby, you've sprung from nowhere, sure, and you have!"

"Good morning, captain, I mean Mr. Dunbrody, sir." Archibald Ormsby, a South Carolinian, had served aboard CSS *Old Dominion,* Rory's first command, in Chesapeake waters, and later with Rory as part of Taylor Wood's "naval cavalry", river raiders on the Potomac and Piankatank. "It's a pleasure to see you again, sir," said the diminutive and witty midshipman. "We all arrived a day before the *Martha* left England, and Commander Bulloch seized us as crew before anyone else could put a claim in. There are three other middies, two master's mates, the purser's mate, a surgeon, two assistant engineers and a warrant gunner."

"Well, I hope you won't be too upset working on your Sabbath, but even 'though it's Saturday, we need to get these stores loaded."

"Sir, you Catholics have only ten commandments to follow. We Jews have 613 laws or mitzvahs. It leaves us a bit more latitude than you. I don't recall a commandment regarding ammunition on the Sabbath." He grinned at Rory.

Rory took a launch ashore through the surf, with a Portuguese member of the crew as translator, to secure fresh stores. Porto da Cruz, a center for sugar cane, provided water, vegetables, fresh meat and fruit, all paid for by Commander Bulloch's specie. These acquisitions were brought to the shore from the terraced slopes of the mountains and willing crewmen loaded them aboard the ship's boats.

After three long days of toil, the *Mesopotamia's* guns were mounted and her stores and ammunition struck below. She'd not used her precious coal on her run south, even when pursued by *Tuscarora.* She was ready for commissioning into the Confederate States Navy. During the loading, Captain Canby had observed the men and officers of what would now become his crew, and had moved from the *Martha* to the captain's cabin aboard *Mesopotamia.*

Canby assembled the men on the morning of the fourth day, in the overcast of a typical eastern Atlantic early-April morning in latitude 33 degrees north. Most of the hands wore tarpaulin jackets against the chill of the wind.

"Men, as you all know by now, I'm Captain Ashton Canby, Confederate States Navy, here to commission the *Mesopotamia* as the Confederate States Ship *Star of the South.* "I've watched you do fine work in arming and loading the *Star* in these last few days, under the able leadership of your interim commander, Mr. Cadwallader. He will now become first lieutenant. Allow me to name your other officers, including those who arrived with me aboard *Martha.*"

Canby introduced each of the ship's officers and petty officers, and gestured toward a table set up amidships. "Now, each of you must choose whether to sign aboard the ship and join the Confederate Navy, or return to England aboard *Martha. Star* will be a commerce cruiser. We'll face no men of war unless unavoidable. We'll capture prizes and prisoners, and periodically parole the prisoners and send them away aboard neutral vessels. Your pay is handsome by British merchant standards, and you'll have a bonus for signing today. Your prize money will be twice the Royal Navy shares. Who'll be the first in line?"

All but a handful of men signed the articles and accepted a bonus from the purser. The ship was still undermanned, but Canby was confident he could recruit the remaining men needed from among the crews of the prizes he would take at sea. As the few men returning to England filed aboard *Martha,* the captain stepped forward. "Welcome to the CSN, men. Say adieu to the *Martha* for a time. She'll be our tender, and will join us later at our first rendezvous. We'll cast off *Martha*, Mr. Cadwallader, and as soon as we're outside the Portuguese territorial limit, I'll commission this ship as *Star of the South.* We'll pay a port call on the governor of Madeira, and be at sea tomorrow afternoon. The Union whaling fleet should be plentiful in these waters."

Within an hour, the CSS *Star of the South*, now a Confederate cruiser, was flying the Stars and Bars from her spanker gaff, with its 13 white stars in a circle in the blue canton. Each star represented a state of the Confederacy, including Missouri and Kentucky. Neither of the latter had seceded, but each had held secession caucuses whose votes for secession led the Confederacy to count them, somewhat wistfully, as member states.

Star was sailing east to round Point das Pocas and the small island of Sao Lourenco. She would then bear southwest toward the thatched roofs and the church spires of Funchal. Her war had begun.

CHAPTER 5
THE MISSION TO JUAREZ
FEBRUARY 1863

Sailing Master Tobias St. John of the sloop of war *Woonsocket* tugged at his navy-blue frock coat, making sure the fit hung just right as he made his way to Allan Pinkerton's Washington, D.C. office. The new U.S. Navy uniform regulations had been in effect since the previous month, and Tobias had received his new uniform from the tailor only yesterday, in this first week of February 1863. Masters now had gold lace on their sleeves, two rings in contrast to the 1862 coat, which had none. One gold bar and a silver fouled anchor shone against the blue of his gold-edged shoulder bars, and his peaked cap carried a silver fouled anchor over a gold cap wreath. *Quite the picture, I am,* thought Tobias. *I must ask for leave after this assignment so I can visit Dad in New Bedford. As a Free Quaker, he's never taken the uniform amiss on his only son.* When Tobias had visited his father, Carlyle St. John, the previous autumn, he had remarked with pride on the six pointed bronzed star his son wore around his neck on a red and blue ribbon. It was America's highest award for valor, the Medal of Honor, and Tobias had been the first black man to receive one.

Notwithstanding the honor, Tobias had undergone a court martial in January. He'd been unjustly charged by his ship's commander, who had caused the wreck of the USS *Wilkes-Barre* and tried to shift the blame to Tobias. The charges had been withdrawn for lack of evidence, and he had been fully restored to duty. Allan Pinkerton, former Secret

Service chief now under personal contract to President Lincoln, had
been a character witness for Tobias during the trial. At the celebration
following Tobias' exoneration, Pinkerton had told Tobias of Lincoln's
desire to send him on yet another espionage mission. His first, in mid-
1862, had taken him behind Confederate lines posing as a slave pilot, and
had resulted in the Union capture of three rebel blockade runners. *Maybe
I shouldn't have done such a good job,* Tobias thought ruefully.

Pinkerton's office was in the same building that housed the Navy
Department. The mission he'd recruited Tobias for had its resources and
support provided by the Navy. "Come in, Mr. St. John, yer a sight for
sore eyes!" Pinkerton exclaimed in his Glasgow burr. "Dinnae stand on
ceremony, Tobias. Let me take your coat."

Pinkerton and Tobias were soon deep in the details of the
mission to Mexico, where Tobias would be met by an agent of the
Reformist president, Benito Juarez. Although the Juaristas had lost
their lengthy control of the port of Veracruz to the French when Louis
Napoleon's forces had flooded Mexico in late 1862, it was still a hotbed of
liberal resistance against the conservatives and the French. Juan Francisco
de la Montoya y Hinojosa, "Paco" to his friends, a trusted agent of Juarez,
would meet Tobias as he slipped ashore from the Union sloop of war, USS
Woonsocket, the ship Pinkerton had arranged for Tobias to be assigned to.
Tobias had, coincidentally, met *Woonsocket's* commander, Captain Oakley,
the previous autumn in Brooklyn Navy Yard, when Kekoa Kalama, a
friend of Tobias', had joined the *Woonsocket* as a master's mate.

The French had been careful to maintain Veracruz as an open
port. Union ships came and went frequently as they patrolled the Gulf
of Mexico looking for Confederate blockade runners. The French were
determined not to force the Union to invoke the Monroe Doctrine.

Tobias and Paco would travel north from Veracruz to the Juarez
stronghold of Xalapa to carry Lincoln's solemn promise of continued
personal support of the Juaristas. There, they would meet Juarez himself.
The beleaguered president believed it better to meet away from spy-
ridden Mexico City. Then, Montoya y Hinojosa and Tobias would
reboard *Woonsocket* and travel north to Matamoros, where, with the
help of Mexican army officers sympathetic to Juarez, they would steal a

Confederate shipment of rifles and ammunition brought to Matamoros by a British blockade runner, the shipment bound for Brownsville, Texas, across the Rio Grande from Matamoros. That was the plan.

"Aye, laddie," said Pinkerton, "I ken ye've been behind enemy lines before, but ye must be especially careful this time. "T'is a different language, a divided country, and none of your own kind tae provide support when needed."

Tobias smiled at the Scot's concern. "I'll be on guard, Allan. And I've been honing the Spanish skills I learned in Paraguay and Nicaragua in the fifties, ever since the court martial and your offer of the mission."

"Aye, none would be the wiser if ye turned me doon, but I know that's no' your nature," said Pinkerton, with a tone of admiration tinged with regret. "The president's called for you tae meet with him, before he sends you on your way. He's joining us here at the Navy Department, so as not to attract attention to you at the White House." It was a familiar sight in the Capital to see Lincoln walking to the gray Navy Department building, next door to the White House. He often wore slippers and a shawl as he consulted with two of his most trusted policy advisors, Gideon Welles and Gustavus Fox, the Navy secretary and assistant secretary. Lincoln knew that his appearance at the Navy offices would evoke no curiosity, even in gossip-ridden Washington.

"After you meet with Mr. Lincoln, you and I will explore more details of the mission. We'll be joined by *Señor* Matias Romero, Juarez's envoy tae the United States."

Lincoln was already in the conference room when Tobias was ushered in. "Mr. President, it's an honor to see you again. Thank you, a thousand times, for the emancipation proclamation." Lincoln had issued the proclamation in early January, and Tobias, born into British slavery, revered the president for his action.

Lincoln rose to greet the tall sea officer, his homely face alight with a smile. "Ah, but don't you see, sailing master, it was you who helped give me the time to make the proclamation possible. I needed a gesture to keep the Abolitionist movement from tearing me down, without moving precipitously to the proclamation absent the reinforcement of a major victory. Your medal of honor gave me that time. That was in May, was it not, before your spy mission to Wilmington?"

"It was, Mr. President."

"Valorous as you were, sailing master, it was your being at the right place and at the right time that brought you the medal. Life is unfair."

"I don't mind the randomness of the honor, sir, if it enabled you to help my people in the end."

"That's the irony, sailing master. I never intended the war to hinge on abolishing slavery. I would have sacrificed the freedom of the slaves in the South, reluctantly, if that sacrifice would have served to hold the Union together. The Southern leadership never stepped away from their perceived blot on their honor long enough to realize they could have had all they wanted."

"Still and all, sir, the right thing was done, and it was done by you."

"And now I ask you to help me again, and again, no one will ever know."

"It makes not the least difference, Mr. President. I welcome the chance to conspire once more with you."

The president threw back his head and laughed. "It's a privilege to have such a co-conspirator, Mr. St. John. The honor is mine. Let me tell you what I need. Mexican President Benito Juarez, a true man of the people, is about to be deposed at the behest of a European power. We cannot allow this infringement upon the Monroe Doctrine."

"Yes, sir, Mr. Pinkerton has outlined my mission and the policy concerns which make it necessary."

"You must tell Mr. Juarez that I will be issuing a public warning to France, Austria, and all of Europe, that those who infringe upon the bastions and redoubts of the Doctrine will ultimately be made to pay the penalty."

"I'll carry the message, Mr. President."

"Express to President Juarez my personal admiration and my pledge of support, one lawyer to another."

"Aye, aye, Mr. President."

"And then you must explain to him why I will use the word 'ultimately' in my declaration. I am unable at this time to confront the European powers with anything but a threat of future action. Mr. Seward, my secretary of state, is quite right that we have not the resources both to fight the rebels and enforce the Monroe Doctrine. Formal action will have to wait. But, as you've learned from Pinkerton, we have our own plan, one that will secretly kick the Confederacy in the rump and help Juarez in the same action. You're the one to carry out the plan, Mr. St. John. God speed and God bless you, sailing master." As Lincoln shook his hand and clasped his shoulder, Tobias basked in the glow of the president's gratitude and approval.

As for the president, he walked back to the White House with seriously conflicted thoughts. *Intercepting this British arms shipment and getting it to Juarez instead will kill two birds with one stone,* he thought. *But oh, the irony I could not share with my young sea hero! We issue permits for hundreds of arms shipments each year from New York traders to Matamoros, and we know that the arms reach Texas in return for cotton that provides Union Army uniforms. The trade bolsters the textile industry, the whole Union economy, and it keeps the New York Copperhead Democrats, who grow rich from it, from rising against me. I hope I never have to explain that to St. John.*

Back in Pinkerton's office, Tobias met Matias Romero, like Juarez, a Oaxacan and graduate of the Oaxaca Institute of Sciences and Arts. "*Muchisimo gusto, señor,*" said Tobias as he shook hands with the handsome Mexican.

"It is a pleasure to meet you also, sailing master," Romero responded in excellent English. "I wish you good fortune in your mission. I have some information concerning the northeastern states of my country that may help you be successful."

"*Gracias, señor,* I know President Lincoln has great confidence in your advice." Tobias saw a pleased look on Romero's face at the compliment.

"President Juarez understands Mr. Lincoln's inability to formally recognize the Liberal regime while the French are present in Mexico," Romero continued. "He wishes me to help all I can in your informal efforts to support him. So, let me tell you of Governor Vidaurri and the northeastern states. Vidaurri has extended his control from the states of Nueva Leon and Coahuila to Matamoros, your target, in the state of Tamaulipas. He controls the border trade and revenues along the Rio Grande. He has declared for Juarez, but sends no money to our Mexican federal government. We believe he will not interfere with our taking a Confederate arms shipment so long as he loses no revenue."

Tobias reflected for a moment and then asked, "Even though he claims to support Juarez, won't Vidaurri's troops resist our raid?"

Romero grinned conspiratorially at Pinkerton and Tobias. "His former general, Escobedo, and many of his troops and officers are intensely loyal to Juarez, and have left the northeastern states for San Luis Potosi, the next state south. Vidaurri has not replaced them, and many of the remaining troops support General Escobedo. The general's forces will transport the arms from Matamoros to San Luis Potosi. *Pues,* there is just one problem." Romero paused, and shrugged his shoulders. "A little thing."

"What might that be, sir?" Tobias was enjoying the verbal game Romero was playing. *Here comes the part I won't like,* he thought.

"A Mexican who is an agent for the Confederacy commands the warehouse guards in Matamoros. Great quantities of cotton are shipped to Europe from his warehouses, and the arms and ammunition landed in exchange are stored there until the Confederates can receive them. His name is Jose' Agustin Quintero. He is a Harvard-educated *Cubano.* His men are numerous and dangerous. They will transport the arms upriver to a place where they can slip unnoticed into Texas. The men of Escobedo will intercept them on the river. But we must leave them leaderless on their trip, to ensure capture of the muskets. You will be the bait to lure Quintero into our hands, and leave his men without their commander. As I say, a small thing for a man of your experience and courage." Romero smiled again. "Mr. Pinkerton actually suggested this approach."

"Och, it's right up your alley, laddie," said Pinkerton with a wink. "Tae ensure your safety, I've persuaded Mr. Lincoln to provide a Henry .44 caliber rim fire repeating rifle from his special cache of weapons for his agents. It has a 15-shot magazine and a 24-inch barrel, like a carbine. Very handy in case you're outnumbered, nae doubt!"

CHAPTER 6
COASTING TO THE GULF
FEBRUARY 1863

The *Woonsocket* provisioned at the Washington Navy Yard for her voyage down the coast of the Confederacy and on to Veracruz. Tobias took the opportunity to get to know the two master's mates who reported to him in his position as sailing master or chief navigator of the *Woonsocket*. One of them was Kekoa Kalama, a Hawai'ian former harpooner whom Tobias had helped find a billet aboard *Woonsocket* the previous autumn. Tobias had known Kekoa's father Kele, a Hudson's Bay Company employee, when Tobias had served in Puget's Sound before the war. In addition to being versed in European navigational techniques, Kekoa had another body of navigational knowledge at his disposal for Pacific waters. He had studied Polynesian and Micronesian star navigation under the grandson of the famous Tahitian navigator, Tupaia, who had sailed with Captain James Cook of the Royal Navy.

Later in February, Tobias took the opportunity, as the ship lay in the Navy Yard, to visit his friend and former shipmate, Roswell Lamson, at the Bureau of Navigation. Tobias had watched Lamson grow in skill and confidence when they were both aboard USS *Wabash* in the Port Royal campaign, and on blockade off Charleston. Tobias had been happy to act as Roswell's navigational mentor, a task his service in the Coast Survey had thoroughly prepared him for. The US Coast Survey was among the elite cartographic organizations in the world, and its members and former officers played a central part in the success of the Union's sea-land operations, as Survey personnel knew the coasts of North America better than anyone else.

Lamson had come on board *Wabash* as a midshipman fresh from his third year at the Naval Academy in Annapolis, and had risen through the grades to his lieutenancy, passing Tobias in the process. Tobias had no illusions about his future advancement in rank. There was to be none. He'd come as far as any man of color could expect. He was pleased that Lamson, an exceptionally competent and courageous officer, had advanced so quickly. The two shipmates understood their positions amid the protocols of promotion, and thought no more about them.

"Tobias," Lamson exclaimed, "I heard about your Court. Congratulations. They should cashier that dilettante!" The commander who had brought charges against Tobias was Jeremiah Oldham, a former yachtsman from New England. Oldham had accused Tobias to cover up his own culpability in the loss of USS *Wilkes-Barre,* and had withdrawn the court martial charges in the face of an overwhelming lack of foundation.

"Thank you, Roswell. You look as if you've settled in here at the Bureau." Lamson sat at a high stool before a canted accountant's desk, overlooking the street below and the distant Potomac.

"I'm chafing to get back to sea, my friend, as you most certainly know, although I must say Commodore Davis is a good man to work for. You're the lucky one, with an assignment aboard *Woonsocket.*"

"I am lucky, indeed, Roswell, more than you know. And I empathize with your desire for sea duty. Do you remember our days on the St. Johns River, raising the *America*?"

"I remember vividly, my friend, sailing up the river to Dunn's Creek and finding that great old yacht scuttled and resting on the river bottom. Lord, how we worked to raise her!"

"And to good purpose," said Tobias. "She captured a blockade runner that October!"

"You'll be interested in this, Tobias, as a US Coast Survey graduate. Commodore Davis has scheduled an audience next week with the great savants, professors Agassiz and Pierce of Harvard, and Professor Alexander Bache, the superintendent of the Coast Survey. We're going to talk navigation. Are you crushed to miss it, oh prescient pilot?"

"I am, being an admirer of Dr. Bache. I'm convinced my service in the Coast Survey got me my commission, despite being black. I'd love to be a mouse in the corner, particularly with all the wisdom that Bache brings, being a great grandson of Ben Franklin, and having built the Survey into the best in the world. But remember, Roswell, I'll be at sea and you will not." They both laughed.

"*Touché*," said Roswell. "With luck, I'll not be far behind. The commodore tells me I may soon be assigned to *Minnesota*." The big 44-gun frigate had been present at the Battle of Hampton Roads.

"I'll think of you as we work our way down the Carolina coast, Roswell. I wish I could bring my young Hawai'ian master's mate, Kekoa Kalama, to the meeting with Bache and Agassiz. He has studied the ancient Polynesian and Micronesian star navigation techniques, and would engender a sparkling discussion, I'm sure!"

"So he would, Tobias. I want to ask Dr. Bache more about the Gulf Stream investigation, and whether the Survey will expand its geodectic land work after the war. Right now, he has your former Survey colleagues going in with the first wave on our land-sea operations, sounding and replacing harbor bouys while under sniper fire!"

The two friends conversed on matters navigational, said their goodbyes, and within two days, Tobias was navigating his way to *Woonsocket's* next landfall, Charleston Harbor. The *Woonsocket's* course to Veracruz enabled her to pause at Charleston to receive dispatches from the commander of the South Atlantic Blockading Squadron and to relay them to the flagship of the Gulf Blockading Squadron off Mobile Bay.

As they drove south in the Gulf Stream, Tobias reflected on his service in the U.S. Coast Survey, and upon the leadership of Alexander Bache. *We would not know of the Gulf Stream's effect on navigation and weather, if Dr. Bache had not moved the Survey beyond the charting of the coasts to collecting temperatures and flows in the Stream itself,* he mused. *What vision the man has! And how lucky I was to serve!*

Tobias was reviewing his charts in the wardroom when the captain's clerk found him. "Captain's compliments, and could you join him in his cabin, sir?" said the clerk.

"My respects to the captain, I'm on my way," Tobias replied. Tobias looked forward, as always, to an encounter with his commander,

Captain DeWitt Oakley. Oakley was cut from the same cloth as one of Tobias' previous captains, Henry French of the *Preble*. Like French, Oakley was a good sailor, fair, decisive, and respected by his crew.

"Sailing master reporting as ordered, sir."

"Come and sit down, Mr. St. John. You'll recall last autumn when I took Kalama aboard as an acting master's mate, I gave him a six month trial period."

"Yes, sir, I remember."

"Now that you've been his superior for a time, I'm interested in your assessment of his performance. Should I make him a master's mate?"

"His performance is excellent in every way, sir, in fact it matches or exceeds his more senior counterpart."

"Excellent. I'll make him, then," said Oakley. "You may deliver the news. Now, for a more immediate question, what's your estimate of our arrival time in Charleston?"

"Just before sunset, sir," said Tobias, thankful he'd had all his calculations at his fingertips.

"Very well, sailing master, we'll deliver our dispatches to Admiral Du Pont that night and make our formal call upon him in the morning."

"Aye, aye, sir," Tobias replied, wondering where this unusual sharing of detail to a subordinate was going.

"You and the admiral have a history together, do you not?"

"Yes, sir, I was aboard *Wabash* during the Port Royal and Florida landings, and I was detached from the admiral's command for espionage in Wilmington."

"Excellent! I'll ask you to accompany me on our formal call. I'm sure he'll be delighted to see you."

"Aye, aye, sir. My pleasure, sir, and thank you." Tobias appreciated the honor Oakley was bestowing on a junior officer to partake in an admiral's call.

"That will be all, then, St. John. Eight bells in the morning watch."

"Aye, aye, sir." Tobias exited the cabin as the blue-coated Marine sentry closed the door behind him.

Tobias and Oakley sat in the sternsheets of the captain's gig as they left the hove-to *Woonsocket* for the pull to the flagship *Wabash*, several miles off the mouth of Charleston harbor. As they entered the admiral's cabin aboard *Wabash*, Tobias saw the admiral and two officers already seated at the table. Robert Smalls rose, his face breaking into a grin. "Mighty fine to see you, sailing master," he said warmly, extending his hand. Smalls wore the silver-edged shoulder bars and ship's wheel of a US Navy pilot on his uniform coat. As a slave pilot, Smalls had escaped with the other slave members of the CSS *Planter's* crew and delivered the gunboat to the union blockade. The navy had then made him a pilot.

The other officer, a lieutenant with piercing eyes and shoulder-length hair, rose as Du Pont said, "May I present Lieutenant William Cushing. I wanted you to see the results of the information network you set up, St. John. Mr. Cushing here has been taking *Commodore Barney* into the Stono River and Folly River based on information we get from your pilots' network and the rest of the 'Black Dispatch', and Mr. Smalls and the *Planter* have just returned from supporting the First South Carolina Volunteer regiment of colored troops in an expedition up the St. Mary's River in Georgia. *Planter* was transferred to the War Department last September. When Mr. Smalls delivered *Planter* to us in 1862, he also brought some valuable information about the abandonment of the Stono River. You were among the first to greet him, Mr. St. John. I'm sure you remember."

"Yes, I do, admiral. It's good to see you again, pilot," Tobias said to Smalls. "And a pleasure to meet you, Mr. Cushing." Cushing was tall, although not as tall as the towering Tobias, who stood six feet, two inches. Cushing's calm countenance gave no hint of his record in action: slightly wounded at Hampton Roads, surviving storms of gunfire on Pamlico Sound, the Carolina coasts and the islands below Charleston, and having his first command sunk during an attack on Jacksonville, North Carolina at New River Inlet.

"The network you uncovered has enabled us to contain the Charleston defenses on James Island, Mr. St. John. I'd enjoy taking you up the Stono to see for yourself."

"I know St. John would like nothing better, lieutenant, but we're proceeding to Mobile Bay with dispatches," said Oakley.

"Another time, then, Mr. St. John?"

"I'll look forward to it, Mr. Cushing."

"We're liable to have plenty of action here soon, gentlemen," said Du Pont. "Washington is determined to make an attack on Sumter with our monitors and other ironclads, against my advice, I might add."

"You think it can't succeed, sir?" Oakley asked.

"At close range, gentlemen, I'm convinced we're more vulnerable than the fort. It won't sink. But, we'll follow our orders as they come." Du Pont shrugged his shoulders and his subordinates were silent, each contemplating the results of an assault on the formidable fortification.

After the call on the admiral, Smalls and Tobias spoke on deck. "Are you enjoying your service as a free pilot, Robert?"

"I shorely am, Tobias. I don't know where dese changing times will take us, but it's good to be part of it. And I haven't run us aground yet!"

"We'll keep our hopes high, and our expectations low, my friend."

Smalls grinned at the tall Antiguan. "Dat's de way to face each day!"

CHAPTER 7
ADVENTURE IN VERACRUZ
MARCH 1863

The strong natural and man-made defenses of Veracruz were evident from the foredeck of *USS Woonsocket* where Tobias stood beside the rail. He was glad that they were in harbor several weeks in advance of the April onset for the malaria season.   Veracruz had been the seat of the Liberal regime, led by Juarez, during the Mexican civil war begun in 1858.   Now, it was a French-held port, as the French and the Mexican conservative forces strove to oust President Juarez from the capital, Mexico City.   In a careful balancing of national interests, the French allowed free use of the port to Union ships as well as those of other nations.   The French base for their interests and for their puppet conservative Mexican government was seventy miles west of Veracruz, in Orizaba.   Several French warships lay in the harbor.   Tobias put his telescope to his eye to read the name of the nearest: *Cuirassier.*   The *Woonsocket's* surgeon, Doctor Willard Miles, stood beside Tobias at the rail.

"You're looking at the source of a dangerous disease in the coast around Veracruz, Tobias, come next month," said the surgeon.   "When I expressed my concerns about the malaria season, the captain assured me we won't linger that long."

Tobias smiled at the surgeon.   "I like that you're always thinking of us, your potential patients, Willard."   Tobias and Willard had become friends on the voyage south.   Willard was a Philadelphia Free Quaker, like Tobias' father, and willing to serve in the navy as long as he could save lives instead of taking them.   The kindly gray-haired surgeon and Tobias had spent many hours off watch talking together. Although Tobias no longer considered himself a practicing Quaker, he had been raised and educated in the Society of Friends, and he and the doctor shared many beliefs. Miles was also a strong abolitionist.

That evening, Tobias was rowed ashore with Captain Oakley in the captain's gig. They were to meet the agent of Juarez, Montoya y Hinojosa, at the Hotel Independencia for dinner. The gig secured at the *muelle* or mole, a long masonry dock extending into the harbor, to await the return of the two officers. Oakley and Tobias walked a short distance up the Paseo de Malaco'n to the hotel where they were greeted at the dining room by the maitre d'. "*Señores*," he said, "*Señor* Montoya y Hinojosa is already at your table and is expecting you." Tobias noticed the ill-concealed surprise of the maitre d' at the sight of a black officer. They were shown to a table where a stocky man of middle years rose to meet them.

"Juan Francisco de la Montoya y Hinojosa, at your service, gentlemen. Please call me 'Paco'."

Montoya was a full-blooded member of Oaxaca's Zapotec tribe, as was the man he served, Benito Juarez. He was fully conversant with the political situation in Veracruz and in Matamoros, the border city at the mouth of the Rio Grande. "Governor Vidaurri has decided it is better to cast his lot with the Liberals, who are not strong enough to diminish his independence, rather than with the conservatives, who, with the French, will most certainly interfere with his monopoly of customs fees. After we meet with the president at Xalapa, we will go north, with the help of Captain Oakley, to Vidaurri's stronghold. I'm confident he won't interfere with our 'confiscation' of Confederate muskets as long as he loses no profit in the transaction. Of course, the president has appointed him only as the military governor of Tamaulipas, but he exerts more influence than the titular governor of the state."

"*Señor* Montoya," Tobias began.

"Paco, please," said Montoya.

"Paco, the French are here in strength since their defeat at Puebla last May. Can your forces withstand an attack on the capital?"

"I will let the president answer that question, *señor*. We will see him soon enough. He has asked me to bring you to Xalapa as soon as possible. He is most eager to meet Mr. Lincoln's envoy."

They agreed that Tobias would return to *Woonsocket*, dress in his native Caribbean costume, and be rowed to a point across the harbor from the island fortress of San Juan de Ulua. There, Paco and a small mounted escort would accompany him to Xalapa, outside the area of French control, to meet Juarez. It would be a three-day ride to accommodate the modest pace of an inexperienced rider like Tobias.

As they parted company, Oakley encountered an Annapolis classmate from a U.S. frigate in the harbor. "Oakley, come join our party and meet my officers," said the frigate commander, ignoring Tobias.

"Go ahead, sir," said Tobias. "I'll wait on the veranda at the Plaza de Armas."

Tobias walked to the nearby plaza and took a seat at an outside table of a café. The wide plaza, a block square, was bordered by a veranda upon which many shops opened. It was evening, and friends and couples were gathering for the evening *paseo*. The Veracruzans seated on the shaded veranda viewed the plaza through dozens of archways. The roof of the veranda protected those below from the sun, and in the evenings, funneled a cool breeze through the archways to dispel the heavy evening humidity. Tobias ordered a cool cup of chocolate. At the next table sat a burly, middle-aged officer in French naval uniform. "*Bon soir, capitaine,*" he said politely in his passable French.

"Good evening, sailing master. Do I detect a trace of Breton accent?" The French captain, with graying blonde, shoulder-length hair, had a kind face and a quick smile.

"*Oui, capitaine,* I was born and raised in Antigua. I fell in love with a woman in *les Iles des Saintes*. She is half Breton, and I learned French from her."

"Permit me to introduce myself. I am Jean Gilbert Duquesne, captain of the *Cuirassier*. Please join me at my table."

"Thank you, sir. I am Tobias St. John, sailing master of the *Woonsocket.*

With a flash of recognition, Duquesne said, "I believe I know a friend of yours, a Lieutenant Dunbrody? I met him at the Battle of

Hampton Roads."

"He is, indeed, my dear friend, but how did you connect us, sir?"

"He described you as a tall man of color, and a sailing master. You are most probably the only man of that description in your navy. And he painted you as a man of action. I can see that in you. I merely used my powers of deduction, as any good navigator would, *vraiment?* Do you know how Dunbrody is faring?"

"He is well, sir, as of December when I last had word. He received the Thanks of the Confederate Congress for action against Union gunboats on the Piankatank River."

"He, too, is a man of action. I met him just before the battle of Hampton Roads, which we were privileged to observe. My fellow observer there, Capitaine de Jonquines, commands the corvette you see in the harbor, the *Berthollet.* What brings you here, sailing master?"

"Why, captain, I'm but a junior officer of a ship on patrol."

"Oh, assuredly," said Duquesne with a conspiratorial smile. "But, a junior officer who wears the Medal of Honor. Yet, I would always take the word of an officer and gentleman, and a neutral, as well, regarding Louis Napoleon's little excursion here." He sighed. "How I hope *Cuirassier* is gone from Veracruz before the malaria season."

"Your troops seem numerous, sir."

"*Mais oui,* numerous and largely unwelcome. The British and Spanish negotiated a settlement of Mexico's debts to them, but not we French. We press on, hoping to impose a monarchy. But mine not to question, simply to do my duty. As sailors, we understand that, do we not?"

"Yes, sir. We have our duty to do. I have heard officers far more knowledgeable than I am about international affairs say that the European powers would be pleased if the United States became fragmented as a result of this war, and therefore less able to insist on favorable U.S. trade policy in this hemisphere. Is this a valid point of view?" Tobias sipped from his chocolate and awaited Duquesne's answer.

"That view goes hand-in-hand with our Emperor's desire for a stronger presence in your northern hemisphere, it is true, sailing master." Duquesne shrugged his shoulders. "But having seen the industrial strength of your Union, I have doubts about the ability of the South to prevail, and I have observed that even our ostensible supporters here, the conservatives, are none too enthusiastic about accepting a European monarchy. The issue is definitely still in doubt, my friend."

Tobias glanced toward the plaza. "This conversation has been both pleasant and illuminating, *capitaine*. I'm grateful for your insights and your courtesy. I wish we could continue, but I see my commander is ready. By your leave, *capitaine?*"

"*Au revoir* and *bonne chance*, Mr. St. John. Perhaps we will someday have an opportunity for more of this pleasurable discourse."

At midnight, a boat from *Woonsocket* landed Tobias on the Mexican shore across the harbor from the gloomy bulk of Fort San Juan de Ulua, a massive, multi-bastioned stone fortress that dominated the harbor. He carried a small pack, two navy six Colt revolvers, a nondescript cutlass, and his Henry repeating rifle. The pack contained a tarpaulin jacket, and he wore a tarpaulin hat, a loose-fitting Antiguan shirt and white duck trousers ending at mid–calf.

Paco and four other mounted men greeted him as he left the light surf, and he mounted a decidedly docile bay mare. They rode north, northwest and inland, climbing through the steepening terrain, past cattle and sugar cane toward Xalapa Enriquez, fifty miles distant as the crow flies, and 4000 feet in elevation. The gradual ascent took the party past Cerro Gordo, an 1848 Mexican War battle site, and a hilltop fort near Plan del Rio, where the hills grew more pronounced. On the third day, Paco cautioned Tobias as the wind rose. "This is a '*sur*', amigo. These winds rush down from the mountains during the dry season and blow heavy clay tiles from the roofs. Hang on!" Among his companions, Tobias' limited riding skills were a frequent source of amusement.

They arrived late the next night at a secluded hacienda in the high, mountainous country outside Xalapa. Lencero was an ancient hacienda, an appropriate meeting place for history in the making. The next morning, after breakfast, they met with President Juarez and an aide in the great room of the hacienda. After introductions, they sat at a large table, set with fruit, wafers, breads and juices. Tobias noted how similar in appearance Montoya and Juarez were, both short, stocky, dark, and intensely focused.

"Mr. St. John," Juarez began, "I apologize for not receiving Mr. Lincoln's emissary with the pomp and ceremony due him. I deemed it best to meet away from the intrigues of my government in Mexico City."

"Quite understandable and most prudent, your Excellency. Mr. Lincoln sends his warmest regards and his great admiration, as he said, 'lawyer to lawyer and president to president.'"

"I reciprocate those regards. Please convey them to President Lincoln."

"Aye, aye, sir." Juarez looked a bit startled at the naval response, and then smiled. Tobias returned the smile and continued. "The president asked me to convey his regrets that he cannot enforce the Monroe Doctrine while the outcome of the war with the Rebels is still seen to be in question. He hopes that we will soon be seen as the inevitable winner, and he can then be more assertive with the French."

"Tell Mr. Lincoln that I fully understand his dilemma, and that I am grateful for the degree of support he is able to manifest. You should know that our government is still being courted by the Confederates. Their zeal, however, has diminished as the French grow stronger, and I fully expect they shall court the Conservatives and the French as assiduously as they have my Liberals, when the French army forces me to flee the capital, as they surely will."

"Do you expect this soon, sir?"

"I do. The French will soon attack Puebla again. We defeated them last year on *el cinco de Mayo*, but they will be many times stronger in this attempt. After they take Puebla, we cannot deny them Mexico City. I will leave, but I have many supporters in the north and south, and we will hold out until the French grow weary of holding up the Conservatives."

"Mr. Lincoln hopes eventually to be in a position to send you muskets directly from Louisiana. Secretary of State Seward advises him strongly to avoid the risk of angering the French by sending you arms or extending a loan. The president recognizes the value of this advice, but I know it still rankles him to be unable to provide you direct aid."

"In the mean time, *Señor* St. John, Mexico appreciates the risk you will take in order to 'divert' the shipment of Confederate muskets in

Matamoros to our cause."

"It will be a triumph for your nation and mine, Excellency. Let's hope for success."

"Ultimate success may be a longer time coming for Mexico than for the Union. It is clear that Napoleon III will set up a puppet monarch who will support the resurgence of the Church as a political power here. But I think the French will eventually find that the Conservatives are not monarchists, any more than we Liberals. We have interesting years ahead."

"Excellency," said Montoya, "*Señor* St. John must depart now if he is to intercept the Confederate arms shipment. Can you leave him with an uplifting word?"

"Tell Mr. Lincoln that we both may yet defy the trends of history, and that men of courage and goodwill may, indeed, prevail!"

"I will carry your message, Excellency. *Buena suerte!*"

"And the best of good fortune to you in return, my friend."

CHAPTER 8
STANDOFF IN MATAMOROS
MARCH 1863

Paco stood next to Tobias near the *Woonsocket's* entry port five nights later. Kekoa and the senior master's mate, Kelso, held their gear, ready to hand it down into the jolly boat. The sloop of war was hove-to in the darkness off Boca de Sandoval and Laguna Madre, a number of miles south of Matamoros and the mouth of the Rio Grande, or the Rio Bravo, as it was called in Mexico.

Matamoros, thirty miles as the crow flies from the gritty little village of Bagdad at the river mouth, was a port at which runners of the Union blockade were able to land arms shipments with impunity, and, in return, ship cotton cargoes to Europe. The mighty river deposited vast quantities of silt at its delta. Blockade runners were obliged to anchor three to four miles off its mouth because the depth of the channel in the delta was only four to five feet. The Mexicans sent shallow-draft steamers as lighters from Bagdad to the ships, and then back up river to the wharves at Matamoros. There, the incoming cargoes of both luxury items and contraband of war were accepted by Matamoros merchants, sometimes transferred ashore to Matamoros warehouses, but often on paper without off-loading, and then lightered across the river to Confederate merchants at Brownsville, Texas, or up-river 300 miles to Piedras Negras, the "Black Stones." Cotton was then brought from Matamoros to the anchored blockade runners by the small steamers. While it was only 35 miles from Matamoros to Bagdad, the meandering trip by river was closer to sixty.

Captain Oakley left the quarterdeck to bid them goodbye as

they disembarked. "Mr. St. John, we will patrol off the mouth of the Rio Grande, as a good blockader ought, until we receive the signal from the Juaristas to recover you. Good luck to you and *Señor* Montoya in seizing the Confederate muskets."

"Aye, aye, sir. Thank you, sir." Tobias and Paco swung down the boarding ladder into the waiting jolly boat.

"*Malama pono*, sir," said Kekoa.

"What did he say?" asked Kelso of Oakley.

"I believe he just told Mr. St. John to take care, Mr. Kelso," answered Oakley. "Don't trouble yourself."

"*Mahalo nui loa.*" Tobias' response could just be heard over the wind and surf.

Ashore, they were greeted by the local Juarista agent, on the shores of Laguna Madre, accompanied by an armed escort. "*Señores*, I am Miguel Ignacio Morelos, at your service. Please call me 'Nacho'." They rode slowly and silently to the outskirts of Matamoros, through the acres of chaparral and mesquite thorn bushes that surrounded the city. They entered the city, where they found shelter and instant sleep on pallets in a low brick building near a riverside warehouse. "There," whispered Nacho, "is where the cotton is housed, and where the muskets will be kept for acquisition by *los Confederates*."

As Tobias awoke at daybreak, he stumbled groggily to the dirt-caked window overlooking the riverside and the cotton-filled warehouse. Steam lighters from a blockade runner bore slowly toward the warehouse wharf. Tobias could barely see the shallow-draft boats, masked further by the encrusted window he looked through, but he recognized the men aboard as blockade runner crewmen, English, Scots and Irish. While he and his companions ate cold breakfast rations, they watched Mexican stevedores stagger under the weight of the musket crates they carried from the lighters to the warehouse. Late in the morning, a relief crew of 'longshoremen began the two-day loading of the cotton bales aboard the steam lighters for the downstream trip to the blockade runner anchored off the river mouth.

Nacho slipped out of their brick hideaway and returned some hours later with rations and news. "The ship, she is the *Albion*, a British blockade runner commanded by a man named Ludlow. While the stevedores load the cotton aboard the down-stream steamers, Quintero's men are preparing the muskets to be loaded in boats for the trip upriver. They'll begin loading at nightfall. Quintero will be there, supervising."

"My God, Ludlow again," exclaimed Tobias. "This man recurs in my life like a nightmare!"

Paco chuckled. "Not a favorite of yours, *amigo?*"

"We've tried to kill each other before, Paco, *es verdad*," Tobias responded with a smile. "He'd not be happy if he knew I was near. But, in theory, he is an unarmed blockade runner, and if we come to combat, he becomes a pirate, under international law."

"At what point should we try to seize Quintero?" Paco glanced out the window at the warehouse, and then at Nacho as he asked his question.

"Quintero has an office two blocks up *Calle Rio*, River Street, from the warehouse. He'll return to it for a meal and a glass of wine around midnight, if his past behavior holds true. That is our moment!"

"Is General Escobedo ready upriver?" Tobias asked. The Mexicans spoke English in deference to his poor Spanish.

"Assuredly. I sent word myself," said Nacho.

As night fell, the three conspirators spotted Jose' Quintero, sporting a peaked campaign hat, addressing his men as they prepared to load the muskets aboard the pulling boats that would transport them upriver. They then fell asleep on their pallets for brief catnaps. They were, after all, veterans of combat and campaign, with the combatant's knowledge that opportunity for sleep was precious, and not to be squandered.

Tobias awoke at eleven o'clock, being used to sleeping in four hour stretches, the length of a watch at sea. He looked first at his Henry rifle, cutlass, and pistols beside him, leaning against his saddle. Then, he peered out the dingy window and saw Quintero's men still loading the muskets in the boats. He woke his companions, and, before midnight, they slipped out of their lair and hid in a dark alley opposite Quintero's office.

Footsteps echoed from the cobblestones and brick walls of

the buildings on this section of the *avenida*. Quintero, still wearing his campaign hat, fumbled for his keys at his doorway, directly across the street from the alley mouth. Tobias, in stocking feet, glided silently across the street and seized Quintero, clapping one hand across his mouth as he crooked his arm around Quintero's neck from behind. Montoya and Morelos hurried to the struggling men. They quickly gagged and bound Quintero, and slipped back through the alleys to their hiding place, carrying the bound Confederate agent.

The three took turns watching the loading and keeping an eye on Quintero. As each boat was loaded, it cast off from the dock and headed upriver, soon out of sight. At two in the morning, Tobias was at the window, and saw several of Quintero's men in animated discussion. Four of them ran toward Quintero's office, as the last boat pulled away, loaded with musket crates.

"We've done it!" Tobias was jubilant. "Quintero's men, leaderless, are on their way upriver, into the hands of Escobedo. All we have to do is keep Quintero out of sight, and then rejoin *Woonsocket*!"

"Tobias," cried Nacho, "I'm going to check the warehouse while they're looking for Quintero!" His eyes alight, Morelos ran to the front door opening on to the *avenida*. Tobias leaped to his feet to stop him, but it was too late.

"Paco, why does he need to check the warehouse? The guns are gone and we have Quintero!" Tobias sighed in exasperation. "He's exposed out there. I have a bad feeling about this."

"*Yo tambien, amigo*," Paco replied. "He just needed to act, I suppose. Too much waiting. I'll guard the door. Let's hope he returns soon."

"He's coming this way," said Tobias, looking out the window. "My God! There're Quintero's men! They see him coming toward us. They've got him!" Tobias looked at Quintero. The Confederate agent's eyes were narrowed in triumph and he smiled through his gag.

"Paco! Quick! Out the back door! Ride for Bagdad and the coast. Quintero's men will soon find that we're here. I'll hold them. You must report our success to Mr. Lincoln and your government! *Woonsocket* will be anchored off the river mouth. Find her!"

"They'll kill you, Tobias!"

"It will take them some time, *amigo*. I have my repeater. Go! Now!"

Paco shook his head in dismay as he grabbed his pistols and saddle and rushed for the back door. Tobias broke a front window with the butt of his Henry rim-fire. Quintero's men had bound Nacho and were pointing a gun at his head when the crash of breaking glass riveted their attention on the brick building. Tobias sent three quick shots toward the man with the pistol at Nacho's head, hitting him in the leg. The four men scattered and returned fire. Tobias crouched below the window as the hoof beats of Paco's horse echoed up the street. A fusillade of pistol fire crashed through the windows facing the river. Tobias bolted the door through which Paco had exited, and quickly dragged a desk and several heavy timbers together against the rear wall as a makeshift barricade facing the front door.

"Surrender, or we'll kill this cockroach!" Quintero's men shouted to Tobias.

"If you kill him, we will kill Quintero!" Tobias shouted back. *The longer a lead I can give Paco, the better his chances of signaling Oakley from Bagdad's shore and bringing the report to Lincoln,* he thought. *Now, if I can only give Nacho a fighting chance.*

"Perhaps we can arrange an exchange, *amigo?*" A voice floated in through the smashed-out window.

"I'm listening!"

"Bring Quintero to the door. We will free your *compadre*. They will step slowly in unison, Quintero toward us, your friend toward the alley and escape. When your friend is gone, you must swear not to shoot Quintero in the back. When both hostages are safe, we can discuss terms of the surrender of you and the rest of your party."

"*Un momento*. I must discuss this with my men." Tobias smiled crazily to himself. *The great battalion commander St. John addresses his troops!*

"We will agree to your terms." Tobias left Quintero's gag and bound wrists in place. He would wait for any reaction on the part of Quintero's men.

"Let us see *Señor* Quintero in the doorway!"

Tobias reached for his seaman's clasp knife, razor sharp, and cut the cords around Quintero's ankles. He seized him beneath a shoulder and hoisted him to his feet with one powerful arm, his other holding his rifle. "You understand the arrangements, *señor?* Nod if you do."

Quintero nodded once, and glared hatefully at Tobias.

Tobias guided Quintero's unsteady course to the front door, and stood slightly in the shadows behind him, the Henry trained on his back. "They will count, *señor.* Take a step for each. *Buena suerte.*" Tobias smiled at the irony.

As each numeral was called out, each man stepped forward, Nacho toward the relative safety of the alley, and Quintero, toward his men. When the count reached *diez y seis,* Nacho ran down the alley. "We will come to claim *Señor* Quintero, *amigo,* as agreed."

"As you wish, *señor.* Then, we will talk."

Two men emerged from the shadows of the warehouse and assisted Quintero to the warehouse doorway. Tobias could hear him try to speak as his men removed the gag, gasping at first and then after a drink of water, sputtering with rage and indignation. "Imbeciles! There is only one man! Go! Take him now!" Tobias' limited Spanish could make out most of the words: "*solo un hombre,*" "*adelante,*" "*ahora,*" "*imbecil*". He laid two navy six revolvers on a plank in front of him and picked up his Henry .44. He fired and cocked six shots from the repeater in rapid succession, then three from a pistol, then seven more from the rifle, then three from a pistol, then two more distinctive heavy barks from the rifle and two from the second pistol.

"Does that sound to you like the gunfire from one man, *amigo?* We are many and we are armed!" As he reloaded, Tobias went to the window. Silence greeted him.

Finally, a voice called, registering at once confusion and skepticism. "Many or one, you must surrender or you will receive no quarter! We have a field piece from our British friends we can use. We will soon bring the building down around your heads."

"You must give us some time to discuss this."

"You have five minutes, *señor.* Then, only the Fates can save you, and your chances are slim!"

Tobias waited as the first hint of dawn lightened the night sky. Five minutes, then ten. Finally, he heard: "Your time is up, *señor*. Surrender now and live, or later die!"

"We are coming out, *señor*."

"First, throw your weapons out the front door."

Tobias threw his four pistols, his cutlass, and his Henry rifle out the door and on to the cobblestones, rattling and echoing, one by one. *Paco should have an hour lead on pursuit, by now,* he thought.

"Throw out the rest, *señor*."

"That is all I have," Tobias replied. "I am coming out now. Your leader was correct. I am alone." Tobias stepped through the doorway, his hands raised, and stepped slowly toward the warehouse. Quintero and his men came forward, guns trained on the tall Negro, their faces a mix of anger and disbelief, discernible in the burgeoning light of daybreak.

"Seize him, tie his hands and put a halter about his neck," cried Quintero. They lead Tobias to the warehouse, threw him down on a wooden loading pallet, and secured his neck halter to an iron ring set in a massive wooden pillar supporting a roof beam. He heard a man report to Quintero. "No more men or weapons in the building, *señor.*"

Tobias listened to a murmured discussion of his fate, unable to discern words, conscious of angry tones, exhausted, his hands bound behind him and his wrists in excruciating pain. He closed his eyes and drifted, slowly, thankfully, into drowsiness. He jerked upright, startled by the supercilious, nasal whine of an upper class English accent from a voice he recognized only too well. "I say, can one of you chaps sign this bill of lading? This evening's tide will be favorable, and I'm bound down river to return to my ship, and weigh anchor with your cotton."

Ludlow! Tobias grit his teeth in frustration.

"Hello," said Ludlow in surprise, "what's this?" laughing as he saw Tobias tethered to the pillar. "My word, it's that damned Yankee blackamoor! I might have known you'd be in the thick of this melee."

"*Señor Capitan*, you leave with this evening's tide, *si*?" Quintero smiled ingratiatingly in the early morning sun. "Perhaps you would be willing to assist us in a delicate matter?"

"How might I be of service, *Señor* Quintero?"

"This man is an agent of President Lincoln. I know from overhearing him talk to the other agents, who escaped. It would be embarrassing and inconvenient for Governor Vidaurri if this man remains within his jurisdiction. In turn, that would adversely affect our arrangement with your ship and the Confederates."

"It would be helpful if he disappeared, then?" Ludlow smiled at the Mexican.

"Si, muy util, capitan."

"Won't the other agents raise questions if he should vanish?"

"But *capitan,* they are gone. We will insist that this one too, escaped. Who is to say otherwise?"

"Finnegan!" Ludlow roared in a voice that would penetrate a gale. A stocky boatswain appeared in the doorway. "Put a tarpaulin over this man so he can't be identified and secure him aboard the steam lighter. Post a guard. Post two! Oh, and gag him first."

The efficient Finnegan bound and gagged Tobias, wrapped him in a tarpaulin, and transported him in a cart to the steam lighter at the wharf, where four seamen carried the still-cloaked sailing master to be shackled to a thwart amid the cotton bales. Lying uncomfortably on the bottom-boards, Tobias listened to the sounds of the steamer casting off. She headed downstream toward the dingy village of Bagdad, at the mouth of the Rio Grande. After a twelve hour trip amid frequent groundings on the river's shifting sandbars, the steam lighter headed off-shore in the fading daylight to the anchored *Albion.*

CHAPTER 9
PERFIDIOUS ALBION
MARCH 1863

Tobias lay on a bunk in the crew's quarters aboard *Albion*, the British blockade-runner. His hands were still shackled, but no longer behind his back. His leg was shackled to the bunk. "Sorry, sir," Finnegan the boatswain had apologized, "Captain Ludlow's orders, and you're to remain triced-up. But he didn't say your hands shackled front or back, so we'll make you more comfortable and we'll take that gag off as well."

"I'm grateful, bo'sun," Tobias had responded. He now listened to the hiss of the boilers as the swift blockade-runner raised steam and prepared to weigh anchor. The crew's quarters were in the deckhouse abaft *Albion's* after stack. Through a grimy port, Tobias could make out other blockade runners anchored nearby, waiting for their cargoes. In the distance toward the low shore, he could see small schooners thread their way south behind the low coastal barrier islands, bringing more cotton from Texas to Bagdad. Tobias knew that as soon as night had fallen and the tide was favorable, the ship would make her dash to the open sea. *And my departure point from the ship to Davy Jones' locker, unless I think of an escape plan,* thought Tobias. Exhausted, he closed his eyes and fell asleep.

Tobias awoke with a start thirty minutes later, to the sounds of the anchor being weighed. The beat of the paddle wheels began. Through the port, he could see stars. *A clear night!* Tobias thought. *If Paco made his way to the Woonsocket, I may have a chance. Oakley is as savvy a commander as you could wish for. Let's hope visibility stays good, and that Ludlow strays close enough to American waters to give Oakley an excuse to intercept.* Tobias' thoughts raced south of Guadeloupe, to his love,

Monique. *I'll see her again or die trying,* he vowed. *Maybe I can get some concessions out of our Irish boatswain.*

No sooner had he thought of Finnegan than the boatswain appeared at the door of the tiny crew's quarters. "It's sorry I am to tell you, sailing master, but I've orders to put you over the side. May heaven bless you, sir."

"Mr. Finnegan, if you'd find it in your heart to slip me the shackle keys as you toss me overboard, the saints will line up to greet you on your way into heaven, as my dear friend Rory Dunbrody might say."

Finnegan thought for a moment. "Sure, what harm could it do? You'll not last long out there, sir, but if it will ease your passin', I'll put the keys in your hand at the proper moment, I will. The least I can do for a fellow sailor, and the friend of an Irishman. I don't mind tellin' you, sir, my heart's not in this kind of work, but the captain, he's a hard man."

"As Dunbrody would say, God save you, Mr. Finnegan."

The *Albion* drove into the chop of a freshening breeze blowing onshore. Her speed had increased to thirteen knots. The onshore wind blew scattered clouds fitfully across the stars of a moonless night. As Finnegan and a crewman brought Tobias to the 'midships rail, they heard Ludlow's voice from the open bridge deck above the wheel house, "Now's the time, Mr. Finnegan."

"To the rail, if you please, sailing master." Finnegan gripped Tobias firmly by one arm and carefully pressed the shackle keys into his hands. "There'll be a longboat sweep followin' you overside to buoy you up, me lad. The saints preserve ye, now."

Tobias was led to the rail, consisting of wires led through stanchions to reduce the weight of the speedy ship. At that moment, he and Finnegan were blinded by an exceedingly bright yellow flash. *Have I died already?* He wondered.

"Blockader to starboard," came a lookout's cry. "She's fired a flare!" Finnegan shoved Tobias back inside the crew's quarters. "You're a lucky man, sailing master, I'm waiting for orders before I throw you overboard, which means I'll not need to be dreadin' my next confession."

On the bridge, Ludlow's night vision was likewise destroyed. He rushed to the engine room voice pipe on the conning bridge. "Engineer, give me all you have, we've a blockade ship to starboard." He spoke to the helmsman in the wheelhouse below through a second voice pipe, "Hard a port! We'll be changing course back to starboard in two minutes. I want to throw off their aim. Be ready."

Shots were falling close aboard the *Albion* as she headed away from *Woonsocket* and toward Texas. Ludlow heard a tremendous crash from the starboard side and looked aft to see the starboard paddle box still disintegrating from a direct hit. The ship slewed around to starboard, losing speed as a fire started by an exploding shell reached the cotton bales stacked on deck. Finnegan climbed to the bridge. "The way's off her, sir, and the engine room crew is coming on deck." Another shot, a 32-pound ball this time, struck the longboat suspended in davits just forward of the bridge. Finnegan and Ludlow could see their pursuer clearly now in the starry night, a Union sloop of war, swinging to a parallel course to starboard close alongside and launching boats.

"Get those burning bales overside, Mr. Finnegan, and lower the flag. Did you get our prisoner overboard?"

"Sure, and he's in the crew's quarters, sir. I thought y' might not want to commit murder with the Union Navy watchin'."

"You're not paid to think, old fellow. Carry on then. I'll deal with him myself." Ludlow left the bridge and made his way aft. He drew a revolver. Crewmen were shoving smoldering bales of cotton overboard with long boathooks. He could see no light in the crew's quarters as he peered through the port. He opened the door quietly, stepping inside cautiously. The door slammed violently against his face, trapping him momentarily against the door jam. He stumbled forward, just as Tobias swung a heavy bunk stanchion against the back of his skull.

Ludlow lay motionless. Tobias turned him over with his foot. *I'm torn between wishing that you're dead, and hoping you'll survive to be tried for attempted murder. I surmise your bo'sun failed to mention he'd given me the shackle keys.* With that thought, Tobias began to laugh uncontrollably.

A fusillade of pistol shots brought Tobias' hysterical laughter under control. The boarders from the sloop of war were on deck. He heard shouts through the open door: "Hands in the air! Drop that boat hook!" Then Kekoa's voice: "Mistah St. John, Mistah St. John!"

"Over here, Mr. Kalama, abaft the paddle wheel box!" Tobias retrieved Ludlow's revolver and kept it trained on his inert form.

Kekoa led a boarding party up the ladder over the port paddle wheel box, still intact, and down again to the deck where Tobias stood at the crew quarters door. He stopped, a look of relief on his face. "You all right, sir?" he asked.

"I am now, master's mate." Tobias beamed with relief at seeing his shipmate. "Now this one," he said, pointing to Ludlow, "he's an evil man, who almost had me overboard." Tobias stepped through the door, and retrieved the shackles and keys from the deck. "Secure him in these, Mr. Kalama. He'll be on trial for attempted murder, if my wishes come true."

"Aye, aye, sir. Captain Oakley said to bring you aboard *Woonsocket* as soon as we found you, sir. The boat's alongside."

Oakley stood at the entry port as Tobias came aboard. Juan Francisco de la Montoya y Hinojosa stood beside him. "You're a sight for sore eyes, Mr. St. John," said Oakley, grinning broadly. "*Señor* Montoya and I were worried we'd not find you on this broad ocean."

"As was I, captain. *Buenas noches*, Paco. Thank you for carrying the message to Captain Oakley. You saved my life."

"*No hay de que, amigo.* It was you who took the risks and prevailed against misfortune! When I heard you say you had a history with the captain of the blockade-runner, I suspected he would be compelled to assure himself of your death. Captain Oakley agreed that it was our best chance to effect your rescue if we intercepted *Albion*. Fortune smiled on us all!"

"Indeed, *señor*. Captain, the *Albion's* boatswain saved my life by an act of compassion. His conscience led him to contravene the intentions of his commander, which were to murder me. Can we reward the one, and see to the punishment of the other?"

"We'll do our best, sailing master. The trial of a British subject and a furloughed Royal Navy officer make this a case more complicated than most. But I'm sure of my bearings. *Albion* was in American waters when we sighted her. We're all exhausted from the heat of battle. Let's sleep on the challenge and meet in the morning."

CHAPTER 10
LEGAL ADVICE FROM ABE LINCOLN,
ATTORNEY AT LAW
APRIL 1863

The screw sloop of war *Woonsocket* made her way across the Gulf of Mexico and up the Atlantic coast to Washington, District of Columbia. Her most recent prize, the blockade-runner *Albion,* had been entrusted to the care of a U.S. Navy tug. After *Woonsocket* anchored in the Potomac, off Washington, her captain and her sailing master reported to the office of the Secretary of the Navy. Within the hour, Gideon Welles, Assistant Navy Secretary Gus Fox, Tobias, and Captain DeWitt Oakley had been joined by the President of the United States and Allan Pinkerton, a frequent consultant to the president on espionage matters.

"Gentlemen," said the president, "It's a pleasure to join you to learn details of our Mexican adventure."

"Mr. President, I'd like to ask Captain Oakley to present a summary of the Mexican mission, and have Mr. St. John fill in certain details."

"Splendid, Gideon. Mr. St. John, I'm pleased to see you in one piece." Tobias smiled in response, as Oakley began. Oakley described the meeting with Montoya, the subsequent landing of Tobias and Montoya south of Matamoros, and the interception of *Albion* with Tobias aboard. Tobias then gave the details of the meeting with Juarez, the clash in Matamoros, Tobias' capture by the Mexican agent of the Confederacy, Quintero, and Ludlow's attempt to commit murder. Lincoln listened intently, puffing on his pipe. Oakley concluded. "Mr. President, I was at a loss to know how to proceed with Captain Ludlow. We have a willing witness in his bo'sun, Finnegan, who will testify as to his orders to kill Mr. St. John. But given the difficulties with Britain over Captain Wilkes stopping the British packet *Trent* and removing the Confederate commissioners in '61, and the recent complaint from the British about taking their merchant ships off Matamoros in Mexican waters, I thought I should wait for guidance before trying Captain Ludlow, to preclude another international crisis, sir."

"Very prudent of you, captain," said Lincoln. "Clearly, you made the right decision. This is a very delicate situation. And congratulations on your decision to bring *Woonsocket* to confront *Albion* before she could get to the open sea. I realize your log shows you were north of 25 degrees, 55 minutes North Latitude, and therefore in American territorial waters. I'm confident we'll have no argument from President Juarez and his government that you might have been in Mexican waters."

"Thank you, sir," Oakley responded. "I should tell you that Captain Tatham of HMS *Phaeton*, stationed in the waters off the mouth of the Rio Grande, confided to me that the Royal Navy understands our difficulties in confronting English blockade runners that use the proximity of Brownsville and Matamoros as a ploy to thwart the blockade. He very graciously had me to dine aboard *Phaeton* and we discussed the diplomatic sensitivities of the situation."

Lincoln nodded appreciatively. "Captain Tatham's conciliatory attitude mirrors that of the British government. Lord Russell himself has said that Her Majesty's government cannot deny us the exercising of rights which they have previously claimed themselves." The president cleared his throat and continued. "When the citizens of a neutral nation undertake to break a blockade declared by a belligerent nation, they become subject to the international laws of war. If captured, they may be treated as prisoners of war."

Tobias smiled to himself as he listened. *I do believe the president is addressing us as a lawyer would a jury. He's taken himself back to the bar of the court!*

"If blockade-runners resist our blockaders by force," Lincoln went on, "under the law they may be treated as pirates. I believe that is the case here. Even though the port Ludlow left was Mexican, we have witnesses, Finnegan and *Señor* Montoya, to testify that he carried contraband of war which was trans-shipped to enter the Confederacy at Piedras Negras, and that it was intercepted by Mexico's General Escobedo, representing another neutral. And he gave orders to kill a US naval officer, an act of piracy."

Welles spoke up. "Let me play the devil's advocate, Mr. President. Could the British argue that *Woonsocket* stopped a ship from Matamoros, a neutral port, bearing a non-contraband cargo, the cotton, and therefore was not subject to blockade?"

"They might, but not effectively, I believe, now that they allow their subjects to construct ships in Great Britain built solely for the purpose of breaking our blockade. I realize *Albion* was not such a vessel, but our British cousins know that even converting *Albion* to the purpose stretches the rules of neutrality as never before. After all, *Albion* carried contraband in, no matter what it took out of port. That's why they don't protest our near-blockade of their Bermuda and Nassau ports, even though it galls them."

"Right, sir," said Fox. "They know we can demonstrate that their ports are *de facto* bases for the breaking of our blockade! And Port Isabel and Brownsville, on our side of the Rio Grande, are in Rebel hands. *Woonsocket* was stopping a ship which arguably carried cargo from a Confederate port!"

Lincoln smiled at Fox's enthusiasm. "We may have you try the case, Gus!"

"Mr. President, we may have one more high face card to play with the British." Oakley leaned forward, his elbows resting on the large conference table. "Mr. St. John told us he was threatened by Quintero's men at the warehouse standoff. They said they could persuade Ludlow to loan them a field piece he had hidden on *Albion*. Isn't that another violation of international law?"

"Indeed it is, captain. We'll use that as another hole card, to continue your analogy. Gentlemen, all this being said, here's my proposal. Ludlow and the crew will be detained as prisoners of war. Ludlow will be charged with piracy in federal court. We'll be sure to depose Finnegan, *Señor* Montoya, and perhaps General Escobedo, as well as all the *Woonsocket* crew involved. We'll move Finnegan to a comfortable facility, and promise suspension of any sentence in return for his testimony. The trial will take a long time. The war may end before it concludes. If we have a conviction, we'll allow the British to plead for commutation of the sentence. They can hardly ask for more than that, after we present them with the case we have. What say you all?"

Lincoln's summation was met with murmurs of assent by everyone. The president rose to leave, and all stood with him. "Gideon, we'll have to keep *Woonsocket* in the Caribbean and on the Atlantic coast so our witnesses are within reach as the trial goes forward. Mr. St. John, once again, you've carried out a dangerous assignment most successfully. Mr. Pinkerton's labors on our behalf are made easier by your efforts. Am I right, Allan?"

"Och, aye, sir," the Glaswegian replied. "'T'is bra that the lad came intae some more prize money, to salve the cruelties of combat, mind." Amid appreciative laughter, the meeting ended.

CHAPTER 11
THE SUFFOLK CAMPAIGN
APRIL 1863

Woonsocket swung gently to her anchor in Hampton Roads, off
Newport News, Virginia. She had been assigned to the North Atlantic
Blockading Squadron, still commanded by Admiral Samuel P. Lee, or
"Old Triplicate," as he was known in the navy. Lee was a "stickler"
crossing every "t," and dotting every "i." Tobias had been under his
command when he went behind enemy lines in Wilmington, North
Carolina, to effect the capture of three blockade runners while posing as a
slave pilot of the Cape Fear River. Lee had said at the time that he would
have recommended Tobias for a Medal of Honor if he didn't already have
one.

The North Atlantic Squadron was acting in support of Union
ground troops defending Suffolk, Virginia, several miles west of Norfolk,
and some eighteen miles up the Nansemond River, as the river meandered.
The Great Dismal Swamp was not far away. The Union forces in Suffolk
were threatened by two divisions under highly regarded Confederate
General "Pete" Longstreet, facing Union commanders of considerably less
competence. "At least, that's what Admiral Lee informs me," said Captain
Oakley as he spoke to Tobias in his cabin.

"It's fortunate the admiral had all his major ships begin infantry
and field artillery training for our crews," Oakley continued. "We'll be
asked to provide replacements for crews lost in this campaign, and to
augment the landing forces." Oakley paused. "The admiral specifically
asked for you. He said he's endorsing a request from the flotilla

commander, your old friend Lieutenant Lamson. You've been on several landings together and it seems he wants to add this one to the list. You'll meet Mr. Cushing again as well. He's commanding the *Commodore Barney*."

"It will be a pleasure to serve with them both, sir. What will my command be?"

"A battery of field howitzers, Mr. St. John. You'll have one hundred men in your command. Mr. Lamson is using USS *Stepping Stones* as flotilla flagship. He lost his own command, USS *Mt. Washington*, to the very battery you'll be assaulting, just a week ago. You may pick your men. I assume you'll want those you've been training."

"Yes, sir. I've had the gunner as second in command, and Mr. Kalama as third officer."

"Carry on then. You may use the launches to transport you to the flotilla. The *Commodore Barney* has room for the battery, being a converted ferry boat."

"Aye, aye, sir, I'll see to it immediately."

Late that evening, the *Woonsocket's* launches carried the limbers, wheels and howitzers of the battery and its 100-man contingent up the broad lower expanses of the Nansemond River. Its broad estuary joined the James River just west of the Elizabeth River, gateway to Norfolk. The *Commodore Barney* waited for them two miles upstream. As the sailors of the battery, under the urging of Gunner Cramer and Master's Mate Kalama, unloaded their guns and stowed their gear aboard, Tobias made his way to the pilot house. Lieutenant William Barker Cushing, commanding, shook his hand warmly. "Welcome aboard, Mr. St. John. This should be an interesting little enterprise, of a kind I know you're familiar with." Cushing's gleeful anticipation was palpable, and his reputation as an aggressive risk taker was widely known throughout the navy.

"I'm delighted to be a part of it, sir, and have a chance to take you up on your invitation to action when we met off Charleston earlier this year." Tobias smiled in response to Cushing's warm greeting.

"We're getting under way, sailing master. Please keep me company on the bridge, and I'll introduce you to the nooks and crannies of the mighty Nansemond. It's sixteen miles to Suffolk, where we'll rendezvous with Mr. Lamson. He'll be briefing us tonight on the assault, along with Mr. Brown of the *Couer de Lion*, our third gunboat, and Mr. Harris, commanding *Stepping Stones*. You outrank both Brown and Harris, by the way. They're both acting masters."

As they wended their way south up the Nansemond, Cushing eagerly pointed out the Union landing places and targets along the river bank. "Here's where the west branch of the Nansemond joins the river," Cushing said, pointing to starboard. "The river narrows considerably upstream of this point. Dead ahead is Fort Huger, the Rebel's battery on Hill's Point. It commands the river and forces us to pass it only at night. Mr. Lamson lost the *Mt. Washington* here last week when they put a shot through her boiler and she drifted aground. We had to tow her to Hampton Roads at night."

"Is Roswell all right, Mr. Cushing?"

"He was unhurt. Have you met him? Of course, I remember now. He told me you're friends and have served together in several operations from the *Wabash*. You need not be concerned. He's rarin' to go!"

They entered a bend in the upper river. "Here is where we've anchored before and laid down enfilading fire on the outer works of Fort Huger. We've forced them to abandon some of the rifle pits." Tobias could envision the enfilade, or sweeping fire from the side, cutting along the length of the rifle pits like a scythe.

Later that evening, they came to anchor off Suffolk. Roswell Lamson soon joined them aboard *Commodore Barney*. "Tobias, good of you to help us out. I promise you some excitement!"

"I don't doubt it, sir. I'm pleased to be included."

"Gentlemen, I have a suggestion," said Roswell. "The last time Tobias and I met, he was in command of our expeditionary force. We're all three of us with similar combat and command experience, and close in rank. Unless others are present, I'd like to proceed on a first name basis, as comrades and shipmates. Will, Tobias?"

"As you wish, sir-Roswell," said Tobias, smiling.

"Fine with me, Roswell," Cushing said.

"Excellent! Now, I propose to land elements of the Eighth Connecticut at the bend just upriver of Fort Huger at midnight tomorrow, from *Commodore Barney* and *Couer de Lion*. The *Barney* is by far the largest of our gunboats, and can carry the most men. They will then lay down an enfilading fire as the troops advance, alarming the enemy from his rear. Next, we'll land a howitzer battery from *Minnesota* under my command, and Tobias' *Woonsocket* battery, 200 sailors in all, from *Stepping Stones* and USS *Teaser* directly under the upper end of the Rebel fortifications. The landing place is quite close to the fort, and none of its guns can be depressed sufficiently to touch us. Four hundred of the Eighty-ninth New York will land with us and help drag the howitzers up the bank. Questions so far?"

Will spoke. "When will *Teaser* join us, Roswell?"

"She's bringing the men from the *Minnesota* up tonight. There's a tale! She was in the attack against *Minnesota* at the battle of Hampton Roads. We captured her from the Rebs last July. Is that irony? Listen! I hear Brown and Harris being piped aboard now. Let's fill them in on the battle plan."

The *Teaser,* when she arrived before dawn, brought the 100 men of the *Minnesota's* howitzer battery and half a dozen launches under tow to aid in landing the infantry. The day passed slowly. Tobias, aboard the *Commodore Barney,* spent his time with Gunner Cramer, Kekoa, and their gun captains. "You must designate 'boarders' from among your gun crews to be ready in case we need to augment the infantry as they assault the fort. Twenty-five men ready to seize cutlasses and pistols will do nicely."

"Sir," asked Kekoa, "will we be firing as the infantry come up to the fortifications? I fear for hitting our own troops."

"Good question, Mr. Kalama. Have you attacked a fort before?" Kekoa, Cramer and Tobias all began to laugh.

"Many a battery's forgotten to cease fire during the assault, sir," said Cramer. "It's truly a good question, young Mr. Kalama."

Tobias responded. "The infantry will fire red flares when they're within fifty yards of the fort, Mr. Kalama. At that point, we'll cease fire and stand by with our 'naval infantry', as needed. The *Commodore Barney* and the *Teaser* will also cease fire."

In mid May, Carlyle St. John, Tobias' father, found the following letter awaiting him after his day teaching at a Quaker Academy in New Bedford, Massachusetts.

Dear Father,

By now, I'm sure you've read of the recent actions on the Nansemond River, where we took Fort Huger from the Confederates, and repulsed the efforts of General Longstreet to cross the Nansemond and advance on Suffolk and Norfolk. Longstreet has now retired from this theater to rejoin General Lee against General Hooker's advance on Richmond. My friend Roswell Lamson hopes our infantry will advance towards Petersburg in Longstreet's absence, but our army seems to move slowly, if at all, when opportunity appears.

Young Kekoa and I were in the thick of the action. We landed our howitzer battery alongside Roswell's just below Fort Huger at midnight. The infantry helped us drag the howitzers and ammunition up the bank, and we set up a scant 150 yards from the fort. Lieutenant Will Cushing, another "fire-eater" like Roswell, opened fire from two gunboats upriver at the same time we did. Our sailors fired half again as fast as the gunners in the fort. The Rebs' fire slackened and our infantry attacked. We ceased fire and Roswell and I led 50 of our sailors in support of our infantry. We were through the embrasures in no time. The Rebs surrendered 160 men and five cannon. Kekoa was right along side of me with his cutlass and pistols!

The capture of the fort meant we could use the whole length of the river in daylight, which was a good thing, as our infantry attacked Longstreet the next week. They were thrown back, but because we held Fort Huger, our ships were able to give them covering fire as they retreated. Longstreet attacked across the river several days later, and again we enabled the army to defend against the Rebs successfully.

We're back aboard Woonsocket now, as Longstreet is gone. It was exciting to serve with Roswell's little flotilla and to see how well a man I once commanded did on his own hook. It's a far cry from the whaling you and I both practiced, but afloat, nonetheless. Serving with two officers like Will and Roswell was a great experience for me, as they are among the few who don't care about my race, only how I do my duty.

We hear that Woonsocket is going to the Caribbean to search for the

Florida and other Rebel raiders. It will be nice to be in open waters again. My anticipation is tempered, however, by the news I've just received. Daniel Fell, my old tormentor from Preble, will join us as we leave for the Caribbean, replacing our current first lieutenant.

> *I hope you are well, and still inspiring young minds at the Academy. I will write again soon,*
> > *Your loving son, Tobias*

CHAPTER 12
THE STAR OF THE SOUTH
MAY 1863

Rory had the watch as the foliage of Madeira's southern coast gave way to the stone buildings of Funchal. The Desert Islands, "*Ilhas Desertas*," were visible 18 miles distant off the port quarter. Sunlight shone on this protected southern side of the island, in contrast to the mists of the northern side. The town was visible from several miles up the coast, as it rose up the steep volcanic slopes of the island. "Deck, there! Crossed yards in the bay," the lookout called. Rory called the captain, and ran up the mizzen shrouds.

Canby came on deck with his glass in his hand, and trained it on the town as Rory returned to the quarterdeck. "The lookout spotted topmasts in the bay, sir," said Rory. "She looks like a man o' war to me."

"Very well, Mr. Dunbrody, ease her two points to port." *Star of the South* was running easily before the wind out of Africa. "We'll gain some sea room in case our new friend is a Union cruiser." As they rounded Ponta do Garajau, the bay, Escada do Funchal, opened up to Rory's line of sight and the hull of the anchored warship came into view. Rory squinted into the setting sun and saw the stars and stripes flying from the stern, against a backdrop of purple jacaranda and red bougainvillea.

"It's the *Tuscarora* again, sir. She must have bet we'd arrive in these waters, and come straight here."

"We'll hope she doesn't have her steam up, Mr. Dunbrody. Cadwallader tells me she's got a foul bottom. We'll out-run her, I'm sure.

We'll have to wait on the Governor of Funchal another time."

The crew of the *Tuscarora* could be seen slipping her cable and setting sail, but Rory knew that *Star*, with a mile and a half lead, wouldn't be caught by the Yankee. *And this time we have our after pivot mounted for a stern chase. It won't be so easy for her now,* thought Rory.

The *Star of the South* continued her course just south of west past the 1500-foot bluffs of Cabo Girao. At that point, eight miles off Madeira's southern shore, Canby opted not to wear to starboard in order to head northwest on a beam reach for the whaling grounds off the Azores. "The *Tuscarora's* captain is no fool, gentlemen," Canby explained to his officers gathered on the quarterdeck. "I don't want to give him a hint of our intention to head northwest to the Azores. So, we'll wait for dark to alter course." The sun set soon after with the Union sloop two miles behind. Rory was disappointed to miss an opportunity to try the after eight-inch pivot, but he realized he'd have many more chances among the Union whaling fleet.

Dawn two days later brought a call from the masthead. "Smoke two points to starboard!" Rory could see a column of black smoke from the deck.

"Call the captain," he told the midshipman of the watch. Canby came on deck moments later. "Sir, there'll be a whaleship under that smoke trying blubber, 'tis my belief."

"No doubt you're right, Mr. Dunbrody," Canby replied. "They still find sperm and right whales in these waters, even though they've over-fished the stock for years. You sound as if you know something of whaling."

"I had a shipmate, a good friend, who was a whaler before he came to the navy. We used to yarn about his whalin' days. The whalers call hunting in these grounds 'plum pudding cruises.' Not as dangerous as the Pacific grounds."

"We'll soon see about that," grinned Canby, as they grew closer to the sooty column. Soon, masts and rigging became visible through the oily smoke.

"Sail ho, whaler with a whale alongside!" The *Wessex* of New Bedford, 120 feet long and full of whale oil, was in the wrong place at the wrong time. Rory took the cutter as *Star of the South* hove to a hundred yards away in a moderate sea, upwind to avoid the awful stench of the whale rendering. The whale was secured to the ship's starboard side with a massive chain around the flukes. Men with cutting irons stood on a stage rigged out from the ship's side above the whale carcass, while blubber hooks and tackle hoisted huge slabs of blubber from the carcass. Rory steered to the port side and boarded. The captain, taken unawares, left his monitoring of the cutting and confronted Rory with obvious annoyance.

"What'r you about, mister?" he asked, "I've got a whale to try out here. State your business!"

"I'm Lieutenant Dunbrody of the Confederate States Ship *Star of the South*," he announced politely. "I'll just be looking at your ship's papers, if you please, captain." The captain's expression changed from annoyance to dismay, and he led Rory below. Rory examined the papers that the captain took from the ship's safe. "I regret to tell you, sir, that your ship and its cargo are a prize of war. Please have your crew gather their personal gear and assemble amidships. I'd be obliged if you'd hoist out your boats, and make sure they're provisioned. I suspect you'll be rowing the thirty miles to the Azores." Rory returned topside and used the *Wessex's* speaking trumpet to report to Canby as the captain swore and stamped across his quarterdeck and dashed his cap to the deck.

Rory hailed the *Star of the South*. "She's a New Bedford ship, sir, with 500 barrels of oil already aboard."

"Excellent, Mr. Dunbrody!" Canby's reply carried down from windward. "Take her instruments, any weapons and get her boats ready for a long pull. They can row to Terceira and we won't have to feed prisoners!"

The fires from the tryworks made easy the task of lighting the combustibles the cutter crew placed around the oil barrels in the blubber room and the hold.

Rory stood by the port quarter rail as a mate, harpooner and five black sailors hoisted out a whaleboat. Several other black crewmen were in another whale boat. *Typical of a New Bedford whaler,* Rory thought. *A quarter of her crew is colored.* "Any of you men know Tobias St. John?" An older crewman looked up from the after fall.

"I does, suh, years back. I heard he went to the navy and made it out of the foc'sle."

"That he did, lad," smiled Rory, and then addressed the officer at the tiller. "If you have your boat compass and you're ready for sea, Mr. Mate, row to the *Star*, and wait for our captain's word."

Four boats and thirty men backed water off the quarter of *Star of the South*. Rory stood with the other officers beside Captain Canby as he addressed the prisoners. $25,000 worth of whale ship and whale oil burned brightly as a backdrop to the scene. "You're 20 miles from Sao Miguel." He turned aside to his officers. "I've half a mind to keep those blacks aboard and see what they bring on the block!"

"With respect, sir," countered Rory, "They'd eat up all the profits before we could return to the South, and the Confederate Admiralty Court has ruled that captured black seamen are not subject to prosecution under the laws prohibiting introduction of free Negroes."

"Indeed? When was that?"

"Summer of '61, sir, Judge McGrath," replied Rory. "I'd guess that most of these men are freemen from New England and the Cape Verdes."

"Thank you, Mr. Dunbrody. I've been away from the South too long. You've a good point on eating up the profits." Turning back to the boats of the *Wessex*, Canby called, "The course is nor', nor'west. Good luck."

Star of the South bore off southwestward toward the sea lanes for ships bound to and from the South Atlantic. Rory was off watch, but remained on deck, gazing at the whaleboats until they disappeared on course for the Azores. *Maybe I saved some grief for an old shipmate of Tobias,* he thought, his eyes on the horizon. *I wonder where the war has taken Mr. St. John?*

The morning watch had just come on deck as a string of six days with no Union merchant ships sighted came to an end with a cry of "sail ho off the port bow!" They had reached 55 degrees west longitude and 17 degrees north latitude; square in the middle of the shipping lanes from the southern capes to the northeast United States. Rory was officer of the watch and Ormsby, his midshipman.

"Mr. Ormsby, to the foretop and see what you can make of her," said Rory. Ormsby, a brass telescope in his belt, scampered to the foretopgallant crosstrees.

"Full-rigged ship, and a Yankee clipper by the cut of her, sir," called Ormsby to the deck.

"Aye, aye. Hastings," Rory said to the signalman standing by, "my respects to the captain and say we've sighted a clipper."

"Call all hands, Mr. Dunbrody," said the captain when he came on deck. "We'll set the stu'nsails and see if we can run her down." The starboard studding-sail booms were run out and the studding-sails set. Studding sails were used in moderate airs and set outside of the "plain" sails already set, increasing the sail area and the speed of the ship.

One half hour's run produced no gain on the clipper. Canby gave the command "down screw," and the screw was lowered and engine started in order to increase speed. Four hours later, the *Star* had closed to just more than a mile astern. "Try a shot for range, Mr. Dunbrody," said the captain. Rory went forward to his waiting crew at the bow pivot. Their first shot splashed a ship's length ahead of their quarry, and slightly to port. The clipper hove to and lost way, backing her yards so that the wind blew into them from ahead of the ship, and raising the clews, or lower corners of each sail. Rory could see her captain's crestfallen look through his glass.

Star of the South hoisted the Stars and Bars. "Mr. Sutherland," said Canby, "take the longboat. It's your turn to lead the boarding party. Look at her papers. I've every confidence she's a Yankee. Take six extra men. That's a large clipper."

Indeed, the *Silas Matthews* was American-owned, eighty days out of China with a cargo of tea and silks valued at over a million dollars, and bound for New York City. She carried a crew of forty, and several passengers, as well as the captain's wife. She, and one female passenger, a missionary's wife, Mrs. Anderson, were hoisted aboard in a large rattan chair with a whip rove from the mainyard. As soon as she set foot on deck, Mrs. Anderson began a harangue, starting with the captain and ascending to Secretary Mallory and President Davis, denouncing all as scoundrels and pirates. Ormsby and Rory stood on the quarterdeck, at a distance from the diatribe.

"Sure, she seems to lack some of the Christian tolerance one might associate with her husband's calling."

Ormsby smiled at Rory's remark. "She may soon be inspired to more colorful language. The captain sent Mr. McGuiness off with the cutter to salvage linens and china for the wardroom and gunroom. I'd guess that some will have lately belonged to Mrs. Anderson. Standby for a broadside, sir."

Ormsby's prediction proved accurate. As the cutter crew came aboard carrying spoils from the prize, the missionary's wife spied her favorite tablecloth under the arm of McCafferty, a burly quartermaster. "Thief! Pirate! Spawn of the Devil!" Mrs. Anderson jumped up and down on both feet, so distraught was she. McCafferty, a man customarily cool and resolute amid the din of cannon fire, turned tail and scuttled below to escape the shrill invective. The observers on the quarterdeck could not conceal their smiles and the poor woman turned on them next.

Rory pushed Ormsby ahead of him. "Get below and don't slow me down, Mr. Ormsby, we're outgunned, and that's a fact." The two young officers ran down the companionway, enjoying a lighthearted respite from pressures of wartime life at sea.

It was not until noon the next day that the transfer of prisoners was complete. Because the clipper's crew was so numerous, Canby was forced to shackle them, as there was no other way to secure the ship from the possibility of a prisoner uprising. Rory commiserated with the *Silas Matthews'* captain and his wife, an engaging couple from New York, as they stood on the quarterdeck. It was common, particularly in the China trade, for captains to be accompanied by their wives on the long voyages. Captain David Webster and his wife, MaryAnn, were occupying Captain Canby's cabin while aboard, and had been spared the shackling required for their crew.

"We regret the necessity of the shackles, sir," Rory said. "We'll work hard to find a vessel that will accept you all and transport you to a safe haven. I've told the guard detail to make sure no crew member is chafed by the shackles."

Mrs. Webster, a tall and slender brunette, smiled at Rory. "We're receiving much kinder treatment than the New York papers have led us to expect, lieutenant."

"Sure, it's a terrible evil t'be fightin' against friend and family, ma'am. There's no use makin' it worse than it has to be."

"It sounds as if you've friends or family yourself on the Northern side, lieutenant," said Captain Webster.

"Aye, sir, my closest friend is a Union sailing master and my brother Tim is a captain in your infantry. 'Tis a constant weight upon me, t'be sure."

They set the *Silas Matthews* afire as the Websters watched, the captain holding his wife while she struggled to hold back the tears. The pillar of smoke was visible long after her hull and masts were below the horizon. The next day, they encountered another ship, but she proved to be a British merchant and unwilling to take the prisoners. Two days later, they stopped a Danish bark bound for St. Thomas. Her captain agreed to take the captives aboard, and Rory helped the Websters into the waiting boat, wishing them smooth sailing. The crew of *Star* breathed a noticeable sigh of relief as the missionary's wife, Mrs. Anderson, was lowered into the boat, still haranguing.

"We've not heard the last of her, Diarmund, sure as I'm a Dillon," Rory said to McGuiness, the officer of the watch, as they stood by the starboard rail.

"How so, Rory, and the dear lady out of earshot, and all?"

"Faith, we'll be readin' the Northern newspapers in two months time and she'll be on the front page, on about her gross mistreatment by the pirates of the South, see if we don't."

"And a good point y'make, my friend," said McGuiness.

They were at the latitude of Martinique, a French island with coal available at the harbor of Fort-de-France. As they had last fueled at a British port, and now were a vessel foreign to Britain, they were precluded from fueling at a British port for three months. Canby wanted to fuel before word reached the Union that a new Rebel cruiser was afloat in the Atlantic. As they traveled toward the Caribbean, Canby exercised them at the guns twice a day, knowing that the *Martha* would be well stocked with powder and shot. Three days later they anchored in the harbor of the lush, green island with the *Tricolore* flying above the stone and brick fort at the harbor entrance.

Coaling took two grimy, sweaty days, while the U.S. Consul tried to delay their departure by demanding the French authorities allow two American merchant ships to depart with a 24-hour escape window. The French acquiesced, but a day later, no Union warships had appeared as *Star of the South* eased out of the harbor entrance under all plain sail. Canby had let it be known that he intended to cruise off the coast of Brazil, and *Star* headed southeast until Martinique was below the horizon, then headed west and north toward Guadeloupe, where she hoped to find her tender, the *Martha,* awaiting in the secluded little harbor of Deshais with fresh provisions and ammunition.

Each ship had two anchors out for stability in the strong wind gusts that roared down the "chutes" on the side of Mont Soufriere, Guadeloupe's tall volcano. The *Martha* had, in addition to stores and ammunition, two more nine-pounder smooth bore cannon. "Stow those below, Mr. Cadwallader," said the captain to his first lieutenant, "we'll hope we can duplicate ourselves. If I can find the right prize, we'll arm her and set another cruiser to hound the enemy." Canby smiled at the prospect. He gave the crew shore leave, confident of few desertions. "After all," he explained at dinner with his officers, "we've taken two valuable prizes, and every man knows we'll have to reach the Confederacy before they can be compensated with their shares by our prize court. Besides, we've no Frenchmen aboard, and these town folk speak only that and their patois."

As the ships shuddered and the rigging sang amid the violent gusts from Soufreire's slopes, the crew sat ashore in the two tiny grog shops Deshais boasted, trying hand gestures and broken French to converse with the amused local beauties. But Canby was right, the lure of prize money owed outweighed the freedoms of Basse-Terre. Not a man deserted.

Canby was aware that word was now spreading that a Confederate cruiser was at sea in the French Caribbean. "We've taken rich prizes in the sea lanes, so we're going back but in a different spot," he told his officers. "We'll head north through the Antilles and wait off the Bahamas, beyond the blockading squadrons, but close enough for both Caribbean and South Atlantic traffic." Several days later, they were 200 miles north of Canal de la Mona, the strait between Puerto Rico and Hispaniola, on a northerly heading. But their first sighting was not a merchantman. It was the side wheel gunboat USS *Shoshone County*, on her way south to join the squadron searching for *Star of the South*.

The *Shoshone County* carried one eight-inch Dahlgren pivot in the bow and four 24-pound smooth bores in broadside. The ships were mismatched, and Canby decided the superior strength of his ship made risking damage away from repair yards worth the chance.

Shoshone County and *Star of the South* were on opposite courses, starboard side to starboard side as the Yankee headed south and the Rebel north. Canby took advantage of his ship's appearance, that of a Royal Navy dispatch cruiser, when only a mile separated the two ships. "Hoist the Blue Ensign," he ordered. The British rear admiral commanding in the Caribbean was of the "blue" squadron as the Royal Navy was then divided, and the Union captain would expect to see the Union Jack in the canton of a blue flag on a warship of British design in these waters. "Down behind the bulwarks, officers and gun crews! We want to look unconcerned and British." Canby took off his gray jacket, and his steward brought him an old blue British merchantman's coat he'd worn aboard *Martha*.

As the ships drew nearer each other, the Confederates quietly cleared for action. Rory took his station at the forward eight-inch pivot gun. His gun crew had already removed the tompion and lashings, sponged and readied the gun for loading. *Those days of gun drill are payin' off, t'be sure,* Rory thought. He gazed back aft at the 32-pounder broadside gun crews, four to a side. McGuiness and Sutherland each commanded a broadside battery, and Cadwallader crouched behind the rail aft with the captain, at the after pivot. The well-protected inverted cylinder engine gave the *Star* ten-knot speed as they came abreast of *Shoshone County*, both pivots trained to starboard. The Blue Ensign was lowered and the Confederate flag rose to the spanker gaff as Canby called for the first broadside. "Aim at the paddle wheel box, lads," he cried. Rory's crew swung open the hinged gun ports in the bow, unmasking the big pivot gun. "Fire!" Three hundred weight of shot hurtled across four hundred yards of open sea before the unsuspecting *Shoshone County* could train her guns on the *Star.* Rory saw two round shot from the starboard 32-pounders strike the Union steamer, but his gun's eight-inch shell did not find the target.

"Quoins," he called to his gun captain. "We were over. Depress two degrees!" *Star* was past the Union ship and swung to starboard as *Shoshone County* continued on, her gun crews trying desperately to ready their guns for action. Four minutes later, the ships were 1000 yards apart as *Shoshone County* came to port and her first ragged broadside howled overhead. *They're firing high too,* he thought. Rory's second shot, a shaped exploding shell, was short, but his third struck the Union steamer's port paddle wheel box. The paddle wheel disintegrated in a burst of splinters, and a fire started in the debris. As the *Shoshone County* slewed around to port, driven by her starboard paddle wheel, she pointed her bow toward the onrushing *Star* for a moment and her bow pivot gun fired a shot that struck the *Star's* forward port 32, dismounting it and killing every man in the gun crew as well as Lieutenant Sutherland. The *Shoshone County* continued her uncontrolled turn.

"Sand, there," called Canby as the blood of the gunners covered the deck around the dismounted gun. "Get those bodies below!" As *Star* overtook the Union gunboat, Canby steered to a position just off the starboard quarter of the *Shoshone County,* where neither the Yankee's bow pivot nor her broadside guns could be brought to bear.

Canby grabbed a speaking trumpet. "Do you strike? I can pound you to pieces. You've fought as well as any could!" The Union captain looked at his blaze amidships, his paddle wheel in shambles, and the big Rebel cruiser at now point blank range. He stepped to his flag halyard and slowly lowered the Stars and Stripes. "Mr. Dunbrody, Mr. McGuiness, take the longboat and cutter, extinguish that fire and bring the prisoners off. We shouldn't linger, in case there's a bigger Yankee in the neighborhood!"

USS *Shoshone County,* surrendered and still afire, drifted in the waters of the Gulf Stream. Rebel and Union sailors alike joined in extinguishing the fire by rigging hoses, some from *Star of the South.* Volunteers from the recently vanquished crew of the gunboat worked side by side with the Confederate prize crew to quell the flames. While the shackled prisoners watched, an honor guard of their shipmates then buried eight of the Union dead at sea, the sewn hammocks containing the corpses sliding over-side from under Union flags, while a similar ceremony for the seven dead Confederates, including Lieutenant Ian Sutherland, late of Scotland, took place aboard *Star*. Canby allowed the Union captain to raise his ensign to half-staff in honor of the dead. A three-gun salute was fired from *Star* in honor of the dead from both sides.

Canby quickly removed all the arms and supplies that his ship could use, scuttled the *Shoshone County*, and then turned his ship south toward Hispaniola. Making land-fall near Cap Haitien, he turned west, northwest to Cuba, staying just outside the three-mile national limit claimed by Spain as he moved west up the Cuban coast toward *La Habana*, ready to avail himself of the safety of neutral waters if a Federal cruiser should be sighted.

The mood of the Confederate sailors and their Union captives had elevated sharply since the sad duty of burying their comrades. The prisoners were cheered by the knowledge that they would be paroled in Havana, and the Rebel crewmen looked forward to the possibility of shore leave in a Spanish port. The cynics among them tempered their regrets over the loss of shipmates by the assurance that their shares of prize money already earned had been increased by the reduction of shipmates to share it with.

Three days after the battle, they lay within sight of Morro Castle, the massive brooding fortress guarding the harbor of Havana, seat of the Spanish governor of Cuba. They hove-to just outside the harbor mouth, and a pilot boat with a port official aboard soon came alongside. "*Señor*," Canby began as the harbormaster's deputy came aboard, "we wish to enter harbor to repair damage, and to coal and replenish our stores. Also, we have 100 prisoners who are parolees, and we wish to land them. *Por favor, señor.*"

Rory and Diarmund McGuiness watched this exchange with curiosity. "Sure, it's a lot to ask of a neutral," whispered Diarmund with a grin. "Are y' thinkin' he'll turn us away now, for our temerity, and all?"

The two Irish lieutenants were surprised and astonished at the

Spanish reaction. *"Muchisimo gusto, capitan.* It is our great pleasure to aid the brave *marinaros* of the Confederate States Navy in their endeavors. Please, follow my pilot boat as we lead you to your anchorage."

The pro-Confederate attitude of the government was mirrored by the warm welcome of the Cuban people. Small boats of well-wishers surrounded the ship, and those granted shore leave were mobbed by enthusiastic crowds with bands playing "The Bonnie Blue Flag," whose tune was identical to Rory's favorite Irish chantey, "The Girls of Dublin Town." In vain did Robert Schufeldt, the U.S. consul, arrange for U.S. ships in the harbor to leave one each day, and then implore the Spanish to hold *Star of the South* until the last one had departed. Canby completed replenishment in two days and was allowed to leave. A bare twelve hours later, the USS *Dacotah* steamed into the harbor, but the quarry had fled. While in harbor, the Confederates had read southern newspapers that described the new "second national flag" of the Confederacy, the St. Andrew's Cross of the flag of the Army of Northern Virginia in the canton, set in a field of white. The papers noted that the flag had also been designated by the Confederate Congress as the new Naval Ensign. Canby had the sailmaker at work on several as they left harbor.

CHAPTER 13
WOONSOCKET ON CARIBBEAN PATROL
MAY 1863

USS *Woonsocket* left the broad estuary of the St. Mary's River in northern Florida under steam. Captain Oakley was on the quarterdeck as the ship pitched in response to the first Atlantic rollers. Beside him stood his new first lieutenant, Daniel Fell, brought aboard at Fernandina, where the man he replaced had left *Woonsocket* for his own command, a paddle wheel gunboat.

Tobias stood on the foredeck, having guided the ship out the river mouth in his capacity of sailing master, or chief navigating officer. Tobias wore a worried look, and its source was not a problem of navigation. Daniel Fell had tried to court martial Tobias when they both served aboard USS *Preble* at the start of the war, and Tobias knew Fell's animosity toward him and blacks in general had not diminished. *Thank heaven I was able to tell the captain about my history with Fell,* he thought. Oakley was a fair and thoughtful commander, and had reassured Tobias upon hearing of Fell's earlier attempt to bring charges. "Just do your duty, Mr. St. John," he had said. "I'll do mine as well, and I'll make sure that Mr. Fell does his."

Tobias walked aft to the quarterdeck where Oakley was addressing Fell. "Mr. Fell, stop the engine, lift the screw, and set all plain sail. Mr. St. John, I need a course for Martinique. We've been ordered to patrol French possessions in the Caribbean. The Navy Department believes the Confederates have a raider afloat that will try to coal at a French harbor next."

Tobias quickly gave Oakley a course that had *Woonsocket* bowling along the outside of the Leeward Islands several days later on a beam reach under brisk northeast Trades. In one afternoon watch, just after the noon sun sight, Tobias and Kekoa found themselves alone at the wardroom table as Kekoa checked his position against Tobias'.

"Excellent work, Kalama," said Tobias, as he found their positions in agreement.

"Thank you, sir," the Hawaiian replied. He leaned toward Tobias and dropped his voice. "Sir, I overheard Mr. Fell and Mr. Krotemann talking about you. They mean to do you harm, sir." Karl Krotemann was the master-at-arms, a warrant officer and the ship's policeman.

"Thanks for the warning, Kekoa. Where were you, and what did they say?" Tobias matched Kekoa's caution, speaking in almost a whisper.

"I was in da chart locker, aft of da master-at-arms office. Dey no can see me, I wait 'til they bot' wen away before I come out." Kekoa was visibly upset, and was lapsing into the cadences of Hawaiian pidgin. Usually, he spoke the perfect English he'd learned in a Honolulu missionary school. "I hear da exec say if you go ashore while we in da Caribbean, dat Mr. Krotemann should try make big *pilikia* for you, make it look like you desert."

"You've lost me, Kekoa. What is *pilikia*?"

"Is trouble, Mr. St. John, big trouble!"

"Well, Kekoa," said Tobias, conspiratorially, "forewarned is forearmed. If I go ashore to collect information, as I well may, it will be in my back yard, among my people. We'll see just who make *pilikia* for whom. I'm grateful for your loyalty."

"Dey're two bad sailors, Mr. St. John. You be careful. *Malama pono!* De don' like blacks. Kanakas, neider."

Woonsocket touched at Fort-de-France, and learned of *Star of the South's* recent visit. As they left the harbor, the midshipman of the watch found Tobias in the wardroom. "Captain's compliments and may he see you in his cabin, sir."

"My respects to the captain, mister, I'll be there directly." When Tobias reported, Oakley was seated at his day cabin table, charts before him.

"Mr. St. John, our orders are to patrol French possessions hereabouts as our raider, calling herself '*Star of the South*,' may attempt a rendezvous with a tender for re-supply. I know that these are the waters of your birth and childhood. I wish to call upon your local knowledge as we try to find our quarry."

"I'm happy to oblige, sir. We're only a day's sail from *Les Iles des Saintes*, and two days from Antigua. I have friends and family in each place, who are sailors as well."

"Very well, we'll be putting you ashore in each place. Do what you must to discover the raider's track."

"Aye, aye, sir." *I think I'll not burden this good commander with what I know of his executive officer's plan for my demise. He'll know soon enough,* Tobias thought.

Star of the South swung to her best bower anchor 24-hours later in the harbor of Bourg, the town of the isle of Terre-de-Haut. As Tobias was rowed ashore in the jolly boat, he saw the longboat just astern, with a boat's crew ready to obtain fresh vegetables and replenish the ship's fresh water supply. He could see Krotemann among the shore party. *Re-supply! A new duty for the master at arms,* Tobias thought.

Tobias instructed the coxswain of the jolly boat to return to the quay in four hours' time. He watched from the shadows of a doorway up the cobbled main street as the longboat secured to the quay and Krotemann leapt ashore, spoke briefly to the jolly boat's coxswain, and then walked swiftly up the main street toward Tobias' doorway. Tobias strolled leisurely up the street, Krotemann keeping pace 200 feet behind, then down a narrow side street. Soon, Tobias came to the door of the Duvalliere house, of a kind one might find on the Breton shore, home to his lover Monique's father and several of her half-Breton, half-African brothers. Monique's father, a Breton fisherman on the island of Terre–de-Haut, had fallen in love with a slave woman on nearby Terre-de-Bas who had saved him from drowning. He had purchased her freedom, married her, and they had raised a family.

Monique's brother Etienne answered Tobias' knock. "*Mon ami* Tobias!" he exclaimed. "*Entre vous*. It is grand to see you!" As Etienne closed the door, Tobias glimpsed Krotemann in an alleyway just down the street. Etienne and Tobias were soon joined by Pierre, the Duvalliere patriarch, and Etienne's brother, Claude, a genial giant of a man.

"What brings you to Terre-de-Haut, my son?" Pierre smiled warmly as he asked. Tobias and Monique had been childhood sweethearts, and the Duvallieres had long treated Tobias as one of the family.

"My ship is pursuing a Confederate raider which was recently in Martinique, *mon pere*. My captain has asked me to inquire ashore among my friends here and on Antigua as to her whereabouts."

"*Mais oui*, the near islands were abuzz last week with word of her," said Claude. "She missed an American cruiser in Fort de France by hours. She spread rumors that she would go south, but my friend Jean says he saw her headed north two days later, off Montserrat."

"Oh, my friends, this is most useful. I knew you would have heard of any strange ships." Tobias paused, and leaned forward anxiously in his chair. "I need to ask a favor, and it could lead you to danger if you agree. You must feel free to tell me 'no' if you wish."

"I can think of nothing you might ask which we would refuse, *mon fils*," said Pierre. "Ask, I beg of you."

"Very well, Pierre. There are men aboard my ship who wish me harm. My shipmates have heard them conspiring to injure me while I'm ashore and make it appear I've deserted. One of them has followed me and is hiding down the street from your door. If he could be induced to follow me to a secluded spot where he could be beaten unconscious, and then be left where he could be found before we depart, it might dissuade them, at least for a time."

By the time Tobias had finished his tale, all three fishermen were grinning broadly, and Claude was rubbing his hands together in gleeful anticipation. "Life can be very ordinary here, Tobias," said Etienne. "You must visit more often. Who are these evil shipmates?"

"One is the first lieutenant, who hates blacks. The one outside is the master-at-arms, who is both bigot and toady. But fortunately, my captain and many of the crew are sailors first. With them, my seamanship balances my color."

The senior Duvalliere rose, his eyes bright. "The three of us will arm ourselves with fish cudgels and slip out the back, down side streets to our warehouse at the harbor. Wait 15 minutes and join us there, leading your friend down the main street. Enter and leave the door open. It will be dark inside. He will surely follow. You must leave out the back. We'll take care of everything! Now, describe him to us so we may be sure of our target."

"He is a big man, shorter then me but heavier. Big shoulders, big belly, and dark, bushy eyebrows."

Etienne laughed. "We will recognize him, *mon ami*! This will give you time to visit our sister without interruption. After dark, we'll leave him beside the quay. If you are in the search party, you'll find him there."

Tobias pursed his lips in thought. "Even though he will suspect my involvement, he can only tell Lieutenant Fell. I'll need to be even more cautious aboard, 'though, after this setback for their plans."

"It is possible that one of them may find his capacity for devilment diminished," said Claude with a rakish grin.

"Thank you, my friends," said Tobias.

"Our pleasure, *mon ami*," said Etienne. "You will be seeing your cousin Mitch in St. John's, no? Ask him to share the final chapter of the story with us next time he comes south." Mitchell St. John, Tobias' fisherman cousin, lived in Antigua's principal town, St. John's. That would be *Woonsocket's* next stop. The three Duvallieres left through their back door to begin their adventure.

Tobias left 15 minutes later, and made sure Krotemann was following as he made his way to the Duvalliere warehouse. He entered as planned, leaving the door open. "Get out the door quickly, Tobias," came a whisper from the shadows. He left and walked to Monique's shop and apartment with a spring in his step.

"*Cherie*," he called as he opened the door. Monique looked up from the counter joyfully at the sound of his voice.

"Tobias, love, it's been since last September. Far too long," she cried as she filled his arms.

"You're as beautiful as ever, Monique," he said as he held her at arms length and gazed at the tall and winsome love of his life.

"What strange and exotic assignment brings you to this far corner of the sea, love?"

"I have only two hours to tell you, *cherie*."

"Then we had best insure no interruptions," she said as she hung a 'closed' sign on the door of her shop and locked the door. "I know a place where we can talk very privately," she said as she led him up the stairs to her apartment above the shop. Later, lying among the pillows on her bed, Tobias explained his ship's presence in the harbor, and her family's defense of her lover.

"Can't you experience an ordinary, boring voyage for a change?" she asked. He winced.

"It's all right, love," she reassured him. "I remember the letter you wrote after your court martial, telling me how you felt reborn and ready to use your talents to make a difference in the way our people are seen now that the Emancipation Proclamation has been made. I understand your resolve, I just worry."

Tobias sighed. "Sometimes it seems I can make no difference at all."

"We may not see the results, but I have faith they are there," said Monique. "You have just time for a glass of wine and a bite to eat."

"You've already fed my soul, woman, but I won't turn down food!"

In mid afternoon, Tobias walked down the hill to the harbor. The jolly boat was at the quay, as he had ordered. The midshipman in charge of the longboat approached Tobias. "Sir, have you seen the master-at-arms? No one has seen him since we first landed, and we're ready to return to *Woonsocket* with our last provisions."

"I haven't seen him either, mister. I thought he was assigned to the provisioning. Did he say what he was about?"

"No, sir. He left the boat when we first landed without a word."

"Well, when you go aboard, report to Mr. Fell. Perhaps he can shed some light on Mr. Krotemann's location." Tobias was thoroughly enjoying himself at this point. As he stepped into the jolly boat, he spoke to the coxswain.

"Mr. Krotemann is missing, O'Leary. Did he speak to you when the boats arrived at the quay this morning?" Tobias assumed his most innocent expression.

"He asked me if you'd told me where you were going in town, sir," O'Leary replied.

"Thank you, cox'n."

The jolly boat reached *Woonsocket* ahead of the longboat, and Tobias reported to the captain immediately as he'd been previously instructed to do.

"What did you find, Mr. St. John?" The captain was seated in his day cabin.

"The raider was seen off Montserrat headed north a week ago, sir. I'm confident of my source."

"Just as I thought! He's headed for the shipping lanes into Union ports where his chances are best." Oakley stood, and began pacing the cramped cabin, his hands behind him. "We'll check your sources in St. John's, as it's on the way, but I'm confident we'll be on the right track," he said with conviction. "As soon as the long boat's aboard, we'll weigh anchor!"

"Sir, the middie commanding the longboat says the master-at-arms hasn't been seen since morning."

"What was the master-at-arms doing ashore with a provisioning party?"

"I don't know, sir. I assumed he was assigned by Mr. Fell."

The Marine sentry knocked at the door. "Captain, the first lieutenant would like to see you, sir."

"Enter, Mr. Fell." The first lieutenant strode through the door and stopped, taken aback at the sight of Tobias.

"Sir, may I speak in private?"

"You may say what you wish with Mr. St. John present, Mr. Fell, but I have a question for you. What was Mr. Krotemann doing ashore with a provisioning party?"

"Why, why, sir, I sent him with the longboat to...to keep an eye on pilfering, sir." Fell exhaled as a marginally plausible explanation occurred to him at the last moment.

"And did Mr. Krotemann discover any sticky fingers among our provisioning party?"

"I don't know, sir, he seems to be missing." Fell actually looked crestfallen, a condition Tobias had never encountered in the man in the year and a half since they'd met.

"Missing?" the captain exclaimed. "What are you doing to find him?"

"I was about to send St. John to find him."

"Mister St. John is an excellent choice, first lieutenant. He's the only officer or crewman who knows this terrain. Kindly refer to him by his proper honorific. Carry on!"

"Aye, aye, sir. Mr. St. John, please take a search crew to locate the master-at-arms."

"Aye, aye, sir," replied Tobias, struggling not to smile. Fell almost ran from the cabin, so relieved was he to escape a most uncomfortable confrontation with his commander.

"By your leave, sir," Tobias said to Oakley, "I'll be starting the search."

"Carry on, sailing master."

Tobias came on deck. "Mr. Murdoch," he called to the boatswain. "A bo'sun's mate, if you please, and pass the word for Master's Mate Kalama. I'll take both of them in the cutter, if you'd be so kind. And put half a dozen lanterns aboard. It's growing dark, and there is no twilight in these latitudes."

"Aye, aye, sir," replied the boatswain. As they lowered the cutter from the port quarter davits, Tobias was joined by Kekoa and Boatswain's Mate Jon Halvorson, who had begun his sailing days aboard a Swedish merchant ship before emigrating to America and joining the navy. The boat's crew clambered down the boarding ladder.

"Bosun's mate, take the tiller, if you please," he said to Halvorson. "I'll ask you and Kalama to divide the crew. We're searching for any sign of Mr. Krotemann who's not been seen for several hours. As we land Kalama and I will go to the left down the main street. You take your men to the right."

"Aye, aye, sir," they each responded. Halvorson turned to Kekoa. "Ve vill each take three lanterns, ya?"

As the cutter came alongside the quay, the crew tossed oars and the bow oar shipped his, then climbed to the quay with the bow painter in hand. They lit the lanterns and spread out to both sides of the street, the lanterns bobbing in the dark like slow-moving fireflies. One of Halvorson's men approached a pile of driftwood near the quay just off the street. "Sir," he called, "I think I've found him!"

Tobias, Kekoa and Halvorson all converged on the driftwood pile. Halvorson knelt. "Ya, sure, its Mr. Krotemann all right. And he's yoost barely breathing." Krotemann still wore his blue jacket, missing one sleeve. His straw sennet hat was missing its top, and hung around his neck like a collar.

"We'll need to be careful moving him, in case of broken bones," said Tobias. "Halvorson, use a tarpaulin from the cutter."

They rowed swiftly back to the ship, and carried Krotemann below to the surgeon's station on the orlop deck, where they were joined by Surgeon Miles. "Ease him down to this cot and let me have a look at him," said Miles. "When you report to the captain, Mr. St. John, tell him I'll be up directly with a report of my own on the patient's condition."

"I'll do that, doctor," Tobias replied as he left the orlop.

Tobias reported to Oakley. "Sir, we found him in a pile of driftwood near the quay. He's unconscious, and there is no way of telling where he's been from his condition. I should mention one more thing, sir. When the longboat's middie told me Krotemann was overdue, I asked O'Leary, the jolly boat cox'n, if Krotemann had spoken to him when the boats arrived. O'Leary said Krotemann had asked if I'd mentioned where I was going in town."

Oakley stared at Tobias for a moment, nodded, thanked him for his diligence, and dismissed him. As Tobias left the cabin, he overheard the Marine sentry announcing Dr. Miles.

Miles reported. "He's concussed, sir, but I believe he'll be conscious in a few hours. His right arm is broken. I've set it and restrained him as best I can. He'll have quiet in sickbay. He's my only patient."

"Very well, doctor. Let me know immediately when he regains consciousness. And I'd be grateful to hear anything he might utter in a semi-conscious state. There is a mystery surrounding his presence ashore that the first lieutenant has been unable to illuminate. Perhaps the master-at-arms can help."

"Aye, aye, sir," the doctor replied. As Miles left the captain's cabin, he found Fell standing in the passageway nearby.

"Doctor, notify me immediately when the master-at-arms regains consciousness," Fell ordered.

The plot thickens, Miles thought to himself.

Several hours later, Miles was in the sickbay on the orlop deck when Krotemann began to stir. The orlop was the lowest deck, and typically unventilated, but reforms in the early part of the century instituted by the Royal Navy's Admiral Lord St. Vincent set a standard for ventilation through scuttles and better sanitation. Survival rates of patients at sea confined in the surgery or "cockpit" on the orlop deck had increased. "Coming out of it, Mr. Krotemann?" Miles leaned over the patient as Krotemann moaned and opened his eyes.

"Oh, my God, what a headache!"

"Williams," Miles called to his orderly, "get Mr. Krotemann here some water while I find the first lieutenant." *As he's not uttered anything while unconscious, perhaps the exec can elicit a remark now, so I have something to report to the captain,* he thought as he climbed to the wardroom area and Fell's cabin.

Fell and the surgeon descended to the sickbay. "I'll need a word in private with the master-at-arms, surgeon," said Fell.

"Aye, aye, sir. Williams, go to the scuttlebutt for fresh water. I'll be in my office, sir," Miles said to Fell. The surgeon's office was separated from the sick bay by a heavy canvas curtain, but Miles was able to hear normal conversation through the screen, the better to monitor his patients.

Miles sat at his desk, listening intently. He had no compunction in eavesdropping. He had been ordered to do so, and further, he was aware of Fell's bigotry, which ran contrary to his deeply-held Quaker beliefs. He had seen Fell's harsh treatment of the several black sailors aboard *Woonsocket*, and had felt powerless to counter it.

He heard Fell whisper to Krotemann, who, still befuddled,

responded in full voice. "Sir, I followed him into a warehouse to knock him out, but a gang o' men jumped me. Maybe the nigra was one o' them."

"Quiet, you fool, Keep your voice down!" Fell's whisper was so forced that Miles could distinguish the words, even through the canvas. "He may be on to us. We'll be on our guard. Say no more. We'll talk later." Miles carefully noted the exchange in his pocket journal, and sat back in his chair until he heard Fell climb the companionway.

When Miles shared his notes with the captain, Oakley said, "well done, surgeon. This won't be enough in a court martial, but it puts us on alert. I'll caution Mr. St. John. They'll slip up further, and we'll get proof for court next time. Not a word to anyone, now!"

"Aye, aye, sir," the surgeon responded, nodding with satisfaction.

Oakley sat in his cabin, gazing out the stern window and deep in thought. *I have no doubt St. John was aware of this plot, but he strove to keep me out of it and found a way to thwart it himself, at least for a time. He must have seen this as the best approach for all concerned, including me, and he may have been right. The sooner I can get rid of Fell, the sooner I'll have a healthy ship. And I already have two witnesses, of a sort, O'Leary and the doctor.*

Woonsocket lay at anchor a day later in St. John's harbor, Antigua. The morning sun glinted off the twin silver turrets of the cathedral, halfway up the hill on the north side of town. Tobias had been sent ashore in the jolly boat to confer with his sources in the town of his birth as to the whereabouts of *Star of the South*. As his cousin Mitch's schooner was in the harbor, he walked up High Street to the house at number four, and was greeted by his eleven year old cousin Daniel, Mitch's son, who leaped into his arms for a hug.

"Cousin Toby, where you been? How long can you stay?" Daniel was jumping up and down in excitement.

Tobias squatted down and looked his little cousin in the eye. "I wish I could stay for months, like the last time, but my ship sails this afternoon. Maybe nex' time, Daniel!" Tobias had stayed for many weeks in 1862, growing a beard and changing his appearance for his clandestine mission posing as a slave pilot behind Confederate lines.

Tobias heard Mitch coming down the stairs. The cousins embraced as Tobias found himself abandoning his Massachusetts accent for the lilt of the islands. "Oh, mon, you a sight!"

"And you, Tobias. I hear you tell Daniel you sail today. Mus' be important, mon!"

"Oh, yes, mon, you may be sure of dat!" Tobias exclaimed. He explained his mission, and Mitch smiled in response.

"You know Edward, live down on Church Street? He say he saw big barque-rigged screw cruiser, British cut to her jib, pivots fore and aft and four ports a side, four days ago off St. Croix!"

"Mitch, this is just what we need!" Tobias explained the Duvallieres' sighting. "I t'ink we can be sure she's heading to the New York shipping lanes. Now, I must tell you of a problem aboard so you can tell the Duvallieres nex' time you see dem. Daniel," he said with a very solemn glance at his little cousin, "dis nex' story is jus' for our family, no one else, very secret!" Daniel nodded just as solemnly. Tobias then explained Fell's plot and asked Mitch to share the results with the Duvallieres.

"Before you leave, mon, I give you dese newspapers," said Mitch, handing Tobias several different English-language news sheets from various Windward islands. Tobias hurriedly scanned them.

"Thank you, Mitch. The *Florida* is still at large and arming prizes as raiders. My commander will be interested to see these."

"More hunting for you, cousin," said Mitch. "Good luck!"

After another hour's conversation, Tobias said his goodbyes and walked down High Street under the hot afternoon sun to the quay where he signaled for the jolly boat. After his report to Oakley, the captain asked Tobias for a course. "We'll traverse some of the shipping lanes and then touch at Port Royal for further orders and intelligence," said Oakley. "Through Anegada Passage to the shipping lanes?"

"Mona Passage, I'm thinking, sir," Tobias said.

"Carry on then," said Oakley, and went on deck to weigh anchor.

Tobias came on deck shortly with the requested course. "Thank you, Mr. St. John," said the captain, and the *Woonsocket* sailed north to continue her pursuit.

A week later, *Woonsocket* steamed into the broad entrance to Port Royal, now the Union Navy's repair center and headquarters along the South Atlantic coast. They had encountered several ships; British, Danish, Spanish, that had reported encountering *Star of the South* in the shipping lanes to the northern states. Tobias stood on the foredeck, conning the ship toward her berth at the navy quay close to the army wharf on Hilton Head Island. As usual, when Tobias saw the Hilton shore, the desolate beaches and scrub pines reminded him of his first encounter here, as he had stormed ashore in the assault and capture of Fort Walker.

They secured *Woonsocket* across the quay from the old line-of-battle ship *Vermont,* converted into a receiving ship, barracks and hospital. On several hulks just down the beach, the navy had built a series of shops including a foundry and a boiler shop. Mail call created excitement throughout the *Woonsocket* after months at sea.

Tobias sat in the wardroom, looking at his pile of letters. One from Rory via Connemara told him that his Irish friend hoped to be at sea again soon, and that he had read with approval New York papers with the results of the USS *Wilkes-Barre* court martial exonerating Tobias. Tobias would burn this letter at first opportunity, avoiding another court for "communication with the enemy."

His next letter was from Charlotte Forten, the comely black abolitionist he had met during his involvement with the "Great Experiment" in which hundreds of northern free blacks had taught in schools created by the Union government to teach newly freed slaves to read, write and cipher. He felt a twinge of longing, sprinkled with guilt, as he remembered his infatuation with the erudite Miss Forten. She wrote that after a year in Port Royal, she was even more dedicated to her teaching, and gratified with the results. She mentioned that she had been tutoring Tobias' friend Robert Smalls, a Union Navy freedman pilot, until he was wounded in the April assault on Fort Sumter, and removed to the hospital in Fortress Monroe, Virginia.

The third letter was from Smalls, himself:

Dear Tobias, it read,

This letter is being written for me by my new tutor in Fortress Monroe. Your friend Miss Forten tutored me in Port Royal until I was moved to hospital here. *When you met me, I could read a chart and keep a log, but my master in Charleston, who let me do much, never allowed me to learn to read and write well. Now, I am learning slowly to do both, but I am not yet able to write my own letters. I hear the Rebels have offered $50,000 for my capture. I'm flattered. I had no idea of my worth while I was a slave!*

I hope you are well. I enjoyed seeing you aboard Wabash in February. You may remember Admiral Du Pont's fear that armored ships could not take Charleston Harbor. It was confirmed on April 7, when six monitors and the New Ironsides and Keokuk were pounded and repulsed. I had been transferred to the ironclad USS Keokuk from USS Planter as pilot. In the April attack on Sumter, we took many hits, one of which temporarily blinded me at my station in the pilothouse. Keokuk sank in the channel the next day. I am repairing well, but I fear our friend and leader Admiral Du Pont will not recover from the repulse we suffered. It is rumored he will be relieved of command of the South Atlantic Blockading Squadron, succeeded by Admiral Foote. I personally doubt anyone could mount a better attack by sea on Charleston's defenses. Miss Forten taught me the word 'scapegoat.' It seems Admiral Du Pont is being made one. I am still in Fortress Monroe hospital until my vision fully repairs, but my new tutor visits me daily.

I wish you well and hope to see you soon.

Your friend,

Robert Smalls, Pilot, USN

How far he has come, Tobias thought. *And there will be many more freedman pilots.* Tobias put his letters in his notecase, placed it in his cabin and went on deck. Lieutenant Fell stood by the port gangway, a look of disgust upon his face.

"Mr. St. John, I've just learned we're being required to accept contrabands to bring us to full complement. As these are your people, I want you to take a bo'sun's mate, report to the *Vermont* where they've been training, and march them back aboard. I doubt that I can make sailors of these contrabands," Fell said, spitting out the word, "but I'm required to try."

"Aye, aye, sir." Tobias took refuge in the only response unlikely to provoke Fell further. He turned to the midshipman of the watch. "Pass the word for Bo'sun's Mate Halvorson, if you please." The husky Swede met Tobias at the entry port and together they descended the gangway to the quay. "We're going to bring back a detail of new men for *Woonsocket*, Halvorson. They're contrabands." He looked at Halvorson, searching in his mind to find words that would subtly evoke the Swede's attitude toward black sailors. "Have you any questions for me on our duty here?"

Halvorson paused for a moment. His knowing look told Tobias he understood the question fully. "I vork with all sorts of sailors, sir. The blacks ve have all ready, de're mostly good hands, do their vork vell, sir. Some are freemen, some contraband. These contraband, if they learn like the ones ve already have, ve'll make sailors out of them, yoost you vatch, sir."

"Thank you, bo'sun's mate." *Nice to find another enlightened shipmate*, Tobias thought. Aboard the *Vermont*, a detail of 20 blacks in sailor's uniforms was drawn up in the waist of the upper deck.

"Call the men to attention, bo'sun's mate, and then have them stand easy, if you please," said Tobias, loud enough so that all could hear him. *Might as well teach them to treat subordinates with respect,* he thought. Halvorson gave each order and patiently explained the commands to the men.

Tobias stepped forward, and every eye was on him. "Men, welcome to the United States Ship *Woonsocket*. I'm Master Tobias St. John. I'm an officer, the ship's navigator. You'll find very few black officers in the navy. Just a few former slave pilots. Bo'sun's Mate Halvorson here is a petty officer. You must obey his commands, just like mine. There are more than a few black petty officers in the navy, now – master's mates, quartermasters, firemen first class. So Bo'sun's Mate Halvorson's rank is not out of reach for you if you work hard. How many of you have been to sea?" Eight men raised their hands. Slaves along the Carolina coasts were frequently hands aboard their owner's coasters and barges, or pilots who could guide ships through the treacherous and ever changing harbor entrances of the Atlantic coastline. "I ask you experienced men to help the more lubberly learn the ropes." Several of the contrabands smiled.

"How many can read and write?" Five raised their hands. Slave owners frowned on educating their slaves, but many were allowed to attend church, and several denominations encouraged slaves to read so as to better follow the scriptures. "I'm going to ask the captain to allow me to hold classes for you off watch. If he approves, we'll get the names of any who want to learn or improve your reading and writing. Now, let me tell you what you'll face aboard. There are a few white sailors and officers who will judge you on your seamanship and attention to duty rather then your race. Many more will tolerate you, but ignore you and avoid you if they can. But, you will quickly notice those who despise you and will make your life miserable, with insults, and beatings if they find opportunity. Try to endure. There is less of that aboard *Woonsocket* because our captain is a fair man and a good sailor. Halvorson will march you to the ship. Remember, you're free men now. Welcome and good luck. Carry on, bo'sun's mate." Tobias thought he could recognize looks of hope or encouragement on the faces of several of the new recruits.

Oakley was just returning to the ship from his visit to Squadron Headquarters as Tobias stood on deck aboard *Woonsocket*, watching the last of the new men file below. "Good afternoon, sailing master. The Navy Department appears to feel beset by these rebel raiders. *Florida's* reported to be sinking ship after ship off Brazil, and now *Star of the South* is doing the same, from the Azores to east of the Bahamas. Our orders are to go east into the shipping lanes and then north to find her."

"I'll have a course for you directly, sir," said Tobias as he turned to go below.

CHAPTER 14
PRIZE-MASTER ORMSBY RUNS AGROUND
JUNE 1863

Star of the South, under sail, sped north along the 70th meridian of longitude, 600 miles south of Bermuda and east of the Bahamas. "Sail, ho, dead ahead, sir," came the cry from the masthead. "Small barque with stunsails set."

Archibald Ormsby was officer of the watch. After the death of Lieutenant Sutherland, Captain Canby had made Ormsby acting fourth lieutenant. Canby had consulted Rory before his decision, as Ormsby had served under Rory aboard CSS *Old Dominion* and in John Taylor Wood's "Naval Cavalry" raiders. "He's a cool one under fire, sir," Rory had told the captain, remembering Archie under the guns of the *Monitor* at the battle of Hampton Roads.

When the barque was sighted, Ormsby called the captain who gave the order to drop the screw and start the engine. With the increased speed, it was still several hours and twilight before their shot across the bow of the barque brought the *Starry Night* to a standstill. She was 30 days out of Rio de Janeiro with a cargo of saltpeter. Canby was ecstatic when the boarding party returned. "What a capture for the Cause, if we can get it through the blockade! Think of the tons of gunpowder this will produce! Mr. Cadwallader," Canby said, as the officers were collected on the quarterdeck, "which officer has the best chance of running the blockade?"

"Sir, three of us grew up in the British Isles and are only marginally familiar with Charleston and Wilmington, the only open

Atlantic ports. You, Lieutenant Ormsby, and the two middies are the only southerners, sir, but Mr. Ormsby is the only one from a port still in Confederate possession." It was the first lieutenant's duty to know everything about the makeup of the crew. Ormsby was from Charleston.

Canby smiled. "Aren't you forgetting Mr. Dunbrody in your list of 'Southrons'?"

Cadwallader laughed. "Yes, sir, it's always difficult to know where to place an Irishman. He did cruise the South Atlantic coast as a midshipman, it's true, but his experience in Wilmington was as a passenger on a blockade runner, sir."

"Well, Mr. Ormsby, it looks like you're the choice for prize-master. I declare, young man, from midshipman to acting lieutenant to your own command in ten days. You're traveling fast. Can you bring her in?" Canby smiled at the stunned young officer.

"Well, suh, I grew up sailing from the Ashley River to Morris Island. I believe I can find my way back, if anyone aboard can."

"Very well, Mr. Ormsby, I can let you have twelve men and a master's mate. The barque is small enough that you should be able to handle her under plain sail. We'll take their crew aboard, and leave your hands free. If you can bring this off, it will be a great boost to the war effort. But you know, I'm sure, how difficult this will be. We ceased using sailing ships to run the blockade way back in the first year of the war."

"Yes, sir, I know we've little chance against steam-powered blockaders. Where is the moon in five nights, sir?"

Canby turned to Rory. "Mr. Dunbrody?"

"Perfect, sir, a new moon. No light at all."

Canby smiled at the young acting lieutenant. "There you are, Mr. Ormsby. A good omen as you set sail!"

Five nights later, *Starry Night* ghosted along under topsails, jib and foretopmast staysail. The white line of the surf was visible to starboard. Ormsby had made landfall northeast of Charleston Harbor, at Isle of Palms, easing in while casting the deep sea lead, until he struck soundings near the now-visible surf line. In arriving so far northeast, he had avoided the blockading squadron off the harbor mouth, and was now inshore of them, headed southwest close along the coast on a beam reach. He knew the distance from Isle of Palms to Sullivan's Island, and he was determined to try the very narrow channel just off Sullivan's, "Maffit's Channel," past Breach Inlet, rather than risk the well-used main ship channel further west. The main ship channel was dotted with the wreckage of hulks that the Federals had sunk there in an effort to seal it off to blockade runners. As the channel most used by Rebel blockade runners, it attracted the heaviest concentration of blockaders. *My only chance is to try where they least expect an attempt,* he thought. *The only problem is, the best and darkest hour for the approach is at low tide.*

Starry Night was just off the mouth of Breach Inlet, barely discernable in the moonless night and a scant mile from the entrance to the channel off Sullivan's Island. A lookout in the waist pointed to the port side, and called in a hoarse whisper, "blockader to port!" Ormsby could see the silhouette of a Union side wheel gunboat 200 yards off the port side. *Starry Night* showed no lights. The binnacle light by which the quartermaster steered was hooded. The men had been cautioned to speak in whispers and make no sound. Under their reduced sail, they crept past the blockader at four knots, or about five statute miles per hour. The only sound was the crash of the distant surf. Everyone held his breath.

Then they were past. The blockader's silhouette altered from a beam view to bow-on and then faded into the night. Suddenly Ormsby could see the hexagonal bulk of Battery Beauregard on Sullivan's Island, just off the starboard bow. *Starry Night* wore slightly to starboard, the wind coming aft, and entered the narrow north channel, "Maffit's Channel." "Well done, men! Well done, Armstrong," he called softly to his crew and his helmsman. And then they struck.

The barque eased gently on to the bar, her starboard side grazing the sand at first and then the bow sliding over a sandbank dead ahead. The grounding was so gradual that no mast or spar was lost. "Get those tops'ls in," called Ormsby. The men scrambled aloft and furled the fore and main topsails quickly. The afterguard tailed on to the spanker halyard and lowered the spanker. "Mr. Whitby," he called to the master's mate, "call away the cutter. I'm going to the battery for reinforcements. The Federals may try to board and burn us, come daybreak."

"Aye, aye, sir. Six men here for the cutter." The boat was hoisted out, manned and soon pulled the short distance to the shore. Archie Ormsby sprinted across the sand, a white flag in his hand.

"Ahoy the fort!" The fort garrison had not yet noticed the barque aground in the channel. Ormsby's coxswain was carrying a lantern. Ormsby held the flag so the lantern's light shone on it. "Ahoy the fort, Confederate States Navy ship aground in the channel. I'm the commander. We need assistance!" The gunners from the battery's night watch advanced cautiously as Ormsby and the coxswain stood motionless. "Lieutenant Ormsby, CSN, and a Charleston native," Archie announced to the Confederate Army artillery officer commanding the garrison party.

"Ormsby? Archie? I do declare, it's Albert McClatchy, your old classmate. What have you brought the city of your birth?"

Archie quickly explained his dilemma to his old friend, Albert. "It's four in the morning, Archie, we don't have to worry until daybreak, most likely."

"Then we should be all right, Albert, if we can have sharpshooters aboard, and with your guns from the battery to keep any Union boarding parties at a distance, we can kedge off. The high tide's at 8:30."

"We can telegraph navy headquarters in Charleston, Archie. Let them know you're here. They could send a tug."

"Splendid, Albert. Ask for some marines as well, to hold off any cutting-out expedition from the blockading squadron."

"I will, Archie, but I doubt they'll send ship's boats under the guns of our battery. And they don't know what valuable cargo you're carrying."

"Good point, Albert. Who is the commander of our squadron here?"

"Commander John Tucker. He has two small ironclads and a bevy of tugs and gunboats."

"Handsome Jack Tucker!" Ormsby exclaimed excitedly. "I served in his squadron at Hampton Roads!"

"I'll be sure to let him know who the prize-master is," said McClatchy.

"Thanks, Albert. Tell him I'm an acting lieutenant now. He

knew me as a midshipman. I'd best get back and prepare the kedge."

Ormsby stood on his quarterdeck in the darkness just before dawn. He glanced at the loom of the cutter's bulk in the darkness, 75 yards astern. The cutter's crew had just set the kedge anchor, and the cable attached to it was run through the stern windows of the *Starry Night* and forward to the drum of the capstan amidships. Six men strained at the capstan bars, trying to haul the ship off the sandbar, stern-first, as the rising tide began to lift the bow off the bar. "Heave a pawl, you men. Heave away! Whitby, do you know a capstan chantey?"

"Aye, aye, sir," said the former whaler, and broke into a Dundee whaling capstan chantey. *"Did nae see ye doon the glen, bonnie laddie, heeland laddie, did nae see ye 'roon the barn, bonnie heeland laddie. Way-hay and away we go, bonnie laddie, heeland laddie,"* Whitby sang, and the men pushed on the capstan bars with a will.

Ormsby looked forward, past Fort Sumter to Fort Ripley in the distance. He realized he could distinguish their shapes. It was then just six o'clock, and it had brought the first blush of daylight and two side wheel tugs from the Cooper River navy pier in Charleston. A squad of Confederate Marines was aboard the lead tug, as well as the station commander, John Randolph Tucker. Tucker had distinguished himself as commander of the James River Squadron at the Battle of Hampton roads in early 1862.

"Good morning, sir," Ormsby called from his quarterdeck.

"Good morning, young Ormsby. Lieutenant McClatchy tells me you've brought us a cargo of saltpeter. Well done! We'll come alongside to disembark our Marines, and then weigh your kedge and take the cable aboard as a towline. Stand by to take a line forward from *Suwannoochee*." Tucker pointed to the second tug, just off *Starry Night's* bow.

"Aye, aye, sir. Mr. Whitby, 'vast heaving. Belay the cable. Tell the cutter's crew to weigh the kedge and pass the cable to the commander's tug."

As Ormsby looked aft to the cutter, he saw the inshore blockader 2000 yards distant. A puff of smoke rose from her bow and an instant later Ormsby heard the dull 'thud' of her bow pivot's report. A splash appeared 250 yards seaward of the cutter. *Extreme range,* thought Ormsby, as Battery Beauregard returned fire with a four-gun salvo.

The blockader was joined by two more inshore gunboats, but
the fire from the battery kept them at a range that precluded success.
Shots fired from a stationary platform such as Battery Beauregard were far
more accurate then those fired from a ship rolling in the Atlantic swell.
The rising tide and Tucker's tug soon had *Starry Night* off the bar and
the CSS *Suwannoochee* took up the strain on the towing hawser. *Starry
Night* passed out of range of the Union ships and into Charleston harbor.
Ormsby waved his hat at the battery. "Armstrong," said Ormsby, "hoist
'well done, Albert.' You'll have to spell out 'Albert,' but it will be worth
it."

Whitby and a Confederate Army ordinance captain supervised
the transfer of saltpeter bags from *Starry Night* to the drays along the pier
that would start them on their journey to the gunpowder factory. Ormsby
sat in Tucker's pierside office, reminiscing on James River days. Finally,
Tucker leaned forward with a smile.

"It's always gratifying, Mr. Ormsby, to see one of my officers
distinguish himself in action. That was a brilliant stroke to bring a
sailing ship through a blockade of steamers. We'll get *Starry Night* into
prize court tomorrow. Meanwhile, I'm confirming Captain Canby's
action. Effective immediately, you are commissioned a lieutenant in the
Confederate States Provisional Navy."

"Thank you, sir," said Ormsby, his head in a whirl.
Commissioned rank, and in the provisional navy! Ormsby smiled to
himself. The provisional navy had been created by the Confederate
Congress in May 1863 at the urging of Secretary of the Navy Mallory.
Since the war's beginning, Mallory often had been unable to promote
and assign daring and competent officers because the Confederate
Navy was devoted to seniority as a basis for promotion. Some senior
officers, like Semmes, Buchanan and Tattnall, were open to Mallory's
innovative and revolutionary methods and policies. Many more were
not. In the provisional navy, parallel to the existing service, promotion
and assignment were based only on merit and the needs of the service.
Ormsby thought to himself, *promotion based on merit! Mother and dad
will be pleased.*

"There's another 'Old Dominion' stationed here, Mr. Ormsby," said Tucker. "I'm sure you'll want to say 'hello' to Lieutenant Glendenning during your stay." Quentin Glendenning and Archie had served aboard the Confederate armed tug *Old Dominion* in Chesapeake Bay during the early days of the war.

"I'll be sure to do that, sir." Ormsby glanced out the office window as an old lightship with a tall derrick mounted in the bow was towed by. He could see diving equipment on deck. "Sir, what is that lightship being used for?"

"We're trying to salvage the eleven-inch Dahlgrens from the wreck of the *Keokuk*," said Tucker. "Mr. LaCoste of the Ordinance Department has his hands full. But if we're successful, we'll improve our defense considerably."

The rush of his promotion news had begun to wear off, and the strain of the last week was taking its toll on Ormsby's ability to stay awake. Tucker smiled as he noticed his lieutenant's eyes struggle to stay open. "Lieutenant, it's time you took a bit of leave. Your family lives here. I'm sure you'd benefit from two weeks to get reacquainted. When you get back, we'll see about new orders, as well as a nice sum of prize money!"

"My parents will surely be surprised, sir. I'm most grateful." Ormsby could already picture himself on the verandah or "piazza" of his parent's long house, taking his ease.

CHAPTER 15
THE CONFEDERATE RAIDER FLORA
JUNE 1863

The CSS *Star of the South* rolled north under her courses and topsails in the warm waters of the Gulf Stream. The 18-man crew of the Union merchant ship *Starry Night*, prisoners aboard *Star*, were taking their morning hour of exercise on the main deck, closely supervised by the Master-at-Arms and his guard detail. As Lieutenant Cadwallader, officer of the watch, followed the exercise regimen from his post on the quarterdeck, he heard a call from the lookout aloft. "Sail ho, two points off the starboard bow! She looks like a Dutchman."

"Call all hands and set the royals," Cadwallader ordered. "Hoist the Blue Ensign." The British colors appropriate to the Atlantic coast of North America fluttered to the peak of the spanker. The additional sail spread enabled *Star* to overtake the ship ahead. The quarry made no attempt to outrun *Star*. The British cut of *Star's* hull and suit of sails may have reassured the ship, indeed a Netherlands merchant, that she was in no danger.

Star fired a shot, and the Dutch brig hove to. "Mr. Dunbrody, please board her and check her papers," said Captain Canby, now on deck.

"Aye, aye, sir." The jolly boat and a crew of six brought Rory to the side of the *Maartin de Groot*, out of 's Gravenhage, whose papers showed a Dutch cargo bound for Bermuda and Havana.

"That is not a Royal Navy uniform," smiled the captain as he led Rory below to examine the manifest.

"Sure and you're right, sir, and you'll note the Blue Ensign is down and the Confederacy's new 'stainless banner' flyin'," said Rory, gesturing toward *Star of the South* as she tossed a cable's length to starboard. The southern papers had given that nickname to the flag for its white field. After a brief examination, Rory was able to say, "Your papers are in order, sir. Thank you for your forbearance."

"Would you be interested in what the New York papers are saying about you, lieutenant? We picked these up yesterday in Bermuda." He handed a packet of newspapers to Rory. "You certainly look like a British cruiser, but since the crew of the *Shoshone County* were released, your description has apparently been given to the twenty Union ships searching for you." The Netherlander smiled. "Good luck to you. You'll need it."

Canby read the papers with interest. "We are being preceded, gentlemen, by a colleague, Lieutenant Charles W. Read, in a raider that has taken three ships this month. At last report he was off Hatteras," he said to his officers gathered on the quarterdeck.

"Savez Read, sir!" Rory exclaimed. "He's a bold one, sure and he is. He was my second in a duel in New Orleans, and fought the *McRae* 'til she sank!"

"Well, the papers say his current ship, the *Clarence*, was a prize of the *Florida* under Maffit, and that Maffit armed her and sent her forth to sink more Yankees."

"Sure, now, captain, just the trick I've been suggestin' for us," smiled Rory.

"Yes, lieutenant," sighed Canby, "I assure you I haven't forgotten. According to these reports, it seems we won't be fooling many potential prizes with our present appearance, gentlemen, as *Shoshone County's* crew have given a very accurate description of us." "Mr. Cadwallader, see what you can do to re-rig the mizzen. We'll be a full-rigged ship by tomorrow. That should throw them off for a week or two! They report we've got a dozen or two scouring the seas for us. That should weaken the blockade!"

"Aye, aye, sir," said Cadwallader, eying the two fore and aft sails flying above him on the mizzenmast. To effect the change, he would have to strike the fore and aft topsail and use two valuable spare spars for the crossed yards of a mizzen topsail and a mizzen royal. The spanker would remain. The barque rig would be transformed to that of a full-rigged ship.

Canby turned to Rory. "Where did your friend Read get a name like 'savvy'?"

"At the Academy, sir, he was a terrible student in French. He only learned one word, 'savez,' the word for 'you know' and he used it incessantly. The nickname stuck."

"It's certainly memorable."

The next morning, a Monday, the *Star* flew the Union stars and stripes with her new rig. The day provided a bumper harvest. First they stopped and burned an American barque with a cargo of Muscavado Caribbean sugars valued at $17,000. As was the rule among the Confederate raiders, the captured crewmen were allowed to keep all personal belongings. Upon reaching *Star of the South,* one of the barque's sailors complained that his pocket watch had been taken by a boarding-party member. The barque's captain relayed the complaint to Canby.

"Mr. Dunbrody!"

"Sir," replied Rory who had eavesdropped as the complaint was being made.

"It appears we have a theft to investigate. See to it, if you please."

"Aye, aye, captain," said Rory as he turned to go below. The boarding party was shackling the barque's crew on the gun deck as Rory called them to attention. "Men, one of you has disobeyed orders and relieved one of our prisoners of his pocket watch. I do not wish to know whom. I want the watch returned. I will go on deck and leave you to discuss this among yourselves. Send an innocent man to me with the watch. No questions asked. Should you fail to follow my orders, your grog will be stopped until a search and interrogation turns up the guilty party. Punishment will follow, sure and it will, twenty-four lashes, I'm thinkin', at the least. So, if the watch fails to appear, the cat's out of the bag. Are we clear, men?"

Rory heard affirmative mumbles. Most of the men looked at the deck, their heads bowed and their eyes avoiding Rory's. A few began to glare at some of their fellows. He left abruptly and climbed the companionway to the upper deck. Ten minutes later, a young Welshman saluted and handed Rory the watch. "It warn't me, sir," he said, earnestly.

"I know that, Evans. Thank you." Canby watched from the starboard side of the quarterdeck, a bemused look on his face. Rory handed him the watch.

"Nicely done, Mr. Dunbrody."

"Thank you, captain."

"Sail ho, off the starboard beam," came the lookout's call.

"What d'ye make of her?" McGuiness had the watch, and posed the question.

"Ship-rigged, and New Englander by the cut of her, sir," came the reply.

"Lower the screw, and set all plain sail, Mr. McGuiness," said Canby. "Hoist the stars and stripes." The courses converged and the *Star of the South* ran swiftly under her new rig, proof that Cadwallader knew what he was about. As they closed to within a half mile, the Stainless Banner rose to the peak of the spanker, and Rory's forward pivot fired a blank cartridge. After no response from the Yankee, Rory fired a shaped solid shell. The Yankee, an East India trader, came up into the wind.

"Board her, Mr. Dunbrody, if you please." She proved to be the *Parmeter,* bound for Boston out of Calcutta with a cargo of jute and linseed. Also aboard was Lester Eliot, U.S. consul to Madagascar, his wife and their three young daughters. The linseed oil made a fine and spectacular blaze as they burned her that afternoon, and the ladies were soon made comfortable on the afterdeck, among the *Star's* young officers. The midshipmen were particularly (and unusually) well-behaved. The captains of the barque, the *Starry Night,* and the *Parmeter,* and their families, together with the Eliots, were given the captain's and senior officers' quarters and made most comfortable. After the war, when Canby would face charges for inhumane treatment of prisoners, Eliot would appear on his behalf, and charges would be dropped.

As the afternoon wore on, the sun shone on a blue sea clear of sails and smoke, and Rory, watching on the quarterdeck as the officers chatted and flirted with the Eliot girls, found his thoughts wandering to Carrie Anne. *I hope she misses me as I miss her,* he thought. *I wish I could see a time when we're reunited, but this cruise seems destined to carry me farther away, with little hope of reunion.*

He sighed, and then turned to more immediate and pressing concerns, the assignment of crewmen for prisoner guard duty. The combined crews of the three destroyed vessels were a significant threat to the safety of the ship, as they outnumbered the *Star's* crew.

Tuesday dawned and managed even to surpass Monday's good fortune. The ship *Lorena* of New York, laden with pork, ham, flour, beef, lobsters in ice, and a variety of fine alcoholic beverages, fell prey to the *Star of the South,* and markedly improved the menus of her various messes, from the captain's larder to the lower deck. Moreover, Canby bonded her for $10,000 to be paid the Confederate government 30 days after war's end, and put every single prisoner, properly paroled, aboard her for delivery to her next port.

Rory was the boarding officer, and talked at length to the owner-captain and his family while the cargo was being unloaded, and the prisoners brought aboard. "Are you a gamblin' man, Captain Terry?" Rory asked as they stood on the quarterdeck. "You'll only pay your bond if the South continues to exist after the war ends, and you're already ahead, not havin' t' watch your ship burn, as many others have had t' do."

"I'm in the game, like it or not, lieutenant, but judging from the news, I have a fifty-fifty chance," said Captain Mark Terry. His wife Kim stood next to him, her arm around her daughter Lorena, for whom the ship was named.

"How did you come to have a mermaid as a figurehead, sailors thinkin' mermaids are bad luck, and all?"

Mrs. Terry laughed. "My daughter Lorena loves mermaid tales, and my husband is a classicist, lieutenant. Mark had read of the ancient Syrian goddess, Atargatis, half woman, half fish, who drew power from the moon and controlled the tides. It is she you see as the figurehead."

"Yes, and I decided goddesses were exempt from the mermaid's curse, and managed to convince my crew," added the captain.

"So I have my figure, minus the bad luck," said Lorena, smiling. "I hope you haven't lost any relatives in the war, Mr. Dunbrody?" she asked. "Our cousin Jesse was killed at Gaines Mill."

"No young miss, I've lost no one yet," said Rory, crossing himself. "Sure, it was kind of y' to ask." The last of the prisoners had just come aboard *Lorena.* I'll excuse meself, now, and wish you all smooth sailin'."

The Terrys waved as the ship bore off. Captain Canby, having rid himself of his prisoners, heaved an audible sigh of relief as the *Lorena's* royals dropped below the horizon. Canby had secured several New York newspapers from the *Lorena,* and was able to bring his crew up to date on Savez Read. "He's burned the *Clarence* and taken a new prize as a raider, the *Tacony.* He took a prize three days ago off Delaware."

No sooner had the *Lorena* disappeared then a call from the lookout announced a brig on a southerly course. Canby bore to port to intercept her, flying the flag of the Union as usual as the gavotte of chase and boarding began. "A sprightly vessel from the looks of her topsails, Mr. Dunbrody," said Canby, lightheartedly. The disposition of the prisoners and the ever-increasing number of prizes were improving Canby's mood noticeably.

"No doubt about it, captain. Perhaps she's the one we could be usin' those two nine-pounders in the hold to arm and set loose, d' ye think?" Rory knew he was close to the edge of self-aggrandizement, but his desire for another command drove him to press the issue.

"Time will tell, Mr. Dunbrody," said Canby with a smile. He recognized Rory's aggressiveness for what it was, the desire to excel in the performance of his duty. *A valuable trait,* Canby thought.

The brig hauled her wind at the first warning cannon shot, and proved to be just the vessel the raiders had been looking for. She was freshly coppered, 300 tons with fine lines, and innocuous enough to be allowed to close with most merchant ships to a range where a brace of nine-pounders could be put to use. The name she bore was *Flora,* and she carried ammunition, arms and four brass howitzers for the Union forces at Port Royal, as well as a Union army paymaster.

On deck after the capture, Canby asked, "if I were to give you command of the brig, what would your course of action be, Mr. Dunbrody?" Canby was clearly still enjoying himself, and the sparring with his lieutenant was a pleasurable game for him.

"Captain," said Rory, in a rare serious moment, "I'd take her north to the George's Bank, and decimate the fishing schooner fleet. Sure, the cries of outrage from Boston and New England would then be heard for miles at sea, and Secretary Welles would be impelled to divert more ships from blockade to quash my impudence, sir."

"And then?"

"I'd follow the fine example of my commander, disguise myself, and then attack New York!"

"I declare, lieutenant, you're the equivalent of a catamount at sea. I'm inclined to give you command for the entertainment value, alone! You're in command of the brig, to carry out attacks against northern shipping, and we'll arm you with the nine-pounders and two of the howitzers!"

Rory beamed, his smile bright enough to light the quarterdeck. "Thank you, captain. We'll make the *Star* proud of us!"

"I'm sure you will, Dunbrody. I can give you a midshipman, a master's mate, a bosun's mate, and twenty men. She's a brig, and a crew that size can handle her."

"Indeed it can, sir. Might I have a blackganger, sir, just in case we need to convert to steam? Tryin' to think of contingency, now, d' ye see, sir?"

"Very well, you may approach Chief Engineer Allison with my blessing and ask to recruit a volunteer from among our three firemen first class. We'll make the volunteer 'acting third assistant engineer.' That should evoke a response."

"You're very kind, sir, thank you. By your leave, sir." Rory hurried below to assemble his crew. *If I do need to abandon this brig and can find a steamer, I'll have a chance with a fireman first class,* Rory thought as he ran to the engine room. *I think I'll ask Duffy. He's been studyin' in hopes of promotion.*

Lieutenant McGuiness had led the boarding party, many of whom were still aboard the *Flora*. The cutter had returned to Star with the brig's crew as prisoners. Rory had assembled his men, and the ship's officers had come to the quarterdeck to bid him a hasty goodbye.

"Best of good fortune, Rory," said Cadwallader. O'Toole the boatswain shook his hand earnestly. Engineer Allison had brought Fireman First Class Niall Duffy on deck and groused at Rory as he said goodbye.

"You're taking my best fireman-first, young man. Use him well!"

"Aye, aye, chief," Rory smiled in response.

"Tell Mr. McGuiness to bring back two of the four howitzers when he returns in the cutter, Captain Dunbrody," said Canby.

"Aye, aye, sir. That title has a nice ring to it, sir. Thank you for your confidence."

"You've earned it, Dunbrody. We're expecting great things of you with those howitzers in addition to the two nine-pounders. I also want you to take this, for contingencies," said Canby, handing Rory a small cloth bag that clinked audibly. "We took 5000 Union dollars in specie from the paymaster aboard *Flora*. I'm giving you $500."

"Thank you, sir. I'll not disappoint you."

The nine-pounder cannons *Star of the South* had carried for arming an auxiliary raider were being swung into the cutter by O'Toole and a work party, as Canby and Rory watched from the quarterdeck. "I believe we'll head south and perhaps draw pursuit away from you as you head north," said Canby.

"We'll be grateful for that, sir, t' be sure. By your leave, sir." Rory saluted the captain, then the Confederate ensign at the mizzen peak, and walked to the rail to board the cutter and join his crew, his seabag in his hand, with the specie inside.

The new crew of the CSS *Flora* and the original boarding party labored for two hours to mount the two nine-pounders in broadside and assemble the two howitzers and lash them in position on the foredeck. The carpenter's stores aboard *Flora* provided tools sufficient for the cutting of rudimentary gun ports for the nine-pounders and the rigging of their recoil tackle.

Two days later, on a course for George's Bank, the lookout's call heralded their first prize, the *Westwind*, a barque carrying a cargo of coal for the Union squadron in New Orleans. Rory took the crew aboard as prisoners, shackled them below, and burned the barque. In the hour before midnight, Rory stood by the lee rail, watching the phosphorescence of the wake trail behind the ship. The endless list of command concerns tumbled in his mind, keeping him from sleep. *We can't take many more prizes without the risk of being outnumbered by our prisoners,* he thought. *And Savez Read could well be on the same course, a week ahead of us, stirring up a hornet's nest of federal cruisers!* Thomas Walsh, the master's mate from County Cork, was officer of the watch. He and Beaupre, the midshipman, were Rory's two watch-keeping officers. *They seem competent enough,* thought Rory. *Walsh led the boarding party and handled it well.* Rory strode up the slanting deck to the binnacle, lit by a small lantern and hooded so as not to destroy the helmsman's night vision. *On course and making ten knots,* he thought with satisfaction. "Mr. Walsh, I'm turning in. Call me if you need to."

"Aye, aye, sir," said Walsh, his Cork brogue causing Rory a pang of homesickness.

Union Secretary of the Navy Gideon Welles was having a very bad fortnight. In mid-June he had learned of the captures by the *Clarence.* Then, word of captures by *Star of the South* reached him. The newspapers gave the Rebel "pirates" front-page coverage. He sent twenty federal ships to sea and chartered more with acting captains and crews. Savez Read burned the *Clarence* and seized the *Tacony.* More ships burned and more headlines screamed for protection. A storm cloaked the track of the Rebels. And through it all, Robert E. Lee advanced on Pennsylvania. Exasperated, Welles rose from his desk and walked to the office of his assistant navy secretary, Gus Fox. "Look at this, Gus! The Boston *Evening Journal,* the New York *Daily Tribune,* the *Herald,* the Portland *Press,* all screaming that I haven't done enough!" He dropped the stack of newspapers on Fox's desk. "Twenty ships! If they'd found *Tacony* promptly, the same papers would be blaming me for needless and expensive over-reaction!"

Fox leaned back in his chair. "Gideon, you know we'll find her, and the Army will have another battle loss, and the papers will have forgotten you within days. We just need to keep searching, and fending off panicky politicians like Governor Andrew and Senator Morgan." The Massachusetts governor had blasted Wells for "absence of action," and the New York senator along with New York City mayor Opdyke had demanded that the frigate *Roanoke* be stationed in New York harbor to defend the city.

"I know, Gus. It's just frustrating to be harassed while our only recourse is diligence and patience."

"Well, Gideon, let's just resolve to out-wait the panicky populace. Not much else we can do." Another week proved Fox to be correct regarding Lieutenant Read, as he was captured while seizing the revenue cutter *Caleb Cushing* in Portland, Maine. Rory's ship, however, was still a thorn in Secretary Welles' side.

While Savez Read was being captured in Maine, the CSS *Flora* arrived at George's Bank, a wide and extensive shoal one hundred miles east of Cape Cod. It was an excellent fishing ground, shoaling to as little as 15 feet in some places, and crowded with fishing schooners. "Mr. McCafferty, hoist out the gig, if you please." Finn Mccafferty, formerly a quartermaster, had been selected by Rory as his boatswain's mate, and as the acting boatswain of the *Flora*, he was addressed as a warrant officer, by "mister." "Mr. Walsh, take eight men," said Rory to his master's mate, "secure each crew in shackles, and take as many as six of those schooners. Then we'll transfer the crews to one, bond her, and burn the rest. That'll give Gideon Welles heartburn, sure, and it will!"

"Aye, aye, sir. Cutlasses and pistols, sir?"

"T' be sure, Mr. Walsh." Rory had been able to arm his crew with Colt Navy Sixes, part of the *Flora's* cargo, rather than use the European revolvers that were the best Bulloch had been able to provide when *Star of the South* armed from *Martha*.

Walsh was able to take five schooners before some of the other became wary at the gig's approach and began slipping their cables and sailing away. When Rory saw that *Flora's* presence had become suspect, he raised the new Confederate flag, the "second national ensign" with its blue saltier, and hoisted his Irish battle flag, green with a gold harp, at the main course yardarm. Then he fired a few shots from his nine-pounder smoothbores to scatter them.

As most of the fishing fleet scrambled to sail out of range, the gig laboriously gathered the shackled crews of the five still-anchored captured schooners. "Which one appears to you to be the oldest, Mr. Beaupre?" Rory waited as his midshipman and second in command scanned the little squadron with his glass.

"The one furthest east, sir, the *Myrtle*."

"Very well, kindly direct Mr. Walsh to put the crews aboard her. Bring the captain to me. We'll bond her and send her with all the prisoners to Gloucester. Then have Mr. Walsh burn the others. I'm going below to enter all this in the log."

As night fell, a fog descended over the Bank. Rory sailed cautiously north toward the edge of George's Bank and anchored at midnight. He gathered his officers and acting warrant officers for dinner in the brig's cramped captain's cabin. Beaupre, Walsh, Duffy and McCafferty sat, two to the side, with Rory at the head of the table. As was the naval tradition, they were arranged by rank, with Beaupre and Walsh closest to the captain, and McCafferty and Duffy at the end opposite Rory. Beaupre was Acadian, or Cajun, used to dining well among Louisiana society. Walsh had dined in the gunroom of several ships as a master's mate, and was at least familiar with some of the niceties of more formal navy dining. McCafferty and Duffy, promoted from the lower deck, were visibly uncomfortable as the meal began, but Rory quickly put them at ease. The brig's previous captain had laid by a nice store of wine and Rory had selected a bottle of Madeira. With no steward, Rory poured the wine himself. "Now, gentlemen, to a successful cruise so far!" Each glass was raised with enthusiasm. "Barnwell is no chef, t' be sure," said Rory of the sailor acting as ship's cook, "but the beef is still good, and the vegetables still fresh. And since four out of five here are Irish, I know the potatoes will find your favor!" At this, laughter rippled around the table.

"As good as Liverpool pub food, sir," countered Walsh.

"Carry on then, lads." Rory, at twenty-six, was older than all but McCafferty. "When the meal is finished, I'll ask your leave to break with dining-at-sea protocol, and discuss some ship's business."

It was a memorable meal for all. The last ship Rory commanded, *Old Dominion,* had been part of a squadron. *Flora* was his first independent command, and he was enjoying every minute. His dinner companions had never been senior officers before, and though the brig was small, it was theirs and they relished the experience.

"Now, then, lads," said Rory as they finished the meal, "a bit of planning and then another bottle and a song or two. Our next target will put us all in harm's way, but I assure you I'll find a way for all of us to make it through. I don't believe in futile gestures. We're going to attack New York!" He sat back and smiled at his guests.

Beaupre was the first to recover from the shock. "Sir, aren't we a trifle under-gunned for such an attack?"

"Ach, sure, and we are, Mr. Beaupre, but they won't see us comin' and we'll cause such a fuss that we'll escape in the hullabaloo! Here's how." He had their attention now. "The fishermen we sent to Gloucester will tell all to look for a brig. We'll trade *Flora* for a steamer. You'll be a real chief engineer, Mr. Duffy!" Niall Duffy smiled uncertainly.

"We're lying right in the track of coastal packets here. A steamer will turn up soon. We'll burn or scuttle *Flora*, and bond the next prize and send the prisoners with her. We'll head for New York. Their pilot schooners compete for ships as far as 150 miles from New York. We'll capture one, and then use her to lure ships to us. They'll think they're following a New York pilot.

"Won't we become overburdened with prisoners, sir?" Walsh leaned forward with a quizzical look, his glass of wine forgotten in the midst of Rory's narrative.

"That's our goal, Mr. Walsh, sure and you've put your finger on it. As soon as we have more prisoners than we're comfortable with, we'll take the next ship, bond her and put them aboard. Then comes the last and best part of the plan!"

Beaupre laughed. "It's so exciting now, I can't imagine it getting any better, captain." His humor cut the tension in the cabin and everyone relaxed.

Rory continued. "We cut every halyard, sheet and brace on the prisoners' ship to keep them from following immediately. Then we put a crew of four aboard our captured pilot schooner, rig her as a fire ship, and she'll appear to lead us in to the Brooklyn Navy Yard just at dusk. She'll grapple and burn the best target, we'll swing close to pick up her crew, fire a broadside or two and escape out Hell Gate, a pistol at our pilot's head!"

Walsh stood, applauding with a look of amazement, and the others joined him. "Incredible, sir," said Beaupre. "Sure, and it's like a fairy-tale sir," said McCafferty. "Will it work?"

"Probably not, bo'sun. And we'll probably have to change it half a dozen times. That's where my pledge to give everyone a survival chance comes in," said Rory. "There are a host of things to go wrong! We'll be running up the East River in the dark, with a reluctant pilot. We could easily run aground. Or the batteries guarding the river and Hell Gate might sink us. So, any of the crew who are British subjects shall have the opportunity to leave us as we try our exit. The men have never had uniforms anyway. They can get ashore, work their way to a crimp or the ships at South Street or the Hudson River, and be away and free of Federal prison."

"I don't think you'll get many takers, sir," said Walsh.

"Then they're all proper rapparees, they are, rebels without equal. That offer extends to all of you British subjects, by the way, even though you are acting warrant officers. You'd be able to melt into the crowd, as well. I'm afraid Beaupre and I are in a different boat. He has a southern accent, and I have a commission. You and I can go down with the ship, midshipman."

As Beaupre smiled with some display of pride, Walsh rose in mock indignation. "Sir, I am shocked that you might believe I would desert another Irishman in his moment of need, and I'm sure I speak for these two other rapparees. Sir." The other "rapparees" nodded in agreement

"Well, I stand corrected, and that's a fact. But I want the men to understand that they have the choice. A federal prison is just short of a death sentence, by all reports, not that ours are any different. Now, another glass, and a song and Mr. McCafferty has the mid anchor-watch. Make sure the masthead lookout is alert through this fog, bo'sun." A second bottle, and then a third accompanied the renditions of chanteys from across the world. Beaupre offered a New Orleans stevedore capstan chantey, "One More Day," in a haunting baritone, followed by McCafferty leading the British merchantman's paean to Napoleon, "Boney was a Warrior," a mainsail chantey.

CHAPTER 16
THE BELLE OF BILOXI
JUNE 1863

As the morning dawned and the fog lifted, they weighed anchor and set a course southwest toward the approaches to Sandy Hook and New York City. They were in the midst of a shipping track and it soon yielded prizes, first a barque out of Maine, with 1200 bales of hay and straw for Federal horses aboard, and the next day, a clipper, also from Maine, with 1800 sacks of rice aboard. Rory valued her at $35,000. *I hope this tally of prize values isn't just an exercise,* he thought as he made his entries in the log. *We'll all have to reach the Confederacy in order for the men to benefit.*

The barque had made a fine fire the night before, the hay and straw blazing away. While the smoke from the clipper still ascended into the blue July sky early the next day, they found the prize they'd been looking for, a side wheel packet from the New York – Charleston Line, now carrying passengers from Halifax to New York, the war having precluded Charleston as a destination. She was a brig-rigged passenger steamer of 700 tons. The name *Peter Stuyvesant* was painted on each of her paddle wheel boxes. She had a pilot house-bridge forward, a tall smokestack between the masts, and boats in davits on either side. There were railed command stations atop each paddle wheel box. *Flora* fired a blank cartridge as the packet approached, and she stopped her engines and drifted to a stop as the brig drew alongside her.

"Mr. Walsh, sure, and she looks like a Union packet," said Rory. "Board her and confine the passengers and crew, once you've examined her papers. We'll transfer our prisoners from *Flora* next, and then the nine-pounder cannon and the howitzers."

"Aye, aye, sir," said Walsh. McCafferty already had the crew hoisting out the cutter. They had a long and exhausting day ahead of them, but at its end they had 70 prisoners confined in the packet's main cabin, the two howitzers assembled and ready to fire, and the nine pounders aboard. The crew had been energized by the prospect of a new raider, and the realization that the Union cruisers would still be looking for the brig. Rory had given a spirited appeal to the captured sailors of the three ships, promising prize money and a short cruise if they joined his crew. *Well,* he smiled to himself, *I'm not stretchin' the truth too far. This cruise is liable to be very short.* He was surprised to have four crewmen, two of them firemen and recent Irish immigrants, volunteer.

At dusk, Rory gave one more order. "Mr. Beaupre, go aboard *Flora,* scuttle her, and bring our last few lads off. Tomorrow, we'll mount the smoothbores, and look for a ship to take our prisoners." It was a clear night, and from the deck of his new command, Rory could see the *Flora* settle slowly in the water. *Sure, she was a good old bucket,* he thought, *and I'll miss her, but we'll be safer aboard the Peter Stuyvesant.*

"Well done, Mr. Beaupre," Rory smiled in the darkness at his second in command. "She's takin' her sweet time in sinkin', sure and she is."

"It's a slow process, sir, with only a few sea cocks," replied Beaupre. "Will we rename this one, sir?"

"Well, now, you're from the Gulf Coast, Mr. Beaupre. What would you think of "*Belle of Biloxi?*"

"A fine choice, sir. Alliteration always makes a name stand out."

"Then that's what she shall be, but I'm thinkin' we'll leave 'Peter Stuyvesant' on her paddle boxes, to help us if we try our little expedition to New York."

"A prudent decision, I'm sure, sir," said the Louisianan. "There were recent Halifax papers in the main cabin, sir. It appears Mr. Read was captured in Portland, Maine, on the 26th of June."

"Sure, we'll have to take up the slack for old Savez, then. Put them in my cabin, if you please," said Rory.

The next morning, Rory awoke to the sight of *Flora's* decks awash. It was clear she was about to go under. *Belle of Biloxi* was hove to, under topsails and headsails, a cable's length away. "Sail ho," came the cry from the lookout. "She's a coasting schooner, sir, and she's in ballast."

Perfect, thought Rory. "Mr. Walsh," he said to the officer of the deck, "we've a schooner with no cargo, and plenty of room for our prisoners, 'bibbin' down on us, straightway,' in the words of the song. I'm thinkin' she sees *Flora* goin' down, and us hoverin' nearby, and she wants to join us in renderin' assistance. Keep those Union colors flyin' and ready a boat to board her. Hands to quarters, if you please, and have the howitzers ready."

The schooner *Compass Rose* of Philadelphia was indeed in ballast, and her captain at once dismayed at his capture and relieved that he'd be bonded as he took on Rory's prisoners. *At least he's not losin' his livelihood,* thought Rory as he filed the bond away in his ship's papers. *Three days to Philadelphia,* Rory calculated. *Plenty of time to carry out our New York adventure, if we can convince a pilot to get us through Hell Gate.*

As the *Compass Rose* sailed out of sight, Rory went below. "You have the deck, Mr. Walsh. I'm going to the engine room and see if Mr. Duffy and his new firemen can move this tub!" The *Peter Stuyvesant* was powered with an inclined, direct acting engine. The cylinder and piston were nearly horizontal, and connected by lever-arms and a cam to the crankshaft of the sidewheels. It was efficient, simple, and located below the water line. Duffy was busy with his "black gang," the nickname for the often-sooty firemen who fed the coal into the fires of the boilers. They were raising steam.

"We should be able to move you right along, sir," Duffy said, brightly.

"Splendid, Mr. Duffy. We'll move slowly down to the Sandy Hook approaches and see if we can snare a pilot schooner. No high speed chases, I shouldn't think."

"Aye, aye, sir," said Duffy. "We'll ease into it, then."

"Carry on then Mr. Duffy. Oh, one more thing," said Rory, turning to the two new firemen. "Have you lads spent any time ashore in New York?"

"Aye, sor, the bot' of us," said one in a Dublin accent. "I'm

Coogan and this one's O'Flaherty."

"That's grand, men. I may be talkin' t' ye later about conditions ashore."

Belle of Biloxi moved at moderate speed down the shipping lanes. McCafferty and Rory oversaw the mounting of the two nine-pounder smoothbores on their gun carriages, and the cutting of the gun ports. The freshly armed packet was 50 miles southeast of Montauk Point at nightfall. Beaupre had the midwatch. A seaman shook Rory awake just after midnight. "Sir, Mr. Beaupre says he thinks a Union cruiser is overtaking us, sir."

"I'll come, thank you, Wagner."

When Rory reached the bridge, Beaupre had the night glass on the black shape looming on their port quarter. *Belle* had her running lights on and minimal passenger cabin lights, as would befit the Halifax to New York packet she hoped to be mistaken for.

"Federal cruiser, suh, or I'm a blind lubber," said Beaupre, handing Rory the telescope.

"Sure, and you're right, number one. Call the hands very quietly and keep 'em out of sight. We look like an innocent packet, I'm hopin'."

Ten minutes later, the USS *Dai Ching*, a 175 foot screw gunboat carrying seven guns, hailed the *Belle of Biloxi*. "What ship's that?"

"Packet *Peter Stuyvesant*, Halifax to New York."

"There's a Rebel pirate cruising the coast, burning merchantmen. She's a brig. Better keep a sharp lookout."

"Thanks for the warning. Good hunting!"

The *Dai Ching* steamed on by, and Rory realized he'd been gripping the rail so hard, his knuckles were white.

Regardless of his tension while alongside the Union gunboat, Rory was asleep within minutes of returning to his cabin. He was awakened, per his standing orders, at daybreak. The captain's quarters aboard the side wheeler were abaft the pilot house and bridge. Barnwell, the cook, had made the most of the fresh stores carried by the packet, which was rarely at sea for more than a week at a time. "Fresh eggs, bacon and toast," Rory exclaimed to seaman Wagner, who had brought the meal from the galley. "And coffee, real coffee! The coastal packet run's the life for us, Wagner!"

"Aye, sir, it beats crossin' the Atlantic," Wagner replied with a grin.

That's a good sign, now, a sailor with a smile, Rory mused as Wagner left the cabin. *We'll see if we can keep the morale up this day.*

After the luxury of a breakfast uninterrupted by a ship-sighting, Rory rose from the table, stretched, and put on his gray uniform jacket. The door to the chartroom was not latched, as he made his way into the pilothouse. It swung back and forth to the motion of the ship as she rolled through the moderate sea. Rory pushed it open and leaned over the chart. He could see the last entry from the officer of the watch placing *Belle of Biloxi* about 75 miles from Sandy Hook. *Good place to troll for a pilot,* he smiled to himself.

"Sail ho, dead ahead, schooner with tops'ls, sir!"

Rory left the chartroom for the bridge in the Belle's spacious pilothouse. Walsh had the watch. "God bless us, Mr. Walsh, that could be our next customer!"

"I wouldn't be surprised at all, at all, sir."

"If she runs down to us, Thomas, call the gun crews but keep them out of sight."

"Aye, aye, sir," said Walsh, obviously pleased with Rory's familiar form of address.

Sure, these lads are beginnin' t' seem like brothers, thought Rory. *Would that we were in another line of work, and I could be sure t' keep 'em safe.*

"Deck, there. She's runnin' down to us. A New York pilot schooner, sir, sure as a gun!"

"Well, now, Mr. Walsh, let's look as if we need help. Mr. McCafferty, a boarding party at the port side quarter boat, away from the schooner. Get her into the water as soon as the schooner hauls her wind. Mr. Walsh, get a boarding ladder overside, and call the hands to quarters, if you please."

"Aye, aye, sir." Walsh trained his telescope on the onrushing pilot schooner, close hauled against the easterly wind, with mainsail, foresail and triangular topsails all set and drawing. Walsh watched her rush up to a cable's length distance and luff up into the wind, losing her way, and smartly launching a small pulling boat. The oarsman was dressed in a black suit and vest, and a stylish beaver top hat, a symbol of his pilot's status, was visible beneath the sternsheets. He secured to the boarding ladder, jammed his hat firmly onto his head, grabbed a valise and with a practiced air, climbed the ladder to the deck.

As the top hat rose above the level of the entry port, Rory said to Walsh in a whisper, "Strike the stars and stripes and hoist our battle ensign, Mr. Walsh."

Walsh strode to the flag halyard himself, rather than give an order, so as to preserve the surprise about to startle the pilot.

The pilot walked forward to Rory, who had descended the ladder from the bridge to the main deck. "Curtis Abernathy, licensed New York harbor pilot, at your service, sir. I'd be pleased to guide you to the harbor of our metropolis, and if you'll be so kind as to sign these papers, we can begin!"

"Och, and a fine fellow you are, Pilot Abernathy! Accordin'ly, it pains me mightily t' inform you that I'm Captain Dunbrody of the Confederate States Ship *Belle of Biloxi*, and you, good sir, are my prisoner!" Rory pointed above to the Confederate ensign flying from the main peak, and Abernathy's jaw dropped as he sputtered, "My God, what flag is that? What ship is this?"

"There, there, now, you're in no danger, my friend. As you can see, my boarding party is about to secure your lovely schooner, and we'll just be havin' a grand cruise t'gether, for a day or two!" Rory winked at seaman Wagner, who was leading the guard detail. "Wagner, would y' be takin' Mr. Abernathy t' the guest quarters, please. I'll just relieve you of that heavy valise, now."

Rory returned to the bridge. With the call to quarters, Beaupre had come to the bridge. Rory turned to Walsh. "That was easier than I thought, Mr. Walsh. Dismiss the gun crews. I'll ask you to select a crew of six and take command of yonder schooner. Your first command, Thomas! A meteoric rise!" Delighted, Walsh joined in Rory's laughter. "Your assignment, as we've discussed, is to play the part of Mr. Abernathy. You're a New York Harbor Pilot, and you'll guide the unsuspecting New York-bound ships straight to us. We'll maintain station at this position. You'll take McCafferty with you to command the schooner whilst you're aboard our victims."

"Aye, aye, sir. Thank you sir. May I take the valise, sir, so I can study for my 'part'?"

"Indeed you may, Captain Walsh." The two young men were enjoying themselves greatly. "Mr. Beaupre," Rory said to his second in command, "I know you understand that I need you aboard, as the officer who'll command if I'm unable."

"Of course, sir. I'm looking forward to my role, as well."

"Sure, and there's a bit of drama in store for us all, Mr. Beaupre. Now, with Walsh gone, I'll take the other watch."

"Aye, aye, sir. Thank you, sir."

"Ach, don't mention it, at all. I believe I'll have a chat with the schooner's crew, now." Rory went aft to the main passenger cabin where the schooner's crew was sitting, with wrist shackles, drinking coffee brewed by Barnwell, who seemed to be enjoying his new duty as ship's cook. "Ah, there you are now, and how are all you lads farin' under the cruel imprisonment by the dread Rebel pirates?"

Several of the twelve-man crew smiled in spite of themselves, sitting in the comfortable passenger chairs and drinking reasonably good coffee. Mr. Abernathy was an exception. He scowled at Rory, as menacingly as he was able. "What do you intend to do with my schooner, you, you brigand?"

"Well, now, we brigands are notorious for our reluctance to divulge our evil plans, d' ye see? But as you asked so nicely, I'll let you in on our secret. We're going to convert her to a fire ship." Abernathy gasped, a most stricken look upon his face.

"You'd burn my beautiful schooner?"

"I'd rather not, if it's all the same to you," replied Rory. "All that depends on how familiar you are with Hell Gate."

"I'm, I'm not at all familiar with it. It's a very dangerous passage," Abernathy sputtered.

"Ah, now, such a pity. I was hoping I could spare the *Waterbury*, is it? She's truly a fine vessel. I guess we'll have to cast our nets for a pilot who knows Hell Gate."

The *Waterbury*, with Walsh, McCafferty, and their crew aboard, set out to lure ships entering New York harbor into the clutches of the CSS *Belle of Biloxi*. It proved to be much easier than anyone suspected. Walsh played his part with relish, and as the first new capture "happened" to cruise within short cannon shot of the hove-to *Belle of Biloxi*, a shot across the bow brought her up, all standing, and the cutter loaded with the boarding party sprinted out from the counter of *Belle*, and swiftly boarded the new prize.

The first prize was an 800-ton U.S. Mail screw packet, carrying freight and passengers, as well as mail. She was valued at $800,000. Rory was forced to shackle his prisoners as the numbers became dangerous. Rory raised his speaking trumpet and shouted across the fifty yards separating the raider and the *City of Troy* as the cutter brought the last load of passengers to *Belle of Biloxi*. "Mr. Beaupre, scuttle her, if you please. Can't risk smoke this close-in."

The next prize Walsh brought by was the key to Rory's New York raid, a 400-ton Maine brig with a cargo of gunpowder for the Brooklyn Navy Yard. Beaupre transferred the crew to *Belle* and left a four-man prize crew aboard under an able seaman. The brig *Joseph Lincoln* maintained station just off *Belle's* starboard quarter. The long July day was moving toward twilight when the lookout called, "Sail ho, pilot schooner off the starboard beam!"

"Mr. Beaupre, I believe we're attractin' a crowd." Rory laughed at the bizarre effect the collection of three vessels hove-to seemed to be having.

"Curiosity killed the cat, suh," Beaupre replied. "I declare, this new pilot is just dyin' to know if he can cut himself into the game and guide one of us in. He'll regret it."

"That he will, Mr. Beaupre. Send the hands to the guns, and have a boarding party ready." Rory lifted the speaking trumpet. "Mr. Walsh, make as if you're going to pilot the brig in. We'll ask for the new pilot for *Belle*."

The schooner came south to the little squadron on a beam reach, with the east wind blowing over her port side. She came to within fifty yards of the three innocent-appearing vessels, and wore to starboard, heading west toward New York with the wind aft. As she saw the *Waterbury* move alongside the *Joseph Lincoln*, she drew up abeam of the side-wheel packet.

"Ahoy, the *Peter Stuyvesant!* Do you require a pilot?"

"Aye, aye," Rory responded through his speaking trumpet. He watched as the pilot on board the schooner stepped over side into his dinghy and began to pull for the *Belle*. Rory leaned over the port gunwale and called softly to the cutter below. "Mr. Walsh, pull for that schooner as soon as you hear the gun." He then stepped to the entry port amidships, right next to the starboard nine-pounder gun crew. "As soon as you see that pilot's hat in the entry port, open the gun port and fire a shot across the schooner's bow," he said to the gun captain.

When Rory saw the pilot's beaver hat appear at deck level he called to the afterguard, "Hoist the colors!" Meanwhile, the gunport swung open, the crew ran the gun out, heaving on the tackles, and the gun captain pulled the lanyard, igniting the primer and firing the gun. The pilot looked about the deck, taking it all in, and calmly turned his gaze to Rory. "Captain Dunbrody of the CSS *Belle of Biloxi*, sir. I beg to inform you that you and your schooner are captives of the Confederate States Navy."

"Daniel Phelps, pilot and captain of the *Oliver Griffith*, at your service, sir." The man's quiet resolve was obvious and impressive. "You may not be quite the captor you purport, sir," he continued, gesturing toward his schooner, which had headed north and away from *Belle* after gybing, a dangerous maneuver for a vessel with a sail area as large as the *Oliver Griffith's*.

"A valid observation, sure and it is, captain," said Rory as he watched the schooner sail away. "Gun captain, fire as she bears."

The nine-pounder's next shot was astern of the schooner but the third snapped her mainmast twelve feet from the deck, and carried her foretopmast down with it. The cutter's crew, pulling like madmen, boarded the cutter a half-mile from the *Belle,* as the schooner's crew tried in vain to clear the wreckage.

"You've a well-trained gun crew there, Captain Dunbrody," said

Phelps, quietly, as he surveyed his dismasted pilot schooner.

"Kind of you to say, sir," said Rory. "Mr. Beaupre, run down to the schooner, if you please."

It was still twilight when Rory met with the two pilots in his cabin abaft the pilothouse. "Gentlemen, I have a proposal for you. I need to take my ship up the East River and through Hell Gate. If you will guide me through, I'll bond your schooners and you need not lose your livelihood." Abernathy was perspiring heavily. His handkerchief was soggy as he once again wiped his neck and forehead. He looked at Phelps, beseechingly, and then at Rory.

"As I told you before, captain, I don't know Hell Gate, but I will take you into New York's upper bay if you'll not burn my *Waterbury*."

"Very well, Mr. Abernathy. Captain Phelps?"

Phelps looked at Rory with a steady gaze. He inclined his head slightly, a faint smile on his face. "If you'll bond my schooner, I'll take you through Hell Gate. I know it well."

"You've saved two handsome vessels, gentlemen," said Rory. "I'll ask each of you to sign an $8,000 bond. I have them here." *Belle of Biloxi may enter the East River*, thought Rory, *but I've my doubts of making it out. Mr. Phelps strikes me as a hard-boiled man.*

As night fell, the little squadron consisting of the raider, the pilot schooners and the *Joseph Lincoln*, hove to in close proximity to one another. Rory made an "officer's call" and brought Beaupre, Walsh, McCafferty, and Duffy to his cabin for dinner. The boarding party aboard the *Oliver Griffith* had cleared away the wreckage and the schooner was capable of sailing, albeit slowly, with only her foremast able to carry sail. "Gentlemen, we've much to discuss," said Rory, after the meal had been cleared away by Seaman Wagner, the acting steward. "Help yourself to more wine." His smile faded to a more serious aspect as he looked at each officer in turn.

"We're overburdened with prisoners from four vessels, and we're exhausted from captures and crew transfers. I intend to bond the *Oliver Griffith,* and put all aboard in the morning." His officers nodded their approval, and their energy was visibly restored by the prospect of bidding farewell to 90 prisoners.

"We'll proceed with the brig and the *Waterbury* as her pilot consort, and the *Belle*, as the *Stuyvesant*, will tag along behind, just the regular packet from Halifax returnin' to New York. Mr. McCafferty, you'll be my second in command aboard *Belle* for that segment. I intend to reach The Narrows an hour before sunset."

"Sir," asked Beaupre, "do you still foresee an attack on the Brooklyn Yard?"

"I do, and a grand spectacle it will be, sure as I'm a Dunbrody! Mr. Beaupre, you'll command the brig, with a three-minute slow match fuse to her cargo of gunpowder. The *Waterbury*, with Mr. Walsh in command, will come alongside the brig as she's off the Whitehall Street Pier, lookin' as if she's takin' off her pilot. Put all but four of your crew aboard. We'll follow, and take all of your men that are aboard *Waterbury* aboard the *Belle*, after you've anchored *Waterbury* off Whitehall, honoring our bond. As we move upriver to the Brooklyn Yard, we'll select a target anchored there. I'm thinkin' a fat transport, with no battle crew aboard. Tow the jolly boat, lash the helm of the brig, light the fuse, run her at the target's anchor chain and bowsprit, and get into the jolly boat. We'll pick you up and head upriver to Hell Gate."

Walsh leaned forward and offered the wine to his fellow officers as he questioned Rory. "Will the pilots be aboard *Belle,* sir?"

"Faith, and you've figured out the plan already, Mr. Walsh! We'll have both aboard, Abernathy to bring us through the Narrows, and Phelps to take us out Hell Gate. A word here, lads. We must plan for treachery! I can't bring myself to trust the word of Phelps. He's a man too clever, by half!"

"I agree, sir," said Beaupre, "but what can we do?"

"First, we'll plumb the depths of his Hell Gate knowledge in the presence of Abernathy. Phelps won't dissemble much, as Abernathy might be clumsy enough to expose the lie! But we'll ensure the crew has a chance to escape if we're run aground, by accident or purpose. We'll have the quarter boats ready to drop from the davits, and the crew ready to board 'em. I've talked to our New York lads, Coogan and O'Flaherty. They tell me Harlem Village has a commuter ferry six times a day to Peck's Slip near Beekman. Anywhere south of 49th Street, our men are in the city and can find their way to the docks. Our lads have never had uniforms, and they're all Irish, Scots and English. If they can land from the quarter boats, as sailors, they can melt into any waterfront crowd and get a ship. I don't want any of them in Federal prison. And I'll distribute their share of the specie we have with us."

"Do the pilots know our plan, sir?" McCafferty asked.

"No, but I wouldn't be surprised if Phelps has tumbled to it. We'll keep a close eye on them both aboard *Belle*. Oh, and gentlemen, wear your side arms tomorrow, or keep them close at hand. Revolvers, and swords or cutlasses. As John Paul Jones would say, we're definitely going in harm's way. Now, gentlemen, one more glass. 'T is a long day tomorrow."

CHAPTER 17
NEW YORK CITY BURNING
JULY 1863

It was past noon aboard USS *Woonsocket* on Sunday, July 12, 1863. The ship was re-provisioning after months at sea in pursuit of the *Star of the South*, the *Florida,* the *Clarence* and *Tacony,* and then the *Flora.* The *Woonsocket,* and the rest of the Union naval establishment, was still unaware of the CSS *Belle of Biloxi,* as no prisoners of that raider had yet made landfall. *Woonsocket* was anchored in the East River, just down stream from the Brooklyn Navy Yard and on the Manhattan side. She was waiting her turn to have her hull cleaned after many months at sea, and to be re-provisioned.

Throughout the morning, officers and petty officers who had gone ashore to Manhattan Island on ship's business or on liberty had reported a condition of tension and unrest in the city. President Lincoln's newly-imposed military draft had begun the day before. Moneyed citizens could purchase replacements for $300 each, but the poorer New Yorkers, mostly Irish, who barely subsisted on low-paying jobs, were unable to evade the conscription. They saw the loss of their work, low-paid though it was, as a benefit to the equally-low–status Negroes who were not subject to the draft. The US Army had accepted black enlistees for more than a year, but they were not drafted.

Criminal gangs controlled life in much of the tenement areas of the city, in particular the Five Points, at the intersection of Baxter, Water, Worth and Pearl streets. Five Points was only a few blocks from South Street, off which *Woonsocket* was anchored. Returning crewmen reported gang leaders near the docks inciting crowds of Irish workers and toughs to violent action against the draft when it resumed on Monday morning.

Tobias had the afternoon watch, from noon until four p.m. His two master's mates, Kelso and Kekoa Kalama, reported to him as they returned from a ship chandlery with navigational supplies. The Navy Yard was across the river and too far away for supply runs. "I'll be glad when we're in the Yard," said Kelso as he reported. "We'll have more of a selection with navy supplies."

"Our berth should be ready Wednesday," said Tobias, "according to Mr. Fell." Tobias raised his eyebrows as he uttered the first lieutenant's name.

"Bumbye, I t'ink," said Kekoa with a smile, lapsing into to his Hawaiian pidgin. *By and by,* Tobias translated to himself.

"Sir, said Kelso, "we passed by several saloons on our way back to the shore boat and-"

Tobias interrupted, laughing. "Are you sure you passed them by, Mr. Kelso?"

"Oh, yes sir! We was scared to go in, in uniform." Kelso was in dead earnest, his eyes as big as saucers. "We could hear men inside saying they should attack the armory, seize weapons, burn the draft office and shut down the city."

"You should talk to O'Leary, the cox'n, sir," Kelso continued. "He was ashore on liberty in street clothes, and he said he was in a saloon where they talked of hanging all the blacks, begging your pardon, sir."

"And O'Leary said the leaders were from da New York gangs," Kekoa chimed in. "Dey wen tellin' everyone to meet at da Central Park, and bring pitchforks an' clubs an' crowbars."

"I'm sure Captain Oakley will be interested in what you've learned, you two. Thank you for your report. Now, get those supplies to the chart locker, if you please." As they left, Tobias allowed himself a look of concern. *I'd best report to the captain. Every military unit in the city could be involved if unrest gets out of hand,* he thought. He looked toward

South Street and the city rising beyond. *Woonsocket* was anchored just off the Manhattan shore near Peck's Slip, the ferry terminal for the boats from Harlem Village. The East River was alive with schooners, steamers and ferries of all descriptions. South Street was lined with ships, their bows in to the street, and their bowsprits extending halfway to the red brick buildings across the road as horse-drawn carts and wagons passed beneath them.

At the end of his watch, Tobias was relieved by the fourth lieutenant. Tobias paused at the companionway for a further look. Beyond the Fulton Ferry slip, he could see the tall spire of Trinity Church. He went below to the captain's cabin, and when admitted, told Oakley what he had learned.

"I'm particularly concerned, sir, with the danger to our black sailors," said Tobias when he had recounted the reports he'd gathered. "From all accounts, anyone in uniform is a potential target, and any black, in uniform or no."

"It's a dilemma, that's for certain, Mr. St. John," said Oakley. "We've worked hard to show both our black and white sailors that they're sailors first, with no regard to color. Now, for safety sake, I'm going to restrict any shore forces to whites only. Not a very consistent position."

"Sir, I'm sure the men will understand."

"I hope so, sailing master."

****

At 6:30 that evening, two hours before sunset, the *Belle of Biloxi* approached the Narrows, the entrance to the Upper Bay of New York. Rockaway Point was in sight off the starboard side, and Sandy Hook astern and far away to port. They followed the brig *Joseph Lincoln* and the pilot schooner *Waterbury*, innocent craft among dozens approaching New York that evening. Phelps and Abernathy, the two captured pilots, stood on the bridge of *Belle* with Rory as they entered the Narrows.

"Your schooner should reach New York sometime tomorrow, Captain Phelps, and yours will be at anchor this evening, Captain Abernathy," offered Rory to the two pilots. Abernathy scowled, but

Phelps responded with a faint smile.

"That depends on how quickly my crew can re-reeve all the halyards and sheets you cut before we left, captain," Phelps said.

"At least you'll have your vessels, and they'll have done a great service to the Union, bringin' the crews and passengers of our prizes in safely, and all. You might even gain some profitable notoriety for future clients, wouldn't y' think, now?" Rory countered with his own grin.

"You're an honorable man, captain," said Phelps. "Be careful, that can be a danger in this world."

"Good advice, t' be sure, Captain Phelps."

"Well, now, Captain Abernathy, tell me what we face at the Narrows."

Grumpily, Abernathy responded. "We've missed the worst of the Sandy Hook approach, as the weather has been calm. This approach is one of the stormiest in the world, most of the year. And these three vessels are of shallow draft, and need not worry about the bar. But the channel to the East River through the Upper Bay is tortuous, and often shallow." He sighed, with the thought.

"I'm sure your talents and experience will prove equal to the challenge, the both of you," said Rory, "and then you'll be shut of me, and your troubles will be over!" He leaned over to the voice pipe to the engine room. "Slow to ahead one third, Mr. Duffy. The airs are lightening, and our brig is slowin' down a bit."

"Ahead one third," came the response up the voice pipe. Rory smiled at the delight and enthusiasm in Duffy's voice. *Sure, now, our promoted fireman's having a grand time as a chief engineer.*

The trio of vessels moved slowly and carefully up the Bay, as the sun sank lower in the western sky over Staten Island and the Jersey shore. "Mr. McCafferty, walk with me to the bridge wing, please," said Rory. When they had closed the bridge wing door, Rory said, "have the twelve-foot skiff hoisted out and towed astern, Mr. McCafferty. I've a premonition we might be needin' 'er before the night is through."

Up the Bay they went, past Gowanus Bay, the fortifications on Governor's Island coming into view. And with that view, Rory saw the incredible confusion of the craft in the East River, among the busiest waters in the world. Ferry boats, steamers, schooners, pulling boats, lighters, tugs, packets, all on differing courses at disparate rates of speed, horns and whistles signaling to one another. Walsh in the *Waterbury* led the other two ships through the madness of the river with apparent calm. Ships gave way to the pilot schooner as they approached the southern end of Manhattan and the Whitehall pier where many a pilot schooner moored. As planned, the schooner dropped anchor, Walsh and the schooner crew tumbled into a boat from *Belle,* which then swung alongside the brig, by now barely under way, flying just fore topsail and spanker. All but four men left the brig and the boat with the crews from *Waterbury* and *Joseph Lincoln* returned to *Belle.*

"Excellent work, Mr. Walsh," Rory said to his acting master as he came aboard from the schooner. "The action may become a bit more 'free form' from here on out."

"Sure, I expect it will, sir. I'm dying to know which target Mr. Beaupre picks."

Leaving Whitehall, the *Joseph Lincoln* led the packet toward the Brooklyn shore and those naval vessels anchored just off the Navy Yard. Rory diminished his speed until a quarter of a mile separated the two ships. A hoist of signals rose jerkily to the main yard of the brig. Rory snatched his telescope from its mount on the binnacle column. "700-ton cargo ship flying the red swallowtail signal for ammunition transfer. Lighters alongside. Our target." Rory read the signal out loud as McCafferty stood at his side. "Stand by to take the boat's crew aboard from the brig, Mr. McCafferty," he said. "I just hope they can get far enough away from her to survive. May God hold Mr. Beaupre in His hand, the Saints attend. Hoist the colors, Mr. Walsh."

****

Tobias, off watch, stood on the *Woonsocket's* foredeck, looking toward Brooklyn to starboard. The current was from Long Island Sound, through Hell Gate. Steam was down, as the screw sloop had several days before a berth at the Navy Yard would be available. Tobias glanced at a brig easing upstream and bearing for the Brooklyn shore. He noticed she was followed at a distance by a sidewheel packet steamer. He looked again at the steamer, and read the name "Peter Stuyvesant" on the paddle-boxes. *That's odd*, he thought. *That's the New York-Charleston packet that runs now from Halifax. She always docks at the Canal Street pier on the North River.* He continued to watch the packet, musing on the curious New York terminology that called the Hudson the "North River" to distinguish it from the East River. Suddenly, he saw the United States national ensign lowered from the mainmast of the packet, and a white flag with a blue saltier hoisted in its place. The hair on his neck stood, as he saw the brig ahead of the packet hoist the same flag and turn toward the ammunition ship transferring cargo just downstream from the Navy Yard. The brig was towing a ship's boat. Tobias saw three men lower themselves into the boat and cast off from the brig. "Officer of the watch! Call the captain! The Navy Yard's under attack!"

****

Belle of Biloxi bore down on the jolly boat from the *Joseph Lincoln*. Only three men were in the boat as it hooked on to the boarding ladder near the starboard paddle box. As the boat came alongside, Rory leaned over the rail with his speaking trumpet. "Where's Mr. Beaupre?"

The coxswain responded, his reply faint in the wind. "He stayed aboard, sir, to make sure we fouled the bowsprit and anchor chain. He had a grapnel, sir. He ordered us off!"

Damn, thought Rory. *The idjit! The brave, foolhardy idjit. God rest his soul!* A deafening roar and a walloping impact battered the hull of the *Belle of Biloxi*. A towering pillar of smoke rose from the spot where the two ships had been just a moment before, 400 yards away. Debris and bodies were hurled into the air amidst the dark cloud of exploded gunpowder.

"Jasus, Mary and Joseph," swore McCafferty as he watched the column of black soar skyward. Rory turned to the two speechless harbor pilots standing with him on the bridge of the *Belle* as the sun sank behind the forest of masts and spars on the East River Manhattan shore.

"Well, gentlemen, you've carried out half your bargain. You've gotten us this far. I'll release you as soon as we clear Hell Gate."

"You, you damned heartless pirate," sputtered Abernathy. Have you no honor, sir?"

"Well, captain, wouldn't I be assertin' that I've all the honor in the world? I've carried the battle to the heart of my enemy's navy, losing a brave officer in the act, and upheld my oath and the expectations of my service. Will you be as honorable and carry out your agreement?"

"You make a strong argument, captain," Phelps said, entering the exchange. "You've about four miles to Blackwell's Island. I'd stay in the middle of the river." Blackwell's Island, later to be named Roosevelt Island, divided the East River into two channels just below Hell Gate. Only an eighth of a mile wide, it housed the city's charitable and correctional facilities, workhouse, alms-house, penitentiary, lunatic asylum and the like.

"Mr. Walsh, stay in mid stream, if you please. Mr. McCafferty, have the howitzer crew stand by aft, in case we have a stern chase. They may not have tumbled to our involvement at the Navy Yard, in the tumult and the fading light and all. So, we won't fire at them until they do at us."

"Aye, aye, sir," McCafferty replied. "Call away the after howitzer crew," he shouted to the men on deck as they secured the *Lincoln's* jolly boat, towing it and the twelve-foot skiff in tandem.

****

DeWitt Oakley rushed on deck in response to the news the Navy Yard was under attack. As he reached the quarterdeck, still buttoning his uniform jacket, the shock wave from the explosion of the *Lincoln* and the ammunition ship knocked him, off-balance, into the arms of the fourth lieutenant. "Sir, that packet has just hoisted the Rebel flag."

"Very good, Lieutenant Hovey, beat to quarters," said Oakley, recovering his balance. "Mr. St. John, veer to the twenty fathom shackle, buoy the cable, and slip. All hands make sail, Mr. Hovey. Stand by to take us upstream, Mr. St. John." He strode to the engine room voice pipe. "I need steam, chief, and in a hurry! How soon can I get it?"

"Twenty minutes, sir," came the faint reply.

"Half that, chief. Handsomely, now!" The *Woonsocket* soon had courses and topsails set and drawing. The sloop of war moved slowly upstream. Tobias could see the thrashing of the packet's paddle wheels, a mile ahead of her only pursuer. He looked into the Navy Yard, now abeam. Several gunboats were attempting to get under way, but the Yard had been taken by surprise, and no ship had steam up. Boats were now approaching the mid-stream area of debris, all that was left of the brig and the ammunition ship.

"Signal midshipman," called Oakley. "Hoist 'am pursuing packet flying Rebel battle flag, one mile upstream.' That should at least let them know who they should overtake once they're under way."

"Captain, should we try a shot from the forward pivot?" Fell, the first lieutenant, was now on deck, his glass trained on the *Belle of Biloxi*.

"Go forward with your glass, Mr. Fell. If you see the traffic clear out sufficiently that we don't risk hitting a non-combatant ship, take a shot." The first lieutenant walked forward as the twilight descended over the East River.

Tobias approached Oakley. "Sir, we're making about seven knots in this traffic. Until we get steam up, we'll fall behind the rebel, sir. She makes eleven knots, same as we under steam."

"Even so, Mr. St. John, we've got to track her as best we can. We're the only ship under way. She must be making for Hell Gate. She'll have her work cut out for her going through in the dark. Just keep us in the channel and we'll do the best we can. You've got to give credit to the Reb commander, though. What a daring stroke!"

"Aye, sir, you're right. There are few in any navy who could bring this off." A chilling thought struck Tobias. *Damn! We could be chasing Rory! It's just the wild ride he'd undertake!*

****

Rory looked aft from the bridge as the light continued to fade. The dying rays of the sun were just bright enough to illuminate the topsails of the screw sloop of war astern of *Belle*. Blackwell's Island was just ahead in the gloom.

"You'll want to leave the island to port, captain." Rory heard Phelps' voice at his elbow. "After we pass the island, in a mile, we'll leave Astoria close to starboard and bear northeast through Hell Gate. It won't be easy, as it will be dark."

"Do your best, Captain Phelps," Rory replied.

"You're both madmen," exclaimed Abernathy. "You'll not make it through Hell Gate in the dark."

"Mr. McCafferty, would you escort Captain Abernathy below, if you please." Rory smiled at Finn McCafferty in the glow of the binnacle light. "The captain's nerves seem to be a wee bit frazzled."

"Aye, aye, sir." said McCafferty with a conspiratorial wink. "Come along with y' now, captain. "We'll find a nice toddy for ye, in ship's stores. It's always wise to capture a smart passenger ship, sure, and we're feeling clever as can be!" Abernathy, his shoulders drooping, allowed himself to be led below. Finn McCafferty, in contrast, seemed to Rory to draw energy from the danger of the chase. *It must be his wild Celtic warrior heritage, wellin' up, and all,* thought Rory.

"Mr. Walsh, a word with you on the bridge wing, if you please." Rory and Walsh stepped through the bridge wing door, out of hearing of the pilot, Phelps. "Thomas, have the men standing by the quarter boat davits. Lower the boats to just above the waterline. Then go to my cabin and get the specie out of my chart table drawer. Collect McCafferty and the two of you give ten dollars to each man. If we go aground, I want each boat lowered and the men rowing toward the Harlem River. Put Coogan in one boat and O'Flaherty in the other. Tell them to row for Harlem Village, as we planned, and take the steamer to New York. Every man to disappear as best he can. If they can make it to Richmond, Secretary Mallory has the prize share records."

"Aye, aye, sir. The men know you're watching out for them, sir. They're grateful. They wanted you to know."

"Oosh, Thomas. We'll get out of this, yet! And think what we've done already! Sure, and we're the thorn in Gideon Welles' side, and us bein' still young, and all." Rory clapped Walsh on the shoulder. "When you've prepared the men, go below and lay five minutes of slow match to the powder magazine. If we don't make it through, I don't want the *Belle* with the stars and stripes above the Confederate flag as a recapture."

Rory returned to the bridge. As Walsh went aft to ready the men to abandon, if necessary, Rory looked forward. Beyond the north end of Blackwell's Island, he could see the loom of Ward's Island, which they must leave to port as they began to enter the Hell Gate.

McCafferty returned to the bridge. "Sir, the screw sloop astern of us just fired a shell. I could see the flash, but not the splash."

"Carry on, Mr. McCafferty. Keep an eye on her, if you please, but don't return fire. I don't want her sighting off the flash of the howitzer as it gets dark." The volume of boat traffic had diminished considerably now that night had fallen. *I never had time to hoist my harp ensign,* Rory thought. *Sure, and I'm hopin' that's not a bad omen!*

"There are three rocks in mid stream as we go through Hell Gate, captain," said Phelps. "I'll take us through the south or right-hand channel."

"I'll leave it to you, captain," said Rory. "We have our agreement, after all." *Does he believe I'll shoot him if we run aground?* Rory wondered. *He shows no nervousness, at all, at all. I can't tell if he's just a steady hand, or if he is resigned to whatever fate may bring.*

"You may wish to advise the crew we're about to encounter quite a bit of turbulence, captain," said Phelps. "Once we clear Blackwell's Island, the whirlpools and chop will extend across the channel, clear to the Manhattan shore."

"Thank you for the warning, Captain Phelps," said Rory, wondering again at the man's calm demeanor.

"Ease her two points to starboard, helmsman," said Phelps.

"Two points to starboard, aye, aye," the man at the wheel repeated.

"Midships."

"Midships, aye, aye."

The loom of Ward's Island was close to port now, and Rory strained to see through the darkness as they entered the turbulent and narrow Hell Gate. "Frying Pan," "Pot Rock," the names of the obstructions leaped out at him through the darkness as he struggled to remember the chart he'd pored over yesterday. He imagined the promontory of Hallett's Point, protruding 300 feet into the stream. He listened to the thrum of the paddle wheels and the throb of the inclined piston engine, and unconsciously held his breath.

****

"Eleven knots, at last, sir," said Tobias on the quarterdeck as the engine room finally brought the boilers to full steam. "But I've lost sight of the packet in the gloom, sir."

"Very well, Mr. St. John. Go forward and call back course corrections from the foredeck."

"Aye, aye, sir. I believe I'll climb to the foretop. I'll have a more unimpeded view from there." *Anything to stay clear of that bastard Fell,* he thought. "Sir, I suggest we not try the Hell Gate without a pilot at night."

"I agree, Mr. St. John. A screw sloop through the Hell Gate would be foolhardy. And who knows, we could anchor off Ward's Island and find the packet's done the same thing, come morning."

Oakley certainly tries to put the best face on a hard choice, thought Tobias as he climbed the shrouds and ratlines to the foretop. Tobias saw the slender form of Lieutenant Fell, shoulders hunched as he tried to glimpse the target in the darkness. Tobias said nothing, but quietly climbed to the top.

I know he's still waiting his chance to do me in, he thought. *And the longer we wait to accuse him of assaulting me in Terre-de-Haut, the better chance he has of dodging the bullet.*

Tobias took his night glass from his pocket and steadied himself by wrapping one arm around a fore topgallantmast shroud. *Woonsocket* was just abeam of Blackwell's Island. Tobias could see the lights of a steam ferry coming downriver from Harlem Village, but no vessel lights off the starboard bow in the Hell Gate. *Black as the orlop at midnight,* he thought. *God help anyone going through that pass without a pilot.*

****

Rory had just stepped to the bridge wing to peer ahead in the darkness when the throb of the engines was drowned out by a horrendous crash. Rory was thrown to the deck by the jolt as *Belle of Biloxi* went hard aground on a rock to her starboard side. Rory scrambled to his feet and rushed back into the pilothouse. "All engines stop! Have the hands stand by the boats!" As Walsh moved to carry out the orders, Rory drew his Navy Six from his belt and confronted Phelps. He removed a pair of shackles from a pilothouse drawer as Phelps stood stoically by.

"I ran us aground deliberately, captain," said the pilot, "despite our agreement. I'm surprised I'm still alive." Phelps looked at Rory quizzically.

"I'll not be killin' a man for a patriotic act, captain, and our agreement was made under duress. And what would be the point, I'm asking? Another dead sailor? We've too many already! Your schooner's bond, 'though, I'm remindin' you, it's still in effect."

Phelps threw back his head and laughed. "You're an amazing man, captain. Most would have shot me dead. I warned you about your honor being a dangerous thing."

"Sure, I'm about to part company with you and Abernathy, and won't I be safer for it?" McCafferty stepped into the pilothouse. "Mr. McCafferty, I'll be givin' you these shackle keys and the custody of Captain Phelps. Take him and Abernathy to the port paddle wheel box entry port. I'll have the skiff led forward to the port. Unshackle them and cast them off." Turning, to Phelps, he said, "You'll have ten minutes before we fire the *Belle,* pilot. I suggest you row like Hell, and in a direction other then the one we'll take. I may shoot you yet, given another opportunity."

As McCafferty led Phelps below, Walsh returned. "Sir, the men are standing by the boats, and the slow match is laid and ready."

"Very good, Mr. Walsh. Tell Coogan and O'Flaherty they'll have ten minutes before we fire the barky and shed some light on the waters. The Feds will be after us then, so tell them be sure to be out of sight quickly. You, Duffy, McCafferty and I will take the *Joseph Lincoln's* jolly boat. We might just be able to sneak back down river!"

Rory's well-planned exodus worked to perfection. First, the two pilots disappeared downstream, rowing the skiff and arguing about the direction to take. The two quarter boats bore the crew off up the Harlem River to attempt their disappearance and escape. Walsh lit the slow match, and the four officers boarded the jolly boat, rowing hard and downstream away from the wreck, hoping to be beyond the light that the impending explosion and fire would provide. As they rowed, Rory laughed. "Sure, it was a wild ride, lads, and prizes galore! And I never promised more. With luck, we'll creep past the pursuit and see what the morning brings."

****

Woonsocket had just cleared the north end of Blackwell's Island. Oakley had reduced speed to six knots, as the ship closed on the approaches to Hell Gate. A southbound ferry disappeared behind Blackwell's Island, and all was dark beyond. Tobias was still in the foretop, and Fell on the foredeck. A blinding flash lit the night sky ahead to starboard accompanied by a thunderous boom. Tobias cleared his vision by blinking rapidly and focusing on the site of the explosion. "Deck, there," he called aft to the quarterdeck, "there's a ship afire! It looks like the packet."

"Mr. Fell," called Oakley to his first lieutenant, "Launch the cutter and the gig with boat howitzers. I want to secure any crew leaving that wreck!"

"Aye, aye, sir. Mr. Hovey, take the cutter. Mr. St. John, take the gig. We want prisoners!" Fell's voice broke with excitement.

Minutes later, Tobias was in the sternsheets of the gig, Kekoa at the tiller and a six man crew straining at the oars. It was hard going through the choppy waters. Three more men were in the bow with the boat's four-pounder howitzer loaded with grapeshot and ready to fire. The flames from the wreck of the *Belle of Biloxi* backlit the waters of the East River just below Ward's Island and the Hell Gate. "Sir," cried the gunner in the bow, "Boat to port. Looks like two men aboard, sir."

"Give them a hail, Mr. Kalama."

"Boat, there, avast rowing, or we'll put a shot into you!"

The two oarsmen layed on their oars, and one called, "we're New York pilots, escaped from the Rebels!"

"We're coming alongside," called Tobias. Moments later, Phelps was detailing the circumstances of the wreck.

"I ran her aground to stop her escape," he explained. "I thought their captain would shoot me, but he put us in this skiff and let us go. His crew left when we did, in two boats, and then a few minutes later, she exploded."

"Do you know the commander's name?" Tobias asked, while scanning the water between the gig and the wreck a mile distant.

"Dunbrody, an Irishman. So were his other officers. He called me a patriot, strangely enough. In his place, I'd probably have used my pistol."

"Thank you, pilot," said Tobias. "Sit on a thwart amidships, if you please, gentlemen, and we'll search for your recent captors." *To meet like this, after such a long time,* Tobias reflected. *May Rory be safe! Apparently, he hasn't lost his strong sense of the honorable gesture!* They let the skiff drift, and continued their search. Lieutenant Hovey in the cutter was to the east shore of the river, while Tobias and the gig stayed mid-stream and toward the west shore. "In the bow, there, keep your eyes peeled," he called softly.

A hoarse whisper came from the gunner in the bow, "Sir, I see the loom of a boat three points to port." The burning packet threw just enough light to make a four-oared jolly boat visible against the reflective surface of the turbulent river. "Steer for the boat, Mr. Kalama," Tobias ordered. When they were within 200 yards, he hailed.

"Avast rowing and keep your hands on the oars. Way enough, there! We have a four pounder trained on you, loaded with grape."

The oarsmen stopped under the threat of grapeshot, and an Irish brogue instantly recognizable to Tobias floated back over the river. "Sure, and aren't we the innocent fishermen, just out for a quiet troll, now?" *Damn, it is Rory,* Tobias exclaimed to himself. *Well, at least he's safe, so far.* The *Woonsocket's* gig pulled up off the quarter of the jolly boat. Four gray-uniformed officers sat quietly and alertly, hands on their oars. "Hand over your arms, if you please," ordered Tobias. The hulls of the boats pounded together as they bounced and rolled. When the Confederates had given up their pistols and swords, the gig backed water. "Row ahead of us please, down river," Tobias commanded. He reached into a compartment beneath the sternsheets and brought out a flare and a flint and steel. He handed them to Kekoa, who lit the fuse to the flare. The white flare signaled Hovey in the cutter that Tobias was returning to *Woonsocket* with prisoners. Hovey would continue to search until recalled by Oakley.

"Hook to the boarding ladder below the entry port, if you please," Tobias called to the Confederates' boat as they neared the *Woonsocket*.

****

As the black hulk of the *Woonsocket* loomed ahead of them, Rory, rowing the bow oar, called "way enough." As they glided to a stop in the more protected waters off Blackwell's Island, he thought, *I can't suppress my joy at finding Tobias alive, but what a bizarre set of circumstances in which to reunite with a friend!* Looking over his shoulder, he could see the midships entry port of the screw sloop thirty yards ahead. "Let the river carry us down, lads. Be alert, now, for escape opportunities. If we get ashore in New York City, remember it's a hotbed of Copperhead anti-war sentiment. With any luck, we'll find a friend or two."

Thomas Walsh smiled to himself. *Dunbrody is the most relentlessly optimistic man I've ever encountered,* he thought.

When they had climbed the boarding ladder to the main deck, they were greeted by a detail of armed sailors and a beefy, bushy eye-browed warrant officer who declared, "I'm Master-at-Arms Krotemann, and I'm your worst nightmare!"

What a keolaun this one is, thought Rory as they were formed up, two by two and marched aft.

"The captain wants to see you," announced the master-at-arms pompously. "Look sharp, you miserable pirates!" Oakley stood as the four prisoners were halted in front of him.

"You've caused quite a commotion in the harbor, gentlemen. Welcome to USS *Woonsocket*. I'm Captain Oakley. Who is senior, please?"

Rory came to attention and saluted. "Rory Cormac Dunbrody, lieutenant commanding the Confederate States Ship *Belle of Biloxi,* sir. May I introduce Acting Master Walsh, Acting Bo'sun McCafferty and Acting Chief Engineer Duffy?"

"Shades of Galway City, captain," Oakley exclaimed with a smile. "Is the South so short of sailors you've recruited the whole of Connacht and Munster, too?"

"We're a seafaring race, to be sure, sir."

"Where are the rest of your men, captain?" asked Oakley.

"I've not seen them since we abandoned, sir, I've no idea where they are." Rory was studiously formal, with only a shadow of the brogue he usually used.

"We'll keep looking, then," said Oakley. "If you'll give me your parole, I'll not shackle you while you're aboard."

"You have our word that we'll not attempt escape from *Woonsocket,* sir." *Might as well get some rest in comfort. Going ashore is another story,* thought Rory.

"Take them to the wardroom and post two guards, Mr. Krotemann. They can sleep on pallets. Oh, wait," said Oakley, glancing at the entry port. "I want you gentlemen to meet the officer who apprehended you, Mr. St. John." Tobias came aft when he heard his name.

"Good evening, sailing master," said Rory, striving to keep any trace of recognition out of his voice.

"Good evening, captain," Tobias replied, in the same neutral tone.

"Mr. Krotemann, you may take these men below, now," said Oakley. "Mr. Fell, the packet exploded an hour ago. If Mr. Hovey hasn't encountered the rest of the Rebels by now, I doubt he'll find them at all. Wait fifteen minutes, then fire the signal recalling him, if you please. Mr. St. John, when the cutter crew is back aboard, take us down stream to our anchor buoy. Then we can all get some rest."

As Rory and the others were escorted below, a light dawned. *That's Fell, the bigoted bastard Tobias wrote me about last year. He's from the*

Preble. Bad luck for Tobias, getting him as first luff a second time!

While Fell awaited Hovey and the cutter crew on deck, Tobias sought out Captain Oakley. "Sit, Mr. St. John," said Oakley as Tobias entered the captain's cabin and the Marine sentry shut the door. "You did a fine job in cornering our Rebels, and in rescuing our pilots, too."

"Sir, I feel obliged to tell you that Lieutenant Dunbrody and I were shipmates aboard *Active*. We, we are very good friends, sir. I thought you should be aware of that."

Oakley smiled at his sailing master. "Every officer aboard has a friend or relative on the other side, Mr. St. John. The friendships and relations may endure or may not, but we all do our duty, regardless. You're a fine officer. I know you'll do yours. That you told me of your friend proves my point. Go get some rest."

Dawn Monday found *Woonsocket* secure at her Peck Slip anchorage. Her sailors could see crowds of men carrying iron fence posts with pointed tips, crowbars, sledgehammers and axes, with signs which read "No Draft." They were thronging the streets leading from the Five Points district. The Confederate prisoners were allowed a walk for exercise on the foredeck. Rory looked at the crowd ashore. *Sure, some of them look like they're carryin' pikes, just like the last risin' in Ireland*, he thought.

Oakley signaled the Navy Yard of his captures and was ordered to report immediately to the Yard commandant. "Mr. Fell," said Oakley when he had read the signal, "You'll be in command while I report to the Brooklyn Yard. Be thinking about a prisoners' detail to transport these men. I'm sure we'll be shipping them to Boston or Illinois. Oh, and no Negro sailors ashore today, under any circumstances." He paused, deep in thought. "The situation ashore may be more serious than we realize. Rig the boarding nettings, just in case the anti-draft crowds get ambitious."

"Aye, aye, sir," replied Fell, a calculating look on his face, his ferret-like gaze shifting toward the shoreline and then back aboard. Oakley went below, and returned to the deck in his best uniform jacket. "Call away the captain's gig," ordered Fell. "Sideboys to the gangway." Six sailors in uniform jumpers and a boatswain's mate with his silver boatswain's pipe lined the approach to the entry port as Oakley descended the ladder to his waiting gig, the pipe squealing until the moment when the captain's hat disappeared below deck level. Fell watched as the gig pulled toward the Navy Yard in the distance across the river. "Pass the word for Mr. Krotemann to report to my cabin," said Fell to the midshipman of the watch.

Tobias heard that order passed. *Those two together with Fell in command,* he thought. *There's trouble on its way, or I'm a lubber!*

CHAPTER 18
ATTEMPTED MURDER ON SOUTH STREET
JULY 1863

Fell and Krotemann met in the captain's cabin, a secure place for a guarded conversation. "We may have an opportunity, here, Mr. Krotemann, to avenge that black bastard's attempt on your life in Terre-de-Haut." Fell conveniently ignored the fact that he had sent Krotemann ashore in Bourg to bodily injure Tobias. "Keep a close eye on the shore activity in South Street. All the signs point to a riot over the draft by the Irish. If insurrection surfaces, I can argue that the ship was in danger and I needed to move the prisoners to a safer venue."

"Aye, aye, sir, I'll go on deck and call you the minute I see trouble!"

At seven a.m., Krotemann noticed a large number of Negro stevedores on the docks at South Street. This was in contrast to previous days when the stevedores had been mostly white. It later developed that the white stevedores, in the main Irish, had boycotted the docks Monday morning in protest of the draft, and the dock bosses had supplanted them with black stevedores on the spot. Word passed to the strikers, and at just after seven, Krotemann saw crowds of white stevedores marching down to south street from the Five Points area armed with crowbars and cargo hooks, with others from the tenements. They burst onto the docks and attacked the black stevedores without warning. The Negroes fled immediately but numbers were beaten senseless, and Krotemann saw two hanged. "String 'em up!" cried one stevedore as he deftly tossed a line with a noose in the end between the forestay and the jib stay on the bowsprit of a ship extending over South Street.

The crowd began to set fires among the three and five story buildings facing the docks. They enlisted or forced the workers in those buildings to join the mob. Carrying signs reading "No Draft," many in the mob left the docks and marched uptown, gathering strength as it headed for Central Park. Others continued to pillage, burn and search for Negroes.

Krotemann went below to Fell's cabin. "Sir, the mob ashore is burning and hanging and beating the blacks."

"Ah, very good, Mr. Krotemann." Fell leaned back in his chair, folding his hands beneath his chin, a satisfied look on his face. "This is our moment to return this officer corps to its pure state. Send St. John to me now!"

Tobias reported to Fell, his expression guarded. He'd seen the chaos ashore and was seething with frustration at an inability to quell the violence. *I hope the captain makes it back soon,* he thought. *He'll take action ashore!*

"Mr. St. John, you're to take command of a prisoner detail to escort the four Rebel prisoners to Warren Prison in Boston. There's anarchy ashore and I fear for their safety here in New York. The captain was of the same mind when he ordered me to rig the boarding nettings. The safest thing we can do for our prisoners is to remove them to a safe venue."

"Sir, the captain said no blacks ashore today."

"Don't presume to lecture me on my duty, sailing master! He said no black sailors! He said nothing about officers. Pick your detail, secure shackles from the master-at-arms, and carry out your orders. You're to catch the Jersey City Ferry at Pier 17 on Cortland Street, then the train to Boston."

Twenty minutes later, Tobias stood outside the wardroom, his detail behind him. He'd picked the best men aboard, men he knew he could trust, Boatswain's Mate Halvorson, Coxswain O'Leary, and Master's Mate Kelso. Kekoa had begged to be included. "No," Tobias had responded, "the captain meant no men of color ashore when he gave his order. We'll be in enough trouble with me in the detail. I'm sorry, Mr. Kalama, but I'm firm in my resolve. You may not go."

Tobias called the prisoners to attention and explained his orders. "Sure and we've heard and seen what's goin' on ashore, sailing master," Rory responded. "Your commander must be daft to risk us and you in that ruction."

"The orders are my first lieutenant's, captain," Tobias replied. "My commander is at the Navy Yard, reporting to the commandant. I know you've given your parole while aboard. I assume you wish to withdraw it ashore. I'll have to shackle you, as I'm sure you expect."

"Do as you must, sailing master," said Rory. "I don't envy you your task. We withdraw our parole."

"I'll shackle you as we reach the dock, then," said Tobias. His men were armed with Navy Six revolvers and cutlasses, and also Enfield rifles and bayonets Tobias had borrowed from the *Woonsocket's* Marine detachment. As the cutter's crew rowed them to the dock at Peck's Slip, Tobias outlined his plan. "We'll shackle you on the dock, in pairs, right to left hand. We'll turn south on South Street, heading past Beekman and Fulton before we turn to cross the island to the ferry. Halvorson will take the lead. The other three of us will follow you. We'll move quickly."

They ascended the ladder from the slip with Halvorson in the lead, his bayoneted rifle at port arms. Rory followed, his right hand shackled to Walsh's left. Duffy and McCafferty followed them, with Tobias, O'Leary and Kelso bringing up the rear. At the top of the stairway, Halvorson turned to his left and led them down South Street toward Beekman Street. Smoke poured from a three-story brick building in the middle of the block between the Slip and Beekman. Next to it, a crowd of drunken rioters was passing in and out of a ship's chandlery, carrying items out through the battered doorway and through the broken-out windows.

The corpses of two Negro stevedores lay, bloody and beaten, on the sidewalk. The prisoner detail made it past the looters, who were intent on collecting booty and hardly spared them a glance. Tobias glanced to his left and saw crewmen of the ships lining South Street staring, openmouthed, over the forecastle rails as they watched the seething mass of pushing, swearing, stumbling looters pile more in the middle of the street than they could possibly carry away. "Keep moving, if you please, gentlemen," he called as they approached the corner of Beekman and South streets. *This is madness*, Tobias thought.

With a roaring, turbulent, tumbling, mumbling sound, a vast mob of men and women, with staves, metal pipes, and lighted torches in their hands surged out of Beekman Street onto the broad pavement of South Street. A tall, bearded man in a ratty fur jacket and top hat was at their head, waving them on with a *shillelagh* and cursing as he went. "No draft! No saving the damn niggers!" he shouted as the crowd continued to spill into South Street, completely blocking the path Tobias had hoped to take.

"Halvorson, hard a starboard! Into this warehouse!" Tobias hoped the five-story brick building to their right had a back door, as the mob's leader had caught sight of them.

"Look there!" cried the cavorting leader, "a nigger and a bunch of uniforms! After them!" The detail and its prisoners rushed into the warehouse, pushing the ten-foot door closed. The ground floor was crammed with linen and fabric bales, and garments and yarns of every kind.

"Halvorson, you others, man the windows. Fire a shot over their heads." Turning to his prisoners, Tobias reached for the shackle keys. "We're all in this together, now, gentlemen. I'm unshackling you. Detail! Give your pistols to the prisoners. We need a heavier broadside!"

"Do as the detail commander says, gentlemen," said Rory to his officers. "Those bogtrotters out there won't stop to sort us out."

"Break out the windows, men," ordered Tobias. Amid the shattering glass, the small band of sea officers, in blue and gray, fired a volley of shots above the heads of the rioters that halted their advance on the warehouse, at least for the moment.

The gang leader turned to his followers and delivered a fevered harangue, urging his torch carriers to hurl their firebrands through the now-paneless windows of the warehouse. "Sailing master," said Rory, "listen to that *spalpeen*. If we shoot his torch carriers, they'll never rest until we're dead. We've got to convince them to let us go."

Rory and Tobias were now standing together in back of the officers and men of their commands, who were ready to fire again through the windows. "Hold your fire, men," called Tobias over the tumult of the mob outside. Quietly, he said, "I have a thought, Rory. Perhaps we can save the lives of all our men. It means you must kill me. Or, appear to, at least." He burst into a somewhat maniacal grin.

"What blather are y' talkin', now?"

"They're after every black man they can find. They're mostly Irish. And so are our men. Get out there and convince the leader that you, his countryman, hates Negroes as much as they. Bargain a dead nigger for the lives of our mick sailors. Then have the men, from both commands, stand me up on the bull rail above the river across the street, and you put a bullet as close to my head as you can. I'll fake the impact and topple over the rail. You know I'm good for a minute under water. It will look as though I'm gone!"

"Jasus, Tobias, so much could go wrong!" The thought of firing at his friend's head shook Rory's resolve.

"If you want things to go wrong, wait another minute 'til your countryman goads his torch men into burning us out. There're three hundred half drunk men out there, full of booze and hate!"

"You'll ruin your career, losin' us."

"I'll be dead if I don't and so will you. And this riot's going to get worse. It will be a fine excuse! Take command, damn you!"

Rory looked out at the mob and its chief. *By the saints, we must act,* he thought. "That bastard Fell!" he exclaimed to Tobias. "What bad luck getting him again."

"He'll get his, even if I don't survive. Some day I'll tell you the whole story, if we live."

"All right, my friend, here goes!" Rory strode through the door, waving and shouting in his broadest Connacht brogue. "Sure, and I'm on your side. No draft! Up the Irish! I'm a Galway lad, and I'm a Rebel navy man. Look at me, I'm in gray!"

A hush fell over the mob as its leader turned to face Rory. A tall, bearded man with auburn hair almost red stood to the left of the crowd.

"Hear him out, Mulcahy," he called to the leader in a commanding voice. The crowd's murmurs grew louder. Mulcahy shouted at them. "Silence, now, when John Andrews says listen." He pointed to the redheaded man, who was impeccably dressed in a three-piece summer suit. "He's never steered us wrong!"

Rory seized the moment. "Sure, and I'm a Dunbrody, and I've got six Irish sailors in there, three Rebs and three Yanks." *That's gildin' the lily, but only just,* he thought. "They're on your side, no draft and damn the blacks! Let us shoot the black officer that brought us here, and then we'll skedaddle, the Rebs to escape and the Yanks t' run for the ship!" Rory watched as Mulcahy glanced quickly at Andrews, who nodded approval.

"Are we ready to see a nigger get shot?" Mulcahy danced before the crowd.

"Yes!" the crowd roared.

"Duffy, McCafferty, O'Leary, bring 'im out," shouted Rory. Tobias had rehearsed the two contingents. "This is the only way we'll all live through this, men," he'd told them. "We lose enough seamen in battle. Let's not let these scum cost us more!" The officers and petty officers of both contingents rushed out, dragging Tobias. Halvorson and McCafferty each had an arm under one of Tobias'. Tobias was holding his hands behind him and had put shackles on his wrists. He had not locked them, however, and was holding them closed with his fingers.

Halvorson and McCafferty set Tobias on his feet atop the bull rail at the lip of the quay along South Street. The bull rail extended along the quay, made of six-by-six timbers set above the wooden planks of the quay, so that mooring lines could be passed underneath. "Stand away, lads, while I blow this blackamoor to Hell," shouted Rory, raising his pistol. The crowd roared again.

"Fire away, you stupid paddy," shouted Tobias defiantly. "You can't hit the ground with your hat!"

Crack! Rory fired and Tobias jerked his head simultaneously with the report, toppling backwards off the bull rail into the East River, fifteen feet below. The crowd surged to the quay's edge. "He's gone," someone shouted. "He must have sunk like a stone!"

"Off with you, now, lads," Rory called to the Union contingent, not waiting for Mulcahy's assent. Halvorson, O'Leary and Kelso sprinted up river toward Peck's Slip, carrying their rifles. Before the crowd could react, Mulcahy shouted, "Into the warehouse, people! Let's see what fine goods we can lay our hands on." The mob poured into the warehouse, leaving Rory and his officers with a smiling John Andrews.

"Perhaps you'll join me in a walk to a safe house, gentlemen? I think I know one quite close by. Follow me, please."

As they turned to follow the tall redhead, Rory whispered to his men, "Mum's the word on our little charade. We don't know whom we can trust."

****

As Tobias entered the water, he freed his hands of the shackles and kicked powerfully, driving himself deeper until he was sure he was invisible to those on the quay. He headed upstream and after another minute, swam to his left and came to the surface under the quay amid the pilings that supported it. He was a good 40 yards up river. He listened carefully as he caught his breath. He could not see any heads peering over the quay's edge. *I believe we've brought this off,* he thought. *I may consider a career in theater.* He kicked powerfully once again and disappeared beneath the surface. Ten minutes later, after several underwater legs of his journey, he surfaced by the landing dock at Peck's Slip. He could see his prisoner detail at the river end of the dock, and a boat approaching from *Woonsocket.* A few strokes brought him to his men.

"Good afternoon, Woonsockets. I can't tell you how pleased I am to see you."

They rushed to the dockside and reached to pull Tobias from the water. "Ya, sure, you're alright, sir?" Halvorson asked. "Ve vas vorried, ya."

"I'm fine, just a bit weary, bo'sun's mate. You men played your part well." All three petty officers were grinning ear to ear. Halvorson had summoned a boat by firing a shot to get the *Woonsocket's* attention. They watched as the cutter was hoisted out from *Woonsocket,* and rowed steadily, finally coming alongside the dock. *Let's hope the captain's back aboard, or my homecoming will not be a pleasant one,* thought Tobias. *At least I saved my men's lives, even if I threw away my career.* He looked again at the cutter, and saw Krotemann in the sternsheets. His heart sank.

****

Captain DeWitt Oakley had not returned to the ship. Fell stood at the entry port. A rifle shot rang out from the nearby Peck's Slip dock. The foretop lookout called down to the deck. "Sir, it looks like the shore party we just sent out." Fell tore his glass from his belt and focused it on the party at Peck's Slip just as Tobias was being pulled up on the dock. *There he is, that damned moke, still alive! We'll see how he fares when I bring him aboard,* he thought. His lips in a snarl, he called out, "Krotemann, take the cutter in and arrest Mr. St. John!"

Fell struggled to compose himself as the cutter rowed back from the South Street shore. *Damn, he wasn't lynched as I intended,* he thought. *But he's missing his prisoners. That should be enough for a court martial!* "Lieutenant Roessler," he called to the *Woonsocket's* Marine lieutenant, "have a detail take charge of Mr. St. John and confine him to his quarters until I call for him. I want him in shackles!" Fell went below to plan his next move.

Tobias lay on his bunk in his tiny cabin. A Marine sentry stood guard on the other side of his louvered cabin door. His hands were shackled, but not behind his back. "Sorry about this, Tobias," Roessler had said to his wardroom colleague as he put the shackles on Tobias' wrists. Tobias could hear each of the three petty officers that had been ashore with his detail as they were called, one by one, to be questioned by Fell in the captain's cabin. Finally, two Marines appeared at the door of Tobias' cabin.

"Sir, we're to take you to Mr. Fell in the captain's cabin," said one of the Marines.

"Very well, private," said Tobias as he rose and the sentry opened his door.

Tobias stood at attention in the captain's cabin as Fell, seated, glared at him, a smile on his lips. "Well, St. John, you've finally done what I knew you would. You've dug yourself a hole even you can't climb out of. I've questioned each man in your detail. They all tell the same tale. I'm charging you with consorting with the enemy, abandoning your command in the face of the enemy, and failing to comply with a direct order charging you to conduct prisoners to a secure confinement. It's a firing squad for you, you sorry excuse for an officer! Do you have anything to say for yourself before I return you to confinement?"

Tobias stared defiantly at Fell. *I'll be damned if I'll give in to despair,* he thought. *On the face of it, I could be found guilty of each charge. But, he contrived to set up the conditions I had to counter. And, by God, I did counter them! Here's my one chance to tell him what I think of him, and I'm taking it!*

"Sir, you contrived and conspired to risk the lives of my men and the prisoners for your own personal revenge. You, sir, are the sorry excuse for an officer. We'll see who the Court believes!"

"Marines!" Fell bellowed. "Take this man back to quarters. Shackle him to his bunk!" Seething, Fell left the captain's cabin, slamming the door. He ran up the companionway to the quarterdeck just as the lookout shouted to the deck below.

CHAPTER 19
FELL FALLS FROM GRACE
JULY 1863

"Deck, there! Captain's gig approaching!" Fell ordered sideboys for the captain's arrival, and moments later, Oakley came aboard, calling for the first lieutenant.

"Mr. Fell, stand by to get under way. We've been ordered to land our Marines and pick up a Marine unit from Governor's Island and land them also. There're ten thousand rioters marching south on Broadway to City Hall. Every unit under arms in the vicinity has been called out. Pass the word for Mr. St. John. I'll need our pilot."

"Sir, I sent St. John ashore with a three-man prisoner detail to take the Rebels to Boston, sir. I thought their safety was threatened aboard because of the riot, sir. He lost the prisoners and abandoned his men in the face of the enemy. I have him under arrest and I've drawn up charges."

"You did what! You disobeyed my order about blacks ashore? You took it upon yourself to send prisoners away without an order from me? You, you," Oakley stopped himself before he called an officer an imbecile in front of subordinates. "Pass the word for Lieutenant Roessler. You, sir, are under arrest for disobeying an order. That's just for starters. Stand at attention."

Roessler reached the quarterdeck and saluted. "Lieutenant, place Mr. Fell under close arrest. He's to be shackled and confined to the brig. I want your best sentries on duty. No one is to talk to this man without my express order. Am I clear?"

"Yes, sir. Aye, aye, sir. Corporal of the guard!"

"But, sir, you said black sailors, not officers. And you had me rig boarding nettings and said we'd be moving the prisoners to Boston, or, or Illinois." Fell's ferret eyes were doleful, his voice plaintive. "I was exercising initiative, sir!"

"This is the most irresponsible action I've ever encountered." The Marine guards had arrived. "Take this man below. Mr. Roessler, you'll be commanding a Marine landing party ashore to guard City Hall. Give the orders to ready your Marines and report to my cabin for further orders, if you please. Have Mr. St. John released from arrest and have him and his detail report immediately to my cabin."

Tobias and DeWitt Oakley sat in the captain's cabin alone. The three petty officers had presented their accounts of the action on South Street and had been dismissed. "Mr. St. John, you have had one difficult morning."

"Yes, sir. I managed to lose four prisoners I'm sure we wanted badly to keep." Tobias was as drained of energy as Oakley had ever seen him.

"No, I disagree, sailing master. You saved their lives, and the lives of your men. As far as retaining them, the officer prisoner exchange system is still at all ahead full. They'd have been back down south in four months. No, you and your friend Dunbrody did the right and honorable thing. It's Mr. Fell that's the problem. My problem, and that of my good friend and classmate, Admiral Paulding, the Navy Yard Commandant."

"How so, sir?" Tobias was puzzled by the conversation, unusual between superior and subordinate.

"The Navy can ill afford news that one of its officers attempted to murder one of its few black officers. It would be a disaster for the President and the war effort, now that we're accepting black volunteers in the Army. Only three or four regiments are even close to battle readiness. I've already briefed the admiral on the evidence we have of Fell's plot to murder a fellow officer, namely, you. He was appalled, and very cognizant of the political dangers if this became public. Now, I must report to him immediately with news of Fell's latest blunder. Meanwhile, you're to rest in your cabin. I'll ask you to avoid discussion of today's events with anyone aboard until I can confer with Admiral Paulding. You're dismissed, Mr. St. John."

"Aye, aye, sir. I'm glad It's Hiram Paulding, sir. I served under him in the fifties, when he commanded the *Susquehanna* and *Wabash*." Tobias rose and left the cabin, exhausted and somewhat bewildered. *He seemed sympathetic to my case, but will the commandant agree when he hears of this morning's imbroglio?* He wondered as he lay down on his bunk. Even with his future in jeopardy, Tobias was so drained by his ordeal that he fell into a deep sleep. Three hours later, he was summoned to Oakley's cabin. He found the captain with a broad smile upon his face.

"Please be seated, sailing master. I have a tale to tell you." As Tobias took a chair across the table from Oakley and leaned forward expectantly, the captain continued. "The commandant wishes to avoid a Fell court martial if at all possible. He thought your actions ashore today were most resourceful. He remembers you from Nicaragua. I told him I thought we had all the leverage we need to convince Mr. Fell to resign his commission quietly. Do you want to hear how?"

"I'd be fascinated, sir." Tobias brightened.

"I believe I can prevail on Mr. Krotemann to state that Mr. Fell planned to place you in jeopardy of your life by sending you ashore. We have statements from Doctor Miles and O'Leary incriminating him while in *Iles des Saintes*."

"Sir, while you were at the Navy Yard, Krotemann met with Mr. Fell, just before Fell ordered me ashore."

"Excellent, Mr. St. John. That should be the last straw. If we can secure a statement from Krotemann establishing Fell's complicity, we can rid the Navy of both quietly. We'll offer Krotemann the chance to resign, or face many years in prison. I'm confident it will work. But first, we must quell this riot ashore. The commandant is ordering all Marine units in the New York City area to Manhattan. And I order you, Mr. St. John, to consider yourself on temporary recuperative status. No duties. Lots of rest. Doctor Miles concurs in this. No arguments."

Indeed the Marines had their hands full. Along with units from the Army's Invalid Corps, National Guard and ultimately, regular Army units fresh from the Battle of Gettysburg, they fought tens of thousands of rioters over the next three days. Dozens of Negroes and hundreds of rioters were killed. Hundreds of buildings and homes were destroyed and soldiers, Marines and city police all suffered casualties. Arsenals, the Draft Board, and Horace Greeley's New York *Tribune* building were all attacked. The Colored Orphan Asylum was burned. Warships lay off Wall Street and the Battery, ready to sweep the streets with broadsides of grape and canister. Property damage estimates totaled $5,000,000, not including the loss of business and the suspension of trade.

Finally, after several days, the streets were clear of rioters. *Woonsocket's* Marine detachment had returned to the ship. Oakley had made good use of the week by persuading Krotemann to state that Fell had initiated the actions in the Caribbean and on Manhattan threatening Tobias' life. Tobias sat in the captain's cabin as Oakley described his recent meetings with Commandant Paulding.

"The commandant convened a closed board of inquiry, as the most recent murder attempts had occurred within his command. Doctor Miles, O'Leary, your three-man detail, and Krotemann all testified, as did I. Fell was by turns defiant and wheedling." Oakley shook his head disbelievingly at the memory. "The board concluded that the evidence justified a court martial for attempted murder."

"What was Fell's reaction then, sir?"

"Crestfallen and frightened. The next day, Rear Admiral Paulding entered the convening authority's findings. The charge and specifications of two counts of attempted murder of a commissioned officer will remain in Fell's file, but if he would agree to a *nolo contendere* plea, he would be allowed to resign without penalty for the good of the service. He accepted the offer."

"What if he later decides to contest the charges, sir?"

"The *nolo contendere* plea is as good as a confession. He agrees not to contest."

"So, he's gone?"

"He left the ship this morning. I preferred to let you sleep."

"Thank you sir." Tobias laughed. "It was probably just as well. What about Krotemann?"

"Discharged without penalty. He's gone, too."

Tobias sighed heavily, and leaned back in his chair. "Sir, I can't thank you enough for all you've done, and for your support."

"Well, sailing master, don't give me too much credit. This was not for you, but for the good of the service. You're a superb officer with a sterling record. No one wants that tainted. And the whole chain of command, up to the president, was concerned with embarrassment and detriment to the reputation of the navy and, yes, the administration, if this went to a court martial. We were all saving ourselves."

"Yes, sir. Yet, I refuse to have my gratitude deflated. Thank you, anyway!" Both men laughed.

"These draft riots caused enough damage to the war effort without adding your case to the mix," said Oakley. "The commandant will issue a statement noting the destruction of the raider *Belle of Biloxi,* praising our efforts in pursuit. He won't mention prisoners. Nor should he. After four days of mob action, the police force is having trouble accounting for all of its men. No one could attach blame for the loss of four prisoners in those circumstances."

"I doubt he'll mention the ammunition ship explosion, either," said Tobias.

"In a footnote," said Oakley with a smile. "Secretary Welles' office signed off on Commandant Paulding's decision, by the way, and President Lincoln, too. Gustavus Fox telegraphed a 'well-done' for you."

"Am I back on duty, sir?"

"Do you feel you've recovered?"

"Yes, sir, I'm ready!"

"Very well, then. I wonder, on another topic, what became of your friend, Dunbrody?"

"Landed on his feet, sir, without a doubt. He's sure to surface again, wherever the next 'ruction' occurs, as he would say."

"Admiral Paulding has called upon the Navy Department to make a search for them, but I doubt four Irishmen among the 200,000 in New York will be easy to find."

CHAPTER 20
TRAIN RIDE TO TREACHERY
JULY 1863

John Andrews led the officers of the *Belle of Biloxi* up to Pearl
Street, and then toward Five Points until they crossed Fulton. "Left here,
gentlemen. The safe house is up the block. We'll take our ease for the
day, and I'll get your measurements. I know a haberdasher or two with
just your sizes. We'll either have them provide, or the rioters will provide
for us." He laughed gently. "Dearly as I love the Cause, gray will not be
beneficial to wear until we get you further south."

Rory walked beside him. "Do I sense you're an associate of the
fine lads in Richmond, then?"

"I shorely am, Mr. Dunbrody, did I catch the name? We have
a few souls, more than a few, actually, who would like to see this war
end and King Cotton resume his place as a premier trade among men of
property. And they are by no means mostly from the South. Ah, here
we are." They entered a three-story brownstone with an unassuming but
clean entranceway. It was far cooler inside than out. A calm black butler,
with an air of gravitas, greeted them as they stepped in. "Prestwick," said
Andrews, "Take these gentlemen's jackets, and at your own pace, ascertain
their measurements. We must, within days, garb them as adequately-
dressed merchants, not gaudy, but respectable."

"Yes, Mistah Andrews," Prestwick replied, his countenance
unreadable.

"If you'll permit me, you've had a strenuous morning, and I
have much to attend to. We'll assess our situations over a leisurely supper.

Until then, rest and make yourselves at home. Call upon Prestwick for whatever you need." Andrews smiled, waved a good bye, and left the brownstone.

"Let me show you to your rooms, gentlemen," said Prestwick. "After you've rested, should you wish to gather for conversation and refreshment, the parlor is yours. Just ring for me, please, if I can be of service."

They did gather, at three, after each had slept a deep afternoon sleep. Prestwick served what in England would be an afternoon tea, sandwiches, cake, tea and coffee. They ate and drank in silence, famished from their morning's trials. At last they sat back in their comfortable chairs, and grinned at one another. "Sure, it beats the midwatch on a stormy night, sir," said Walsh.

"Aye, it does, Thomas, and I believe we've earned it as well. As we'll be movin' through enemy territory for the next week or so, I think we should suspend the naval courtesies, and address one another by first names. Mine is 'Rory'." Rory leaned forward and picked up his coffee cup. "We'd best be practisin', as it's a hard habit to break. But Finn, Thomas, Niall, it could save our lives."

"Aye, aye, sir, I mean, yes, Rory," said McCafferty, laughing at his difficulty. "You think we'll be posin' as civilians, then?"

"Without a doubt, Finn," Rory replied. "If our new friend is a Confederate agent, as it appears, he'll doubtless provide identities for us all, and a bit of cash. I have it in mind to make our way back to the lines where my old friend John Singleton Mosby has been operatin' of late. The newspaper here in the parlor says he's a major of guerilla cavalry in Northern Virginia. He finally got his promotion. He's a divil on horseback, he is!"

Niall Duffy looked as relaxed as Rory had ever seen him. *It's a long way from fireman first class to acting chief,* Rory thought. *I think he's gettin' comfortable with the thought of bein' an officer, even an actin' one.*

Niall put his feet up on an ottoman. "Can you believe that only four months ago, we'd just boarded *Star of the South?* It's not been tedious, and that's a fact."

"Ah, now, Niall's got the right of it,' said Rory. "We've come a long way together, and we've a long way to go."

John Andrews' voice was charged with excitement as he burst into the brownstone's vestibule. "Prestwick, I'll need those measurements sooner than I thought," he shouted. "Gentlemen, the Jersey City ferry is still running, and I think if we move in the chaos of the riots, tomorrow morning, the Federals will not yet have started to look for you. They've too much else to occupy them. Let's not wait. We'll get you dressed tonight."

He left the room to confer with Prestwick. After fifteen minutes, he returned, a small brass box under his arm. "Prestwick will measure you directly, and then I'll send my men to gather your clothes. I'm going to provide you with thirty dollars each in travel money. It should get you aboard the trains you'll take and to the safe house in Harper's Ferry. Yes," he said in response to their surprised looks, "that's what I'm recommending to you: the ferry to Jersey, the train to Philadelphia and then to Baltimore, and then the Baltimore and Ohio Railroad to Harper's Ferry." He paused. "Catch your breath, gentlemen."

Rory spoke first. "Harper's Ferry is in Virginia, is it not?"

"But it is in federal hands, and will soon be in the new Union state of West Virginia, being formed now. Its most important feature for you four is its location in regard to Lee. Lee is in the Shenandoah Valley, just south of the Potomac, and just beyond Harpers Ferry. Meade is headed toward Northern Virginia with his Army of the Potomac, to Lee's east, and so far, unaware of Lee, and five days behind him."

"How do you see us crossing the line?" Rory leaned forward, eager for the plan to unfold.

"We have a haven for you in Harper's Ferry. Even though it's in Federal hands, there is a strong Southern sentiment there. The agent there will provide you the best route up the river. You'll go fifteen or so miles up the Shenandoah, moving by night. By that time, three days hence, Lee will have crossed the Potomac and moved a distance up the Shenandoah. You'll be within Lee's lines before you know it! But we must get you there while he is still close to Harper's Ferry."

"Won't they be looking for four men?" Walsh opened his hands, palms up, to emphasize his question. "Shouldn't we travel in pairs?"

"I declare, you've the makings of an agent, Mr. Walsh," said Andrews, with a degree of approval. "Indeed, y'all will go in pairs, and in the guise of sutlers, meeting your wares and wagons in Berlin, one stop east of Harper's Ferry, and just on the route of the Army of the Potomac. Sutlers in Harper's Ferry would not excite comment, but Berlin is a more plausible destination for the early part of your trip, when you may be asked for your papers. They will be excellent forgeries, by the way. Sutlers of the Irish persuasion are not uncommon, and you'll look the part. You must practice an avaricious expression, to be even more convincing." Laughter filled the parlor.

"Ah, sure now, lads, we'll all be tinkers!" At Rory's words, they all laughed harder. "I think we can play the part, t' be sure," said Duffy.

"I beg you to excuse me, gentlemen, until supper," drawled Andrews. "We should have your papers by then, and perhaps, your clothing." And with that, he was gone, and the four officers were left to imagine and discuss their next three days.

The next morning, Andrews bade them goodbye. The tumult of the riots was in its second day. Smoke from the fires palled the sky. In the distance, shouting and shots were audible. Andrews waved from the porch of the brownstone, and then turned away quickly. *More divilment on behalf of the Cause on his mind, without a doubt,* thought Rory. Each of the *Belle's* officers was attired in reasonably well-cut jacket and trousers, and bowler hat. They'd retained their comfortable boots. Each bore papers certifying their status as sutlers, accredited to the Army of the Potomac. They made their way 'cross-town to Cortland Street and the terminal of the Jersey City Ferry. So many police and military units were downtown, safeguarding City Hall, Trinity Church, and other edifices of the establishment, that violence along their route was minimal and sporadic.

They boarded the ferry, and without thinking, gathered at the after rail of the passenger deck, gazing at the fires and smoke mounting above the tortured city. "Sure and Andrews had the right of it. They'll not be lookin' for four navy fugitives 'til that ruction's under control." Rory turned to his officers. "We'll make it, lads, see if we don't!"

The train from New Jersey to Philadelphia was uneventful,

although the band of escapees, two by two, and separated by ten seats, started at every loud remark. Rory spent the trip gazing out the window at the beauty of the wooded hills in full leaf, and the breadth of the Delaware River as they crossed into Pennsylvania and its premier city. They mostly slept after the change of trains to Baltimore, and had yet to be asked for their papers.

When they changed to the Baltimore and Ohio line, the air seemed more highly charged. Passengers avoided eye contact. Even the song of the iron wheels over the rails sounded ominous. After all, they were traversing ground that had seen two huge armies move north, collide at Gettysburg, and then stream south again, wary, by turns resolute and irresolute, searching. "Papers, please." A young army lieutenant bearing the insignia of the Provost Marshal held out his hand, his eyes guarded. A trooper with sidearm stood behind him.

"And here you are, your honor," said Rory as he handed his authorization to the officer, and Duffy, his seatmate, followed suit. "Just two sutlers after supportin' the brave lads of the Irish Brigade, and other regiments of our grand army." The provost marshal scanned the authorization, glanced at Rory and Duffy, and handed the packets to each. The provost marshals passed on up the aisle and stepped into the next car. Rory relaxed, thinking, *every click of the wheels singin' on the railroad track brings me closer to Carrie Anne. It's been six months since we last saw one another. Motivation, indeed, t' make it through the lines.*

The train made a stop opposite Leesburg near Conrad's Ferry, (now White's Ferry), and then chugged west toward Berlin and Harper's Ferry. Opposite Harper's Ferry, in the evening, the four left the train, two-by-two, and crossed the bridge over the Potomac. They found their way to the safe house, in a neighborhood of modest but well kept houses, using Andrews' directions. Rory and McCafferty waited for Walsh and Duffy, trailing discreetly. Once together, they knocked precisely, in the code sequence given them by Andrews. The door opened cautiously, and a wizened man in his seventies smiled, gap-toothed. "Y'all come in and welcome to western Virginia. Mistah Smith be with you directly." Their greeter scurried off into the back of the house, and soon they were welcomed by Mr. "Smith," a large man in his early thirties, with cautious eyes.

"Gentlemen, welcome. Come sit in the parlor. I understand you're interested in a leisurely trip up the Shenandoah, perhaps by starlight?"

"Sure, it would be a way for us to relax, and gather our thoughts, away from the hurly-burly of our daily lives, bein' sutlers, and all." Rory took a seat, nodding at his host in thanks. *I'll wager it's a hard life, as an agent. Every knock could mean betrayal,* he thought.

Mr. Smith, sitting in an overstuffed chair, literally beamed at the four young Irishmen. "What a treat for me to encounter men of the sea, this far inland," he said. "We've been expecting you, and your introduction included the tale of your exploits in New York. Congratulations!"

"We were fortunate, to be sure, Mr. Smith. Sadly, our success was tempered by the loss of one of our comrades, a fine young officer from Louisiana. It was he who struck the telling blow, the *coup de tonnerre*, as it were." Rory paused, thinking of Beaupre.

"It were done in a noble cause, sir," replied Mr. Smith. "Knowing of your arrival, we've had four copies of a map of the lower Shenandoah printed. Your route will be along the west bank, and should present few obstacles for active young men."

"I'm surprised, Mr. Smith, that we're not traveling by boat, sailors as we are," said Rory, "perhaps a four oared rowing boat, much like the skiffs used by bateaumen in the coastal waters of Virginia and North Carolina."

Rory smiled to himself at the reference. *Sure, this devotee of the Cause would be appalled at the number of former black slave bateaumen now serving in Uncle Abe's navy,* Rory mused. Tobias had mentioned in his correspondence his astonishment at the number of contraband sailors aboard Union ships.

Smith smiled. "You've obviously not seen the lower Shenandoah. It's shallow, rock-strewn, and replete with rapids. We hear that Lee's lines are about fifteen miles up river," said the agent. "He crossed the Potomac three days ago. Two nights of y'all walking along the banks should suffice. I assure you, by boat would be impossible."

"Sure, and we'll follow your lead, Mr. Smith. We'll be afloat soon enough, and a bit of a stroll in the moonlight will suit us fine. Just the thing we need to work out the stiffness we suffered durin' a two and a half day train ride." Rory spoke in jest, but his companions looked eager to undertake the march.

The four fugitives, for they were still in Union territory, slept for four hours, and then were led to the banks of the Shenandoah near where it joined the Potomac. They carried canteens of water provided by Mr. Smith, and their few possessions and food for the two-day march were packed in knapsacks. They had abandoned their sutlers' valises. In the twilight, Rory could see the massive stone pilings of the railroad bridge over the Potomac, behind him, the one they had crossed earlier on their train ride from Baltimore. They had moved down the steep streets from the Harper's Ferry hills to the flat land along the rock-strewn Shenandoah, among the clapboard houses and shacks that nestled there, homes always at risk from flood.

"Here's where I leave you, gentlemen," whispered Smith, as he pointed south up the river valley. "Just follow the river. God bless you. I expect to read great news of your naval exploits!"

The four sailors moved cautiously along the sandy banks, pausing every hour to drink from their canteens. At dawn, after seven hours, they found a secluded copse of woods a few feet from the bank. "All right, lads," Rory said, "we'll stand two-hour anchor watches. I'll take the first one. Get some sleep!" They awoke in the heat and the insects of mid-day. The riverbank was deserted, and they decided to move during daylight. At dusk, Rory estimated that they'd covered 15 miles since leaving Harper's Ferry, and cautioned his companions.

"Let's move inland slowly and openly, lads, so we draw a challenge before a gunshot," said Rory. The starlight and crescent moon provided enough light for them to recognize a path when they crossed it, 50 feet from the riverbank. "We'll head south again, then. I'll take the van," said Rory, and like the lead ship in a line of battle, he led his men down a winding path that paralleled the river.

"Halt!" came a call. They had reached a rise, a natural post for a picket. "Advance and be recognized," the picket ordered in a Virginia drawl.

"Lieutenant Rory Dunbrody, Confederate States Navy, and three of my officers. We're unarmed." They moved slowly forward.

"Halt," the picket called again. "Corporal of the guard!"

A lantern swayed up the path behind the picket's station. Rory could see the lantern-light glinting off the rifle of the picket, trained on Rory.

The corporal of the guard and two infantrymen arrived at the picket's post. "What's all this, Webly?" he asked.

"These four claim to be naval officers, from our navy, corporal."

"All right, keep them covered and we'll have a look. Advance one at a time, slowly," he ordered. Rory stepped slowly up the path, his hands raised.

"Lieutenant Dunbrody, late of the Confederate States Ship *Belle of Biloxi,* corporal. These are three of my officers. We escaped from the Yankees in New York City."

"You're a long way from New York, and you don't sound very southern to me," the corporal replied.

"Sure, and half the sailors in the Rebel navy are Irish. We were sent by a Confederate agent to Harper's Ferry, and by another one up the river." The four were searched as they stood under the rifles of the guard detail.

"They're unarmed, corporal," said one.

"Good, we'll take them to the lieutenant and let him sort this out." They trailed off through the woods, and soon met the lieutenant commanding the guard detail's platoon, another skeptic.

"Here you are, sir, four Irishmen, with no papers and out of uniform, claiming to be Confederate naval officers. Can you blame me for being cautious?"

"Sure, and you have a point, lieutenant. Can you tell me if General Pickett's division is nearby? The general knows me, personally. We served together on the frontier, before the war, and we've seen each other in Richmond, at the White House, as a matter of fact. Or, is General Stuart's command close by? I rode with his command on the James River."

"You'll pardon my doubts, sir, but anyone could know those names. It so happens that we're in Pickett's division. I am personally going to escort you to the division provost marshal, across the river, and let him investigate your story as he will."

"Sure, y' must do as you think best, lieutenant," said Rory. As the four officers were escorted under guard across the Shenandoah to the provost marshal, Rory whispered to the others. "Sooner or later, lads, we'll find someone who knows me!"

The party of men moved south, paralleling the river, until they came to division headquarters. Troops were bivouacked among the trees, and several tents, the headquarters group, were pitched in a meadow clearing. The lieutenant halted his entourage, and spoke to an orderly, who ducked inside the tent flap of the provost marshal. A tall lieutenant colonel emerged, his dueling scar apparent in the torchlight. *Von Klopfenstein! Damn the bad luck, and all,* thought Rory. *And he's been promoted again!*

"Dunbrody," exclaimed von Klopfenstein, "und mit three other Irishers in tow!" The Prussian, an aide to Pickett when Rory had first met him, was fairly chortling with glee. "You have this 'cock und bull' story, as they say, about escaping from New York. Colonel Donovan, of the secret service, has expressed great concern about your loyalty, given your brother is on the Union side. I would be remiss, I think the word is, if I did not hold you until he can interrogate you about your so-called exploits." Von Klopfenstein smirked, broadly, enjoying himself immensely. "Sergeant Cromwell! Assign a guard to these four men and take them to the stockade!"

"Damn it colonel, I want to see General Pickett!" shouted Rory.

"The general is still recovering from the loss of 2700 men of this division. Ve let him recuperate in peace, Dunbrody."

A provost-marshal sergeant appeared, with a two-man detail, and Rory and his officers were soon marched to a rudimentary stockade, little more than a roped-off open meadow near the river, with guards posted all around. Prisoners were sleeping in small shelter tents. They were mostly the misfits found in any army, malingerers, men who had managed to find alcohol and who could not control it, or the merely insubordinate. It was home for the navy officers for the next two days.

The four were seated around their small campfire at dusk the next day. "Tell us, sir, what the colonel's quarrel is with you," asked Walsh.

"Yes, and who is this Donovan this Proosian says he's waiting for?" Duffy chimed in.

"Well, lads," said Rory in a whisper, "we're a bit too close here to ears we don't want to hear for me t' be explainin'. I promise you the whole story just as soon as we're out of this mess."

CHAPTER 21
MOSBY TO THE RESCUE
JULY 1863

Lee's entire Army of Northern Virginia was resuming its way
south, hoping to outdistance General Meade's Army of the Potomac and
place itself between Meade and Richmond, in a defensive position south
of the Rappahannock River. The two armies struck southward, with the
Rebels crossing to the east side of the Shenandoah, but still on the west
side of the Blue Ridge Mountains, and the Yankees to the east of the
mountains. The Union forces, once across the Potomac, began to lash out
at the Confederates through the passes or "gaps" of the Blue Ridge. Lee
continued filing southward to block any Union threat to Richmond.

The unit from which von Klopfenstein's provost marshal detail
came was Corse's brigade of Pickett's Virginia division. Pickett's division
was assigned to hold the mountain gaps against Yankee incursions. Early
in the morning of their third day in the stockade, Corse's brigade moved
south up the east bank of the river. The first gap it would pass was
Snicker's Gap, a mile ahead. All the stockade prisoners were marched in
formation, but only Rory and his men were shackled.

General Corse was still bitter about having missed the Battle of
Gettysburg. Both his brigade and General Jenkins' had been detached
from Pickett just before Gettysburg to guard Richmond. They had just
rejoined the Army of Northern Virginia as it crossed the Potomac. Rory
and his officers could hear the grumbling among Corse's troops. After
twenty minutes, Rory glanced to his left. In the dim light of the dawn,
he could see the gap, the Blue Ridge tapering to the pass on each side of

the gap. "Be alert, lads," he whispered, "this is a grand place for a Yankee attack." In that instant, the tramp and shuffle of the infantry as they marched was shattered, first by a bugle, then a shout and the thunder of hooves.

"Form line on me!" "Load and fire at will!" The brigade officers called desperate commands as a regiment of Union cavalry swept down out of Snicker's Gap and hurled itself against the flank of Corse's brigade. The provost marshal detail was caught in the middle of the attack. The Union cavalrymen surged through the formation, and sabered the guards. Rory and his officers had taken refuge beneath a wagon just behind them in the column.

"Sir, Rory, look at the sergeant," McCafferty said as they lay under the wagon, cuffed together at the wrist. "He has the shackle keys." The provost marshal sergeant lay just beyond the wagon tongue, his head nearly severed from his body by a saber stroke. The horse pulling the wagon had been killed in the assault, and was still harnessed to the wagon.

"Finn and I will get the keys," Rory said to Walsh and Duffy. "Wait here! Ready, Finn?" The boatswain nodded sharply and gathered his feet beneath him. With a rush, the two scuttled the few feet to the sergeant, and McCafferty removed the keys from the sergeant's pocket. Back they scrambled to their hiding place under the wagon.

"Stand by, lads, here's the order of battle," said Rory. "The fight's still ragin'. We'll leave the shackles on our wrists, Walsh and I, so we can show the federals we're escapees from the Rebels. We don't dare stay with Lee's men. If von Klopfenstein finds us in the mele, he'll shoot us like dogs. Remember, our story to the federals is we were joining the Irish Brigade when the Rebels took us. We'll run for the gap, and hope we can find one of Mosby's men. Mosby's the only army man beside Stuart we can trust."

The Union cavalry was beginning its withdrawal as reinforcements from the rest of Pickett's division began to steady the fleeing men of Corse's brigade. The four sailors ran from the wagon to the slope of the road through the gap and took to the underbrush along the roadside. A troop of federal cavalry, dismounted and in reserve, was firing their carbines to cover their regiment's withdrawal.

Rory boldly approached the troop captain, rattling his shackles. "Your honor, we escaped from the Rebels, we're a levy for the Irish Brigade."

The troop commander scarcely spared them a glance as he fired his carbine. "Get back up the road then 'till you find the next unit. Tell them Captain Stewart of the 5th New York sent you."

"Sure and we will, your honor, and thank y' most kindly." Rory waved frantically to his companions, motioning them up the slope alongside the Snicker's Gap Turnpike.

"Let's get further off the pike, boys," said Rory, after a quarter mile. "The whole regiment of New Yorkers will be ridin' through in a moment or two. We'd best not remind 'em of our presence."

They crested the gap north of the turnpike, just as the Fifth New York Cavalry galloped over the pike and down the slope toward Snickersville. They stood in a copse of woods with a good view of the gap. "Sure, and we've got our work cut out for us, thanks to that *spalpeen* von Klopfenstein," said Rory. "We'll have to dodge the whole of Meade's army while huntin' for Mosby." Then Rory brightened. "Then, again, if I know Jack Mosby, he's likely to find us!"

"So tell us, sir," said Duffy, "what the Proosian fellow has against you, and who Donovan is, and how you met this Mosby, and how he comes to be behind Union lines."

"Well, now, let's have a sit-down," said Rory, taking a seat on an old log. "It's a long haul up the gap, t' be sure. When I was a midshipman, in Puget's Sound on the northwest coast, Pickett was a US Army captain and von Klopfenstein was his lieutenant. We didn't hit it off, Klaus Dieter and me, right from the start, and then we had a mock duel, and he came away a wee embarrassed at his performance, him bein' the expert, and all. He's not forgiven me. And this Donovan fella, isn't he the brother of the man I killed in a duel over my darlin' Carrie Anne? And him in the army secret service, or what passes for it in the South? So he and the Proosian have got their heads together over me, I'm thinkin'. And there you have it for those two *shuilers*. As for John Singleton Mosby, he's had more ups and downs than one of those newfangled elevators Mr. Otis is buildin'. He was a private, and a scout for Stuart. Before that, he'd been a captain. Then he was captured and exchanged, and commended by Lee himself, and now, they've given him a battalion of partisan rangers, like Brennan on the moor, livin' off the land and the help of the ordinary people, and strikin' the enemy when they least expect it, and then just meltin' away into the countryside.

Rory's three subordinates looked slightly dumbfounded, at a story with so many highs and lows. They had only been with him since *Star of the South*, and had no opportunity to talk to anyone who had known him in the war's early days. "That's a tale, indeed, sir," said Duffy. "When did you meet Mosby?"

"Ah, the bold highwayman, did I mention he's a lawyer, too? I met him when he was a scout for General Stuart, the finest cavalry commander in this fight. I rode clear around McClellan's army with him a year ago. He's a fine lad, he is."

"How can we find him, sir?" Walsh, exhausted, was lying flat on his back.

"Sure, Thomas, I wish I knew. The papers say he operates in Loudoun and Fauquier counties, and I believe we're currently in Loudoun, but the whole place is crawlin' with Yankees. If we can't find him, we're in a divil of a fix, we are."

"Well, y'all are in luck!" A voice from deeper in the woods sounded very full of itself. "My name is Hammond, and Ah'm one of Mosby's men. And I've heard tell from the colonel, around many a table in Mosby's Confederacy, of his friend the wild Irish sailor."

The four had automatically leaped to their feet, but then realizing they were unarmed, had relaxed and sat again. "Well, God save y' kindly, Mr. Hammond, it's grand to make your acquaintance."

"I'm fixin' t' step into the clearing, gentlemen." A tall man in a short plain gray jacket with two rows of black buttons stepped from the woods. His low-crowned gray hat had a black hatband and its brim was turned up on each side like a bird about to take flight. Butternut trousers and worn, dusty riding boots completed his outfit. He wore no saber, but carried a Colt revolver on each hip. "Ah can take y'all to the colonel, but I'll need to find four horses. Follow me through the woods to the Springer house. I'll leave you there while I round up some riding stock.

They're friends. Y'all will be safe there."

"Is he far away, Mr. Hammond?"

"Only 15 miles, but as I overheard you observe, suh, the ground is covered with Yankees. We'll wind around, for sure."

"So, there you were," said Rory, "listenin' to us and we suspectin' nothin'!"

"That's my job, cap'n. Not to be seen unless I want to be. The colonel sent me out to keep an eye on the gap. The Yankees have been raidin' over all of them this last few days, Ashby's, Manassas, Chester Gap, we try to keep track and get word of which units are attackin' to Stuart and Lee."

Rory introduced himself and his men formally, first to Hammond and then to the Springers, whose farmhouse had been used many times as a safe haven for the partisan rangers of Mosby's command. Hammond returned with four horses in the late evening. Rory noticed that Hammond had two additional revolvers holstered one on each side of the saddle horn. "I see that Colonel Mosby's command has adopted his 'four-Colt' armament, Mr. Hammond," said Rory.

"It didn't take much persuadin' to convince us, lieutenant. It gives each ranger 24 quick rounds, without fussin' with a carbine or a saber." Rory later learned that everyone in Mosby's command referred to him as "Colonel," even though his substantive rank was major, and he'd only been recommended by Stuart for a lieutenant colonelcy.

Hammond suggested a dawn departure. "With all the Yankees in the area, we'll stick to the ridges, where we can see them from a distance. They'll be crowdin' the turnpikes, towns and railroads. We'll travel by trails through the woods. Let me show you the route." He took a battered map of the area from his jacket pocket, and spread it on the Springer's big dining table. "Here we are, north of Snickersville. We'll make our way through the hills and farmlands, almost due south. We may duck into Rector's Crossroads after ten miles, as the crow flies. Those folks keep a good watch on goin's-on. If the coast is clear, we'll head for Hopewell across open country, in eastern Fauquier County. The colonel's holed-up in a little camp in the Bull Run Mountains there. We call it 'Camp Spindle.'"

"Mr. Hammond, I'm a good rider, but the lads here, they've not spent much time in the saddle, at least not recently."

"Lieutenant, we can take our time. Your men can ride for as long as they be comfortable, and then we'll walk the horses. We'll just keep a good lookout, and be in Camp Spindle before you know it!" In the morning, Hammond was as good as his word. They rode, they walked, they rested in shady groves, and refilled their canteens from spring water. Hammond had grown up in the county, and knew every turn of the trail. He wanted to hear more of life at sea. "I'm a ranger, and far from the ocean. Tell me what it's like, war at sea."

The four sea officers had served on three raiders since *Star of the South* left Portsmouth, and had many a tale to tell. The hours on the woodland trails flew by. On a rise above Goose Creek and Rector's Crossroads, Hammond surveyed the scene below through his field glasses.

"A passel of Yankees in the village," he said. "I can see Clinton's Rector House, but it's got a sight too many blue uniforms around it." He handed the glasses to Rory. Rory saw Union officers lounging along the stone wall fronting the stone façade and verandah of the three-story Rector House, where only the month before, Mosby had officially organized the 43rd Virginia Battalion of Cavalry, "Mosby's Rangers."

"We'll cross the pike between here and Middleburg, and strike east across country," said Hammond. They crossed the creek, and then the pike, and were soon back in the peace of the winding country trails. At dusk, the Bull Run Mountains were rising up against the sky, and they found their way to Camp Spindle in the dark.

Mosby's welcome was effusive. "Rory, you crazy Irishman. What Celtic lunacy have you been up to now?" He turned to Hammond. "James, where did you find him? And how are Lee's men holding up against the Yankees?"

"Well, colonel, they turned up in Snicker's Gap, runnin' from the Yankees and from Pickett. I was hid in the woods, watchin' the Yankee cavalry. These four, they're all Irish, was talkin' about findin' you, as the only Reb army man they could trust, you and General Stuart. They were shorely navy, by their talk, and I 'membered you tellin' tales of yore Irish Rebel navy friend, so I brought 'em."

"Well done, James. You've rescued a great weapon for the South. Rory, who are these people, and how did you come to the Bull Run?"

Rory introduced his officers, and described their odyssey from Portsmouth to Virginia. Mosby, by turns, slapped his thighs and clapped Rory on the shoulder in appreciation, as each phase of the journey unfolded. "What a tale! And everything I would have expected, with you a principal in the drama! I'm sorry to tell you, we've no such magnificent stage on which to present your next act. The damn Yankees are so thick, I've sent my men to their holes for safety, all except these thirty." Some of Mosby's men were guarding about twenty Union prisoners, roped in a compound. "I can't get these prisoners through to Richmond, so many Yankees in the way."

"I'm guessin', then, that it will be as difficult to get us through the lines."

"I'd like to wait a few days to see what develops, before we try. At least you're safe from that damned Prussian."

"Perhaps we could make our stay a fine opportunity for training sailors to ride and forage. You never know when duty will require that skill." Rory smiled at the thought of his three Irish officers in the saddle.

"It would be a good time to bring my men back out of hiding," said Mosby. "I like to give them incentive. We could snatch up a few wagons. We need horses, too. And if we're to capture wagons and share the contents, we need to damage a railroad, as well. General Lee, according to Jeb Stuart, thinks my men collect too many spoils and neglect disrupting the rails that the Yankees move goods upon. We need a balance, to keep Marse Robert happy."

"And doesn't the good general know that a wagon capture draws as many men off the front line to guard the rear as a train wreck?" Rory looked puzzled.

"I think it's more Lee's distaste for keeping the spoils. He considers it unsoldierly."

"The navy will do its best to help keep his honor happy, colonel, darlin'."

"Good, we'll find some action for your sea demons, then. You know, Rory, I'm just a major, but ever since Stuart recommended me for lieutenant colonel, the men call me by that rank."

"They know lieutenant colonels command battalions. At least you've been recommissioned, and field grade, at that."

The next ten days brought adventure, wonderment and saddle sores to the former officers' cadre of the CSS *Belle of Biloxi*. Mosby called in 100 more men of his battalion. He paired up each navy man with a veteran ranger. Two days after Rory's party had reached Camp Spindle, thirty men, including the sea officers, rode through Hopewell's Gap to cross the Bull Run and strike twenty sutlers' wagons on the Little River turnpike near Chantilly, where Washington Territory's first governor, Isaac Stevens, had died as an embattled Union general. Hammond rode with Rory. The rangers overwhelmed the Union guards, loaded as much as they could of the food, alcohol, clothing and tobacco into three wagons, and burned the others, leaving the sutlers looking on, hopelessly. They mounted the guards, now prisoners, on their own horses, and allowed them to share in the captured goods as they galloped back toward Hopewell's Gap.

"These Yankee boys, they don't cotton much to the sutlers," Hammond said to Rory as they rode west. "They think the prices are too high, I guess. When we captures the escorts, we always let 'em have their pick of the goods. They always make sure the sutlers know that their goods are bein' consumed for free, when we're riding off!" Hammond laughed at the thought. "We'll have us a little party ourselves, tonight, what with the liquor supply we just captured. 'Course, the colonel, he don't hold with drinkin', himself. He'll just try to make sure we're ready for action tomorrow, and he'll drink his coffee. Shore do love his coffee, the man does."

As Meade's forces streamed south, he placed guards along the railroad lines he used to bring supplies and ammunition to his advancing troops. The Orange and Alexandria Railroad was a major supply route for the Union forces, and Meade placed heavy guard details along the line as quickly as he could. He first secured the line at vulnerable points furthest from Alexandria, thinking that the tracks were safer closer to Washington, D.C. Mosby was able to scout a wooden trestle over Pohick Creek east of Fairfax Station and discovered that the federals were not yet concentrated in great numbers there.

Rory once again rode alongside Hammond as the twenty men led by Mosby left the Bull Run Mountains and passed south of Centreville and Fairfax Courthouse. They picked their way carefully through the dark. They carried captured incendiary charges and sacks of tinder as saddlebags. Halting up the creek from the trestle, they counted the guard detail. "Four," whispered Mosby. "Let's ride!" With an ear-splitting yell, the twenty rangers charged up the slope paralleling the creek to the tracks over the trestle. Rory rode with reins in one hand and his Colt revolver in the other. Two guards fell in the fusillade, and the other two fled south down the creek.

"Set the charges and place the tinder, men," called Mosby. "James, Mr. Dunbrody, take five men each as pickets to guard the track, east and west. You others, gather as much dry wood as you can. Three minutes and we'll set her off!"

The trestle burst into flames as the riders returned the way they'd come. "Sure, and that will attract some attention," laughed Duffy as they rode away.

"Even better, Mr. Duffy," said Mosby, "it will warm the heart of General Lee!"

Mosby's battalion was always in need of mounts. Two horses per man seemed to be the preferred number, Rory noticed. He was not surprised, then, when riding with Mosby and thirty of his men two days after the bridge burning near Centreville, that they attacked a larger number of federals who were herding 100 horses near where Little River Pike joins the Warrenton Pike. "Two groups, men," called Mosby. "Lieutenant Turner, take fifteen men and attack the rear. You others come with me!" Rory and his men were in Thomas Turner's group as the ranger lieutenant led them downslope toward Difficult Run where the Union troopers were watering the herd. The yelling and shooting of the rangers scattered the Yankees who soon regrouped in a copse of trees and began to return fire. Two rangers were killed, but the Confederates rounded up most of the herd, split into small groups and galloped west into the setting sun over the Bull Run Mountains.

By the naval contingent's tenth day with Mosby, Lee had moved his army through the Shenandoah Valley and eastward to a position south of the Rappahannock. Meade's forces faced them over the river. Mosby talked to the four navy men over a Camp Spindle campfire. "The Yankees have moved their front-line units through here to the Rappahannock. All we have here in Northern Virginia are the supply lines, and the units trying to find us. I think it's safe to take you down through the Shenandoah Valley to Lee. I'm going to escort you personally. I'll persuade Stuart to take us to Lee so you can tell him first-hand how you were imprisoned by that damned Prussian! Treating our naval heroes that way! I'll bet Lee will have a fit!"

"Sure, it would be a great comfort to us if you're our guide, colonel. We're fish out of water, and that's a fact!"

"Good, that's settled. We'll leave in the morning. I'm sure your officers will be glad to move you closer to that beautiful blond in Richmond. They've noticed, I don't doubt, you gazing moodily into the campfire every evening."

"Mr. Walsh," said Duffy, "is the captain blushing?"

"It must be the heat of the fire, Mr. Duffy," Walsh replied. Everyone laughed, even Rory.

It was a careful, yet relaxed entourage, Mosby, four nautical Irishmen, Hammond and two other rangers. They made their way without incident through Manassas Gap, and down the Blue Ridge above the river to Sperry's Gap and on to Culpeper Courthouse, where Lee and Stuart had their headquarters. As they traveled southeast toward Culpeper, Mosby said, "I wish I could keep on south, Rory. My parents left our old home, Tudor Grove, near Charlottesville, and relocated near Lynchburg. I haven't seen them in a long time, and the war is hard on them."

"Sure, and I miss my family, too. My da and sister, they're in Edward's Ferry, on the Roanoke. Who knows where brother Tim is, in the Union Army, and all? May we live to see them again, and the war end soon."

"This must be Stuart's headquarters, up ahead. He'll be glad to see us." Indeed, Stuart seemed genuinely glad to see Rory again, in the company of his protégé, Mosby. He was even more pleased to hear of their recent successes. The piercing eyes of the big full-bearded general flashed dangerously at the story of von Klopfenstein and the stockade stay of the naval officers.

"Unconscionable. General Lee needs to know of this." Stuart seemed to have largely recovered from Lee's expressed admonishment at Gettysburg, when Stuart, Lee's eyes, had arrived two days late. "Pickett has not been the same since the decimation of his division," Stuart said. "He needs to refocus on the enemy, and put the defeat behind him. There are battles still to be won." He paused. "Come, we'll go to General Lee with this news. He needs to know, for several reasons. Come with me, Colonel Mosby, and we'll present our naval heroes."

"Sir, I'm just a major," said Mosby, smiling.

"I'm anticipating, colonel. It's my duty as a cavalryman to anticipate." He grinned through his magnificent beard.

They needed to wait only a few moments before Lee, himself, came to his tent front to welcome them. The courtly man with the silver-white hair inclined his head. "General, Major Mosby, who have you brought me?" He looked at the four naval officers, in their put-together gray tunics, and focused on Rory. "You're the young Irish naval lieutenant. We met at Drewry's Bluff. I've just been reading of your raider exploits in the northern newspapers. A raid on the Brooklyn Yard! Of course, they call it piracy. Well done, young man."

"Thank y' most kindly, general. Permit me to introduce my officers, Walsh, McCafferty and Duffy. General Lee." They all saluted, beaming.

"A pleasure, gentlemen. General, major, how did you come by these heroes?" Lee led them inside his tent.

Stuart told Rory's tale of escape, incarceration, escape again, and schooling in the Mosby academy of guerilla warfare. Lee nodded approvingly at each phase, except at the report of von Klopfenstein's arrests. When Stuart's report concluded, Lee did not respond for a time, visibly processing the information.

At last, he spoke. "Major, congratulations on your zeal and effectiveness, and for safeguarding Lieutenant Dunbrody and his officers. I'm particularly pleased at the recent railway disruption. Lieutenant

Dunbrody, I congratulate you and these fine officers on your successful and daring attacks. But, I apologize for the actions of an officer of my command. I pledge to you that I will personally take appropriate action."

"Thank you, general," said Rory. "Most kind of you, sir."

"Not at all. I'll pen a note to Secretary Mallory assuring him that I'll deal with the question, and send it with you to Richmond. General Stuart, would you be so kind as to provide an escort to the capital for these officers?"

"Yes, general, my pleasure, sir!"

"Then, I must take my leave, gentlemen. Thanks to you all for your service to the nation." They stood, saluted, and left the tent.

Walking away, Rory murmured to his officers, "Sure, and when I meet that man, my knees turn to jelly." The three nodded in empathy. As they stood near the headquarters tent, Rory thanked Stuart and Mosby for their aid. Mosby laughed. "General," he said to Stuart, "I think that after ten days in the saddle, each of these sailors will be glad to get back to sea!"

CHAPTER 22
HANDSOME JACK AND THE DEFENSE OF CHARLESTON
AUGUST 1863

Rory's three-day ride to Richmond with Stuart's troopers in the August heat was uncomfortable, but uneventful. Rory was unable to keep his thoughts very far from Carrie Anne. The late morning of the third day found them at Capitol Square. They thanked Stuart's escort, dismounted, returned the horses to Stuart's men with gratitude bordering on glee, and entered the Mechanics Institute Building, just across the street from Capitol Square, where the Secretary of the Navy had his offices. They waited only moments before navy secretary Stephen Mallory rushed out of his office to greet them. "Gentlemen, come in, come in. You've escaped the clutches of the Union! I am delighted."

Mallory, an enthusiastic man with a round face and great energy, seated them around a conference table in his office. "Lieutenant, do introduce me to these young officers." Rory introduced the three, and Mallory shook the hand of each. "I have read the accounts of our agents, correspondents, and the northern newspapers. With your ships, and Maffitt and Charles Read operating almost simultaneously, the Confederate Navy has struck with impact and severity. Our northern foes are still gnashing their journalistic teeth!" Mallory sat back, a grin of great delight on his face.

"Sir, I should give you this note from General Lee before we go on. He was most helpful in providing for our return, as were General Stuart and Major Mosby." Rory handed the secretary Lee's note, which apologized for von Klopfenstein's actions. Mallory took a moment to read the note. Notes from Marse Robert always took precedence in the Confederacy of 1863. After reading the note twice, Mallory looked up at Rory, his expression serious.

"Our Prussian friend surfaces again, Mr. Dunbrody. I have confidence that Lee will bring this forcibly to Pickett's attention. Rumor here in the capital, which is always with us, has that Lee is less than happy with Pickett's morose behavior since the charge at Gettysburg. But how much a reprimand from Lee will influence a foreign national with no deep connection to this country is another matter. You must have severely bruised von Klopfenstein's self-esteem in Washington Territory so long ago!" Mallory leaned back in his chair. "Well," he exclaimed, "we must put all that behind us, and examine the details of your exploits, so important to us here at the Navy Department. Mr. Dunbrody, if you'd check this list of prizes, I'd be obliged."

Rory looked at the list of prizes from his days on the *Star of the South*, the *Flora*, and the *Belle of Biloxi*, 23 ships worth a total of 2,230,000 dollars. "Sure, and it's more impressive cumulatively than it was individually, Mr. Secretary. It's accurate, to the best of my recollection."

"I declare, young man, it's worth far more than the monetary value, and we have you and your shipmates to thank. The chaos that our raiders have caused, the naval resources diverted from blockade to scour the seas for our few ships, these outcomes of your commerce-raiding have been of inestimable value, both militarily and in raising the spirits of the South!"

Mallory turned toward the door of the conference room. "Cartwright," he called to the clerk in the anteroom, "bring some refreshment, please, for our naval heroes. And then arrange for lodging for them this evening." He swung back to them in his chair. "It's a long ride from northern Virginia, gentlemen. I apologize for not caring for your thirst after such a journey. Now," he said, "I have a request of you all. We desperately need experienced naval officers and men for the defense of Charleston harbor." Mallory looked at each man in turn.

"In April, Commander John Randolph Tucker relieved Commodore Duncan Ingraham as the senior naval officer in

Charleston. The overall defenses are under the command of General Pierre Gustave Toutant Beauregard." Mallory rolled his eyes as he intoned P.G.T. Beauregard's name. "General Beauregard, to give him his due, understands naval matters as much as any army officer I've ever encountered, and, he's aggressive and innovative. Nonetheless, he is a mercurial, arrogant and testy commander. Poor Ingraham and he just couldn't get along. "Handsome Jack" Tucker is the soul of diplomacy, and Beauregard actually holds him in reasonably high regard. But, as an underling, of course." Mallory paused, while his audience marveled at how much he had disclosed of the higher politics of the naval command. "Tucker needs experienced naval officers capable of commanding landing parties, serving aboard every variety of vessel from picket boats to ironclad rams to the new spar torpedo craft. Will you gentlemen volunteer?"

Rory turned to his officers. "Lads, I can vouch for Jack Tucker as a commander. I've served under him twice, and he's the best! Further, the people of Charleston are among the most hospitable in the world. We can't go wrong by volunteering!"

His three subordinates grinned. "Sir," said Walsh, "you know we can't resist a hooley." The others nodded enthusiastically.

"Sir, we're all of a mind," said Rory to the puzzled Mallory. "Being Irish as you must be, with your name, I'm sure you understand."

Mallory looked pleased, and relieved. "Excellent, gentlemen. Now let me apprise you of the tactical situation in Charleston. For the last month, Battery Wagner on Morris Island, at the south of the harbor entrance, has been under assault by the Federals. They threw one of their first Negro regiments at us two weeks ago, the 54th Massachusetts. Their monitors can bombard the battery from the sea, and they are out of range of our naval guns. Moreover, the shoals extending into the harbor from Morris Island preclude our small ironclads, the *Chicora* and the *Palmetto State*, from firing on the Union regiments attacking the battery."

He sighed, resignedly. "We need small boat commanders to take fresh troops into the battery, and take off the exhausted defenders, all in the dark. That, and serving as officers aboard *Palmetto State* and *Chicora*, will be your first duties."

Rory and the others took all this in, nodding with determination.

"Splendid," said Mallory. "We'll arrange for two days of rest for you here in Richmond, not a particularly inviting city in these times, and then send you south. May I have a word with Mr. Dunbrody, gentlemen?"

As Rory's officers rose to give Mallory a private word with him, Rory said, "sir, before they leave, can you tell us of word from *Star of the South*, or from our crew aboard *Belle of Biloxi?*"

"Of course, I was remiss in not telling you all. The good news first. To my knowledge, none of the *Belle's* crew has been captured, and a number have returned to Richmond. Several of those I've already sent to Commander Turner in Charleston. The ones who had prize money coming from the adjudication of the prize courts have received theirs."

"And the bad news, sir?"

"The *Star* was seized by a Union cruiser while she was in a neutral Brazilian harbor. Captain Canby was of course relying on his neutral status and took no precautions against the seizure. The Brazilians are outraged, of course, and the Yankees are making polite noises about a court martial for their commander, but they aren't giving *Star of the South* back. It's a *fait accompli*. We are negotiating for exchange of prisoners."

"Any casualties, sir?"

"Just a few bumps and bruises. It was a complete surprise. And Lincoln calls us pirates!"

"Thank you, Mr. Secretary," said Walsh. "We'll wait in the anteroom."

"Mr. Dunbrody," said Mallory when the others had left, "I have some more good news for you. President Davis has exercised his authority to make dual army-navy commission appointments, and has made you a major of cavalry, to accompany your navy rank of lieutenant, or, when called for, lieutenant-commanding. Congratulations!"

"Thank you, Mr. Secretary. Whatever do you suppose prompted the president to do that? Aside from my recent visit with Mosby, I haven't ridden since the Chesapeake raids in '62 with Taylor Wood."

"I believe that's the answer, 'major,'" said Mallory with a smile. "John Taylor Wood was made colonel of cavalry last January because of those Chesapeake raids, where he learned how useful joint army-navy commands would be for land-sea operations. I happen to know, that under the president's auspices, he is planning a third Chesapeake raid this month. He's tried to keep the raid secret from this department, and everyone else, for fear of the enemy learning of the attacks. Of course, it hasn't worked, but I haven't complained. He is the president's nephew, after all. And I know he's advised the president to consider a raid this winter to recapture New Berne. I think that's what prompted your promotion. Because of your record with him, and your home in New Berne, it's my guess he wants you on that raid, and able to command army troops as well as naval forces."

"By all that's holy, sir, that's a lot to digest in one meal. D' ye suppose he's goin' to let me in on his plan, at some point?" Rory softened his sarcasm with a smile.

"I just know that while you're under Commander Tucker's command in Charleston, you should be prepared to move quickly to North Carolina, if ordered. That's my advice, my boy. As you now have an army commission, you may find a general officer you can turn to in Charleston, one less volatile than Beauregard. Brigadier General Clyde Cherberg has recently been assigned by Davis as Beauregard's second in command. He has a reputation for tact and inter-service cooperation."

"Aye, aye, sir. I appreciate you sharing all this with me, sir. It makes it easier to prepare the men for action. These three officers have begun their riding in the last weeks. I think I'll have them continue, just in case."

"Very prudent of you, Mr. Dunbrody. I'm sure you want to be on your way, and no doubt pay a visit to the Farwells on Church Hill."

"Just what I had in mind, sir. By your leave." Rory and his officers left the navy department for their temporary hotel quarters. Rory could not stop thinking of Carrie Anne, so close by at the Farwell house, her aunt and uncle's. He made sure his officers were settled in and then excused himself for the evening. There were no longer horse-drawn taxis available in the capital. Horses were reserved now for the cavalry, and townspeople made their way on foot, in all but the most unusual cases. Rory began the walk to nearby Church Hill, walking through Capitol Square and then across town to the hill toward the east. Forty minutes later, he stood on the portico of the Farwell's Federal-style mansion just off Broad Street, and rang the door pull. "Cicero!" he exclaimed as the Farwell's black coachman answered the door. "Grand to see you, Cicero! Sure, and they've expanded the range of your duties, haven't they, now?"

"Mistah Dunbrody, welcome back! Yas, suh, we all be doing more than we used to, 'cause of de war. The coach house is now a conbalescent hall for de wounded soldiers. So, I help wid de butlin', most times."

"Cicero, I apologize for just dropping in, but I've just escaped from the North. Is Miss Eastman at home?"

"You just come on in, suh, and I'll tell folks you be here. Ever'one be wantin' to see you, I'm sure!" Cicero ushered him into the sitting room, and disappeared into the depths of the mansion.

Aunt Harriet Farwell was the first of the household to appear, sweeping into the room, and clasping both of Rory's hands with her own. "Mr. Dunbrody, Rory, I am so relieved to see you, and all in one piece! Carrie Anne, my sister, and Natalie will be down directly. Mr. Farwell is away on business, but we expect him home this evening. He'll be delighted to know you've returned. You must tell us all your adventures, but do wait, so you only have to tell the story once! Please, be seated."

Sure, she's a most gracious woman, is Carrie Anne's aunt, Rory thought. Carrie Anne, her mother, her cousin Natalie, and Carrie Anne's brother Beau soon joined them in the sitting room. Cicero and several other servants hovered just down the halls from the doorways into the room. Rory had been very popular with the family and staff when last he had visited, in November of 1862. Carrie Anne rushed to him, and they embraced and kissed chastely, in front of so many family members. Her eyes conveyed passion far in excess of her embrace. "Oh, my dear, I've been so wondering what's happened since your last letter from England."

"Portsmouth was the last port we touched where I could mail a letter, love."

"Now," said Aunt Harriet, taking charge in her own home, "we must hear how you came here, and all your battles since last winter!"

"Aye, aye, Aunt Harriet," Rory replied, to much laughter throughout the room. "Well, now, Commander Bulloch put me to work finding a ship to buy and bring out of England, me not bein' readily recognizable to the Union spies, on account of me bein' just another Paddy, d' ye see? And it worked! Away we went to Madeira, off Africa, and commissioned *Star of the South,* a fine ship and crew, to boot, and then the captain gave me command of a prize, the brig *Flora,* and then I switched to another prize, the *Peter Stuyvesant,* which steamer I renamed *Belle of Biloxi,* and we took 23 prizes, altogether." Rory paused, out of breath, and looked about him at his audience. Astonished looks greeted him.

"My stars," said Aunt Harriet, "you've had two more commands!"

"Aunt Harriet, y've become an astute observer of naval affairs! And I'm sure you've noticed I've salted a bit of prize money by, so as to strengthen me suit for the hand of your lovely niece!" More laughter ensued. Carrie Anne winked at Rory. "So then, I decided to attack New York City, and did so with some explosive results, so t' speak, but, alas, I was captured with three of my officers, but we escaped in the confusion of the Draft Riots, and crossed the Potomac to be rescued by my old friend Jack Mosby, who turned us into cavalrymen, and then General Lee and Secretary Mallory said I should come visit the Farwell House!"

"I declare, Rory Cormac Dunbrody, that's a whirlwind tour if I ever heard one. I suspect you left some details out!" Carrie Anne raised her eyebrows.

"Nothin' of importance, Carrie, darlin'," Rory replied, "but you can interrogate me at your leisure, as if I could stop you."

"We have set a place for you at dinner, Rory, and I'm sure Mr. Farwell will want to hear more details, as will we. Meantime, I suspect Carrie Anne and Natalie will want to show you the grounds and the coach house, and demonstrate how we do our little bit for the war effort."

"That's most kind of you, Mrs. Farwell. I look forward to catching up with you all. I'd enjoy a pre-prandial tour, t' be sure."

Carrie Anne and Rory toured the house, much changed in the ten months he'd been away. Cousin Natalie was her usual droll self, as she assumed the chaperone's role thrust upon her by her mother and the mores of the time. "Now you two walk on ahead, and I'll follow," said Natalie, "desperately trying to adjust to my frequent difficulties with sight and hearing."

Many rooms in the house were taken up with bandage and hospital supply storage. Women volunteered to wrap bandages in one of the large bedrooms several days a week. The coach house had been transformed into a bunkhouse and common room for a number of wounded Confederate soldiers recovering from their wounds.

"Many families in town are doing what we're doing here, Rory. The need is so great, after Gettysburg." Carrie Anne frowned, and then continued, her tone stern. "Then we have those ladies who moved here from Washington when Virginia seceded, not wishing to stay in the north, who recently found the living conditions here unsuitable for their taste. 'Too many wounded.' 'Not enough gaiety.' 'Impossible to entertain with the food shortages.' Do you know they've all moved back to Washington! My stars!" Carrie Anne tossed her head, indignantly.

"Oh, my dear Carrie, there are those whose lives are entwined with the trivial, and then there are people like you, God bless you and the Saints preserve you." Rory took her hand in his as they walked through the Farwell's formal garden. "The day after tomorrow, love, to change the subject to selfish concerns, I must leave for my new duties in Charleston."

"My goodness, aren't they going to give you more time to recover, after all you've been through?"

"Sure, my dear, there's a war on, as you've said, yourself. My old commander, Jack Tucker, is in dire need of officers and men in Charleston. I must go, as much as I'd rather bide here with you." He smiled through a mist of tears, and noticed she was doing the same. "Here's a thought, love. Surely the Farwells or the Eastmans have friends in Charleston, the Heart of the Confederacy! You and the ever-faithful, sometimes-watchful Natalie could come visit. By all accounts, 't is a charmin' city."

His heart melted as she smiled a devilish smile. "What a grand idea, as you might say, lieutenant."

"And haven't I forgotten to tell you what I just learned! President Davis has made me a major of cavalry, along with my naval commission. I can command army troops, now, when we have sea-land attacks. 'T is a great honor, and no doubt the work of Taylor Wood, fine lad he is!"

"Oh, Rory, congratulations! I'm so proud that the president thinks so much of you. You see, I was right! You left out quite a bit in your little summary. You can fill us all in at dinner."

Rory returned to his hotel, exhausted yet exhilarated from his visit. *Sure, I am never so comfortable and loved as when I'm with that woman and her family,* he reflected.

At dinner that evening, Carrie Anne raised the question of visiting Charleston. Aunt Harriet smiled and nodded imperceptibly at her sister, Carrie Anne's mother, and at her husband Fred. *Sure, Carrie Anne's already broached the idea, and they've had a family sit-down about it,* thought Rory. *This family's way ahead of me in the future–planning department.*

"We have some dear friends in Charleston, Rory," said Uncle Fred. "We're thinking of sending Natalie and Carrie Anne down to the Mills for a visit, after you're settled in your new station. They live on Meeting Street, not far from the harbor."

"That would brighten the city considerable, to be sure," replied Rory with a grin. After dinner, Uncle Fred took Rory aside.

"I know it's hard to think of the mundane, such as investments, in the midst of this war, but I'd like to offer some advice on investing your newly-received prize money."

"Sure, I'm always grateful for suggestions on money from a man of your experience, sir."

"You might wish to consider moving a substantial portion of your funds to a British bank in the Caribbean, or Bermuda. After our retreat from Gettysburg, I don't think we can expect substantial help from Europe. The North has too many resources for us to expect an outright victory. And if the cause is eventually lost, fortunes in Confederate money will be worthless." Uncle Fred sighed, and leaned back in his chair. "While remaining loyal to our country, it's important for us to maintain loyalty to our families and their interests, too."

It's the truth you're talkin', Mr. Farwell. Would you have an idea of a safe bank for several thousand dollars, now? You bein' an export-import merchant, as y' are?"

"I'd be happy to arrange an exchange to British pounds and a deposit in a Bermuda bank well known to me, my boy. You and Carrie Anne will have needs that outlast the duration of this war, for certain!"

Rory left the Farwells with a sense of confidence in his future he'd not experienced before. *D'ye suppose I'm growin' up, at last?* he wondered.

The next morning, a navy department clerk brought the accumulated mail for the four officers. Rory sorted through his letters of the last six months. *Timothy writes he's asked for transfer to the New Berne area to be closer to Da and Siobhan. Here's one from Tobias, sent through Uncle Liam, saying he's chasing raiders and hoping it's not me. Oh! One from Da and Siobhan, telling me all about buildin' ships in a cornfield. I'll make sure I see them on my way to Charleston! And a letter each from my uncles, tellin' me how grand a visit it was in January.*

Rory carefully destroyed Tobias' letter, and set about packing. He would leave a day earlier than his officers, and make a stop in Weldon where his father Patrick would meet him to take him for an overnight visit to Scotland Neck, near Edwards Ferry, North Carolina. Then, he'd go on south and take the railroad to Charleston.

Patrick Dunbrody met his son, Rory, in Weldon, as was his custom, with a four-oared wherry to carry them down the Roanoke River to Scotland Neck. Their route took them by Peter Smith's cornfield at Edward's Ferry, transformed into a shipyard where the CSS *Albemarle*, ironclad ram, had been laid down the previous April.

As they swept slowly around the bend above the cornfield, Rory glanced at the bank, and stared. "Da, the ram is gone! You've launched her!"

"The first of July, son. She banged up a rib or two as she went into the river, so we've towed her up to Halifax for repairs. Gil Elliot is still rounding up iron and trying to expedite the rolling at Tredegar Works in Richmond, so we've quite a bit of time before she's commissioned, but at least she left the cornfield!"

"When we went past Halifax, I didn't see her!"

"Ach, she's hauled out and in a shed. They'll repair her and get her in the river, and put the plates on when they come from Richmond."

"What are y'doin' now, at Edward's Ferry?"

"We're readyin' for another ram, to lay down next year. Here we are at the road to Scotland Neck. Your sister will be eager to see you!" After a short horse ride, they arrived at the rented Dunbrody bungalow.

The Dunbrody home in Union-occupied New Berne was being lived in by Patrick's shipyard foreman, who was continuing to operate the shipyard in hopes that war's end would restore normal ship construction operations for the Dunbrody family and their employees.

Rory's sister Siobhan rushed out to greet them. "Bless you, brother, you're still in one piece!"

"Well, not for lack of the Yankees' tryin', sister dear. They've had their chances."

"And isn't it a wonderful day, and all, with you here and a letter from Tim just come that his transfer to New Berne and the Neuse has been approved!"

"He'll be here, then in North Carolina?" Rory's shock was tinged with apprehension, as he realized that John Taylor Wood's plan for a Neuse attack could bring him face to face with Tim in battle. *I must not mention the prospect,* thought Rory, *for they would worry the more and might be tempted to talk about it, and the plan compromised as a result.*

"Oh, aye," Siobhan replied, "he's been assigned to the 17th Massachusetts."

"We hope he'll be able to look in at the New Berne properties, from time to time, just to be sure there'll be something left at the end of the war." Patrick winked at his younger son. "Up north of Plymouth, folks are havin' the divil of a time with the 'Buffaloes,' groups of brigands the Yankees have put into uniform to terrorize northeast North Carolina. It's already full of Union sympathizers. It wouldn't hurt to have a Union officer keepin' an eye on our property."

"Just be careful, Da. And if you need any money, I've come by the way of a bit of prize money, for emergencies, like."

"You're kind to offer, son. We're doin' all right, so far, but it's nice to know there's somethin' in reserve. Here's a little toast to the Dunbrody family. May our tribe increase!"

Two days later, Rory arrived in Charleston, and made his way to the CSS *Indian Chief,* CSN receiving ship and headquarters of John Randolph Tucker, Commodore, commanding the Charleston Squadron afloat. "Mr. Dunbrody! Welcome to Charleston," Tucker exclaimed as Rory was ushered into his cabin. "Please take a seat. I'm delighted to have you back in my squadron. I understand you're bringing some officers from your most recent command!"

"Yes, commodore, we should have an engineer, a bo'sun and a master's mate here within days."

"That's welcome news, lieutenant. We've already profited from ten of your crew from *Belle of Biloxi*. Let me bring you up to date on why we need officers and seamen so desperately here in Charleston. We must maintain control of Morris Island, south of the harbor, in order to keep the main channel open for blockade runners. A month ago, the Yankees began an all-out attack. We threw them back in their frontal assault on Battery Wagner, and now they've settled in to siege and bombardment. The harbor between Fort Sumter and Morris is too shallow for us to take our rams, *Chicora* and *Palmetto State*, close enough to give fire support to Battery Wagner and our other positions. They, on the other hand, can bring their monitors up to the ocean shoreline and give heavy cannon support to their attacking infantry."

"Our defenders must be exhausted, sir, what with the constant bombardment and attack, and all."

"Precisely, lieutenant! And that has led General Beauregard to give us one more mission, in addition to the two we're already carrying out. Every third night, we must bring in replacements for the infantry and artillerymen on Morris Island, and take off the exhausted men who have been in combat the previous three days. All by small boat, under oars. It leaves me short of men for our other duties: defending Sumter and the rest of the harbor from the Yankee squadron, and attacking them with our newest weapon, spar torpedoes. You can see why I'm so glad to have you and the others from *Belle of Biloxi*!"

"Sure, and I can, commodore. Tell me about the spar torpedoes."

Tucker settled back in his chair. "It's quite a story, Mr. Dunbrody. General Beauregard is a very imaginative commander. He also appreciates the value of seaborne attack. Several months ago we began talking about attacking the blockade squadron's close-in ships with a torpedo ram. First we tried rowing boats with spar torpedoes mounted at the bow. That didn't work. Too slow! Then, one of Beauregard's engineer captains, Francis Lee, found an old gunboat hull and put a spar torpedo at her bow. The engine's undependable, and so underpowered we can't armor the gunboat, but in the dark, we're going to try for an attack, in about ten days. It's an Army venture, so we've agreed to a volunteer blockade-runner captain, James Carlin, to command. We've christened her the *Torch*."

"So this is an 'all-or-nothing' try, sir?"

"No, no, it's just the first of several! A group of investors, inventors, and Army Engineer Bureau officers have designed and built a submarine! They started in New Orleans, and moved to Mobile when we lost New Orleans to the Yankees. You know Commander Mathew Fontaine Maury, do you not?"

"Yes, sir, from my duty in England, under Commander Bulloch."

"His nephew, Dabney Maury, is commanding general at Mobile Bay, and very supportive of these submersibles. Unfortunately, they've already sunk two while testing, the *Pioneer* and *American Diver*. The third is still operating, thank Heavens! She sank a barge in a test recently and so impressed Admiral Buchanan in Mobile that he wrote to me to urge Beauregard to use it here. The general is all excited about it and agreed. It's scheduled to arrive tomorrow by rail, with its investors and inventors as part of the crew. One of them is from the sewing machine family, the Singers."

"It sounds as if you've got your hands full, sir."

"That's not the whole of it, lieutenant. Captain Lee also teamed up with two Charleston civilians to design and build a semi-submersible they call the *David*. Theodore Stoney put up the money and Dr. St. Julian Ravenel designed her. She's 54 feet long with a six-foot beam, powered by a small boiler and steam engine. She's built to ballast so as to lower her to only inches of freeboard, except for the stack, of course. She carries a 20-foot spar torpedo extending from her bow, and should be ready for action this fall. As you can see, there is a lot of talent and imagination here in Charleston."

"Please tell me where I fit in, sir."

I'd like you to assume two duties, Mr. Dunbrody. The first is liaison officer to General Beauregard. It's a good fit for your Celtic charm." Tucker laughed at his own humor. "You'll be working directly with Beauregard's chief of staff, Brigadier General Clyde Cherberg. You two should hit it off well. He's pleasant, tactful, and energetic. He manages to smooth Beauregard's rough edges, and believe me, the major general has them. Your new dual appointment to army major makes you even more qualified for this work."

"Yes, sir, I heard about the Beauregard-Cherberg team from Secretary Mallory. What's the second duty, sir?"

"Initially, I'm assigning you as second lieutenant aboard *Chicora*. You served with her commander, Rochelle, in the James River Squadron. I suspect you'll be first lieutenant before long. These torpedo boats will demand officers from both my gunboats. Your first duty will be in command of a squadron of ship's boats transporting the Army to and from Morris."

"Aye, aye, sir. Do the squadron officers bunk here aboard *Indian Chief?*"

"They do, lieutenant. The interiors of our ironclads are like the insides of steam boilers. No one could actually sleep aboard. It's all we can do to fight aboard them. And Dunbrody, I have no illusions about how long I'll be able to keep you in this command. Mallory will pluck you away for some new adventure soon, without a doubt. But I'm pleased that you're here, as I said."

"Likewise, commodore."

"I'm sure you'll want to renew your acquaintance with Glendenning and Ormsby, your old shipmates. They should be aboard this evening."

"I'll make a point to do so, sir."

"Good! Get settled, then, and tomorrow I'll introduce you to the generals and the squadron officers you've not met."

"Aye, aye, sir. Good afternoon, sir."

Rory came to attention, and left the cabin. *What a tumultuous station this will be,* he thought. *I think I'd rather be at sea, thank you very much!* That evening, Rory sat in the *Indian Chief's* wardroom, yarning with his friends and former officers from his first command, the armed tug *Old Dominion*. He had parted from Archibald Ormsby when they were both aboard *Star of the South*. Quentin Glendenning, *Old Dominion's* first lieutenant, had been assigned to Charleston after the battle of Drewry's Bluff.

"What a fine job you did, Archie, bringing *Starry Night* in through the blockade!" Rory beamed at Ormsby, who had begun as a green midshipman under Rory's command, and now was a lieutenant with command experience.

"And he's been lording it over me, in his quiet way, ever since, as I've yet to have my own command!" Glendenning said, affectionately teasing his former shipmate.

"Just the luck of the draw, Quentin, nothing more," replied Ormsby. "We'll each have lots more action while on this station!"

"How are your parents, Archie?" Rory asked. The senior Ormsbys were long-time Charleston residents.

"Like many downtown residents, they've moved beyond Calhoun Street, Rory. The 1861 fire destroyed hundreds of homes close to the harbor, and the threat of Yankee bombardment is causing even more folks to relocate in the northern part of the city. We'll give you a tour and you'll see the devastation, yourself."

"That doesn't bode well for a visit from Carrie Anne. The Farwells had friends on Meeting Street, but if it's as you say, they may be gone."

"I'm doubtful I'd ask my sweetheart to visit Charleston at this turn of its history, Rory," said Archie. "You'll have to see, and make your own judgment. Has the commodore told you of your duties yet?"

"I'm to be second of the *Chicora*, and lend a hand with the relief and supply of our infantry and artillery on Morris Island, I'm also to be liaison with General Beauregard's staff."

"We'll be seeing a lot of each other, then, Rory," said Glendenning. "Archie and I are both assigned to the *Palmetto State*, and we are commanding relief flotillas every third night. Once a week, we go ashore with our sailors and marines and move against the enemy's pickets on Morris."

"Here's luck to us then," said Rory, and raised his glass.

CHAPTER 23
RORY AND THE SUBMARINE SERVICE
AUGUST - DECEMBER 1863

The next few days were filled with action and encounters for Rory. He was at the railroad yard the next morning, when "Whitney's submarine boat," soon to become the CSS *Hunley* after another one of its investor-designers, was unloaded from two flatcars. Workmen removed the tarpaulins that covered the 32-foot long craft also known as the "fish boat," which had been constructed from an augmented boiler.

She was tapered on both ends, with a propeller at the stern turned by eight of the nine-man crew operating a crank inside the five-foot-wide craft. They entered through two hatches, and the boat submerged by flooding ballast tanks. Pumps emptied the tanks in order to surface again. Fins extended on either side to control depth. The onlookers cheered as the craft was trucked to the harbor at a dock near the *Indian Chief.* Later that day, Rory met with generals Beauregard and Cherberg at Charleston Army headquarters.

"You saw the submarine boat come in today, lieutenant?" asked Beauregard.

"Sure and I did, general, and it's a most curious craft, it is. I'm more than ever convinced that I'm a surface sailor."

"Well, surface you may be, suh, but as you're an experienced naval officer and a major of cavalry as well, I'm asking you to join General Cherberg in devisin' an attack plan for this boat and our other torpedo vessels." Beauregard smiled and awarded Rory a look of certitude.

"Aye, aye, general," Rory replied. "I'll be eager to help General

Cherberg confound the Yankees."

"The first thing we should do, major," said Cherberg, "is get you together with our Captain Lee, and examine the *Torch*."

"Whenever it is convenient for you, general," Rory replied. Over the next several days, Cherberg and Rory met with the designers of the *Torch*, and the Charleston designers of the *David*.

They first met with James Carlin, a veteran blockade runner, and Captain Francis D. Lee, who had designed the *Torch*, a steam torpedo ram assembled from the hull of an incomplete gunboat, the engine of which was too underpowered to move the vessel if it were armored as in Lee's original plans. Lee detailed the armament. "We've mounted a torpedo at the end of a fourteen-foot spar," he explained. To compensate for the lack of power, Captain Carlin will pass Sumter on the last of the ebb tide, sweep out to our target, the USS *New Ironsides,* run the spar under her hull, detonate it, and return on the flood tide."

"Ah intend to pick up a squad of sharpshooters at Fort Sumter," added Carlin, "to keep the crew of the *New Ironsides* from disruptin' the delicate business of plantin' the charge."

Rory glanced at Cherberg, seated next to him at the table, and saw his look of skepticism. "Major," said the general to Rory, "have you any comment?"

"Sir, I admire the captain's courage and resolve, particularly as the success of his plan hinges on the continuing operation of a second-hand engine."

"I share your apprehension, major, but as these are willing volunteers, we'll do all in our power to give them the support they need."

Their next meeting took them 35 miles up the Santee River to the site where the *David* was under construction. Ravenel and Stoney gave them a quick tour of the blue-gray semi-submersible with the tapered ends. "We'll be bringing her down into the city for trials within the week, gentlemen," said Dr. Ravenel. "We look forward to joining Captain Lee, our co-designer, and getting the *David* into action!"

"It can't happen too soon for General Beauregard, doctor," Cherberg replied.

The next night was Rory's initiation into the nighttime relief of the Morris Island defenders. Men from two Confederate regiments were loaded into ship's boats manned by the sailors of Tucker's squadron. They were towed under a new moon to the shores of Morris Island by several steam launches. Then they silently cast off their tows, and rowed with muffled oarlocks to the sands of the island beach. Rory steered a cutter from the *Chicora,* with Glendenning in a boat from the *Palmetto State* rowing alongside. Their oars were so close that the oarsmen had to time their strokes to avoid the clatter of blade-on-blade. Rory strained his eyes through the gloom. To his left, he saw a cluster of dark figures, distinguishable against the lighter hue of the sand. "Quentin," he whispered hoarsely, "there they are, two points to port."

"I see them, Rory! Easy, now, men. Half power. Way enough." The boats glided gently on to the sand of the beach.

"Get your men over the side, lieutenant, if you please," said Rory to the army officer commanding the twenty men in his cutter. "Quietly, please." As the infantry eased over the gunwales, Rory could hear unavoidable "clinks" and "clanks" of rifles hitting canteens and bayonets. The troops being relieved surged forward as their relief disappeared inland through the dunes in back of the beach. The "crump" of mortars being fired startled the Confederates as they loaded the weary island garrison.

"Rory, the Yankees have tumbled to us," called Glendenning. "Load as quick as you can."

"Twenty men here, please!" Rory called in his best half-gale roar to the oncoming troops. *No need for silence now,* thought Rory as a round from a Union mortar exploded just above the surface of the harbor between his boat and Quentin's. The two boats soon had their 20 men apiece on board, as did five boats to either side of them. Two hundred and forty Rebel infantry were drawn away from shore by the flotilla of squadron boats, with only a few casualties. One of those was Quentin Glendenning.

"Mr. Dunbrody, sir," called the midshipman in the *Palmetto State's* cutter as they pulled toward the steam launches waiting to tow them past Fort Sumter, "Mr. Glendenning took a shrapnel shard in the neck and he's bleeding, sir."

"Put a compress on it, mister, and pull for the first steam

launch!" Rory shouted across the water. When they reached the first
steam launch, Rory cried to the coxswain, "Get Mr. Glendenning back to
the *Chicora's* surgeon. *Chicora's* abeam of the Fort. Never mind the other
boats!"

Rory directed the steam launch towing his cutter to lay alongside
Chicora. Rory climbed aboard through an open gun port and went
directly below to the surgeon in the cockpit. It was below the waterline in
the iron craft, the dank, rust-colored bulkheads beaded with condensation,
and not a breath of air stirring. Rory mopped his brow. "How is
Glendenning, surgeon?" He asked.

"I'm sorry, lieutenant," the surgeon responded, "I did all I could
but he was gone just after he reached us. The shrapnel severed his artery
and he bled to death."

Rory pulled back the sheet covering Glendenning's face. "He
was a fine officer, doctor." Rory's voice broke. "He could admit when
he was wrong, and he was as brave as anyone. Thank you for all you did,
doctor. I'd best report to Commodore Tucker."

Rory walked slowly from the cockpit, the iron stairs of the
companionway echoing with his footsteps and the memories of Quentin
Glendenning, his first lieutenant aboard *Old Dominion,* initially disdainful
and insubordinate, then, after experiencing and acknowledging Rory's
courage and leadership in battle, becoming the firmest of friends and
comrades. "God bless you, Quentin!" Rory sobbed, aloud.

Tucker and Lieutenant Rochelle were in the *Chicora's* pilothouse.
"I'm saddened as you are, lieutenant," said Tucker. "You should return to
Indian Chief and get some sleep."

In the ensuing week, Rory needed every bit of sleep he could
accumulate. A veritable hurricane of activity overwhelmed the Charleston
Squadron. On August 17, under the command of Union General Quincy
Adams Gillmore, the guns of the fleet and the army mounted on Morris
Island began a week-long shelling of Fort Sumter. The fort was soon
reduced to rubble, and artillery could no longer be mounted there. Rory
joined the men of the squadron in transferring the battery from Sumter
to Fort Moultrie and other batteries on Sullivan's Island to the north of
the harbor. Walsh, McCafferty and Duffy arrived during the shelling and

immediately joined in the transfer operation.

Beauregard, Cherberg, Tucker and Rory met to devise a new defense strategy for Sumter. They decided they could hold the fort against Union Marine and infantry attack by stationing riflemen in the bombproof cellars of the fort, ready to man the jumbled remains of the parapets at the first sign of a Union landing. *Chicora* and *Palmetto State* would station themselves each night close to the fort, to assist in repelling an attack. When the new flagship *Charleston* was commissioned, she would join them. *Another intrusion into sleep already in short supply,* thought an exhausted Rory. *I'm going to be one tired Irishman!* He didn't know the half of it.

James Carlin and the *Torch* attacked the USS *New Ironsides* twice during the next three nights. Rory, as submarine and torpedo craft liaison, was up each night waiting for results. A disgusted Carlin reported at four in the morning after the second attack. "I caught the ebb tide, just as we'd planned," said Carlin, sinking disconsolately into his chair in the quiet wardroom of the *Indian Chief.* "We ran down to the Yankee as she was anchored in the channel east of Morris Island. I was abeam of her. She was to port. I put the helm hard over and charged, or limped, down to her. The tide swung her away from us and our engine was insufficient to compensate. We ended up fouled in her anchor cable, just as our engine quit. They gave the alarm, and her crew began peppering us with musket and small arms fire. After five minutes, we got our engine restarted and made it back to the harbor. *Torch* is just not fit for combat!"

"I'm inclined to agree, captain," said Rory. "I'll pass the word to General Beauregard. Congratulations on escaping a dangerous situation!"

The next day, Horace Hunley arrived from Mobile, and joined the submarine he had designed with his fellow designers Whitney, Watson and McClintock as crew at a base in a cove behind Fort Moultrie on Sullivan's Island. Test runs began immediately.

Beauregard had other distractions to deal with. General Gillmore announced he would follow his reduction of Fort Sumter with bombardment of the city itself, and its civilian population. Beauregard was outraged. Gillmore paid no attention to Beauregard's strongly worded response, and opened fire from his 200-pounder Parrott gun, the "Swamp

Angel," mounted in a battery on Morris Island. Shells began raining on the lower city, driving many more residents north of Calhoun Street. Although the Parrott exploded after a day of firing, the threat of resumed bombardment hung over the city like a cloud.

By the end of the week, the submarine strategy group was called to meet once more, by a perplexed P.G.T. Beauregard. "Gentlemen, our own General Clingman, in command at Sullivan's Island, is concerned that Mr. McClintock may be too timid to command our submersible with any effect. They've been out to attack five times, and have yet to close with the enemy. Clingman says they've cited tide, wind, and weather. He suggests a change in command, and I'm inclined to agree. We must keep the Yankees off balance. Commodore, do you have an officer who might be active in command?"

"Yes, general, I can think of two I'd recommend. Lieutenants Payne and Hasker of the *Chicora* have already asked about the possibility of assignment. Payne is eager to the point of recklessness, at times. It seems to me we'd see some results with him in command."

Cherberg cleared his throat, and evoked a glance from Beauregard. "Have you something to offer, general?"

"Yes, general," said Cherberg. "It might smooth any ruffled feathers among the designers if we brought the boat into the Navy, and named it for one of them, say, the 'Hunley'."

"A very diplomatic idea, Clyde!" Bearegard smiled. "Cut the orders please, if the commodore has no objections to adding to his squadron."

"A good idea, sir," said Tucker. "As you know, I'm commissioning a new and bigger flagship, the ironclad *Charleston*, this week. I believe I'll ask Dunbrody here to be lieutenant commanding of *Charleston*, and move Ormsby and Walsh to replace Payne and Hasker aboard *Chicora*." Rory sat in stunned silence. It was news to him, but welcome news, indeed.

I wonder if he decided that on the spot, or if he just wanted to surprise me? Rory looked at Tucker for a sign, but could see nothing on the commodore's face that answered his questions. *Well, now,* thought Rory, *it just doesn't matter. I've my fourth command, and that's a fact! I'll have to dig*

*out the "bonnie green flag and the harp without the crown," and find a place
to fly it aboard Charleston!*

Four days later, the "fish boat" was officially christened CSS
Hunley, with Lieutenant Payne in command. Forty-eight hours later,
the *Hunley* sank, drowning five of its crew after a training dive at Fort
Johnson, on James Island. Payne inadvertently stepped on a dive fin
as the boat was underway, and she submerged with her hatches open.
Payne, Hasker and two crewmen managed to escape through the hatches.
Cherberg and Rory met the day after the sinking.

"Sure, and it's not an auspicious beginnin' for our submersible,
general," said Rory with a sigh.

"No, major, but General Beauregard takes solace in the fact that
this was an error of operation, not of design. He believes the *Hunley* can
still be an effective weapon. What are the arrangements for raising the
boat?"

"Horace Hunley will oversee the salvage, sir," said Rory. "We
had divers down yesterday afternoon. We'll have to tunnel through soft
mud under her keel to get chains round her for a derrick to raise her. And
you should be aware, sir, Mr. Hunley told me he intends to ask General
Beauregard to return her to his charge, sir. He thinks the navy crew
largely incompetent, sir."

"I'll pass that on, major."

The ten days it took to raise the *Hunley* were strenuous for
Rory. He assumed his new command, the *Charleston*, Tucker's new
flagship, longer than *Chicora* and mounting six guns. On September 6,
the Rebels evacuated Morris Island. General Beauregard realized they
could no longer hold Battery Wagner against federal siege. On September
7, Admiral Dahlgren, commanding the Union forces, demanded the
surrender of Fort Sumter, now defended by 300 riflemen, the great
guns having been removed. The Rebel command group met at army
headquarters in response to the demand.

"I'm going to tell them they can have Sumter when they can take
it, gentlemen," said Beauregard with a laugh. "They don't realize we have
their signal book from the wreck of the *Keokuk,* and that we know they're
planning to attack tomorrow night!" The ironclad USS *Keokuk* had been

sunk in Charleston harbor during Du Pont's attack on Sumter in April. "Are we ready for them, commodore?"

"Aye, aye, general, we'll have all three ironclads off the fort and ready to fire on their boats with grapeshot and canister as they approach."

"Excellent, commodore. This will be small consolation for having to give up Morris Island, effectively removing Charleston as a port open to blockade runners, but at least we'll retain the symbol of southern freedom in Fort Sumter!"

In the darkness after midnight on September 9, 1863 the screw tug *Dandelion* of Dahlgren's command towed boats loaded with 500 sailors and marines to a point 400 yards from Fort Sumter. The boats then rowed silently toward Fort Sumter in three waves. As the first landed, it was greeted by a hail of musket fire from the infantry of the garrison, who had been waiting. *Charleston, Palmetto State* and *Chicora* steamed out from behind the fort and drove off the second and third waves of Union boats, which were also under fire from Confederate batteries on Sullivan's Island. The ironclads then turned their guns on the Federals ashore at the fort. "Grape and canister, men! Pour it into them," Rory called to his crew aboard *Charleston*. Boatswain McCafferty stood beside Rory in the *Charleston's* pilothouse with a night glass in his hand.

"Sir, I see white flags on the beach. They're surrendering!"

"Cease fire," cried Rory. Union forces lost 130 killed, wounded, and captured that night, and Sumter remained in Confederate hands.

The nights on patrol around Fort Sumter and the days of fitful sleep while commanding the *Charleston* left Rory with a feeling of ennui. "Sure, I'm glad to have my own command again, Archie, but night after night to sail her a mile in each direction, and then ease around in the dark off the fort with the steam up 'til dawn, its got me totterin' about the barky in a most *downie* state, it does, altogether with Quentin's dyin' and all." Rory said to Ormsby at the *Indian Chief's* wardroom table one humid and drowsy afternoon.

"'*Downie*' meaning?" asked Ormsby.

"Och, wretched, miserable," Rory responded. "I'm not fit t' be with meself!"

Rory brought a proposal to the submarine strategy group toward the end of September. Addressing Beauregard, he said, "Sir, I suggest we turn the *David* loose against our old target, the *New Ironsides*. Captain Lee and our two civilian designers tell me she's ready for action. I'd like to ask for the commodore's torpedo specialist aboard *Chicora*, Lieutenant Glassell, to command. Sure, and he's a fine officer, sir, and knows his way around spar torpedoes, he does! And he's told me he's eager for the challenge. And I'd like to go along as observer, being the submarine liaison officer, and all."

"I like your proposal, major," said Beauregard. "We'll discuss this. But first, any news of the *Hunley*?"

"Yes, sir, after your recent order putting the *Hunley* under the control of Mr. Hunley, he oversaw her raising. It was complete this morning. Sure, and it's a sad thing. We'll have some burials to attend to. Mr. Hunley, meanwhile, is completely refitting the craft. He's also sent for Lieutenant George Dixon, an engineer in the 21st Alabama regiment, to take command. Lieutenant Dixon was centrally involved in the design of the *Hunley*, sir. That's all I know, at present."

"And how are you getting along with Mr. Hunley, Dunbrody?"

"Ah, now, general, isn't he a fellow with strong opinions, now? And with good reason, being a young man and a Tulane University graduate, and wealthy and entrepreneurial, and a lawyer and legislator and all. But he knows I've been a place or two, and seen the dark side of war, so we get on fine."

"Gentlemen," said Beauregard, "let's return to Mr. Dunbrody's suggestion regarding the *David* and the *New Ironsides*. Commodore Tucker, what say you?"

"I think it's a fine use of our scarce resources, general, with the chance for success far beyond what we risk. And speaking of risk, knowing Lieutenant Dunbrody's meager swimming skills, I'm impressed with his volunteering to actually go aboard a semi-submersible." Tucker laughed with Rory, who suppressed a shudder at the prospect of sailing aboard a craft with only inches of freeboard. "Glassell's a good choice for commander," Tucker continued. "He and his engineer, Mr. Tomb, have already attempted torpedo attacks with those worthless torpedo rowboats last July. No doubt about their courage, none at all."

In early October, Glassell, Rory and a crew of three took the
David to attack *New Ironsides*. James Tomb, the engineer, and Sullivan,
his fireman, were in the hold tending the engine. Walker Cannon, the
Chicora's pilot, guided the craft while Rory and Glassell peered from the
open hatch into the darkness. Rory could hear the rush of the water only
inches below the hatch combing, as they bore up on the looming hulk of
the *New Ironsides*. *David* was traveling at seven knots. Only the hatch,
the smoke stack, and a small air-vent funnel showed above the glassy
surface of Charleston Harbor. "How big is the charge we're carrying,
Bill?" Rory asked Glassell as they sped toward the Union ironclad.

"There's sixty-pounds of explosive in the torpedo at the end of
that fourteen foot spar you can't see," replied Glassell, pointing to the
water off the bow of the *David*. The spar and its charge were five feet
under the surface. Now, they were within 100 yards of the *New Ironsides*.
Rory could see her starboard gunports open, and her broadside 11-inch
smoothbore cannon run out. "Rory, take this," said Glassell, handing
Rory a single barreled shotgun. "I'm going to lay her up under her
quarter. See if you can get a shot at the officer of the deck, and spread
some confusion."

"Aye, aye, Bill," said Rory, taking the weapon and raising it to his
shoulder as Glassell slowed the way on the *David,* stopping her with the
spar torpedo beneath the Union ship.

A Union lookout called from amidships. "Boat along side to
starboard!" An officer rushed to *New Ironside's* starboard quarter rail,
shouting orders. Rory raised the shotgun and fired as Glassell pulled
hard on the lanyard attached to the explosive charge. The Union
officer disappeared as a column of water shot 100 feet into the air. The
concussion knocked Rory down the hatchway. His head struck the pipe
running between the boiler forward and the engine. He saw stars, and
then water from the water column collapsed through the hatch, knocking
his head back into the pipe again as the weight of the water fell on both
ships.

"All astern!" he heard Glassell shout to Tomb, the engineer.

"Reverse gear is jammed, sir," Tomb replied. "A ballast iron was
knocked loose by the blast and is lodged under the gear wheel!"

"Abandon ship, men!" Glassell shouted. We've taken too much water aboard. Don't get caught if she goes under!" Rory heard Tomb and Sullivan clamber up the hatchway. "Are you all right, Rory?" Glassell shouted down the hatch.

"Sure, and I'll be fine, Bill, get yourself overboard, now!" Rory heaved himself up to a sitting position, and then suddenly lost consciousness.

Gunfire was the first thing he heard as he struggled awake minutes later. Rory's feet were in several inches of water surging slowly back and forth in the hull of the *David*. He braced himself on the boiler pipe and pulled himself to his feet. Peering cautiously over the hatch combing, he saw a figure in the water clinging to a mooring line trailing in the water. It was Cannon, the pilot. "Cannon, what's happenin'?" he called quietly.

"We've drifted away from the Yankee, sir. And we're not sinking. The others swam off, but I can't swim."

"Well, now, pilot, neither can I, enough t' save meself. Let's get you back aboard." Rory grabbed a line loose on the deck near the helm, secured it around a stanchion and threw one end to Cannon. The pilot pulled himself up the curved hull of the boat, breathing heavily.

"Thank you, sir."

"It's the least I can do for another non-swimmer, pilot. I wonder how the others fared?"

"I heard the Yankees pick up someone. Wait! Look over yonder!" Cannon pointed toward the *New Ironsides*, now 200 yards away, and settling slightly by the stern. "Some one is swimming this way." Rory could see the splash of a frantic swimmer only yards from the *David*. Unfortunately for the swimmer, sharpshooters lining the rail of the Yankee steam frigate saw the splash, as well, and began firing. Musket balls pinged off the smoke stack of the *David*. The swimmer made his way to the starboard side of the semi-submersible, away from the frigate, and climbed up the same line Cannon had used. It was Tomb.

"Am I glad to see you all," he gasped. "They picked up Sullivan and the lieutenant, and then I noticed we hadn't sunk, and swam back."

"They'll soon have a boat on their way, now that they've seen you, " said Rory. "As we're not sinkin', could y' have a go at starting the engine?"

"Aye, aye, sir, the water from the blast put out the boiler fire, but we've plenty of combustibles stored dry. Give me a hand, please, sir, if you will." Tomb showed Rory and Cannon what needed to be done to free the engine gear, while he rebuilt the boiler fire. Rory and Cannon cleared the engine machinery, and with the boiler freshly fired, they were able to return to the harbor.

Cannon was at the helm as they approached the *Indian Chief*. Rory stood beside him, shivering violently. *Sure and its not just the cold affectin' me,* he thought. *That was a near thing, and that's a fact!*

Rory reported to the strategy group soon after with the results of the attack. "And wasn't it a most gallant strike against the enemy, now?" He began. "*Ironsides* was severely damaged, but not sunk. I expect she had several casualties, from the severity of the blast. Mr. Glassell and Sullivan, the fireman, were captured, but Mr. Tomb, the engineer, and Mr. Cannon, of *Palmetto State*, stayed with the craft when we took water and the boiler fires were extinguished. We restarted her, great thanks to Mr. Tomb, and brought her home."

"We're glad you've returned, unsunk," said Tucker with a smile. "Do you think the Davids are a worthy weapon?"

"'T is a curious thing now, gentlemen," Rory replied, "but the greatest damage may be to Union crew readiness and their resources. Our intelligence contacts are telling us that all the blockaders now are at battle stations during hours of darkness, and are rigging defensive booms around each vessel every night. That's sure to take a toll on their energies, now, wouldn't y' say? So, even if we can afford to build no more Davids, the fact that we have one is a formidable threat."

"Other observations, Mr. Dunbrody?" asked Beauregard.

"Yes, general. I think the charge was too small. But with a more powerful torpedo, the spar should be longer, too. The *New Ironsides*, among all of the Union ships, may have been particularly vulnerable to night attack. She sent down her masts when she came on blockade, leaving only derrick masts for hoisting boats. Her lookouts were consequently at deck level, and could not see as well as a full rigged ship with masts of 140 feet."

On the day that Dahlgren and Gillmore resumed their bombardments of civilian targets in the city of Charleston, Rory sat in his stateroom aboard *Indian Chief* and composed a letter to Carrie Anne.

My darling Carrie Anne:

I am aboard the Indian Chief, and I can hear the shells exploding a few hundred yards away, among the houses and parks of what used to be a beautiful city. The Yankee attackers of this "cradle of liberty and secession" are employing a policy of unconditional war, wherein they see the support of the civilian populace as a weapon of war, every bit as powerful as guns and ammunition, and so as subject to attack.

We had talked, my love, of your coming to visit Charleston, with Natalie as companion, and to stay with your aunt's friends on Meeting Street. The fact is that the combination of the bombardment, and the devastation from the 1861 fire here has driven your family's friends, the Mills, and my shipmate Ormsby's parents out of the city and into makeshift dwellings unsuitable for visitors. As much as it pains me to ask you not to visit, I must, for your safety is more to me than my own selfish enjoyment of your presence.

I hope you and your family are well, and that your life is full and still enjoyable. I will do all I can to find a way to see you, but the war, at least, my war, is in a stage where sleep is rare, and beyond that, a luxury. They've made me commander of the Charleston, a new ironclad, and I work not only for my dear Jack Tucker, but also for Pierre Gustave Toutant Beauregard, an acerbic, brilliant, knowledgeable general who defends Charleston admirably. Sure, my love, I have my hands full! And I miss you more than I can say.

You have all my love,

your Rory

In October, George Dixon and the crew of the *Hunley* practiced daily, diving under the CSS *Charleston* and the *Indian Chief* in the harbor. James Tomb of the *David,* now promoted to chief engineer and captain of the semi-submersible for his gallantry against the *New Ironsides*, advised Hunley and Dixon regarding the *Hunley's* method of attack. "The risk of fouling the propeller with the tow line to your torpedo is very high," he said. "I strongly recommend the *Hunley* carry a spar torpedo at the bow, and not try to tow a torpedo under the target."

Hunley and Dixon took his advice. And then, on October 15, when Dixon was not in the city, Hunley took his place as commander for the day's training session. Rory, Ormsby, Walsh and Duffy watched through the gray patter of the October rain at the rail of the *Indian Chief,* anchored in the Cooper River off Charleston's shore. They saw the boat submerge, and walked to the other rail to wait for *Hunley's* customary resurfacing after it had dived beneath the receiving ship. Minutes passed. "She should be up by now," ventured Ormsby, voicing their collective fears.

"You're right at that, Archie," said Rory. They focused their gaze on the waters where the *Hunley* usually rose.

"Look, sir," cried Duffy, "bubbles!" He pointed to a spot on the surface toward Mount Pleasant.

"Archie, quick, now. Get a boat overside and we'll direct you to the spot. We'll buoy it. Take bearings, lads!" Rory rushed to the binnacle for the pelorus.

The search efforts continued through October, and into the next month. Finally, the wreck was located in the vicinity of the buoyed area, raised, and yet another memorial and burial was held for a *Hunley* crew. The boat was once again completely refitted, and in December, under Dixon's direction, training and testing began anew, with still another crew of intrepid souls.

That month, Rory received a letter from John Taylor Wood that would change the course of his life.

My dear Rory:

I write to warn you that I need your help in yet another desperate endeavor for the Cause, and to tell you that I have asked for you to serve as the sword at my right hand. As you may know, my Uncle Jefferson still employs me as his aide, and the president and I have ridden together much this autumn, discussing how we might make headway against the Yankee menace. I have persuaded him that an attack in the Carolina sounds, at New Berne, would force the Yankees to divert men and materiel from their main front, and would give us a possible link to the sea, now that Charleston's access has been limited. You more than anyone I know have the knowledge of the Neuse and

New Berne necessary to the success of this enterprise. I know how much you have done in defense of Charleston, by the way, and I am evermore impressed by your diligence and courage!

My uncle tells me that Robert E. Lee has written him endorsing a similar proposal for an attack on the Neuse, advanced by Brigadier General Hoke. President Davis has asked me to visit the lines above New Berne just after the New Year and to report back to him in early January. I believe, my friend, that you may expect orders in early January assigning you to my command. I do not know, at this time, who the army commander will be, but I am hopeful it will be someone of resolve and effectiveness. I have tried to convince my uncle that Brigadier Hoke would be a daring and resourceful commander, but the president is leaning toward Major General Pickett, because of his higher rank. I fear Pickett has lost his resolve after his experience at Gettysburg. I hope I am wrong.

May God bless you and keep you.
I have the honor to be
Your firm friend,
Taylor

CHAPTER 24
RAPHAEL SEMMES WRITES A LETTER
NOVEMBER 1863

While Taylor Wood extended his invitation to Rory, half a world away another former commander wrote a letter with Rory as the subject. Raphael Semmes, Rory's commander in the *Sumter*, had left that ship in Gibraltar in 1862, and embarked on his cruise aboard *Alabama*, a cruise that took him to the distant waters of the South China Sea.

TO HIS EXCELLENCY STEPHEN R. MALLORY
SECRETARY OF THE NAVY OF THE CONFEDERATE STATES OF
AMERICA

SIR: I write to report to you on the state of the war in the East Indian Ocean and the South China Sea, and to beg your assistance in the maintenance of discipline and order aboard the Confederate States Ship Alabama. My ship is weary, and we are far from resources for her physical repair. As you know, any good sailor can cope with the challenges of repair on a remote station, and in that regard we are most certainly able to carry on and faithfully represent the traditions and expectations of the Confederate States Navy. It is the weariness of my crew that moves me to ask your assistance.

My officers are as fine a group of men as I could ever have hoped for. As you know, most are southerners, with a few British subjects among them. The latter have been most beneficial to the cruise, as the great majority of the crew is Irish and English. One of my officers from the British Isles, Lieutenant Low, left Alabama to command CSS Tuscaloosa, a prize I commissioned as a new Confederate cruiser. We left Captain Low and his crew in Cape Town months ago, and I hope he is now on the high seas, wreaking havoc upon the despised Yankee. Yet I miss his talents, as he could speak the language in the accents of his countrymen, and assuage their grievances.

Those grievances have multiplied as the cruise has gone on. Where we took forty prizes in the first year, bringing joy to the hearts of our tars, we've now taken a handful in the past six months. Twenty-two ships of Union registry lie up in Singapore harbor, afraid to seek cargo or to venture out to sea while Alabama is in the offing! Great credit to us, admittedly, for driving the commerce of our enemy from the seas, but little consolation for the prize-hungry foretopman, whose main incentive for enlisting in a cause not his was the promise of "prizes galore."

We recently overhauled a swift clipper, the Winged Racer, which ship we burned as a lawful prize, after stripping her of needed commodities. Among the latter were fine Cuban cigars. In hopes of bolstering the morale of the men before the mast, I distributed cigars to the crew. They responded by pointedly throwing the cigars overside, in a gesture of contempt for my authority. I was compelled to make examples of the ringleaders, which included one of our bravest and most daring hands, coxswain Michael Mars, an Irishman of great talent and derring-do. I sentenced him to one month's forfeiture of pay, three months at menial labor, and to be triced up in the rigging three hours per day for one week. As you can see, I am reduced to disciplining my best men, owing to wide-spread discontent among my Irish and English crew.

I believe that the presence of an Irish officer would do much to raise the crew's morale and bring our effectiveness back to acceptable levels. I request that you assign Lieutenant Rory Dunbrody, formerly of my command in CSS Sumter, to Alabama, and direct him to join ship in Cape Town in March, if at all possible. I found Dunbrody to be an intelligent, daring and effective officer. Moreover, he is a Catholic, like the Irishmen among my crew. I believe his presence aboard Alabama would benefit the ship and the Cause.

I forward this letter in anticipation of its delivery within fifty days, or by February 1864.

I remain your humble and obedient servant,
Raphael Semmes, Captain, CSN,
commanding Alabama

CHAPTER 25
WITH LAMSON ABOARD THE NANSEMOND
AUGUST TO NOVEMBER 1863

Woonsocket, which had been awaiting her turn to refit in the
Brooklyn Navy Yard when the encounter with *Belle of Biloxi* began, was
finally placed in dry-dock at the end of July. Many of her officers received
leave ashore. Tobias reported to Oakley in the dockside building that
housed the officers and crew of the *Woonsocket* while she was in dry-dock.
"Mr. St. John," Oakley smiled at his sailing master, one of his favorite
officers, "I'd say you're entitled to a bit of leave. Take a week and visit your
father in New Bedford."

"Aye, aye, sir. I have to admit, the thought of relaxing in New
Bedford, without reminders of the last two weeks, is very attractive."

"You've earned it, Tobias. I'll see you in a week."

*What a joy it is to be under the command of a man who values me
for my attention to duty, and is not constrained to tell me so,* thought Tobias,
as he packed his sea bag for the packet ride to New Bedford. Later, on
the packet as they steamed through Hell Gate on their way to Long
Island Sound, Tobias thought, *much different from a fortnight ago, when I
approached this passage looking for the raider who turned out to be Rory.* He
left the packet and walked up School Street to his father's home. Carlyle
St. John, former slave, then freedman, whaler and now faculty member
at a respected Quaker academy, greeted his son with surprise and delight.
They spent a long evening catching up on the turns of fate that framed
Tobias' last year. Tobias could see that his father was engaged in every
phase of the year's events. They paused in the talk while Carlyle cooked

supper. "How is young Kekoa?" Carlyle asked as he sautéed the fish that was their entrée.

"Father, he has become a fine master's mate, and a loyal friend. I never would have survived the plots of Daniel Fell had it not been for the actions of Kekoa Kalama."

"Be sure and visit Commander Cavendish, then, while you're here, and share that news with him. He'll be pleased that his recommendation to Captain Oakley has proven a good one." Cavendish, the retired US Navy commander who had guided Tobias into the navy, had met Kekoa, and endorsed his enlistment also. New Bedford, heavily Quaker, was unusually tolerant in its attitudes toward people of color.

When Tobias returned to the Brooklyn Yard and reported to Oakley, he was greeted with a look of pleasure tinged with resignation. "Dammit, St. John. Just when I get a good officer, they take him away!" He laughed, good-naturedly, and handed Tobias a set of orders. "It seems that a former shipmate of yours was so impressed with your talents that he requires your presence aboard his new command, the darling of the fleet!"

Tobias hurriedly scanned the orders. "Report to Captain Roswell Lamson, lieutenant commanding the USS *Nansemond,* for duty as sailing master," he read.

"Sir, I'm at a loss for words. *Woonsocket* has been my home for the better part of a year. Your support and encouragement have helped me cope with everything from harassment to attempted murder. I can't imagine leaving *Woonsocket.*"

"It's been a pleasure to have you under my command, Tobias. You're going to one of the fastest ships in the fleet. She'll do fifteen knots. Lamson is said to be a favorite of Admiral Samuel P. Lee, our North Atlantic Blockade commander. I'd say he is, getting this new ship when dozens of other more senior officers wanted her. And he wants you! I know he's an old shipmate of yours. This should work out well for you. There are no pilots available now, and I daresay you have the fleet's most complete knowledge of the entrances to Wilmington, where *Nansemond* will blockade."

"Thank you, captain. I'm ordered to report immediately. I'll need to say goodbye to my shipmates."

"I know they'll appreciate that, Tobias. You've been through a great deal together aboard *Woonsocket:* your close call in Matamoros when you were behind the lines, the chase of *Star of the South* through the Caribbean, and your next close call, when you foiled Fell, if I may alliterate!" Oakley rose to shake hands, and clasped Tobias warmly by the shoulder. "Stay in touch, Mr. St. John. I want to know of your further exploits. One more thing. Lieutenant Lamson is also short of master's mates, and encourages you to recommend one of your choice. The Navy Office has concurred in this request."

"Sir, that's very generous of Mr. Lamson, and of you. Of course, I'll choose Kalama. Mr. Kelso is also very competent, and I feel pleased and confident to leave him with you."

"Nicely put, Mr. St. John. You could have a future in the diplomatic corps." The two men laughed, at the compliment and at the fantasy of the statement.

Tobias said his goodbyes to his fellow commissioned officers and to his petty officers. The latter caused him quite a surge of emotion. "Halvorson, O'Leary, Kelso, I'll do my best to keep track of you. You're brave and dependable, and good friends, as well." Tobias smiled inwardly as the big Swede wiped his eyes with his sleeve, and the others clustered to shake his hand.

Tobias left the Brooklyn Yard aboard a dispatch steamer bound for Hampton Roads, and Kekoa traveled with him, somewhat anxious about his new ship, but excited, nonetheless. Tobias had learned that Kekoa did not show deep emotions openly, displaying, rather, a stoic reserve when other men might be more demonstrative. The exception to this was laughter, glee, and exuberance. *It must be an Island thing,* thought Tobias.

At Fortress Monroe, they changed to another Navy packet bound up the bay to Baltimore. Lamson had previously found Norfolk to be clogged with refitting ships, and had gained permission to convert *Nansemond* from civilian to war status at the less-crowded Baltimore shipyard. Lamson had exercised his usual intensity during the refit, and the shipyard workers were proud of the good job they'd done so quickly, and, at the same time, glad to see the last of Roswell Lamson. He had overseen the outfitting of *Nansemond* in just eleven days, and managed to get the officers he'd asked for aboard during that time.

The watch-keeping officers, acting ensigns Hunter, Waring and Henderson, had all come aboard to join Ensign Benjamin Porter, the executive officer, and Tobias, the master, as the cadre of *Nansemond*. Lamson named Porter acting lieutenant, so that he outranked Tobias and the watch-keeping officers. The five would get along very well.

When Tobias reported aboard, Lamson greeted him enthusiastically. "Tobias, what a delight to see you. I need a pilot who knows the waters off Cape Fear, and who better than you!"

"Sir, it's a very great pleasure to be serving under you again." Tobias found himself warmly pleased to see his old friend and shipmate again, for he knew Lamson judged him solely on his performance, without regard to his color.

"We have good officers aboard, and my exec, Mr. Porter is one of the best. I'm so glad you brought along young Kalama as master's mate. I remember him from the Nansemond River campaign and the attack on Fort Huger. He's a good petty officer! And you'll meet another one, who remembers you well from *Wabash*. Bo'sun's Mate Hansen still talks about the Coosawatchie landing! Let me show you the wardroom. It's really quite comfortable. And we have our own ship's crockery." Lamson was as excited and proud as only a new commander could be.

In late August, Lamson moved *Nansemond* south to Hampton Roads. As they anchored off Fortress Monroe, Tobias reflected on Rory and his experiences in these very waters in the two-day Battle of Hampton Roads. *What he must have gone through here, trying to tow Virginia off the shoal under the Monitor's fire. And, now, he's saved my life. I hope he's safe and well.*

A week later, *Nansemond* was off Carolina Beach, midway between Masonboro Inlet and New Inlet, just southeast of Wilmington. It was a Sunday morning, where a Rebel battery was firing on several ships of the blockading squadron as they strove to close on the wreck of the blockade runner *Hebe*, which ship they had driven ashore two evenings previous. *Nansemond* joined five other Union blockaders. The Rebels fired effectively from their battery of two Whitworth breech-loading twelve-pounders on wheeled carriages they'd taken previously from another wrecked blockade runner, the *Modern Greece*. The *Hebe* was a fast twin screw steamer loaded with coffee, clothing and medical supplies.

Blockade runners, when facing capture, frequently ran themselves aground so that their cargoes might be taken off by Confederate forces through the surf. The Whitworths, British cannon, were mobile and quick-firing, and they were scoring hits on the Union blockaders that had closed to within 600 yards, particularly the *Minnesota* and the *James Adger*.

"Mr. St. John, Mr. Waring, take two boats and land up the beach from that battery. Ten men in each boat. Rifles and bayonets. Take those guns!

"Aye, aye, sir," they chorused. Tobias stood by the portside cutter, in davits, calling for volunteers. "Mr. Kalama, take the tiller! Bo'sun's Mate Hansen, bow oar, if you please!" The boats were lowered, and away. "Take the wave you like, Kekoa," said Tobias, softly. Kekoa had a knowledge of breaking surf hardly matched among the sailors of any nation. The crewmen of the *Nansemond,* however, could not know this, the two officers having come aboard only days ago. Tobias could read the uncertainty on the faces of his oarsmen, save for the slightly berserker grin of Hansen in the bow. After Kekoa selected a breaker and called to the crew, they soon realized his skill and experience.

"Give way, all," he called to the boat crew as they rode the face of a breaker toward the shore. The boat held its position on the wave face and surged gently to the sand, grounding as Kekoa called "toss oars," and Hansen and the second bow man boated their oars, leapt out of the boat and pulled it further up the slope of the beach.

Tobias assembled the men ashore. Each had a bayoneted rifle. When the men from Waring's boat joined them, they moved south on the beach, their rifles loaded and bayonets fixed. Tobias, as the senior and more battle-tested, was in command. The Whitworth battery crews were intent on their targets afloat, and hadn't noticed the approaching sailors. Tobias halted his naval infantry.

"Two ranks," he called. "Front rank, kneel." "Present, aim, fire!" The Confederate gunners reeled from the volley. Their captain, now aware of the danger, ordered a retreat, leaving the guns. Tobias called for a shout and the men double-timed toward the gun crews in a bayonet charge. The Rebels ran south down the beach, toward Fort Fisher. "Secure the guns, men," ordered Tobias.

Later, as they disassembled the carriages and loaded the Whitworths into the boat, Tobias and Waring talked. "Quite a prize, Mr. St. John," remarked Waring.

"They're beautiful weapons, indeed, Mr. Waring. And most mobile and versatile," replied Tobias. "They can be used ashore and afloat." Now that the gunners had been driven off, Tobias could see the boats from the other ships on their way to the wreck to take off what cargo they could before burning her.

In the next few weeks, Roswell Lamson soon gained the reputation of taking his *Nansemond* closer to the New Inlet bar and the shore than any other blockader. The New Inlet was the principal entrance for Wilmington, and most blockade runners used it. Roswell would anchor right on the bar at night, only 700 yards from the big guns of the Mound battery. Colonel Lamb, the Confederate builder of Fort Fisher, had constructed a 60-foot high earthwork with two heavy guns at its top, known as "the Mound." Tobias was always on deck during the *Nansemond's* "bar episodes," as the piloting challenges came thick and fast. One night, a fast Confederate Ordnance Bureau-owned blockade runner steamed for the inlet as *Nansemond* was quietly anchored on the bar. Lamson immediately opened fire, and the sleek steamer turned around quickly and fled out to sea. Lamson lost sight of her, and had to weigh anchor immediately, as the Mound opened fire on *Nansemond's* gun flashes.

The next morning, the runner was seen aground on the outer edge of the north reef. Through his glass, Tobias could see boats from Fort Fisher taking off cargo, and trying to refloat the ship. She appeared to be a side wheel steamer, perhaps 200 feet long, with two collapsing or retractable funnels, two masts and a steel hull. He read the name on the stern, *Angelique*. *Nansemond* was steaming just out of range of the Mound battery. Presently, Lamson came on deck. He gave the signal midshipman a message to hoist. The squadron flagship replied, and Lamson gave yet

another hoist to the midshipman. The flagship replied again, and Lamson
turned to his officers, all of whom had been casually glancing at the
signals, so as not to appear too nosy.

"Gentlemen, all but the officer of the watch in my cabin, please,"
said the captain.

Porter, Hunter, Henderson and Tobias sat around the dining
table in the captain's day cabin. It was well appointed, with a sofa, a
sideboard, and a secretary, with carpet on the deck, and tweed curtains
on the windows. Waring had the watch, and had remained on deck.
"Gentlemen, you may have noticed I've been exchanging signals with the
squadron commander this morning." Lamson smiled. "I've noticed you
all noticing." Everyone smiled.

"So you probably know what I'm about to tell you," he
continued. "We've persuaded the commander to let us burn the *Angelique*
tonight. We'll take three boats. Mr. St. John will lead, as the officer most
experienced in boarding blockade runners. You other gentlemen may not
realize this, but Mr. St. John led the navy to the capture of three blockade
runners in these waters a year ago. He was aboard one of them posing
as a slave pilot, and ran her aground just south of here. Mr. Henderson,
Mr. Hunter, you'll take the other two boats. I'd like the three of you to
work out a plan of attack and join me here to present it at eight bells in
the afternoon watch. Remember, we're unsure if the Rebs will leave men
aboard, so be prepared. Of course, if they refloat her before nightfall,
this will all be moot. I'm going on deck. Please use my cabin for your
planning."

When they presented their plan at four that afternoon, Lamson
was pleased. "It appears you've covered everything, gentlemen."

Angelique had gone aground while fleeing northeast up the coast
toward Masonboro Inlet. Tobias would board first, through the starboard
paddle wheel box entry port and secure the deck. If Rebels were aboard,
they would engage them immediately. Hunter and Henderson would
board through the portside entry port. If Tobias had met resistance, they'd
engage in support. If no one was aboard, or after resistance had ceased,
Henderson's men would go below and collect combustibles. Hunter's men
would collect any small items of value, navigation instruments, and ship's

papers, and small arms. Tobias' men would remain on guard in case the Confederates tried to reboard.

"Most workable, gentlemen, said Lamson. "Now, try to get some rest. We'll launch at midnight." For the men of the blockade squadrons, sleep was a precious commodity. They were required to be alert and on guard during the hours of darkness, when runners would make their attempts to enter or leave port. Then, the normal working of the ship always took place during daylight hours. It was an exhausting enterprise.

The boarding crews represented more than half of the *Nansemond's* complement. Each man bore a pistol and a cutlass. Tobias carried two Navy Six Colt revolvers, a luxury he had afforded himself from his prize money after the capture of the CSS *Okracoke*. At eleven o'clock, the *Nansemond* approached the grounded runner from seaward. Tobias, on deck with his boarding party, could see lights hanging in the rigging and moving about the deck of the *Angelique*. "Men," he said to his boat crew, "We'll have action tonight. They're taking off the cargo." He had chosen Kekoa as his second in command, and had insisted on adding to his crew Boatswain's Mate David Hansen, the doughty axe-wielding Norwegian from their days aboard *Wabash*. The young Kanaka was a veteran of hand-to-hand engagement now, after the assault on the Whitworth battery defending *Hebe* and the Fort Huger attack.

"Call away the boarding party," ordered Lamson, and the boats were lowered from the davits. The men scrambled down the falls.

"Toss oars. Cast off the falls. Out oars. Stand by to give way together. Give way, all!" ordered Kekoa, confidently. *Angelique* was 250 yards from *Nansemond*. Lamson wished to avoid any chance of being spotted by the workers off-loading the runner, or gunners from Mound battery. The three boats pulled steadily, narrowing the distance to the runner without being detected. Hunter and Henderson's boats rowed under the transom of the *Angelique*, and then pulled frantically up her port side to the paddle wheel box. Tobias' boat had drawn up to the starboard paddle box platform when they heard the alarm given on deck. "Boat, ahoy!" Tobias looked above at the rail but could see no one.

"Kekoa, they've seen the other boats, not us," he whispered.

"Hanson, smash that entry port! Hurry, now!" There was noise enough to mask Hanson's axe smashing the entry port latch to smithereens. On deck, the Rebels were uncertain as to the origin of the *Nansemond's* second and third boats. Their own boats had been shuttling back and forth all night between the runner and the shore, unloading the cargo of guns and ammunition. Before they realized that Hunter and Henderson's boats were not their own, Tobias and his crew had burst on deck through the forward companionway, firing their revolvers, shouting and brandishing their cutlasses.

About 20 Confederates were on deck or in the forward hold, unloading. Several were wounded in the first rush, and others hid abaft the pilothouse. Only two or three were able to draw weapons, and they were quickly cut down. The officer in charge of the unloading operation wore a Royal Navy sword and scabbard at his waist. He drew his blade as Tobias raised his cutlass. *Another British commander,* thought Tobias. *At least, it's not Ludlow!* He parried the first thrust, as Hansen, behind the Briton, promptly clubbed the officer over the head with the flat of his axe. "Ve have them now, ya, sure, Mr. St. John!" Hanson exclaimed with a bloodcurdling shout.

Never bring a sword to an axe fight, Tobias giggled crazily to himself, as the Englishman collapsed to the deck.

The other two boats had boarded to port and their men were on deck now, taking the men who were cowering behind the pilothouse into custody. "Mr. Henderson, Mr. Hunter, well done!" Tobias returned his cutlass to his belt. "Carry out your search and burn duties, if you please. My men will secure the prisoners. Mr. Kalama, Mr. Hansen, take two men each and secure the forward hold. It appears to be the one they were working. Be careful, they're probably hiding."

Tobias turned to two of his boat crew. "You two men, go below to the port side entry port. Watch for Reb boats coming out for more cargo. Don't be seen. When the first men come aboard, disarm them. We'll cover those in the boat from up here."

"Aye, aye, sir," they both replied. The stroke oar, a contraband named Hobbs, was a good sailor and seemed to Tobias to be quick and intelligent. *I must learn more of him,* Tobias thought. *I've not taught contrabands since Woonsocket last summer.*

In 20 minutes, the boarders had prepared the ship for burning, and Hunter's men had collected the ship's chronometer, sextants, papers and the contents of the armory. Hobbs appeared on deck. "Sir, we sees a boat approachin' to port."

"Excellent, Hobbs. Mr. Henderson, could you take your men below and secure the approaching boatload as prisoners when they come on board. Then we'll light the combustibles and leave."

Two hours later, Tobias was on the bridge wing of the *Nansemond*, still awake. The rush of adrenalin was beginning to subside, but he watched, enthralled, as the *Angelique*, with most of her cargo, burned brightly in the predawn darkness. They'd had only two men slightly wounded in the raid, and had captured 22, including six in the boat that had reached *Angelique* at the last moment. Four of the Rebels had been killed in the melee. Lamson had been delighted at the success of the raid, and the "blooding" of two of his less-experienced officers.

Lamson showed Tobias the ship's papers the next day. "She was a Confederate-owned runner, Mr. St. John, assigned to the Ordnance Bureau. The Bureau owns a number of runners, as does their navy. That way, they can control cargoes, and send more war supplies and fewer luxury items. We lost prize money with her destruction, but I know how little you care for that. Nice work last night."

"Thank you, sir. It's a pleasure to be here. Life's not dull aboard your ships!" The two men smiled at each other.

"Boredom is a terrible thing, Tobias!"

Kekoa and Hansen relaxed in the petty officer's mess the day after the *Angelique* action. "You serve with Mr. St. John before, ya?" Hansen smiled at Kekoa.

"Yes, aboard *Woonsocket*, but he wen get me my first billet in the Navy. He knew my father, too, we all three used be whalers. Where you serve wid him?" Kekoa was quite comfortable speaking Hawai'ian pidgin with Hansen, who used his own Norwegian-English. Only with officers and other educated *Haoles* did Kekoa resort to his more formal missionary English.

"Ve vas togedder aboard *Wabash*, in Port Royal. He is a pistol, that Mr. St. John, ya, sure, you betcha!"

The month of October was far from boring for the men of the *Nansemond*. On October 12, they ran the iron-hulled screw steamer *Douro* aground on Carolina Beach north of New Inlet after a chase and then boarded her before all of her crew could escape. She was aground close to a Confederate battery, so they burned the ship and her cargo of cotton, tobacco and turpentine. The $250,000 fire was visible for miles as the turpentine barrels exploded, sending up flames like fireworks.

Three days later, a chase ended in tragedy. The USS *Howquah* and the *Nansemond* pursued a strange sail first seen off Masonboro Inlet in the morning. The chase made very black smoke and behaved like a blockade runner, altering course away from a New Inlet bearing soon after she was sighted and heading north toward Cape Lookout and Raleigh Bay. *Nansemond* and the stranger were each making 15 knots and soon left *Howquah* behind.

Tobias calculated their position continuously as the pursuit continued. He stood on the bridge that extended between the two paddle wheel boxes, a post that afforded the best view aboard, if one excluded the mastheads. Tobias could see the hull of the chase above the horizon now.

Lamson saw the same, with some satisfaction. "She's hull up now, men. We'll catch her, for sure!"

Tobias glanced aft. "Sir, we have a squall coming up from the southeast." Lamson turned to look. It was a big rain and wind squall. It soon overtook them, and after a few minutes they lost sight of the chase. Occasionally, they would catch sight of the loom of the stranger, indistinctly through the weather. As the weather finally cleared, *Nansemond* had come up considerably on her. They were approaching the banks off Cape Lookout. The chase turned to starboard, and closed on the shoals.

"She looks like she's going to beach herself, sir," Henderson said. "She's still showing no colors."

"We're just within range of the bow pivot, sir," said Porter.

"Fire a shot, Mr. Porter."

"Aye, aye, sir. Look! She's heaving to." The chase had stopped, and when the shot was fired, hoisted Union colors.

"Mr. Porter, take three boats and board her. Bring an engineer and three firemen. We'll take her right into Beaufort." Beaufort, North Carolina was just behind the banks near Cape Lookout, only a few miles from their position.

The third assistant engineer, Mr. Strude, and three firemen joined three sailors in the port quarter boat. As they prepared to lower away, the after davit snapped, dropping the boat in the water. "Mr. Porter, life rings and lines for those men," Lamson cried. The captain's gig crew lowered their boat immediately.

"Sir, permission for Kalama and me to save those men," cried Tobias as he stripped off his outer clothing. Kekoa did the same, as Lamson, knowing the two were extraordinarily powerful ocean swimmers, nodded his consent. The two dove over side in graceful, arching dives and swam toward the struggling men. Kekoa and Tobias were supporting three men as the captain's gig approached, rescuing a total of five of the boat's crew. Strude and a lone sailor never surfaced.

"Sir, the boat must have struck them as it fell," said Tobias, returning to the deck and dripping sea water. Lamson looked distraught. A second boat waited a long time, hoping the two men would resurface. Finally, Lamson sighed, and turned to Porter.

"Get the boats over, Mr. Porter, and take the second assistant engineer. We'll close up on the chase. Well done, gig's crew, Mr. St. John, Mr. Kalama."

Ten minutes later, the boarding party could be seen on the stranger's deck, as *Nansemond* hove to within hailing distance.

Porter hailed the *Nansemond*. "She's the USS *Oleander*, sir, Admiral Dahlgren's dispatch steamer from the South Atlantic Squadron."

"Where's her commander?" Lamson demanded. Porter handed the speaking trumpet to a young man in a master's uniform.

"Volunteer Acting Master John Dennis, sir, commanding."

"What're you about, mister? I've chased you for four hours without you once showing your colors!" Lamson was seething. *I've never seen him this angry*, thought Tobias.

"I, I wanted to show what she could do, sir," Dennis replied, haltingly.

"You pulled me off a picket line, and in so doing, aided the enemy! You cost me two good men! You, you, you acting master!" Lamson spat the words, not wanting to insult an officer within hearing of others. "Come back aboard, Mr. Porter. You, there! Volunteer Acting Master Dennis! My report will be in Admiral Lee's hands tonight! You'd best stay clear of my hawse hole!" He dashed his speaking trumpet to the deck and stormed below.

Lamson was rather subdued for the rest of October. Tobias and his other officers could not help but notice his mood, unusual for him. They were all the more pleased on November 5, when Lamson's normal enthusiasm returned during a chase in company with the USS *Keystone* and the army transport *Fulton,* two other Union sidewheel steamers. The three ships were pursuing a blockade runner in heavy seas bound from Nassau to Wilmington. After a five-hour chase on a northerly course, the prize was overtaken. She was the sidewheeler *Margaret and Jesse,* of 700 tons, with an assorted cargo. She was a very fast and successful blockade runner, but was overloaded for this voyage, and had waited too long before beginning to jettison her cargo. A prize crew took her north to Beaufort, North Carolina, and then to Brooklyn Navy Yard to be refitted as the USS *Gettysburg.*

Lamson reported to Admiral Lee aboard the flagship the next morning. When he returned, he passed the word for Tobias. "Come in and sit down, sailing master," he said as Tobias reported. "Admiral Lee sends his regards."

"Somehow, sir, that sounds ominous." They both laughed.

"Nothing ominous, Tobias, but the admiral wants a favor from you."

"Sir, when S.P. Lee asks a favor, the smart officer says yes. What would he like?"

"He's ordered *Nansemond* to Baltimore for a refit, which we greatly need. But he's also received a request from our old friend Will Cushing, for a master with great knowledge of Old Inlet to join him aboard USS *Monticello,* his new command, off the Cape Fear River. He's finally leaving *Commodore Barney. Monticello's* a wooden hull screw steamer, almost 700 tons, with 137 men aboard. The admiral says no one in our navy knows more about Old Inlet than you do. And you know Will, he's always probing ashore. You've lived in Smithville, when you were posing as a slave pilot."

"It's true, sir, I've run ships aground in both inlets! But what about *Nansemond,* sir, when will she be back?"

"She'll be a good six weeks refitting, and then, the admiral's hinting I may get the *Margaret and Jesse,* refitted, as a new command. I hate to lose you, but I could be in the Navy Yard for three months between the two ships. The admiral knows you're due for leave, but it won't be dull with Will Cushing!"

"No one would argue counter to that!"

"Then I can tell the admiral yes?"

"Aye, aye, sir."

"You're a good man, Tobias, and a fine officer. I hope we serve together again."

"Thank you, sir. You never know, with the navy."

Tobias made his way to the gunroom, where he found Kekoa.

"Let's take a turn around the deck, Kekoa."

"Aye, aye, sir. You look like a man who is thinking deep thoughts."

"Perceptive as usual, my Kanaka friend. I've just received orders to report to our old friend Mr. Cushing, on blockade off Cape Fear. Unfortunately, this time I don't get to bring a master's mate."

"That's shipboard life, sir," the young Hawaiian said with a smile. "You and I have sailed the two great oceans. We'll sail together again. And I am in a fine billet, thanks to you. *Mahalo nui loa,* sir."

"I'm going to miss you, master's mate!"

"And I, you, sir. Write when you can, and *malama pono!*"

CHAPTER 26
CAPTAIN ROBERT SMALLS,
US ARMY QUARTERMASTER CORPS
DECEMBER 1863

Tobias reported in mid-November to the USS *Monticello*, a screw steamer 180 feet long, mounting a ten-inch smooth-bore pivot and six 30- and 32-pounder broadside cannon. She was an extremely fast ship in the South Atlantic blockading squadron, capable of eleven and a half knots, with a half-dozen blockade runners already captured. She was Will Cushing's pride and joy, and he, in turn, was the golden-boy of the US Navy on blockade, daring, imaginative and restless. *I'm lucky to be aboard and wanted,* thought Tobias, *with this engaging wild-man for a commander.*

Her station was off Old Inlet, south of Fort Caswell, where the Cape Fear River flows into the Atlantic along the eighteen-mile edge of Frying Pan Shoal. After Tobias had moved into his small cabin, he reported to Cushing.

"Tobias, come in," called Cushing with a smile. "Delighted to have you aboard. I know you have leave coming, but I needed someone who'd been inside the Cape Fear, and you are the one, for certain. I promise I'll get you some time off soon."

"Thank you, sir, but I'm excited to be here, and I'm more interested in your next venture than I am in leave. Sir, I was sorry to hear of your brother's death at Gettysburg."

"Thank you, Tobias. It's a hard thing to accept. Nonetheless, you and I will have some splendid times together here on the Cape Fear, sailing master. Tell me of your knowledge of the river and its inlets."

"I spent two months being tutored by slave pilots who grew up in these waters, from Wilmington to Smithville, and Old and New inlets, learning the bars and shoals and islands and inlets. My contacts have gone, for the most part, but I know the streets of Smithville, still, and the forts, and batteries, as well."

"Just what I need, Tobias. We're going to overrun a battery on Zeek's Island. Do you know it?"

"I know it well, captain. It was one of my bearings when I took the blockade runners out to the blockade squadron trap."

"Good! This evening we'll go over the charts and I'll show you my intent and share my hopes. We did this in August with another battery."

Zeek's Island was situated at the mouth of Buzzard's Bay on the north side of Smith's Island. The south point of Smith's Island bore the name "Cape Fear," also the name of the river emptying to its west. Zeek's Island was in the river proper, across the New Inlet channel from Battery Buchanan, and slightly to its west. Its battery was trained on the entry to New Inlet, intended to guard against enemy intrusion during blockade squadron chases of blockade runners. It was a small battery, with three 32-pounders, smooth-bore cannon. Its central orientation was to the east, and Cushing's plan was to enter the mouth of the Cape Fear River through Old Inlet, quietly row the five miles upriver to the western unguarded shore of Zeek's Island, and strike swiftly across the low dunes of the outer-bank isle to the battery on its east shore.

In late November, on a cloudy but calm night, the *Monticello* drew inshore along the Frying Pan Shoal. The big cutter, with twenty men aboard, was lowered from the midships davit and disappeared into the murk surrounding the entrance to the Cape Fear River. The men were armed with a cutlass and two revolvers each. Cushing and Tobias sat in the sternsheets as the boat, with oarlocks muffled, passed Cape Fear on the tip of Smith Island, four miles to the east across Frying Pan Shoal and then rowed past Fort Holmes on the promontory of Bald Head and next, the darkened Bald Head Lighthouse on the west side of Smith Island, with Battery #4 perched behind it. The cutter then eased by Fort Caswell to the west and they were in the river itself, rowing through the low islands and shoals of the river mouth. The range lights for New Inlet on the river's west bank above Smithville at the Burke signal station were lit for the benefit of incoming blockade runners as the cutter approached Zeek's Island, and Cushing used them for their bearings as they turned east to the island's western shore. The cutter slid softly up the gently-sloping sands of the island. "Sanders, stay with the boat! The rest of you, form on me and Mr. St. John," whispered Cushing, as the men tumbled over the cutter's gunwale. The Union sailors, in two groups looming through the night, crept slowly over the rise to the island's center and then down the slope until the bulk of the battery became visible in the gloom.

Cushing and Tobias conferred, while their men caught their breath. "Take your ten around to the embrasures in front. Wait 'til you hear us yell and open fire, then come through the gunports while they're turned to confront us."

"Aye, aye, sir, it's perfect! Men, quietly now, and follow me! Revolvers in your belts until my command." Tobias and his ten sailors circled silently through the dunes some 50 feet from the sand walls of the battery until they reached a point where they could see the 32-pounders run out through the embrasures. "Three men to each cannon! On my command, revolvers, and then, cold steel!" They crept in clusters of three to the embrasures, and leaned against the sand walls of the battery, pistols in hand, breathless, waiting for Tobias to give the order.

A cacophony of yells, shots and screams rose from the west side of the battery as Cushing's attack began. "Monticellos, through the gun ports!" cried Tobias, as his ten men fired their pistols, screaming and looking for targets. Targets were in short supply, as most of the men of the battery were asleep, save for two sentries and one gun crew. The sentries threw down their muskets and raised their hands at Cushing's first assault, and the gun's crew froze as they saw Tobias and his men storm through the embrasures. Their stacked arms were too far away to be worth the risk of pistol shot.

"Mr. St. John, I want to strike the trunnions off these guns, and fire the magazine. Five minutes, if you please!"

"Aye, aye, sir. What about prisoners, sir?"

"We'll take the battery commander and his sergeants on the

cutter and parole the rest. No room in the cutter. Leave that to me, Tobias, while you deal with the guns and the magazine."

The explosion of the magazine was quite spectacular, lighting up the night sky to the north with crimsons and golds, and plainly visible to the cutter crew, facing aft as they rowed the boat south through Buzzard's Bay and out through the Old Inlet to *Monticello*. "That should tie their smallclothes in a knot at Rebel Army headquarters," laughed Cushing, clapping Tobias on the shoulder. "Well done, men," Cushing called, eyes alight with mirth.

"Tobias," said Cushing at mid-day following the battery explosion, "You need some time off. Ten days for you while we toss about, hoping for the incautious blockade runner."

"Captain, how can I say no?" Tobias realized he did need some time to change his focus, and alter his routine.

"Will you go north to New Bedford, and home?" Cushing asked.

"No, sir, too far to go, and in the middle of winter. No, I'll seek out a friend I made on the Charleston blockade, one you might remember, Pilot Smalls. He's still in the Charleston area."

December 1, 1863, found Tobias aboard a dispatch steamer headed to the blockading fleet off Charleston. His old mentor, Frank Du Pont, was no longer commanding the South Atlantic Blockade Squadron, but the staff of his replacement, John Dahlgren, was most helpful in locating Robert Smalls. Smalls had returned to the Charleston theater in the summer of 1863, having recovered from wounds suffered when he was pilot of the USS *Keokuk,* an ironclad which was sunk in the April 1863 attack on Fort Sumter. During his recovery, the USS *Planter*, the former Confederate gunboat Smalls had delivered to the US Fleet in 1862, was transferred to the US Army Quartermaster Corps. The Quartermasters throughout all theaters of the war, had a fleet of over 4000 craft, mostly sail or steam transports, with quite a few well-armed light draft gunboats such as the *Planter.* Tobias left the dispatch steamer and boarded one such Army side wheeler gunboat bound to an anchorage on the north end of Folly Island, at the mouth of Lighthouse Inlet where he'd been told he'd find Smalls aboard *Planter.*

"Welcome aboard," called Smalls from the upper deck of the *Planter* as Tobias climbed the ladder from the main deck. "Come this way to my cabin, sailing master," said Smalls with a grin. "I have a surprise for you!" Smalls held open the door of the captain's cabin in the large deckhouse abaft the pilothouse. Tobias stepped in, a look of astonishment on his face. "That's right, Tobias," laughed Smalls, "it's my cabin. I'm the captain!"

Tobias took Smalls' right hand in both of his. "Congratulations, captain! Don't keep me in suspense. I want to hear the story."

The two friends sat at the table over cups of coffee as Robert Smalls, former US Navy and Army Quartermaster Corps pilot, now commanding the Army gunboat *Planter*, told his tale. "Two days ago, I was piloting the *Planter* up Lighthouse Inlet with rations for the Union troops on Morris Island, way up the inlet. Lieutenant Nickerson was in command. I'd been with him about four months, an' he always struck me as pretty excitable for an Army officer. Well, the Rebs' batteries on James Island near Secessionville were firing at the *Commodore McDonough,* one of our old New York ferryboat gunboats, and they were firing back. We got caught in the middle. Then a Union battery joined in. We were hit by a short round, and Lieutenant Nickerson told me to head her for the James Island bank and beach her. Then he ran out of the pilot house and went below."

"What a weak-kneed bastard!" Tobias exclaimed. "Obviously, Robert, you had other actions in mind."

"Over half this crew is contrabands," said Smalls. "We beach ourselves and surrender, we's all back in slavery, diggin' trenches for the Rebs around Richmond. No, suh, I wasn't runnin' this boat aground! These side wheelers turn in dere own length. I pointed her downstream and hightailed it out of dere. When we docked at Morris Island depot, Lieutenant General Quincy Adams Gillmore, de big commander here, runs up the gangway. Turns out he was in the Union battery and saw the whole thing, includin' de lieutenant running out ob de pilothouse and hidin' below." Smalls laughed, shaking his head slowly at the memory.

"'Where's your commander?' de general says. 'I don't know, suh, he went below. Suh, I mus' confess I disobeyed his order, suh. He tole' me to beach her, and I ran her back here instead,' I says. Den, Nickerson comes up to de pilothouse, lookin' mighty sheepish. De general say 'You're relieved, lieutenant. I'm having Colonel Ellsworth draw up orders for your court martial for cowardice in the face of the enemy.' Den he turns to me an' says 'What's your name, pilot?' He's a handsome man, wid dis short black beard and piercin' eyes. Looked right through me, he did. I tells him my name an' he says, 'You're in command, then, Smalls. You did well! The colonel will cut those orders, too.' An' so, here I am."

"You've come a long way from the Cooper River, Robert," said Tobias.

"I plan to enjoy it while I can, Tobias."

Over the next eight days, Tobias stayed aboard the *Planter* as an interested observer while the side wheeler moved up and down the Folly River, the Lighthouse Inlet, the lower Stono, and other waterways south of Charleston Harbor. While at anchor, or secured to a depot dock, Robert Smalls and Tobias would enjoy trading stories of the war, and wondering where it would eventually lead them. Tobias was particularly interested as Robert would describe his crew, a rich mix of nationalities and backgrounds. Smalls had managed to bring together a group of very experienced sailors. Most of them were black, and so they were not much sought after by other officers, but Smalls recognized the worth of their varied experiences. Two were Cape Verdeans, half African, half Portuguese, veteran whalers who had left the Cape Verde islands for New Bedford. Most of the rest were contrabands, recently freed slaves with boating or coastal piloting experience from the Sounds of North Carolina and the sea islands around Charleston, Port Royal and Savannah.

The evening before Tobias returned to the *Monticello*, they talked in Roberts' cabin as dusk crept over the ship. "I've noticed that the contraband sailors are treated differently than the freeborn blacks through the fleet," said Robert. As they talked, they watched the light fade over the low, flat islands stretching inland in the short twilight. "The contrabands aren't promoted often, and have the lowest paying jobs, while the freemen and foreign blacks are often petty officers."

"And yet, many of your contraband seamen are prime hands, with years as coastal sailors. The navy could make better use of them, if it could ignore their color. I guess we can't expect the navy to be that much different from the rest of America." Tobias sighed.

"We're just glad to have pay we can keep," smiled Robert. "Some of my contraband sailors came out of New Bedford, with help from the Verdeans. The contrabands got there through the underground railway."

"Yes," said Tobias, "New Bedford was a major terminal. My father was a part of it." Tobias paused, reflecting on his father's work in placing escaped slaves in safe havens in Massachusetts.

"Robert, I've noticed a lack of cooperation between General Gillmore and Admiral Dahlgren. The war effort here seems to be one step forward and two back. This battle for Charleston could go on for a long time at this rate!"

"However long it go on, I don't see America changing much after it ends, not in South Carolina. After the war, you and me may be free, but if we stay in de south, we better be careful."

"You're a careful man, Robert, I know you'll do all right. Let's be sure to stay in touch."

CHAPTER 27
THE ATTACK ON THE NEUSE
JANUARY-FEBRUARY 1864

January came, and with it, orders from the Navy Department assigning Rory to the command of John Taylor Wood on the Neuse River of North Carolina. "You will select two officers and 30 men from the Charleston Squadron with the concurrence of Commodore Tucker and proceed to Goldsboro, N.C., where you will encounter Lieutenant Gift's detachment from Wilmington. You will take command of the combined detachments and proceed to Kinston, where you will place your men under the orders and command of Commander and Colonel John Taylor Wood."

Rory selected Ormsby and Walsh as his subordinates, made sure Boatswain McCafferty was a member of the detachment, said a hurried goodbye to his other Charleston comrades, and sped north by train to Goldsboro. There he found Lieutenant George Gift and 100 Wilmington sailors and marines just arrived on the Wilmington and Weldon Railroad. With them were two 25-foot gigs and two huge, 50-foot launches, which each could carry 40 men easily, plus a boat howitzer.

"Delighted to meet you, suh," said Gift, who clearly realized that Rory was his senior.

"My pleasure, sure and it is, lieutenant," Rory replied. "I realize our orders have placed me in command," said Rory, disarmingly, "but soon we'll both be reportin' to Taylor Wood, so let's proceed on a first-name basis. Mine is Rory."

"Mighty kind of you, suh, - Rory," said Gift. "Mine is George."

The two lieutenants soon had their men and boats transferred to the Atlantic and North Carolina Railroad, bound for Kinston, 20 miles away. Their officers quickly made friends of one another. Wood met them at the Kinston station as they pulled in at noon, on January 31. As they eased into the station, Rory could see Taylor pacing impatiently on the platform.

"Gentlemen, I'm delighted to see you," said Taylor. Gift, Rory, Ormsby, Walsh and one of Gift's midshipmen, Sharf, formed a semi-circle around Wood on the broad platform. "I've sent my ten boats down river early this morning so we'll be in position to reconnoiter off New Berne this evening. I'll take you all with me to catch up to our main body."

"Sir, as I recall from my younger days in this part of the state, it's half a mile to the river from the station." Rory was glancing around for any indication of wagons large enough to bear the big launches. "These wagons will handle the smaller boats, but we'll need teams and big drays for the launches."

Wood looked perplexed. "That will delay us considerably if we wait until the launches can be transferred." Wood paused, then turned to Lieutenant Gift. "Mr. Gift, I'll ask you to take charge of the launches and to follow us with the Wilmington detachment as soon as you can. I'll take the two smaller boats and Mr. Dunbrody's detachment with me now. His home is in New Berne and he knows those waters well."

"Aye, aye, sir," Gift replied. "I'll find some mules and move the boats and howitzers. Where shall I rejoin you, sir?"

"At Swift Creek, lieutenant. Here it is on the chart," said Wood, unrolling a chart on the planks of the platform. "It's five miles upriver from Batchelder's Creek."

Turning to Rory, Wood motioned him to follow. "Have your men move the two gigs to the river. I want you to come with me to Pickett's headquarters."

"Aye, aye, sir. Mr. Ormsby, those two wagons should carry the gigs' weight. We'll meet you at the river."

Wood and Rory walked the three blocks to the hotel where Pickett had established his command. Pickett's office was in a room off the lobby. Outside his door in the lobby, his adjutant and his aide de camp, Klaus von Klopfenstein, now a lieutenant colonel, sat behind desks.

Von Klopfenstein sprang to his feet.

"Herr Colonel Wood, Major Dunbrody, the general is eager to see you. Wait here, please."

"I guess we're in the army, now, Rory," laughed Wood, acknowledging the Prussian's use of their dual-appointment army ranks. Von Klopfenstein reappeared and ushered them into Pickett's office. The animosity of the Prussian toward Rory, always present, seemed subdued. *He's up to something*, thought Rory.

Pickett greeted them effusively. "Gentlemen, we're on the eve of a great victory for the Cause. Let me share my plan with you."

In spite of his bonhomie, it was obvious to Rory that his old acquaintance, George Pickett was a deeply troubled man. His eyes were sad, his face lined and mottled. *Plainly, the man has too much of the drink taken,* thought Rory. *And Taylor tells me his new wife LaSalle is here with him, near Kinston. This may be his last chance to climb back into Lee's good graces. I hope she's not distractin' him!*

Pickett outlined the battle plan originally devised by General Hoke. It was a good one. The federal defenses of New Berne stretched in two parallel lines from the Neuse River several miles to the Trent River. The inner line, four miles southeast of Batchelder's Creek and near the city, was a series of strong earthen fortifications. The outer line of infantry and artillery units would be attacked on the Neuse side by Hoke's brigade. General Seth Barton would attack the Trent River side, take the forts there, crossing the river near Bryce's Creek, and attack the city inner ring of forts. Colonel James Dearing would attack Fort Anderson, across the Neuse, and cut off Federal troops from the north. General Martin would lead troops from Wilmington against Newport Barracks, 20 miles down the Neuse from New Berne, cut the railroad line from Morehead City, and drive the Federals toward Beaufort. Federal gunboats were routinely anchored off New Berne in the Neuse to provide support for the defenders. Wood's men would take these ships, and turn their guns against the Federal troops ashore. "In two days, gentlemen, we'll have retaken the city and captured tons of supplies we desperately need," said Pickett as he concluded his description of the attack.

"You can count on the navy, general, to play its part," said Wood.

"By your leave, sir, we'll get under way." As they left headquarters, Wood said to Rory, "I'm sure Hoke will do well, but I know nothing of Barton and the others. We'll hope for the best."

Von Klopfenstein watched the two navy officers as they left. He contemplated the August reprimand he had received from Lee, himself, for having arrested Dunbrody and his officers as they came up the Shenandoah, and having failed to inform Pickett that he had detained the navy men. He frowned, sat down, and composed a short dispatch.

> *To: Colonel Grenville Donovan, CSA Intelligence Section*
> *My Dear Colonel,*
>
> *I thought you would be interested to know that Lieutenant and Major R.C. Dunbrody is in New Berne and now a part of General Pickett's overall command. He is, as you know, the darling of the navy establishment, yet, there may be an opportunity to pursue your desires regarding his future. Should you decide to join me here, my energies will be at your disposal.*
>
> *Your obedient servant,*
> *Klaus Dieter von Klopfenstein,*
> *LIEUTENANT COLONEL, CSA*

My friend Grenville has carved out his own spy-catching command, he thought, *quite independent from General Winder. I'm sure that his desire for revenge on his brother's killer will inspire him to make life less comfortable for Dunbrody.* "Orderly," he called. "Take this dispatch and make sure it's in the next courier's pouch for Richmond!"

Wood and Rory took the gigs 20 miles down stream and met the ten boats and 200 men of Wood's force where he had sent them to get them out of Kinston and lessen the chance of a security breach. "The less people see of us, the less chance of the Union Navy learning our plans," Wood explained to Rory. Lieutenant Benjamin Loyall, Wood's second in command, greeted them. At sunset, they started down stream for New Berne, hoping to find two or three unsuspecting Union gunboats anchored in the Neuse off the city. At three in the morning, they had reached New Berne. They could see the lights of the city through the fog and light rain. But no Yankee gunboats were to be seen. Puzzled, Wood ordered his flotilla upstream four miles to the marsh beside the mouth of Batchelder's Creek, where they arrived at dawn, February 1. Wood sent a message to Pickett by courier, noting the absence of Union ships. The men slept fitfully and then ate cold rations. They could hear the firing from Hoke's brigade as the assault began.

At sundown they were joined by Gift and the two launches. Wood sent a fast boat down stream. At midnight they returned, having found the USS *Underwriter* anchored off New Berne. Her eight-inch guns and twelve-pounders were trained on the Confederate lines, and the lookouts among her 70-man crew were alert. "Only one ship?" Wood was surprised and disappointed. "We've more than enough men to overwhelm her," he said. Later, they learned that a second Union gunboat had gone aground and a third had sailed up the Trent to defend against Barton.

Wood gathered his men for his customary prayer, and then led his boats down stream. Each man tied a white armband to his sleeve, and memorized the password, "Sumter." Gift's two huge launches trailed the others. Their role would be to tow the *Underwriter* upstream after capture, if feasible. The flotilla was divided into two squadrons. One, under Lieutenant Loyall, would board from aft. The second, Wood's, would board over the bow. Rory and Ormsby each commanded a boat. They rowed quietly past Fort Dutton, a battery on the city shore. Suddenly, the *Underwriter* came in sight. The bulwarks of her 185-foot hull were low, but her towering paddle boxes amidships looked immense in the dark. A hail came from her lookout, "Boat, ahoy! Boat, ahoy!" "Repel boarders, repel boarders," came the cry. Surprise was lost. Union sailors lined the rail, muskets in hand. A shot was fired.

"Give way all, give way," called Wood. They boarded over the bow and stern amid a hail of musket and pistol fire. Rory's bowman tossed a grapnel over the bulwark of the Yankee, and his boat crew clawed their way up the line. Rory parried a Union officer's sword thrust with his cutlass. Behind him, a huge Yankee swung the butt of his musket and knocked Rory overboard. He landed in one of the Rebel boats. *Thank God*, he thought. *At least I'm not in the river.* The thwart had bruised his back. He struggled upright. He could see the crush of Wood's men surge from both ends toward the hurricane deck of the *Underwriter.* They outnumbered the Yankees three to one, but were taking heavy casualties, as most of the Union defenders were under the hurricane deck in the ship's armory, where loaded weapons were close at hand. Finally, the Yankees were overwhelmed and driven into the hold. "She's ours," shouted Ormsby. He looked overside and saw Rory, moving forward in the boat. "Rory, are you all right?"

"I'm not drowning, praise the Saints, Archie!" Wood appeared at Archie's side.

"Mr. Dunbrody, I'm sending down a crew. Please see if we can cast off the chains to the buoys!"

"Aye, aye, sir." As Ormsby and several men tumbled into the boat, Rory, his head splitting, cast off the bow painter.

"Sit down, Rory. You look terrible. Out oars! Give way together." Archie took the tiller. They pulled to the buoy securing the bow line. "Rory, this is a link chain. We'd be forever parting it. We've no cutters for links this size." Ormsby shook his head. "I hate to report this news to the commander." When Rory and Archie found Wood on the bridge of the *Underwriter,* he was not as dismayed as they thought.

"It's little matter, gentlemen, Mr. Loyall reports no steam up. It would take us an hour and a half before we could move, buoys or no," said Wood.

Just then, the foredeck shook under a tremendous explosion. Walsh called out from the foretop. "Sir, Fort Anderson has opened fire!"

"Damned Yankees, we've got 40 prisoners aboard. They're firing on their own men! Mr. Loyall, get the men and prisoners to the boats. Mr. Ormsby, see that Dunbrody is safe aboard a boat. Mr Walsh," Wood called to the foretop. "Take a detail and fire this ship. I want her blown to bits!"

"Aye, aye, sir. Axemen, to the magazine!"

As the flotilla toiled upstream, a thunderous explosion lit the night sky. The *Underwriter* was no more. Sunrise found them at Swift Creek. Taylor Wood went off in search of Pickett. His men collapsed in exhaustion. Rory was determined to sleep, if only to avoid his headache. Before he closed his eyes, he asked, "Archie, what was the butcher bill?"

"Nine dead and 14 wounded, Rory. We lost Wayne and Pickering from our detachment. The Yankees lost 29 dead and wounded and we took 26 prisoners. The rest escaped. And of course, they lost the ship!"

When Rory awoke, at dusk of the same day, February 2, Taylor Wood knelt beside him. "How do you feel, Rory?"

"Much better, sir, thank y' kindly."

"It's a good thing. You have special orders, urgent and direct from Secretary Mallory himself. Apparently, you impressed the great Captain Semmes. He's expressly asked for you to report aboard *Alabama* at Cape Town! You're to catch the first blockade runner out of Wilmington. There's a night train."

"Cape Town! By the Saints, I can't keep up with all this movin' about, at all, at all!"

"It may be the best thing for you, Rory. While at headquarters, I saw Donovan the spy catcher. As I recall, he's nothing but trouble for you."

"Sure and you're right, Taylor. But I hate to leave the lads. What of the rest of the battle?"

"What a debacle, and a disappointment! Barton dithered and never advanced. Nor did Dearing. Martin did well at Newport Barracks. Hoke and I tried to convince Pickett to let us assault the city from the Neuse tonight, but when Barton refused to move, the general lost his determination. I'm off tonight to Richmond to report to Lee and the president. They're not going to like the results. I'd venture that Pickett's reputation is destroyed beyond redemption."

"How is Pickett's mood?" Rory asked, remembering Pickett's mercurial temperament when he first met him in the Pacific Northwest five years before.

"The man is raging," said Taylor. "He's on the verge of despair. He's furious with Barton, and afraid to be candid in his report to Lee. And, he's captured 22 North Carolinian Union soldiers among the 300 that Hoke took prisoner. Most of them were in the North Carolina militia before secession. As near as I can tell, they enlisted in the Union Army before North Carolina seceded. But Pickett swears he'll hang them all as deserters. He's marching them to Kinston as we speak, and has ordered their court martial. Nothing good can come of this."

"Och, the poor man, he's overwhelmed by his own demons. And others will suffer because of his dismay. Well, Taylor, I must say goodbye to my lads, and write a note to Carrie Anne, and to my da' and Siobhan, tellin' 'em how close I was to home. The Saints bless y' and keep y', Taylor. Y've brought great credit upon the navy, once again!"

"Stay safe, my friend," Wood replied. "Give my best to Captain Semmes. We'll get you to your boat and pull upstream."

In Kinston, Rory gathered Ormsby, Walsh and McCafferty around him before leaving for the station. The big boatswain had his arm in a sling, grazed by a Yankee musket ball in the boarding melee. "Lads, I want you to tell the commodore of my orders, and tell all the lads in Charleston we'll be shipmates again, t' be sure. Archie, please make sure these notes get to Carrie Anne, and to me da' and sister in Scotland Neck. God save y' kindly, now!" He waved as he shouldered his sea bag and walked toward the station.

****

FEBRUARY 11, 1864

Bespectacled Colonel Grenville Donovan, of Confederate Army Intelligence, sat with Klaus von Klopfenstein in a secluded corner of the hotel bar where Pickett had established his headquarters in Kinston. They were safe from eavesdroppers.

"How is your esteemed commander?" Donovan asked.

"Ach, mine leader is an angry and despairing man, ready to lash out," the Prussian responded. "Just right for our purposes, Grenville, *nicht wahr?*"

"But Lieutenant Dunbrody has departed, for Cape Town, I'm given to understand," said Donovan. "And he has left still the Confederate hero, beloved of the navy and the army too." He grimaced in disgust.

"Yes, but another Dunbrody has found his way here, my friend. Lieutenant Colonel Timothy Dunbrody, whom your Section, during a board of inquiry, intimated might be subverting our war effort through influence on his brother Rory, is waiting to see the general under a flag of truce. He is aide de camp to Union General Peck, and has come to plead for the lives of his fellow North Carolinians who are facing our court martial for treason. General Pickett hates General Peck!"

"And our General Pickett is thirsting for revenge, and perhaps susceptible to his subordinates' advice?"

"*Ya, wohl!* After all, he was heard to shout at one of our North Carolinian captives, 'God damn you, I'll have you shot and all other rascals who desert!' And this was said before the court martial. Think of this, Grenville. A Dunbrody took a brother from you. Perhaps we can arrange to take a brother from him."

CHAPTER 28
CUSHING AND THE SMITHVILLE RAID
FEBRUARY-APRIL 1864

"What day is it, Tobias?" Will Cushing smiled at his sailing master as they breakfasted aboard the Union blockader, USS *Monticello*.

"Why, Cap'n Will, Ah 'spects you know it be the las' day in February," Tobias replied in a slave patois as familiar to him as his normal New Bedford English or the Antiguan accent of his birth.

"How do you do that, sailing master? You can sound like three different people in the same sentence!"

"You should hear my French and Spanish, sir. What's significant about today?"

"We're going on a fishing expedition. I want two gigs, with ten men each. We'll leave at one bell in the evening watch, dusk, and row to Smithville. I know you're familiar with the territory, as you stole three blockade runners from that very port. We'll visit the commanding general, pay our respects. Sound interesting?"

"Your ideas are always interesting, captain. Sometimes, disturbingly so."

As they had done before, they left Bald Head to starboard and Fort Caswell to port. The ship channel from Fort Caswell north was empty of blockade runners. "Too bad no one's waiting to run the blockade," whispered Cushing. "I was hoping we could take one out on our way back."

They continued with muffled oars to the west bank of the Cape Fear River, landing in the dark just below Smithville. "Leave six men to guard the boats. The rest, follow me," said Cushing. Whispering to Tobias, he said, "I should have said, 'follow you.' After all, you lived and spied here."

They came upon three blacks around a campfire at the outskirts of town. "Let me, captain," Tobias said.

He stood and approached the fire, his Navy six in hand, but at his side. "My name be 'Marcus Aurelius'" he said, using the slave alias he'd operated under in his Smithville spy days. "'Member the name?"

The eldest of the three stood and peered from the light of the fire into the darkness.

"Oh, yes! You be the Devereaux pilot stole the three ships from the rebels! Ah 'member!"

"Well, gentlemen," said Tobias in his normal speech, "I'm back with some more Union sailors, and we need your help. Could you guide us to Confederate Headquarters? We'd like to invite the general for tea aboard our ship!"

The three Negroes looked at Tobias for a moment, and then began to laugh. "Hee, hee," giggled the eldest, "this sound like a fine party. We'd be happy to show you all the way, Marcus Aurelius!" The elderly black man smiled warmly.

"What is your name, sir?" Tobias asked.

"Dey call me Obadiah," he replied.

"Obadiah, this officer is Captain Cushing, and we're both grateful for your help."

Cushing nodded politely, and Obadiah smiled. "Follow me, gen'muns," he said.

General Louis Hebert was the Confederate commander in Smithville, including Fort Johnston, and Fort Caswell. His headquarters was in a large antebellum mansion near Nash Street and the old Devereaux home. A big boarding house, across the street and near the shore, had been converted into a Confederate barracks. Cushing had left the bulk of his command just outside of town, and Tobias, Obadiah and three sailors accompanied him to the general's quarters. Cushing thanked Obadiah. "You'd best leave now, Obadiah, in case anything goes wrong," he explained in a low tone. As Obadiah moved off down Nash Street, Cushing tiptoed silently to the wide veranda and tried the front door. It opened easily. "Unlocked," he whispered. He motioned to the sailors and Tobias to follow him. "Search this floor," he whispered. He left his boots at the foot of the broad staircase and crept up in his stocking feet. At the top of the stairs, he found four closed doors. He tried the one directly ahead of him. Pitch dark and no sound. "Captain, captain!" A shout rang out from his men below. Cushing ran down the stairs three at a time. Tobias and a tall man in a sleeping gown were wrestling for possession of a chair the sleeper had tried to use as a weapon. Cushing drew his pistol and cocked it as he held it against the Rebel's head. Tobias lit a candle.

"Your name, sir, if you please," said Cushing. "Or should I call you 'general'?"

"No, you should not, sir, I'm Captain Kelly, the general's chief engineer."

Cushing was crestfallen. "Are you the ranking officer present, sir?" he asked.

"I am, sir," Kelly replied.

"Captain," said Tobias, "the lights are on in the barracks next door and I hear someone rousing the garrison."

"That would be General Hardman, the adjutant and second in command," said Kelly. "He's no longer present because he ran out the back door in his nightgown." Kelly, Cushing and Tobias all laughed at once.

"Grab every document you can, men," called Cushing, stuffing papers from the front-room desk in his pockets. "Captain, walk with me, please," said Cushing, his pistol in Kelly's back. "Out the front door, now, strolling casually, with not a care in the world." Soldiers and town folk ran to and fro in the dark, stumbling and shoving. No one stopped or questioned the six men. As they passed the campfire of Obadiah and his friends, Cushing paused. "Care to join us, friends? I'll promise you freedom, but not necessarily happiness."

"We'll settle for freedom, Cap'n," said Obadiah, as the three men joined them.

They reached the boats, and rowed in the darkness toward the Old Inlet as the first shots rang out ashore.

The next day, Cushing sent Midshipman Jones under a flag of

truce to the commandant of Fort Caswell. His mission was to collect Captain Kelly's clothes and money, to ease his stay in Union prison. Jones also bore a note from Cushing to General Hebert which read: "My dear general, I deeply regret that you were not at home when I called. Very respectfully, W.B. Cushing." When Jones returned to the ship, he told Cushing that the commandant had been unable to contain his laughter, and had called the raid "a damned splendid affair!"

The Confederate ironclad *Raleigh* was launched in Wilmington, at the Cassidy Yard, in early April 1864. Admiral S.P. Lee, the North Atlantic Blockading Squadron commander, desired greatly to know when she might be ready to sortie against his blockaders off Old and New inlets. And he knew he had just the officers he needed to find the answer, Lieutenant Will Cushing and Sailing Master Tobias St. John.

"Orders from the admiral, Tobias," said Cushing as they talked in the captain's cabin of the USS *Monticello*. "We're to sneak up the Cape Fear River to Wilmington and determine the sea fitness of CSS *Raleigh*. Shouldn't be too hard, and we might just encounter another espionage opportunity or two on the way."

"Why would I doubt our involvement in one or two more unauthorized adventures, knowing you, my captain?" Tobias smiled across the table at the daring, some would say reckless, Captain Cushing. "What do we know about the *Raleigh?*"

"Richmond class ironclad, casemate pierced for four six-inch rifles, 170 feet long, 180 crew, does six knots, downstream, one supposes."

"She'd do a bit of damage if she surprised the inshore blockade."

"We'll go see when she'll be ready, then. Tomorrow at sunset, the big cutter, 15 men, two day's rations, each man with two Colts and a cutlass. Oh, and let's take those half-dozen breech-loading Sharps rifles we just got. Didn't you say you'd used one?"

"Very similar," said Tobias. "It was a Henry repeater from President Lincoln's personal armory. I had to give it up to a Mexican Confederate, unfortunately."

"Well, we'll provide a replacement. Make the preparations, if you please, Mr. St. John."

"Aye, aye, sir."

Into the Cape Fear Estuary they went once more, on a moonlit, partly cloudy night that worried Tobias. *I hope we get more cloud cover before we reach Fort Anderson*, the navigator thought, looking up at the patchy clouds that occasionally obscured the three-quarter moon. After 15 miles, they reached the Cape Fear's Fort Anderson, almost halfway to Wilmington. The river narrowed there and the Rebels had placed obstructions, including a chain across the river and an old schooner lightship from Frying Pan Shoals armed with four guns. It was across the river from the fort. The oarsmen, seven to a side, were tired, and had begun to splash a bit as their oars entered the water during each stroke. The splash at each catch was visible from the fort, and the 32-pound shot was soon flying their way. Cushing steered artfully around the patches of moonlight reflecting from the Cape Fear's surface, and after a close call or two, they were up river from the fort, passing Orton, Lilliput and Old Town creeks to port. At dawn, they drew to the bank, pulled the boat into the thick trees at the water's edge, and rested. The crew slept while Tobias and Will noted the passing river traffic, and two men kept watch.

"Sir," whispered a lookout in mid-afternoon, "there's a small wherry headed this way, two men, look like fishermen!"

The two anglers surrendered immediately when confronted with a dozen desperadoes threatening them with cutlasses, Sharps rifles, and six-shot revolvers. Cushing questioned them and reassured them that they would not be harmed. "We're not here to make war on civilians, gentlemen. Now, let's talk about the *Raleigh!*" The fishermen swore she was still being fitted out at Cassidy's Yard across the river from Wilmington. "We'll see, gentlemen," said Cushing with a measure of skepticism. "We'll pay a visit tonight!"

Towing the fishermen's skiff, the cutter rowed up river after dark. Sure enough, the *Raleigh* was secure to the Cassidy yard wharf. "Mr. St. John," Cushing said formally, as the two friends were in the company of subordinates, "go aboard and see how close she is to commissioning."

"Aye, aye, sir." Tobias went aboard as the cutter came alongside the bow of the ironclad. Like all Confederate rams designed by John L. Porter, her fore and after decks were almost at water level when the ship was empty, and designed to be awash when she was provisioned and armed. Lumber, fittings, and tools were strewn everywhere on the fore deck. The forward gunport had no gunport shutter. Tobias peered inside the casemate. The same chaos prevailed, and neither guns nor gunport shutters were mounted in any of the gun stations. Tobias reboarded the cutter. "She's two weeks away from battle readiness, sir."

"Very well, Mr. St. John. Cast off, there," he called to the bow man. "Let's take a look at the harbor defenses, since we're in the neighborhood!" An hour later, they had catalogued the secrets of Wilmington Harbor; log and chain barriers secured to pilings, two five-gun batteries, and ships sunk at the sides of the channel to narrow the opening. "Take her down river, Mr. St. John, and we'll hole up in Cypress Swamp." At daybreak, they were using their 16-foot sweeps as poles to take them up a small creek in the swamp. They stopped by a log road.

Taking one of the fishermen, Smith, with him, Cushing led a patrol up the log road until it intersected a well-traveled major road. "This here's the main route from Wilmington t' Fort Fisher," Smith declared, helpfully.

"Is it, now?" mused Cushing. Fort Fisher was a huge fortification, stretching from the river to the ocean and fronting several miles of the Atlantic shore until its ramparts turned west to end along the north bank of New Inlet at Battery Buchanan. "The commanding general here is in Wilmington, and Colonel Lamb, commandant of the fort, is at the other end of this road. Couriers will pass here!" Cushing declared. "Hide yourselves in the trees along the road and be prepared to stop a man on horseback," cried Cushing to his patrol.

In less than an hour, Cushing's prediction proved accurate. A Confederate soldier on horseback came whistling down the road, and was quickly surrounded by men with rifles and pistols. They returned to the cutter with their new prisoner, chattering until Cushing told them to quiet down. "Mr. St. John," Cushing called. "Look at this!" He waved the courier's pouch excitedly.

"Gun calibers and emplacements, supply levels, construction problems, tables of organization and equipment, units assigned, It's all here!"

"I'm sure it will gladden the heart of 'old triplicate,'" Tobias responded, using the nickname of Admiral Lee.

"And," Cushing continued, "the mailbag's full of Confederate dollars!"

"If we could find a way to spend them, they could solve our provisions problem, sir. The rations are gone and the men are hungry."

"Mebbe I can be of help, cap'n," said the accommodating Mr. Smith. "I owns the general store that's about two miles down the road!"

"Splendid, Mr. Smith," Cushing exclaimed. He walked to the guards watching the captured courier. "I'm sorry to have to ask you to relinquish your uniform, but Dorsey, here, is of a size with you, and I'm sending him to the Smith General Store to buy rations. With your government's money, of course, but at least we're putting it back into the Rebel economy, and you'll eat tonight." Cushing smiled at the courier, who began to remove his tunic.

Dorsey stuffed his pockets with Confederate greenbacks and made the trek to the store, where Mrs. Smith was greatly pleased to sell enough food to feed a boat's crew.

Fed and rested, the crew gathered around Cushing at nightfall. "Men, we're heading downstream to the *Monticello,* and extra rations all around. We need to leave the river before they know we're here. We'll leave our fishermen and our prisoner the skiff when we pass Fort Caswell. Soldier," he said, turning to the courier, "no one should have to endure prison camp, on either side. I'm turning you loose. Give my regards to Colonel Lamb."

"Thank you, suh," the courier replied, gratefully.

"Let's get under way, then!"

****

"Damn it all, Tobias, I had plans to sneak back up the river for another raid," said Cushing as they talked in his cabin three days later. "But it seems that even Admiral Lee, who wants you here, can't prevail against Gideon Welles and Captain John Winslow of the USS *Kearsarge.* The stalker of the *Alabama* needs a first rate sailing master, and Welles has chosen you! You do know the Navy Secretary, do you not?"

"I have met him, a time or two," said Tobias, smiling wanly at his commanding officer. "I confess I'd rather be here with you aboard *Monticello,* captain, than an ocean away, and a cold ocean at that. But the service doesn't ask us, does it?"

"No, it doesn't, my friend. It's been great good fun having you as an agent for disruption in our little adventures. Be careful, and stay well!"

"And the same to you, Captain Will! It's never been dull."

TO BE CONTINUED IN
"THE PRIDE OF PASCAGOULA"

APPENDIX A:
HISTORICAL NOTE

The Erlanger Loan negotiations were a stumbling block for Bulloch and Maury, as the Confederate Commissioners refused to sign cotton notes while the larger loan was being negotiated, fearing to lose the agreement. Maury did use a time-contingent note as collateral while promising not to draw it for 60 days. It was not from the Hibernian Bank, however.

I have yet to find a definitive source on Juarez's english skills, so I assigned him fluency because of his strong education and his lengthy residence in New Orleans in the fifties.

I am indebted to James Daddysman's "Matamoros" for the irony of Lincoln and the cotton blockade.

The US Coast Survey under Alexander Bache may well be considered a forerunner of the Navy Sea Bees, the "first wave" under fire, as the Coast Survey assistants resurveyed, resounded and rebouyed the entrances to southern harbors under sniper and cannon fire. See **The Chesapeake Command**.

Many details of *Star of the South's* captures are based on prizes taken by *Florida* and *Alabama*. Readers may recognize the circumstances of *Star's* capture as coincident with *Florida's*.

The actions of the Suffolk Campaign occured as depicted with Lamson and Cushing in major roles.

By all accounts, Mosby was as brilliant, daring and even reckless a leader as presented here, and as concerned for his men's welfare.

The CSS *David's* attack on *New Ironsides* unfolded as described herein. Likewise, the blockade scenes of Lamson and Cushing are reported as history outlines them, Rory and Tobias' action excepted.

Robert Small's encounter with Charlotte Forten did not occur, but it well could have, as they were present at Port Royal at the same time, Charlotte teaching, and Robert being tutored after his capture of CSS *Planter.* Accounts of USS *Planter's* 1863 action on Lighthouse Inlet agree on Robert's promotion to her commander as a result.

Many of the scenes along South Street during the New York Draft Riots were taken from occurences in other city locations during the four-day riots.

The "cigar" incident described by Semmes in his letter was recounted in his **Memoirs of Service Afloat.**

John Taylor Wood's assault on USS *Underwriter* occured as described with Rory and his men added. As noted, Wood was deeply disturbed over Pickett's indecision and behavior, and reported this to his uncle, Jefferson Davis. The Midshipman Sharf mentioned was Thomas Sharf, later author of a very detailed and seldom objective history of the Confederate States Navy.

Appendix B:
Ships

Most of the ships appearing in this novel were actual vessels, and most of the officers noted were historical characters aboard these ships. The following are the only fictional ships:

Albion: British blockade runner commanded by Tobias' RN nemesis, Bertram Ludlow. Prize of USS *Woonsocket*.

CSS *Belle of Biloxi:* former steam packet *Peter Stuyvesant*. Prize of CSS *Flora*.

Caitlin: Galway Hooker or "Bhad Mhor," cutter-rigged freight boat owned by Rory's Uncle Liam.

City of Troy: 800-ton US Mail screw packet, prize of *Belle of Biloxi*.

Compass Rose: Philadelphia schooner. Prize of *Belle of Biloxi*.

Cuirassier: French sloop of war on western Atlantic station.

CSS *Flora:* Union merchant brig converted to Confederate cruiser. Prize of *Star of the South*.

Joseph Lincoln: 400-ton Maine brig, prize of *Belle of Biloxi*. Carrying a cargo of gunpowder, Rory converted it into a fireship.

Lorena: Yankee ship outward bound from New York. Prize of *Star of the South*.

Martha: British steamer serving as tender to CSS *Star of the South*.

Maarten de Groot: Dutch merchant ship.

CSS *Old Dominion:* One-gun screw tug, Rory's first command.

Oliver Griffith: New York pilot schooner. Prize of CSS *Belle of Biloxi*.

CSS *Rose of Clifton:* Dunbrody shipyard-built paddlewheel gunboat.

Silas Matthews: China clipper bound for New York. Prize of *Star of the South*.

Myrtle: New England fishing schooner. One of five such prizes taken by CSS *Flora* on George's Bank.

Parmeter: Yankee East India trader, ship-rigged, bound for New York from Calcutta. Prize of *Star of the South*.

USS *Shoshone County:* Union side wheeler gunboat. Sunk by *Star of the South*.

CSS *Star of the South:* former RN dispatch steamer HMS *Mesopotamia*, two pivots, four 32 pdrs in broadside, 10 knots, lift-single screw.

Starry Night: Union merchant barque carrying saltpeter. Prize of *Star of the South*.

CSS *Suwannoochee:* Charleston Confederate Navy tug.

Waterbury: New York pilot schooner. Prize of *Belle of Biloxi*.

Wessex: New Bedford whaler. Prize of *Star of the South*.

Westwind: Barque-rigged Yankee collier. Prize of CSS *Flora*.

USS *Woonsocket: Wyoming*-class sloop of war, 1500 tons, draft of 14 feet, speed – eleven knots.

APPENDIX C:
MAJOR CHARACTERS

Rory Dunbrody, CSN, and father Patrick, sister Siobhan, brother Tim,
Uncle Liam, and the Dillon side of the family.
Tobias St. John, and his family. Antiguan-born former slave, whaler and
now a Union sailing master. Cousins Mitchell and Daniel of St. John's,
Antigua. Father Carlyle St. John of New Bedford.
Kalama, Kele and son Kekoa - Hawaiian seafarers. Kekoa becomes a
master's mate in the US Navy.

Other Important Characters
"*" denotes an actual historical figure.
*John Andrews – rather mysterious New York City figure, certainly a
Southern sympathizer if not southern, himself. He was active in many
aspects of the four-day Draft Riots. Some accounts have him a Virginia
attorney with seagoing experience.
* Pierre Gustave Toutant Beauregard - Confederate major general
commanding the defense of Charleston.
* Commander James D. Bulloch, CSN – Directed raider acquisitions in
Europe.
* Sir Richard Francis Burton: Discoverer of the source of the Nile,
translator, linguist, swordsman, spy, diplomat, bon vivant. To him, slavery
was anathema.
* William Barker Cushing: Union naval officer, friend and commander of
Tobias, notorious for his reckless daring.
* Captain the Honorable Arthur Auckland Leopold Pedro Cochrane, third
son of Admiral Lord Thomas Cochrane, and commander of HMS *Warrior*
in 1863.
* Jefferson Davis – President, Confederate States.
Major, then Colonel Grenville Donovan, CSA (& family)–Confederate
intelligence officer and brother of Thomas whom Rory killed in a duel
over Carrie Anne Eastman in **The Chesapeake Command.**

Niall Duffy: Confederate acting assistant engineer from Ireland, under Rory's command.

* Admiral Samuel Francis "Frank" Du Pont, USN – commanding the South Atlantic Blockading Squadron (and therefore, Tobias) in the first years of the war.

Captain Jean Gilbert Duquesne – French naval officer.

Monique Duvalliere – Tobias' lover and childhood sweetheart in les Isles de Saintes. Monique's father Pierre, brothers Etienne and Claude.

Carrie Anne Eastman - Rory's Southern love interest. Her mother, her brother Beau, her aunt and uncle Harriet and Fred Farwell, her cousin Natalie Farwell.

Lieutenant Daniel Fell: bigoted Union naval officer, Tobias' occasional tormentor.

* John Arbuthnot "Jackie" Fisher: gunnery lieutenant of HMS *Warrior* in 1863, later Baron Fisher of Kilverstone, Admiral of the Fleet, and First Sea Lord. Introduced the 'all-big-gun' capital ship, the *Dreadnought*, in the early 20th Century.

* Charlotte Forten – Abolitionist and teacher from a prominent black Philadelphia family who taught and tutored newly-freed slaves in Port Royal, South Carolina.

* Gustavus Fox, Assistant US Navy Secretary.

Quentin Glendenning, CSN – Rory's subordinate lieutenant.

* Sir Geoffrey Phipps Hornby, Royal Navy officer who befriended Rory in Puget's Sound and helped him in England. Later, Admiral of the Fleet (Britain's highest naval rank).

* Horace Hunley: Confederate inventor of a submarine named for him in which he died.

* Catesby ap Roger Jones, CSN – commander of CSS *Virginia*.

* Benito Juarez: President of Mexico during the American Civil War. A lawyer from the State of Oaxaca.

* Lieutenant Roswell Lamson, USN – Outstanding US Navy officer from Oregon whose assignments are often coincident with Tobias'.

* President Abraham Lincoln

Lieutenant Bertram Ludlow, Royal Navy – Blockade runner, bigot and general trouble-maker in Tobias' world.

* Confederate Secretary of the Navy Stephen Mallory – ran the Rebel navy with creativity and determination.

Finn McCafferty: Confederate acting boatswain from County Cork, under Rory's command.

* Midshipman James Morris "Jimmie" Morgan, CSN – his assignments in New Orleans, Richmond and Great Britain were coincident with Rory's.

* Confederate cavalryman John Singleton Mosby. At first a scout for JEB Stuart, he later commands the 43rd Virginia, a famed guerilla battalion that operated near the present Dulles Airport in Loudoun and Fauquier counties.

Captain DeWitt Oakley: commanding officer of USS *Woonsocket*.

Archibald Ormsby, South Carolinian naval officer often under Rory's command.

* George Edward Pickett, US Army captain and later Confederate major general. Last in his class at West Point. Charming. Flamboyant. He and Rory cross paths frequently.

* Allan Pinkerton – Secret Service Chief for General McClellan and Lincoln's protector. Tobias impresses him with his clandestine abilities.

* Jose' Agustin Quintero: Harvard-educated Cuban Confederate agent in Matamoros.

* Matias Romero: Juarez envoy to the USA.

* Raphael Semmes: Confederate naval officer who commanded CSS *Sumter* and now commands CSS *Alabama*.

* Robert Smalls, slave pilot who commandeered the CSS *Planter* and delivered her to the Union blockade. Later commanded a Union gunboat, served after the war in the South Carolina state legislature, US Congress and South Carolina National Guard (major general).

Baroness Evelyn St. Regis: an attractive and seductive member of the peerage, sympathetic to the Southern Cause.

* James Tomb: engineer and later commander of CSS *David*, Confederate semi-submersible.

Wickstrand Tremaine: Royal Navy commander who befriended Rory and Tobias in Puget's Sound and later assisted Rory in England.

* John Randolph Tucker – senior US and Confederate naval officer in many theaters where Rory fought. Later an admiral jointly commanding

the Chilean and Peruvian navies.

Klaus Dieter von Klopfenstein – aide to George Pickett, formerly a Prussian army officer and duelist, Rory's antagonist.

Thomas Walsh: Confederate master's mate from Ireland under Rory's command,

* Gideon Welles - Union Secretary of the Navy, cabinet adviser to President Lincoln.

* John Taylor Wood – dashing Rebel navy commander and cavalry colonel. Formerly assistant US Naval Academy superintendent. Commanded a "naval cavalry" unit specializing in the capture of Union blockader gunboats. Gunnery officer aboard CSS *Virginia* at Hampton Roads. Jefferson Davis' nephew and aide.

APPENDIX D:
GLOSSARY

Readers of **The Chesapeake Command** and **Gray Raiders, Green Seas** asked for a glossary to be included in this sequel.

ABAFT: Toward the stern of the ship, used relatively, e.g., "the gun was abaft the mizzenmast."

ABEAM: Beside, next to, abreast. At the side of, as opposed to in front or behind.

AFTERGUARD: Seamen whose station is on the quarterdeck.

AVAST: A shipboard order: hold, or stop hauling.

ARMS:

Cannon: **Smoothbore** cannon had no rifling or grooves inside the barrel, and fired roundshot (solid cannon balls) as well as grapeshot (bags of musket balls) or chainshot (two roundshot bound together by a chain) very harmful to rigging. They were muzzleloaders, and usually mounted on wooden gun carriages with wooden wheels to accommodate recoil. Sometimes, they were on Marsilly or "**dumbtruck**" carriages, on which the back two wheels were replaced by a wooden bar sliding on the deck to more effectively reduce recoil. They were classified by the weight of their roundshot, e.g., 32-pounders, 24-pounders. These cannon were used afloat and ashore. **Swivels** were small smoothbores mounted or set in the gunwales of ships or ship's boats and rotated in any direction. Smoothbores were most often mounted in broadside, firing from only one side of the vessel, through a gunport. **Rifled** cannon fire shaped shells, either exploding or solid, with rims so that the rifling causes them to spin through the air for better accuracy. They are classified by muzzle diameter, e.g., 8-inch, eleven-inch, and inventor or manufacturer, e.g., Parrott, Dahlgren (Union), Brooke, the British Whitworth, Blakely, and Armstrong (used by the Confederacy). Their effective range was a bit more than a mile. Most are muzzleloaders, except the breechloader Armstrong.

These cannon were used afloat and ashore. So were **howitzers**, smaller wheeled cannon with elevated muzzles. **Columbiads** were huge 15,000-pound guns used in shore fortifications, with a range of three miles. Rifled cannon were frequently mounted as **pivots**, on tracks secured to the fore or after decks that enabled the gun to be trained in any direction. A pivot might have three gunports through which it could fire, rather than the one customary for a broadside gun. Excellent sources for some of the above are Paul Silverstone's Civil War Navies 1855-1883 – Naval Institute Press, and Ironclads and Columbiads by William R. Trotter – John F. Blair.

Swords: Sabers and cutlasses were the most common used by Civil war armed forces, and were used more often to cut and slash than to thrust, with a single edged blade.

Rapiers, including epees, were double or triple edged and used more to thrust. They were common in dueling.

Sidearms, handguns and revolvers: Very popular was the 1851 Colt .36 caliber Navy Six, a six-shot revolver light in weight and favored by cavalry and the navy.

ARTICLES OF WAR: The disciplinary code for the navy. The US Navy code was adopted, virtually verbatim, by the Confederate Navy. The armies' articles were similar. The modern equivalent is the Uniform Code of Military Justice (UCMJ).

BHAD MHOR, or Bad Mor, pronounced "bawd moor," "big boat": The largest type of Galway Hooker. "Hookers," or "huickers," from the Dutch, are cutter-rigged freight boats used in the waters of western Ireland. Bhad Mhors are from 35 to 44 feet long and carry livestock, turf or peat, hay and other bulk goods. They are now used sparingly for transport, and an association exists for their preservation as a type. Today, they often are raced in Hooker regattas. But in the 19th century, with its poor roads in western Ireland, they were a most effective means of transportation. In addition to the Bhad Mhor, there are three other types, including the gleoiteog (see below).

BEAR UP: In a sailing ship, to sail closer to the wind, or in a steamer, to head for.

BEAT TO QUARTERS: A drum rhythm from the ship's drummer that called the crew to battle stations.

BELL TIME: The striking of the ship's bell to mark the passage of time. Time at sea is divided into four-hour "watches." One bell is struck at each half hour, for a cumulative total of eight bells at the end of the fourth hour. From midnight, the watches are Mid, Morning, Forenoon and Afternoon, bringing the day to 4:00 pm, or "eight bells in the afternoon watch." To preclude sailors from standing the same watch each day, two two-hour watches span the 4:00 to 8:00 pm time. They are known as the First and Second Dog Watches. Four bells are sounded at the end of the First Dog Watch, but in the Second we hear one, two, three, and then at 8:00 pm, eight bells once again. The seventh watch is the Evening Watch, ending when eight bells sounds midnight.

BENS, THE TWELVE: The Twelve Bens, including Benbreen and Benbrack, are a dozen mountain peaks, roughly 2000 feet in height, east of Clifden on the Connemara Peninsula in western Ireland. They were aptly described by Leon Uris as "mountains of naked stone mass."

BEST BOWER: The starboard of the two anchors carried at the bow, as opposed to the SMALL BOWER, the portside anchor, which was, peculiarly, the same weight as the best bower.

BLATHERSKITE: In Ireland, a nonsense talker, a useless individual who talks "blather."

BRIAN BORU, HIS FLAG, HIS HARP: The 11th Century "High King" of Ireland died at his victory in the Battle of Clontarf. A 14th century Irish harp in gold upon a green flag, erroneously attributed to him, became a frequent banner for Irish regiments, and was used by the Irish rebels in 1798. In 1947, the flag was revived as the naval jack of the Irish Navy. It was known as "the harp without the crown," in contrast to the harp included in the British coat of arms during British dominance of Ireland, which had a (British) crown above it.

BROAD REACH: A point of sailing with the wind abeam or slightly abaft the beam.

CAISSONS: Two-wheeled wagons carrying artillery ammunition.

CAPOEIRA: A martial art often disguised as dance and frequently practiced to music, developed first in the slave plantations of Brazil, emphasizing striking with the legs. When slave masters would appear, the participants would subtly shift from confrontational movements to dance form.

CAPSTAN, WINDLASS, CAPSTAN BARS, WINCH: A vertical cylindrical barrel on the main deck of a sailing ship, capped by a drumhead with square pigeon holes in which wooden capstan bars were inserted and pushed by the crew to raise the anchor or yards or boats. Hawsers or cables were wrapped around the drum and held by pawls. With the advent of steam and electricity, a powered horizontal drum, or windlass, performed the same function. The more modern horizontal winch is likewise steam or electrically powered, and a vertical winch is turned by hand on yachts.

CATESBY AP ROGER JONES: The Welsh-named first lieutenant and later commander of the CSS *Virginia*. "Ap" is a Welsh prefix meaning "son of."

CHANDLERY: The store of a ship chandler, a supplier of goods for ships.

CLADDAGH: A shallow boat basin in the center of Galway City, once the old fishing village.

COUNTER: The underside of the after-overhang of a ship, below the transom.

CRANK: In a ship, unstable, in danger of capsizing or overturning, particularly in heavy weather, caused by poor construction, design or improper stowage or ballasting.

CRIMP: A keeper of seamen's lodgings who doubled as a procurer of seamen for ships needing sailors, at a price, of course. Crimps most commonly used spiked drinks as the means to render sailors insensible and easily delivered to ships about to sail.

DALTHEEN: (Irish) impudent fellow.

DAVIT: A set of two small cranes fitted with tackle to lower the boat slung between them along the side or the stern of a ship.

DOUSED HER GLIM: Put out the lantern or other light showing aboard a ship.

DOWNIE: (Irish) wretched, miserable.

DRAFT or draught: The vertical distance between a ship's waterline and her keel. The depth of water a ship "draws" is her draft, e.g., "she drew 22 feet."

DUN LAOGHAIRE: A port south of Dublin, connected by rail.

Pronounced "Dun Leary."

ENFILADE: Sweep (with gunfire) along a line of troops or a trench.

FALLS: The tackle (tackle; two blocks [pulleys] and the rope between them) for lowering and raising boats suspended from davits.

FENIANS: Originally, an American brotherhood of Irish dedicated to the freedom of Ireland from Great Britain, led by John O'Mahoney (1859). They were named for the ancient Gaelic warrior Fiona MacCumhail and his elite legion, the Fianna. Later, James Stephens' Irish branch of the organization adopted the same name.

FORTIFICATIONS: Forts or fortresses consist of **ramparts**, the outer walls, surmounted by **parapets**, upward extensions of the ramparts behind which guns are mounted and fired through **embrasures** or openings in the parapet. Corners of the fortification may project beyond the main walls in hexagonal outward extensions called **bastions**, which contain chambers called casemates in which guns are housed. **Sally ports** are chambered entrances with two doors, an inner door closed after defenders are in the sally port, and an outer door that then is opened to let the defenders "sally forth." **Redoubts** are earthworks outside of main forts and independent of them.

FREE QUAKER: An offshoot of the Society of Friends which, in the American Revolution, and beyond, made exception to the Quaker abhorrence of war and violence for situations in which man struggles against intolerable tyranny.

GAELTACHT: An area where Irish Gaelic is the principal language. In the 21st century, these include significant parts of Connemara, Donegal, Kerry, Cork, and smaller areas in Mayo, Waterford and Meath.

GALLOWGLASSES: in Ireland, originally Gaelic mercenaries of the 13th century who fought for Domnall mac Domnaill, brother of an Irish king, against the Normans. They were heavily armed and armored foot soldiers.

GLEOITEOG: A type of Galway Hooker (see above), pronounced "glochug," 24-30' long, used often for fishing.

GOMBEEN MEN: Rural Irish usurers who exacted exorbitant interest on loans to the Irish peasantry.

GROG: A mixture of rum and water served daily to the ship's crew in the Royal and American navies. Named for British Admiral Vernon, whose

nickname, after a coat he wore, was "Old Grogham." Drink too much and
you were "groggy." The Royal Navy continued the custom through the
20th century, but the Union (US) Navy discontinued it in 1862.

GUNWALE: The upper edge of the side or bulwark of a vessel.
Pronounced "gun'l."

GYBE: or "jibe": While wearing a vessel with a fore-and-aft mainsail
(moving the stern through the wind), the moment when the boom and
sail swing from one side of the craft to the other. Depending on the force
of the wind and the area of the sail, this action can put a great strain
on the rigging and spars. It can be mitigated by strong control of the
mainsheet. If unexpected (e.g., a sudden wind-shift) the swinging boom
can knock a man overside.

HAWSE HOLE: The aperture in the bows of a ship through which the
anchor cable passes. "Stay clear of my hawse hole!" is a admonition to
keep out of my way.

HAWSER: A heavy rope or cable greater than five inches in circumference.
Used for towing, some anchor lines or to secure to a dock.

HOGGING: When the bow and stern of a ship droop below the midship
section of the keel, either on a wave crest, or when aground.

HOKU: In Hawaii, a star.

HOOLEY: In Ireland, an extended celebration usually with "too much
of the drink taken." From a Hindu word for festival, brought back by
Irish soldiers in the Honorable East India Company's army (the "John"
Company).

KAHUNA: In Hawaii, a priest, wizard, minister, expert in any profession.

KANAKA: The Hawaiian word for human being, man, person, individual.
In the world outside the Hawaiian Islands, frequently used to denote a
Hawaiian.

KEEL: The principal member or timber extending the length of a ship's
bottom. The ship's "backbone."

KEOLAUN: In Ireland, a contemptible male.

KERNES or KERNS: Irish light infantry, originally around the 13th
century.

KILO: In Hawaii, a stargazer, seer, reader of omens.

LANYARD: A short length of rope used for a variety of purposes, including the release of the hammer on flintlocks when they were used as firing mechanisms for cannon.

LEAD LINE: A 25-fathom (150 foot) line with a lead weight cylinder attached, used to find the depth of the water. The lead's lower end is cupped and "armed" with tallow, to bring to the surface the nature of the bottom, mud, sand, pebbles, shingles, etc. The line is measured in six-foot lengths or fathoms. The leadsman heaves the line ahead of the ship so that it is vertical as it reaches the bottom. He is positioned in the chains, a platform to which the fore shrouds are attached. The line is marked with specific knots, rags or leathers at most of the six-foot 'fathom' intervals. The leadsman can identify the depth marks by feel, even in the dark. Depths measured by indicators are referred to as marks. Unmarked fathoms in between marks are called out as deeps. "By the mark two" was distinguished by two strips of leather. The "deep six" had no mark but was between "mark five" (white duck cloth) and "mark seven" (red bunting). The deep sea or "dipsea" lead measures depths up to 100 fathoms. It is extended along the length of the ship and held at intervals by sailors who drop their segment of the line in succession.

LEE: The side of a ship or promontory away from the wind.

LIGHTERS: Barges used to convey cargo from ship to shore in shallow waters. They are shallow draft and very steady in calmer water.

LUFF: 1. Slang for lieutenant, from the French and British pronunciation "leftenant." "First Luff" is the first lieutenant or executive officer of a ship. 2. The leading edge of a fore-and-aft sail. To "luff up" is to bring the vessel into the wind so that the luff shivers and the sail spills the wind.

MAHALO NUI LOA: In Hawai'i, thank you very much.

MALAMA PONO: In Hawai'i, be careful, watch out! Take care.

MASSEY LOG: the most accurate rotating log developed in the early 19th century, a streamlined rotator with dials towed at the end of a log-line, invented by Edward Massey. It had to be hauled in for each reading, but was remarkably accurate in measuring ship speed. The rotator varied its speed, and therefore its readings, as the ship varied hers.

MCMANUS, TERENCE: An Irish patriot transported to Australia for his part in the "Young Irelander" uprising in 1848, escaped and died in America, then buried with great pomp and reverence by the Fenians in

Ireland.

MOKU: In Hawai'i, an island, a ship (because the first European ships suggested islands). Sailor is kelamoku, or in pidgin, sailamoku.

MOULINET: In fencing, a circular saber stroke or swing at head level.

MONKEY FIST: An intricately constructed knot, round, and weighty, attached to the end of the light heaving line first tossed from a ship to another vessel or to a dock. Once the lighter, more-easily-thrown heaving line was in hand, the ship's end was tied or "bent" to a heavier line that secured the originating ship to the other vessel or to the dock.

MULLARD: On a Galway Hooker, a bitt or timberhead located near the stern to which sheets are secured.

ORLOP DECK: The lowest deck in a ship. Usually, the location of the surgeon's operating compartment, called the "cockpit." "Orlop" and "cockpit" were sometimes used interchangeably when referring to the surgery.

PA ELE: In Hawai'i, a Negro.

PALU: In Micronesia, a navigator-priest.

PAWLS: A series of metal protrusions at the bottom of a capstan barrel that dropped into slots and acted as a brake on the anchor line. "Heave a pawl": take in the line by the distance of one more pawl by heaving or pushing on the capstan bars.

PELORUS: An instrument for taking bearings, with two sighting vanes, fitted to the rim of a compass and giving the bearings of two objects from a fixed point, usually a ship or boat.

PILIKIA: In Hawai'i, trouble, bad business, bother, adversity.

POINTS OF THE COMPASS: The circumference of the magnetic compass card is divided into 32 points. In the 19th century, they bore names. The four cardinal points were north (N), east (E), south (S), and west (W). Using the northeast quadrant as an example, the names of the seven points between N and E were: N by E, NNE, NE by N, NE, NE by E, ENE, and E by N. In that century, points were used to express the bearing of an object from the ship's heading, e.g., "two points off the starboard bow," or "one point abaft the port beam."

QUOIN: A wedge used to elevate the angle of fire from a ship's cannon.

RAPPAREE: In Ireland, a robber, scoundrel, rebel.

RUCTION: In Ireland, a disturbance, fight, uproar.

SASANACH: In Ireland, an Englishman, sometimes, a Protestant. A term of derision.

SCREW: A nautical propeller.

SCUPPERS: Drains for the weather or upper decks.

SCUTTLEBUTT: 1. A cask of fresh water for daily drinking use, located in a convenient part of the ship. 2. Gossip. As many members of the crew would use the scuttlebutt and pause during the ship's work day, talk and gossip were exchanged there. Gossip exchanged at the office water cooler is a direct descendant.

SHEET: A single line used to trim a sail to the wind and attached to the clew. The clew on a fore-and-aft sail is the lower aftermost corner. On a square sail, the clews are the two lower corners.

SHENANIGANS: In Ireland, tricks or trickery, japes – a practical joke.

SHIP'S BOATS: The dimensions and characteristics of the boats described herein varied with the passage of time and the size of the ships they served. For instance, a cutter, a beamy boat that sailed well, but rowed less well, could be 34 feet long and carry 66 men on a ship of the line or a large steam frigate, but measured 18 feet long on a brig. Smaller vessels had difficulty in hoisting out larger boats using their main and fore course yards. The invention of davits in the 1790s helped the smaller craft to hoist out boats more easily. Generally, the size of a boat from large to small followed this order: Longboat, launch, pinnace, barge, cutter, yawl, gig, jolly boat, skiff, dory, wherry, dinghy. Double-ended whaleboats of 28-30 feet length came into naval use in the mid-19th century. A quarter boat often was one of the above hung in davits at the ship's quarter or after part. The following list from the 1817 Royal Navy Rate Book shows the variety of boats sizes within small boat nomenclature. It is taken from W. E. May's excellent "The Boats of Men of War," Naval Institute Press 1999, the definitive work on the topic:

Launches: in 17 varying lengths – 16 ft to 34 ft.

Barges & pinnaces: 8 different lengths – 28 to 37 ft.

Cutters: 17 different lengths – 12 to 34 ft.

Gigs: 6 different lengths – 18 to 26 ft.

Ship's boats were designed for sailing qualities, rowing qualities, or a compromise combination. Rowing configurations were termed single banked or double banked. Single banked boats had one rower to a thwart, seated all the way across the thwart from the oarlock. For wider or more beamy boats, double banking put two men each with an oar, on each thwart. Oarlocks were first thole pins, upright pegs in the gunwales that the oar pulled against as a fulcrum, with a lanyard around the oar to secure it. Next, a second thole pin was added and the oar set between. Later, notches were cut in a strake above the gunwale and the oar set in. In 1826, metal swiveling oar crutches were introduced.

SHIP TYPES: Beginning with the system of the Royal Navy's Lord Anson in 1751, warships of sailing navies were divided into six divisions or "rates" according to the number of broadside guns carried. A "first rate" carried 100 guns or more. A "fourth rate" carried from 50 to 70 guns, and was the smallest ship of the line, or line-of-battle ship. Fifth and sixth rates were brigs of war, sloops of war, corvettes or frigates carrying up to 50 guns. Steam power brought additional and changing classifications. Ships carried more powerful pivot guns that fired in any direction, in addition to broadside guns. Steam ships came to be classified by how they were powered or armored. Ironclads, sidewheel frigates, screw frigates, sidewheel or screw sloops, sidewheel or screw gunboats, and armed sidewheel or screw tugs were some new types. Specialty vessels, such as spar torpedo boats and handpropelled submarines were introduced in the American Civil War. River combat spawned cottonclads, tinclads, timberclads and rams. It's interesting to note that "second-rate," now connoting low quality, originally meant a ship of the line carrying from 84 to 100 guns, with nothing low-quality about her.

SHUILER: In Ireland, a vagrant, a wanderer.

SIDEBOY: A sailor assigned to attend the gangway when officers or other dignitaries are boarding the ship. The rank of the boarding officer determines the number of sideboys.

SPALPEEN: In Ireland, an itinerant farmhand of dubious reputation or low degree. A rascal. A derogatory term.

STERNSHEETS: In an open boat the section aft of the after thwart, usually fitted with seats for the coxswain, boat commander or passengers.

STOP HER COCKS: To plug any below-waterline pipes opening to the sea on a vessel.

STRAKE: A line of planking in a wooden vessel. The hull is made up of rows of strakes.

SUTLER: Storekeeper selling provisions to soldiers on army posts or in the field.

TEAGUE: A common Irish surname which came to be used as a derogatory term for an Irishman in the USA and Great Britain of the 19th century, like "mick" or "paddy." The "tea" is pronounced "tay." Sometimes, "Taig" or "Teig."

THWART: The transverse wooden seat in a rowing boat on which oarsmen sit.

TIDES: The states of the tides include: slack water, when the tide changes from ebb to flood or the reverse; ebb, outgoing; flood, incoming; high, the greatest level, and low, the lowest level.

TOP HAMPER: A ship's superstructure and upper-deck equipment.

TRANSOM: The athwartship timbers bolted to the sternpost, constituting a flat stern.

TRY WORKS, TRYING OUT: Iron pots set in brickworks on the deck of a whale ship to boil oil out of whale blubber. The process was known as "trying out" the oil.

WARDROOM: The mess and common room for the senior officers (except the captain) in a larger warship, or for all officers (except the captain) in a smaller ship. The gunroom in a larger ship serves the more junior officers.

WAY and WEIGH: Way is to be in motion over the sea bottom. A ship has "way" on her, or is "under way." The command for rowers to begin rowing is "give way all." To weigh anchor is to lift the anchor from the sea bottom. "Under weigh" is an incorrect usage.

WAY ENOUGH: A command to stop rowing.

"WILL NAE BE KENT": In Scots dialect, "will not be known."

YARD: A large wooden or metal spar crossing the masts of a ship horizontally (or diagonally to bear lateen sails), from which a sail is set .

YAW, PITCH AND ROLL: Yaw is the motion of the bow to the left or to the right of the course. Pitch is the up and down motion of the bow caused by wave action ahead or astern of the ship. Roll is the up and down movement of the side of a ship due to wave action from the side or abeam of the ship.

In addition to the sources cited above, the author is indebted to **The Oxford Companion to Ships and the Sea**, Peter Kemp, Oxford Reference, Ship to Shore, Peter D. Jeans, McGraw Hill, **A Sea of Words**, Dean King, Henry Bolt, **Origins of Sea Terms**, John G. Rogers, Mystic Seaport Museum, **Hawaiian Dictionary,** Mary Kawena Pukui and Samuel H. Elbert, University of Hawaii Press, **The Green Flag, Volume II**, Robert Kee, Penguin, and **Slanguage**, a Dictionary of Irish Slang, Bernard Share, Gill and Macmillan.